HIT LIST

Anita Blake, Vampire Hunter, Novels

GUILTY PLEASURES
THE LAUGHING CORPSE
CIRCUS OF THE DAMNED
THE LUNATIC CAFE
BLOODY BONES
THE KILLING DANCE
BURNT OFFERINGS
BLUE MOON
OBSIDIAN BUTTERFLY
NARCISSUS IN CHAINS
CERULEAN SINS
INCUBUS DREAMS
MICAH and STRANGE CANDY
DANSE MACABRE
THE HARLEQUIN
BLOOD NOIR
SKIN TRADE
FLIRT
BULLET
HIT LIST

LAURELL K. HAMILTON

HIT LIST

AN ANITA BLAKE, VAMPIRE HUNTER, NOVEL

headline

First published in the United States of America in 2011 by
the Penguin Group (USA) Inc.
A BERKLEY BOOK

First published in Great Britain in 2011 by
HEADLINE PUBLISHING GROUP

1

ISBN 978 0 7553 5259 3 (Hardback)
ISBN 978 0 7553 5260 9 (Trade paperback)

Typeset in Fournier MT by Palimpsest Book Production Limited,
Falkirk, Stirlingshire

Printed and bound in Great Britain by
Clays Ltd, St Ives plc

Headline's policy is to use papers that are natural, renewable and
recyclable products and made from wood grown in sustainable forests.
The logging and manufacturing processes are expected to conform to
the environmental regulations of the country of origin.

HEADLINE PUBLISHING GROUP
An Hachette UK Company
338 Euston Road
London NW1 3BH

www.headline.co.uk
www.hachette.co.uk

DAVID EUGENE FAVIER

September 25, 1955–December 6, 2010

This one is for Gene,
who loved Anita and Edward as much as I did.
He was always ready to defend my honor online,
but without ever losing sight that he was a gentleman.
He will be missed.

HIT LIST

I

The main piece of the body lay on the ground, on its back in the middle of a smooth grassy field. In the predawn gloom everything looked gray, but there were scuffed and paler places around the field; I think we were in standing in the middle of a softball field. The 'we' was Edward, US Marshal Ted Forrester, and me, US Marshal Anita Blake. Edward was his real name, the real him. Forrester was his secret identity, like Clark Kent for Superman, but to the other marshals he was good ol' boy Ted, once a bounty hunter, now a marshal, grandfathered in under the Preternatural Endangerment Act just like me. I'd been a vampire executioner, not a bounty hunter. But either way, there we stood with real badges; legally we were real cops. Edward still took assassination jobs if the pay was high enough, or the hit interesting enough. He specialized in killing only dangerous things, like wereanimals and vampires. Crime fighting had actually begun to take up most of his time. Work does interfere with your hobbies.

There were other marshals over talking to the local police, but it was just Edward and me standing in the middle of the scattered body parts. Maybe the others had gotten tired of looking at them; we had come straight from the airport in Tacoma to the crime scene. The other cops had been here longer. Dismembered bodies did lose their charm pretty fast.

I fought the urge to huddle in my Windbreaker with *US*

Marshal in big letters on it. It was fifty freaking degrees here. Whoever heard of fifty being the regular temperature in August? It was a hundred-plus with heat index at home in St Louis. The stop before this one had been Alabama. Fifty degrees felt amazingly cold after all that heat and humidity. The light softened around us and I could see the body parts better. It didn't make me like them any better.

'Is the body lying on its back, or its ass?' I asked.

'You mean because it's bisected at midchest and the parts are about ten feet away?'

'Yeah,' I said.

'Does it matter?' he asked. He pushed his hand toward a cowboy hat that he'd left in the car that brought us from the airport. Ted wore a well-loved, well-creased cowboy hat, and the fact that the hat gesture had become habitual said just how much time Edward was spending as his legal alter ego. He settled for running his hand through his short blond hair. He was five foot eight, which seemed tall to me at five-three.

'I guess not.' In my head I thought, *Problems like that are what you think about when you stare down at a dismembered body, because otherwise you want to run screaming, or throw up.* I hadn't thrown up on a body in years, but the St Louis police had never let me live it down.

'They can't find the heart,' he said, voice as unemotional as his face. The light was strong enough that I could see that his eyes were blue rather than just pale. He had a summer tan, light gold, but better than I tanned. It seemed wrong that the blond, blue-eyed WASP tanned darker than I did with my mother's black hair and brown eyes. I was half Hispanic – shouldn't I tan darker than white-bread boy?

'Anita,' he said, and he moved so I couldn't see the body. 'Talk to me.'

I blinked at him. 'They won't find the heart. Just like they didn't find the last three hearts. The killer, or killers, is taking the heart as a trophy, or proof of the kill. Like the woodsman in Snow White taking the heart back to the Wicked Queen in a box, or something.'

'I need you here, working this case, not lost in your head.'

'I'm here.' I frowned at him.

He shook his head. 'I've seen you look at worse than this and be better about it.'

'Maybe I'm tired of looking at shit like this. Aren't you?'

'You don't mean just this case,' he said.

I shook my head.

'Are you asking if looking at things like this bothers me?'

'I would never ask that, it's against the guy code,' I said, and just saying it that way made me smile a little.

He smiled back, but more like it was reflex. It never reached his eyes. They stayed cold and empty as a winter sky. Once the other marshals joined us he'd make his eyes sparkle, or fill with some emotion; he didn't bother when it was just us. We knew each other too well; there was no need to hide.

'No, it doesn't bother me.'

I shrugged, and finally let myself huddle in the thin Windbreaker. At least with my main gun at the small of my back instead of in the shoulder holster, I was able to zip it and not compromise my gun. I still had my backup gun in the shoulder holster and a big-ass knife down my back that attached to the specially made shoulder rig.

'It's more that I'd rather be home.'

'With your men,' he said, and again it was totally neutral.

I nodded. I missed the men in my life when I was away too long, and this was our fourth crime scene in a fourth city. I was tired of planes, tired of other cops, tired of being away.

'I'm missing Becca in *Music Man*. She's just in the chorus, but she's one of the youngest they've ever cast.'

'She must be really good.'

'She is.' He nodded, smiling, and this time it reached all the way up to his eyes. His face was warm and happy thinking about his almost stepdaughter. He'd been living with and engaged to

Donna for years, but never quite married, but the kids thought of him as their dad. Becca had been only six when he and her mother started dating. Edward, whom the vampires had nick-named 'Death', had taken Becca to dance class and sat in the waiting room with the moms for years now. It made me smile just to think about it.

'It was more fun to hunt monsters before we had someone to go home to,' I said.

The smile faded and he turned cold eyes to look at where the head lay to one side of the field. 'I can't argue that. I don't mind the bodies. It doesn't bother me, but I hope we get home before the musical is over.'

'How many nights does it run?'

'Two weeks,' he said.

'Two weeks, starting today?'

'Yes.'

'I don't want to be out here another two weeks,' I said.

'Me, either,' he said, and this time he sounded tired.

The real trouble with this case for me was that I knew exactly why these victims had been chosen. I even knew what was killing them. The trouble was I couldn't tell anyone but Edward, because if I told the police everything I knew, the killers would come after me and every policeman that I told, and everyone that they told. The Harlequin were the vampire equivalent of police, spies, judge, jury, and executioner. They were also some of the greatest warriors to ever live, or unlive. Some of them were vampires and some of them were wereanimals, which was how they were slicing apart the bodies of the weretigers they were killing across the country. The body at our feet looked like a human man. Before he died he'd been able to shift to a big-ass tiger, but it hadn't helped him against the Harlequin, just as it hadn't helped any of the others. If two people were equally fast, equally strong, but one was better trained at fighting, the better trained one would win. So far, none of the weretigers had been anything but ordinary people who just happened to turn into weretigers.

'We're here to work the scene,' Edward said, 'so we do.'

I sighed, squared my shoulders, and stopped huddling in my thin jacket. 'It's partly that we know so much the other police need to know.'

'We settled this, Anita. The . . . ones who can't be named—' He glared at me. 'I really hate that we can't even say their names out loud. It feels like we're in a Harry Potter book talking about He-Who-Must-Not-Be-Named.'

'You know the deal, Edward; if you mention their name without their invitation they hunt you down and kill you for it. If I told the other police, everyone who said their name would be hunted down and slaughtered. I don't know about you, but these guys are scary good, and they seem to have knowledge of modern forensics.'

'They're wearing cloaks, gloves, and hoods that cover their hair, Anita. The outfits that keep them hidden from the other of these . . . guys help them not leave forensic evidence behind.'

'Fair enough.'

'And the Whatevers that are on your side don't know the faces of the others. They wear masks when they meet, like some terrorist cells, so they can spy on each other if they need to.'

'So we have no faces to give them, no names except nicknames, and those match the masks they wear.'

'I don't think assassins this good wear Venetian carnival masks in downtown Tacoma, so the nicknames and masks don't help,' he said.

'So we know everything and nothing useful,' I said.

'If I'd taken the contract to kill the Queen vampire, she'd be dead right now.'

'Or you would and I'd be talking to Peter about why he's lost a second dad.'

Edward gave me the full weight of his cold gaze. 'You know how good I am at my job.'

I'd had years of practice meeting that cold gaze. I met it now.

'You don't understand, Edward. She's the darkness, the night itself made alive.'

'I wouldn't have just blown her body up and called the job done,' he said. 'Something that supernatural needed magic to kill it for good.'

'What – you would have brought a witch along?'

'No, but I would have gone to one and gotten charms, a blessed weapon, something. The mercenaries the vampire council hired to kill her treated her like just another mark and now we're all in the shit because of it.'

I couldn't argue with him; he was too right. The Harlequin had been the law of the vampire council in Europe for thousands of years, but their original job had been as bodyguards to their Dark Queen. Half of them had broken with the vampire council and were back to taking orders from the Mother of All Darkness.

'They thought fire would destroy her,' I said.

'Would you have assumed that?'

I thought about it. 'No.'

'What would you have done?'

'I'd have plastered myself with holy items, thrown more holy items on the body so her spirit couldn't leave the body she's in, and taken her head and heart, then I'd have burned it all separately down to ash, and put the ashes of the head, the heart, and the body in different bodies of running water.'

'You really think she could come back if you put the ashes in the same body of water?'

I shrugged. 'She survived the total destruction by fire of her body and was able to send her spirit out to take over the body of other vampire council members. I wouldn't put anything past her.'

'So even if we find Morte d'Amour, the Lover of Death, and destroy him, she'll just jump to another host.'

'She can survive as a disembodied spirit, Edward; I'm not sure she can be killed.'

'Everything dies, Anita. The universe will die eventually.'

'I'm not going to sweat what happens five billion years from now, Edward; the universe can take care of itself. How do we stop them from killing innocent weretiger citizens, and the bigger question, how do we stop her?'

'You're the necromancer, I'm just a humble killer,' he said.

'Which means, you don't know either,' I said.

'Why doesn't your boyfriend know? Jean-Claude is Master of the City of St Louis, and what's left of the European power structure is trying to make him head of a new vampire council here in the States. Why aren't the vampires and all the other wereanimals you're hanging out with helping to stop this?'

'The other . . . whatevers are hunting these guys. They'll be traveling as they hear about the bodies, but they're behind us, Edward. We've been first on the ground in the last three cities.'

'For preternaturals that are supposed to be the greatest spies and assassins ever, they suck at anything useful.'

'We're not doing much better,' I said.

'So the vampires can't help us. We're cops, let's be cops,' he said.

'What does that mean?'

'We work the scene. This is the kill site. This is where we can learn new things about these bastards. Things that aren't legends, but what they did only a few hours ago. It can help us catch them.'

'You really believe that?'

'I have to believe that, and so do you.'

I took in a deep breath and wished I hadn't. There was a faint bitter smell because we were standing near the end of the body. Death isn't neat, or pretty, or clean; it's all outhouse smells as your body does everything it can do all at once, one last time.

'Fine,' I said, and I squatted beside the body on the balls of my feet. I made myself look at the body, really look at it.

'This body was sliced, neat, very few cuts, very efficient.'

'So why tear the body into pieces?'

'Because they wanted to do it, and were strong enough to do it,' I said.

'You know that doesn't feel right; try again.' He stood over me, and for the first time in a long time I felt like the inexperienced newbie and he was the mentor again, telling me how to kill the monsters. He was one of the few people on the planet I would have taken that attitude from.

'They wanted the bodies to match the other bodies, at least superficially. They hoped the police would think it was the same killers.'

'But it's not,' Edward said.

'The first body and the third were savaged. They were literally torn apart. There were internal organs and guts everywhere. It was like a disorganized killer with maybe an organized partner directing, or controlling him. This is all organized. He, or they, are doing the kills like they've been told to, matching the first kill, but their heart isn't in it.'

'What do you mean?' he asked.

'This was a cold kill like the second one. The other two kills, the murderer took joy in it.'

He came down beside me on the balls of his feet, too. 'My kills are neat and clean, but I enjoy my work.'

'You enjoy the planning and being faster, stronger, just better than whoever you're hunting, but do you actually enjoy the kill?'

'Yes,' he said, and he was looking at the body as he said it.

I studied his profile. I asked him something I'd never asked him before. 'What is it you enjoy about it?'

He turned those pale blue eyes to me. They'd faded so the blue was grayish. It was never a good sign when his eyes changed to that cold winter sky color.

'I like watching the light die in their eyes,' he said, his voice as cold and unemotional as his own eyes.

I met that winter gaze and said, 'That's why you like a close kill.'

He nodded, still holding that winter gaze on me. I don't know what my face showed. We'd started out with him being my teacher, and then he'd paid me the ultimate compliment. He'd told me a few years ago that he wanted to see which of us was better. He wasn't sure anymore, and it was a fantasy of his to have us hunt each other, so we could settle the debate once and for all. When he first told me, I'd been convinced I'd be the one that would die; now I wasn't so sure, maybe I would win. Maybe I could call Donna and the kids and tell them . . . Tell them what? That their family was destroyed because Edward and I had had the ultimate guy moment and I was the better man?

'So you think the killers enjoyed the kill?' My voice was as empty and neutral as any I had, just two killers talking shop over someone else's kill.

'I think they might have enjoyed the killing. There's no way to tell when a killer is this controlled,' he said.

'How does any of this help us catch them?'

He shook his head and looked back at the biggest part of the body. 'I don't know.' He sounded tired again.

I looked down at the body. There was still enough of his chest and stomach left to show that he'd had muscle tone. He'd hit the gym, and it had done him no good at all. He would be another clanless tiger, a survivor of an attack rather than one born into a family group. The Harlequin were killing only the clanless right now, because they were searching for certain tigers. They were searching for gold tigers. A bloodline supposedly destroyed during the reign of the First Emperor of China, but hidden in secret by some of the Harlequin. Hidden from the other Harlequin and from the Mother of All Darkness; the fact that they'd managed to hide them from her when she was at the height of her powers said just how good the Harlequin were at subterfuge. They would have run the world's best witness protection program ever.

We'd hoped they'd stop slaughtering the clanless tigers when the gold tigers made their public debut to the other tiger clans, but though we'd made it public that we had all colors of the tigers with us in St Louis, the Harlequin were still hunting and killing the weretigers. It seemed so pointless.

I stood up, waiting for my bad knee to protest squatting too long, but it didn't. I realized my 'bad knee' hadn't been bad in a while. I was Jean-Claude's human servant and metaphysically tied to several wereanimals. I healed faster than human-normal, but I hadn't realized I'd lost the old aches and pains from past injuries. When had that happened?

Edward stood beside me, and he favored one leg a little. He had an injury on that one from a hunt that went bad. I thought, *How old is Edward? Will he age and I won't? Will my ties to the supernatural keep healing me?* It was a weird thought to think that Edward might grow older faster than I did.

'You've thought of something, what?' he asked.

I opened my mouth, closed it, and tried to think of something else to say out loud. 'Why keep killing the tigers?' I said.

'You mean now that they know you and Jean-Claude have your own gold tigers in St Louis?'

'Yes. They were supposed to kill the clanless tigers to keep us from getting the gold tigers to bond with metaphysically. It's too late, Edward, we've already done that, so why keep killing the other tigers?'

'Maybe they're looking for a specific weretiger.'

'Maybe, but why, or who, and again why? There's nothing to be gained by it.'

'I can think of one thing they've gained,' he said.

'Okay, what?'

'They've separated you from Jean-Claude and all the other people you're metaphysically tied to. In St Louis you have enough bodyguards to make up a small army. Here, it's just you and the police.'

'You think they'd risk attacking me with the cops around? I mean, the whole concept of these guys is that no one knows they exist. They're really invested in being this big dark secret.'

'If Mommie Darkest told them to kill you, would they risk being outed to the human police?'

'Maybe,' I said, and then I had another idea. I wasn't sure it was worse, but it scared me more. 'Her first idea was to take over my body. She wanted to kill me only after she realized I was too powerful for her to move into me.'

'Are you as powerful out here hundreds of miles away from Jean-Claude and the rest?'

I thought about it, really made myself look at it. 'Metaphysically, no. I'm safer if I can touch my master and animals to call.'

'Maybe they're killing the tigers to keep you out here.'

'You think they'll try to kidnap me?' I asked.

'If she still wants your body, yes.'

'And if she just wants me dead, then that works better out here, too,' I said.

'It does,' he said. He was looking out at the edge of the field. He was checking the perimeter for danger, trying to see the Harlequin hiding in the trees along the edge of the green, summer field.

'I don't sense any wereanimals,' I said, 'and walking in full daylight is incredibly rare. I've only met three vampires that could do it.'

'If they're these ultimate spies, would you be able to sense them?'

'I think so,' I said.

He glanced at me, then went back to scanning the area. 'That's pretty arrogant.'

'Maybe, but I'd still know if there was a preternatural close to us.'

He spoke without looking at me, 'Please, tell me this isn't the first time you wondered if this was a trap for you.'

'I thought they didn't know the gold tigers were in St Louis. They should have stopped killing the others after they learned that. It's one of the reasons we made it public.'

'So either it's a trap to keep you away from St Louis or Mommie Darkest forgot to rescind her order.'

'What do you mean?'

'Would they slaughter the weretigers until she ordered them to stop, even if it made no sense?'

I thought about it. 'The ones that are loyal to her are fanatically loyal, so I think they might.'

'So either she forgot to tell them to stop, because she's busy doing something else—'

'Or she's just that crazy,' I said.

He nodded. 'Or she's that crazy, or they're waiting to either kidnap you, or kill you.'

'Fuck,' I said.

'You need to talk to Jean-Claude.'

'I thought you didn't like him,' I said.

'You don't like Donna either,' he said.

'So we each don't like the people that the other one loves.' I shrugged.

'You need bodyguards, Anita.'

'Why not just go home to St Louis?' I said.

'The Marshals Service frowns on us leaving a case in the middle of it, but that's not the problem.'

The other marshals were moving toward us. I moved closer to Edward, and asked, 'Then what is the problem?'

'How would you go home?'

I frowned, but answered. 'I'd get on the first plane I could catch and go home.'

'The police would drop you off at the airport, and then you'd be alone.'

'What?'

'You'd be in the airport, and on the plane alone, Anita. If I really wanted to take you and it was important to not be seen doing it, that's what I'd be waiting for, you alone, away from the other police, and Jean-Claude.'

I leaned close, speaking low. 'So what do I do?'

'Have some guards come in from St Louis.'

'How do I explain that to the other cops?'

'We'll think of something.' And then I knew the other marshals were too close to talk more, because Edward's face folded into a grin. His face lit with that charm that Ted always seemed to have. If there was an Emmy award for hired killers, Edward would so have won.

I wasn't nearly that good, but I managed a pleasant blank face to my fellow marshals. They asked, 'See anything that'll help us catch these bastards?'

Edward and I dutifully said, 'No.'

2

I had been called in to Marshal Raborn's office. It was a neat, square room. The only thing in the room that was messy was the desk, as if he'd straightened every edge in every file cabinet, and then left file folders on his desk overnight and they'd bred into short, unsteady towers of paperwork. Raborn was the local marshal in charge. If I'd been a regular marshal he'd have been more in charge of me, and Edward, but the preternatural branch was rapidly becoming its own entity, which meant Marshal Raborn was frustrated. He seemed to be particularly frustrated with me.

'There have been rumors for decades that Seattle has a weretiger clan,' he said.

I gave him blank cop face, polite, interested, but blank. Every group of wereanimals, or kiss of vampires, runs its business slightly differently. The white tiger clan of Las Vegas and the vampires are very public about who they are, and what they're doing. The red tiger clan of Seattle, not so much. In fact, Seattle wasn't aware they had a tiger clan in residence. The queen of their clan liked it that way. Wereanimals were still people under the law, so they'd never been legal to kill on sight the way vampires had been before the new vampire citizen laws went into effect, but once someone shifted into animal form a lot of people panicked and a lot of wereanimals got shot. I'd been on the receiving end of more than one attack by a wereanimal, so

I sympathized, but at the same time some of my best friends turned furry once a month. I was a little conflicted. Marshal Raborn thought so, too.

He seemed to want me to say something, so I said, 'Sorry, I haven't been on the ground long enough to pick up rumors yet.'

'There are weretigers here, Blake. I know there are.' He gave me a steely, penetrating look out of a pair of gray eyes the color of gunmetal. It was a good hard stare. Bad guys probably folded like cheap card tables when he gave them the stare, but I wasn't a bad guy.

'Obviously,' I said, 'we have a known survivor of a weretiger attack as our victim here.'

'Don't get cute, Blake,' he said, in a voice as hard as the cold stare.

'Sorry, just a natural ability on my part.'

He frowned at me. 'What is?'

'Being cute, or so I'm told.' I smiled at him.

'Are you flirting with me?'

'Nope.'

'Then what's with the smart remark?'

'Why am I getting solo treatment in your office, Raborn?'

'Because you know more than you're telling about these killers.'

Only years of training kept my face blank; only the slightest movement of one eye, almost an involuntary twitch, gave it away. It was the closest thing I had to a tell, as they say in poker. I covered it by smiling at him. I made it a good smile. I'd found that most men got distracted by it. I was buying time while I thought about what to say.

I shook my head, still smiling, as if he amused the hell out of me. What I was thinking was, *Does he actually know anything, or is he just fishing?*

'Do I amuse you, Blake?'

'A little,' I said.

He opened the folder in front of him and started tossing out photos of body parts as if he were dealing cards. I wasn't smiling by the time he finished covering the desk in gruesome pictures.

I gave him angry eyes then. 'You should see it in person, Raborn. It's much worse.'

'I've seen the latest crime scene,' he said.

'Good for you, now what do you want?'

'I want the truth.'

I resisted a terrible urge to say, 'You can't handle the truth,' but the thought helped kill some of the anger. I gave him calmer eyes and said, 'The truth about what exactly?'

'Are there weretigers in Seattle?'

'I haven't been here long enough to know where to get a good cup of coffee. I don't think I should be the one you're asking. You've got a preternatural branch that is local to your area. They should know more than I do about the local wereanimals.'

'They should, but somehow everywhere you go you know more monsters than the rest of us.'

I shrugged, and didn't have to fight to look bored. 'Maybe it's because I see them as people, not just monsters.'

He motioned at the photos spread out on his desk. 'Whatever did this isn't human. Nothing human could have done this.'

I shrugged again. 'I can't speak to that. I'm not in forensics and I've got cop friends who tell some mean stories about humans on PCP.'

'PCP would make them strong enough to do it, but it also makes them crazy,' Raborn said. 'They could do the violent killings, maybe, but not this.' He pointed at one photo. 'This is precise. PCP doesn't make you precise, it makes you a fucking animal.'

Since Edward and I had put that observation into our reports, I wasn't surprised to hear him repeat it back to me. 'Like a wereanimal?' I asked.

'You know what I meant.'

I sat up straighter in the chair because the gun at my back was digging in a little, which meant I was slumping. We were averaging three hours of sleep, and a different time zone every day was beginning to take its toil.

'I'm not sure I do, but if you called me in here to grill me about the local wereanimals, I just got here less than four hours ago. I'm good at gathering information about the local preternatural scene, but I'm not that good. No one is that good.'

'What's killing the weretigers?'

'I'm not sure.'

'Why are they being killed?'

'Why does any serial killer choose his victim?'

'So you know it is a he.'

I sighed. 'Statistically speaking, over ninety percent of all serial killers are male. Using *he* as the pronoun is probably accurate, but, you're right, I don't know that it's a he. Though female serial killers are more likely to use poison or a gun; a blade is more typical of male serial killers. Whoever is killing these victims is sure of his skill with a blade, and that he has the strength to get the job done before the weretiger can fight back. That level of physical confidence is usually male, rather than female.'

He looked at me, but there was a touch less hostility in his face. 'That's true.'

'You seem surprised that I knew that,' I said.

He settled back in his chair and looked at me, but now it was an appraising look. 'I'd been told that the only reason you have more executions than anyone else in the preternatural branch is that you're fucking the monsters, so they talk to you, but maybe that's not all of it.'

I gave him an unfriendly look, and then it seemed too much trouble. I leaned forward in the chair. 'Look, Raborn, if I were living with a group of men and having sex with all of them, and everyone were human, the other cops would still hate it, or they'd see me as a slut. But my live-in sweeties are vampires and shapeshifters, so the other cops really don't like my choice in boyfriends. I accept that, because there's nothing I can do about it, but I want to stop these killers. I don't want to see any more of these bodies. I want to go home to my sweeties, and stop seeing cut-up bodies in my dreams.'

He rubbed his eyes with his thumb and forefinger. 'Yeah, once you start seeing the bodies in your dreams, it's a bitch.'

'Trust me, Raborn, I'm motivated to solve these crimes.'

He looked at me then, and let me see that he was tired, too. 'I believe you want to go home, but how can I trust a marshal who's shacking up with the master vampire of her city?'

'It's illegal to discriminate against me because of who I'm dating.'

'Yeah, yeah, no discriminating on basis of race, religion, or lack of being human, or something like that.'

'I know that other cops say that I'm sleeping my way to all the information, and I do sleep with the monsters. I can't deny that, but the idea that the only skill set I have is sex is just jealousy.'

'What do you mean?' he asked.

'Most of the preternatural branch is male. They actually have a lower percentage of female marshals than the regular branch. Men don't want to admit that a little bitty girl is kicking their asses in the field. They need me not to be better at their job than they are, and the only way they can explain my having the highest number of executions in the entire service is to tell themselves that if they were a woman and could sleep their way to the top it would make all the difference.'

'You are a little bitty thing. You look dainty as my youngest daughter. I've read your cases. I know what you've managed to kill. You've been called in on cases where the first marshals were hospitalized, or killed outright. You, Marshal Forrester, Marshal Spotted-Horse, and Marshal Jefferies are the go-to guys for cleaning up the mess.'

The 'Otto Jefferies' identity was to Olaf what 'Ted Forrester' was to Edward. Olaf was scarier than Edward, though, because among the mercenary stuff his hobby was being a serial killer. He'd promised Edward and some part of some government that he wouldn't do his hobby on American soil. It was one of the ways he kept his day job helping train some uber-secret unit. His victims of choice were petite dark-haired women. He seemed to have a crush on me now, and had flat-out told me he'd be willing to try for normal sex with me, or at least sex that didn't involve my being tortured and dead. Edward wanted me to encourage the attraction, because it was the closest to healthy Olaf had ever been around a woman, but we both agreed that the line between being Olaf's serial killer girlfriend as we killed vampires together, and triggering his own serial killer needs toward me, was probably a thin one. Bernardo Spotted-Horse, like me, just had one name, our real names. Neither of us had ever made a living doing things as harsh as Edward and Olaf.

'We do what we can,' I said.

'They all have military backgrounds, special forces. They're all big, physically imposing men.'

'Ted is only five-eight, not that imposing,' I said.

Raborn smiled. 'Marshal Forrester seems taller.'

I smiled, too. 'That he does.'

'Sometimes, so do you.'

I just looked at him. 'Thanks, I guess.'

'Do the vampires really call you "the Executioner"?'

I shrugged. 'Nicknames.'

'Just answer the question,' he said.

'Fine, I've killed more of them than any other vampire hunter. When you kill enough people, it tends to impress the survivors.'

'You can't be as good at killing as your reputation.'

'Why not?' I asked.

'Because if you were, you couldn't be human.' He gave me that flat, searching gaze.

'My blood work is on record.'

'You carry, at last count, five different types of lycanthropy, which isn't possible. The whole idea of lycanthropy is that once you get it, you can't catch anything else.'

'Yeah, I'm a medical miracle.'

'How can you carry active lycanthropy and not shapeshift?'

'Just lucky, I guess.' Actually, I didn't know for sure, but we'd begun to suspect it was the vampire marks that I carried as Jean-Claude's human servant. It was as if his control and inability to change shape were shared with me. I didn't care what kept me from shifting; I was just happy for it. If I ever shifted for real, I'd lose my badge. I'd be considered unfit for duty due to disability.

'It makes you more than human-strong, though, doesn't it?'

'You'll turn a girl's head complimenting me like that,' I said.

'I've seen your fitness reports, Blake; don't be coy.'

'Then you know I can pretty much lift weight until the mass of the weight to be lifted exceeds my body mass. Any other questions?'

He looked at me and tapped his finger on the edge of the file that had held the photos. 'Not right now.'

'Good.' I stood up.

'The preternatural branch of the service is becoming more and more its own unit; did you know there's talk of forming a new branch of service altogether?'

'I've heard the rumor,' I said, looking down at him.

'Some of the preternatural branch marshals are just killers with badges.'

'Yep,' I said.

'Why do you think the powers that be let you all run wild like this?'

I looked down at him. It seemed like a real question. 'I don't know for sure, but if I had to guess I'd say they're making us into a legal hit squad. They give us badges to placate the liberal left, but they give us enough room in the law to kill the monsters the way the not-so-liberal right wants us to.'

'So you think the government is turning a blind eye to what the preternatural branch is becoming.'

'No, Marshal Raborn, I think they're setting themselves up.'

'Setting themselves up for what?' he asked.

'Plausible deniability,' I said.

We looked at each other. 'There are rumors that the laws are going to change again, and vampires and shapeshifters will be easier to kill legally, with less cause.'

'There are always rumors,' I said.

'If the laws change, which side will you be on?'

'The side I'm always on.'

'Which is?' He studied my face as he asked.

'Mine.'

'Do you think of yourself as human?' he asked.

I went for the door then, but stopped with my hand on the doorknob. I looked back at him. 'Legally, shapeshifters and vampires are human; that you'd even ask that of me is not only insulting, but probably illegal.'

'I'll deny I said it,' he said.

'Well, that answers my question.'

'What question?'

'If you were honest, or a lying bastard.'

His face darkened, and he stood up, sort of looming on the edge of his desk. 'Get out of my office.'

'My pleasure,' I said. I opened the door, shut it firmly but calmly behind me, and walked out through the desks of the other marshals. They'd watched the 'talk' through the glass windows of Raborn's office. They'd seen the body language, and they knew the talk had ended badly. I didn't care. I was just walking, because my throat was tight, and my eyes burned. Was I really going to cry because Raborn had asked me if I thought I was human? I hoped not.

3

Edward found me leaning against the cleanest part of the alley wall I could find. I was crying, not a lot, but still doing it. He didn't say anything. He just leaned against the wall beside me, having to tip his cowboy hat forward so it didn't bump the wall. He looked very Marlboro Man with the hat hiding most of his upper face.

'I still can't get used to you doing the whole Ted cowboy thing.' My voice was steady; if the tears hadn't been visible you couldn't have told I was crying.

He grinned. 'It makes people comfortable around him.'

'Talking about Ted in the third person, when he's you, is a little creepy, too.'

He grinned wider, and drawled in that Ted voice, 'Now, little lady, you know Ted isn't real. He's just a name I use.'

'He's your legal identity. I think it's your birth name.'

The grin began to fade around the edges, and I didn't have to see his eyes to know they were going cold and empty. 'If you want to ask a question, ask it.'

'I've asked before and you wouldn't answer.'

'That was then, this is now.' His voice was very quiet, very Edward.

I tried to read what I could see of his face. 'Okay, is Ted, or rather Theodore Forrester, your birth name?'

He moved the hat so he could look me in the eye as he said, 'Yes.'

I just blinked at him. 'Really, just like that, you finally give me a yes?'

He gave a small shrug, his mouth quirking.

'It was because I was crying, wasn't it?'

'Maybe.'

Then I just went back to the fact that I finally had confirmation that Edward had been born Theodore Forrester. In a way, Ted was the real person, and Edward the secret identity.

'Thank you,' I said.

'For finally answering the question?'

I nodded and smiled. 'And for giving a shit that I was crying.'

'What did Raborn want?'

I told him, ending with, 'I know it was a stupid reason to cry. You'd think I'd get used to being called a monster.'

'It's only been a month since you had to make the hardest kill of your life, Anita. Give yourself a break.'

Edward hadn't been with me for the kill, because it hadn't been a legal monster hunt. It had been Haven, our local Rex, lion king, going apeshit and shooting Nathaniel, my live-in sweetie, wereleopard to call, and one of the loves of my life. Haven had meant to kill him, but Noel, one of the weakest of our werelions, had put himself between Nathaniel and that bullet. He'd lost his life to save Nathaniel's, and I'd barely known Noel. Haven had been jealous, and wanted to hurt me as badly as possible; that he'd chosen Nathaniel's death as the most painful thing he could do to me was something I still hadn't looked at too closely. I had enough pain, because Haven had been one of my lovers. I'd never killed anyone that I'd cared about before. It hadn't felt very good. In fact, it had sucked.

'You're saying I'm still raw from killing Haven?'

'Yes.'

'Have you ever had to kill a lover?'

'Yes.'

I glanced at him. 'Really?'

He nodded. 'Now ask me if I cared about her.'

'Okay, did you care about her?'

'No.'

'And I cared about Haven, so it hurts more.'

'I think so,' he said.

We leaned against the wall some more in companionable silence. Edward and I didn't need to talk – we could talk, but we didn't need to. 'We're going about hunting these killers all wrong. Even if we didn't know what was killing them, and sort of why, we're still doing it ass-backward.'

'We need to consolidate the warrants of execution from the first three cities and just make it one hunt,' he said.

'Yes,' I said.

'But the first three warrants are all in the hands of marshals who were book-and-classroom trained. They were cops, but no one has a violent crimes background. I'm not sure why they're recruiting some of these kids.'

'We were all kids once, Edward, but we need to take over the warrants before some of the other marshals get themselves killed. Raborn said that you, me, Jefferies, and Spotted-Horse are the cleanup crew. We come onto a warrant after other marshals have been killed or injured.'

'It's the law, Anita. The warrant is theirs until they are unable to execute it, through death or injury, or they sign it over to another marshal for some other reason.'

'Let's make them sign it over to us now.'

'How?' he asked.

'We could just ask,' I said.

'I asked two of the marshals. They both refused.'

'You asked the men,' I said.

'Yes.'

'So I'll ask the female marshal,' I said.

'A little girl talk?' he asked.

I frowned at him. 'I don't really do girl talk, but I'll try to persuade her to sign the warrant over to me. If just one of them signs off, then we can hunt the monsters. Stop the crimes by killing the criminal, not by solving them.'

'I like it,' he said.

'You know and I know that we're legal assassins, not cops. Sometimes we solve crimes and catch the bad guys, but at the end of most days we kill people.'

'You sound like that bothers you,' he said. He looked at me as he asked it.

I shrugged. 'It does, and we already discussed that it doesn't bother you. Well, fucking bully for you, but it's beginning to get on my nerves.'

'I think I've figured out a way to use you as bait to lure them out, if it's really you they're wanting.'

I studied his unreadable face. 'But first we'll need someone to sign a warrant over to us, right?'

'That would help, and you getting some bodyguards from home, and maybe calling in Bernardo and Olaf now, before anyone's dead, as backup wouldn't be a bad idea.'

'Olaf still thinks I'm his girlfriend or something.'

'The couple that slaughters people together stays together.'

'That wasn't really very funny,' I said.

'Yes, it was, but I apologize anyway. We both know that someday you, or I, will have to kill Olaf because he's decided to kill you.'

'If he really plans on killing me he'll kill you first, Edward, because he knows that you won't rest until he's dead.'

'You'd do the same for me.'

'True, so he'd kill us really close together, so neither of us could go all revenge on his ass.'

'Probably,' Edward said.

'And yet, you'll call him in to back us up on this case.'

'He's a good man in a fight.'

'He's a crazy psycho killer, is what he is,' I said.

'Technically he's not psychotic.'

'So just a crazy killer,' I said.

'Yeah.' He smiled and it actually reached his eyes; it was a real smile, not Ted's smile, but Edward smiling. I didn't get to see the smile often, so I valued it when I did. I had to smile back.

I shook my head, still smiling. 'Fine, I'll try to get the other marshal to sign off, and then you call in Bernardo and Olaf, but I can't get bodyguards from home to come help us. We're marshals, they aren't, and being able to deputize people isn't a power the Marshals Service has been granted in a very long time.'

'You haven't been keeping up on current events.'

I frowned at him. 'What?'

'Last month a marshal died, because backup didn't arrive in time, but a soldier just home from Iraq was able to take the marshal's weapons and finish the shapeshifter off.'

'I did hear about that. It was tragic and brave and, so what?'

'You really don't check the official emails, do you?'

'Maybe not as often as I should; what'd I miss?'

He got his phone out of his pocket and used his finger to roll through emails, then held the tiny screen up to me. I read it through twice. 'You're joking me.'

'It's official.'

'We have the right to deputize not only if we are without backup, but if we feel that an individual's skill set is of benefit to the execution of our warrant and will save civilian lives. Mother of God, Edward, this gives us carte blanche to form a fucking mob.'

'There's potential for abuse, yes.'

'Potential for abuse, there's potential for pitchforks and torches,' I said.

'Anita, come on, no one would use pitchforks or torches anymore. It'd be flashlights and guns.'

'This isn't funny, Edward; this is a civil rights problem waiting to happen.'

'I didn't know you cared about that, or did that change when you helped get the law passed to spare little vampires when their master is the bad guy?'

'I'm just saying that this little amendment to the law could get out of hand really fast.'

'It could, it probably will, but for us, right now, it's useful.'

'Are you saying we deputize some of the bodyguards from St Louis?'

'It's a thought,' he said.

I opened my mouth, closed it, thought about it, then said, 'Damn, great for us right now, but . . .'

'Take that it helps us right now, Anita. We'll worry about legal rampaging mobs later.'

I nodded. 'Deal.'

'Get her to sign the warrant over to you and I'll call Olaf and Bernardo in, and you pick bodyguards from home.'

'You know most of them now; you want to help pick?'

'I trust your judgment,' he said.

'High praise coming from you.'

'Deserved,' he said.

I tried not to look too pleased, and probably failed. 'Thanks, Edward.'

'Don't mention it, but first you need her to sign the warrant over to you. Get the warrant, and then I have a plan.'

He wouldn't tell me the plan, but since he'd actually admitted his 'real' name to me, I could let him keep his secret plan — for now.

4

The marshal I needed to sweet-talk out of her warrant was female, so we got to split a hotel room. Marshal Laila Karlton was five-six and built solid. I don't mean she was fat, I mean she was all muscle and curves. In too much clothing she looked like it might be fat, but when you saw her just in a T-shirt and jeans, you realized the 'bulk' was half curves and half solid muscle. It wasn't lean muscle and that was the reason it could fool the eye, but when she picked up her backpack of vampire-hunting gear, which probably weighed the same fifty pounds that mine did, her biceps bulged, and you realized it was all camouflage for the fact that she was strong. She didn't see it that way, though.

'God, you're tiny. I bet I can put my hands around that little white-girl waist, and you still have boobs and an ass. That is not fair, girlfriend.'

She'd taken the I'll-cut-myself-down-and-compliment-you-before-you-beat-me-to-it tack. I had the choices of ignoring it, complimenting her in some way, or agreeing that I looked good without complimenting her back. The last choice would make her dislike me more. She'd already let me know, nicely, that my being a few sizes smaller than her made her predisposed not to like me. One of the good things about working with men was that they didn't do this shit.

I tried, but I sucked at these games. 'I know men who prefer your body type to mine.'

'Bullshit,' she said, and was ready to be angry.

'I hang around with a lot of older vampires. They don't like the really thin girls. They like women to look like women, not preadolescent boys with boobs sort of stuck on as an afterthought.'

'You don't look like that,' she said, her voice a little less angry, but still not friendly.

'Neither do you. We both look nice and curvy the way God intended grown-up women to look.'

She thought about it and then grinned at me. It lit her whole face up, and I knew we'd be okay. 'Ain't that the truth. But that booty is not white-girl booty.'

'I'm told I look like my mother, except paler. She was Hispanic.'

'That explains it. I knew you were too round in the right places to be white bread.' She laid out her clothes in a neat line on the bedspread, and then said, 'What do you mean, "told" you look like your mother?'

'She died when I was eight.'

'I'm sorry.' And she sounded like she meant it. In fact, there was an awkward pause as we each unpacked on our side of the room. I had the bed nearest the bathroom and farthest from the door. We hadn't discussed it; I'd just entered the room first.

'It's okay,' I said, 'it was a long time ago.'

'What about your dad?'

'German, as in his was the first generation born in this country.'

'What does he think of you being a marshal and vampire hunter?' she asked, as she dumped her clothes in a pile on the bed and began to sort them.

'He's okay with it. My stepmother, Judith, on the other hand, doesn't like it much.' I must have smiled because Laila laughed, a deep, throaty laugh. It was dark, and sensual like Guinness in a glass. It was a good laugh.

'Oh, yeah, I've been my mom's despair since I could walk. My dad's a football coach and I just wanted to be like my brothers and my dad.'

'No sisters?'

'One and she's the girl.'

'Yeah, I've got a stepsister; she was the girl. I went hunting with my dad.'

'No brothers?'

'One half brother, but he's a little too gentle for hunting. I was my dad's only boy.' I made quote marks in the air with my fingers.

She laughed again. 'I was always competing with my brothers and losing. They're six feet and up like my dad. I'm short like Mama.'

'I've always been the smallest kid in class.'

'I'm not the smallest, just not as tall as I wanted to be.'

'So, does your dad like your job?'

'He's proud of me.'

'Mine, too,' I said. 'He just worries.'

'Yeah, mine, too.' She looked at me sort of sideways and then said, 'They talk about you in the training. Anita Blake, the first female vampire executioner. You still have the highest kill count of any marshal.'

'I've been doing it longer,' I said.

'There's only eight of you from the early days,' she said.

'There were more of us than that,' I said.

'They either retired early like your friend Manny Rodriguez, or they . . .' She was suddenly very interested in getting her clothes in a drawer. 'Is it okay if I take the top drawer?'

'Fine, you're taller.'

She smiled, a little nervous around the edges. 'It's okay, Karlton,' I said. 'I know the mortality rate was high when the vampire executioners first started serving warrants.'

She put her clothes in the drawer, closed it, and then looked at me, sort of sideways, again. 'Why did the mortality rate among the executioners go up after the warrant system was put in place? The books all say it went up, way up, but it doesn't explain why.'

I knelt down and she gave me enough room to put my clothes

in the bottom drawer. I thought about how to answer her. 'Before warrants, vampire hunters weren't always particular about how they killed. We didn't have to defend it in court, so we were a little more trigger happy. After the warrant system some hunters hesitated, worried about what would happen if they couldn't defend it in court and ended up on murder charges. Remember, back then we had no badges. Some of us went to jail for murder even though the vampire killed was confirmed as a serial killer. It made some of us hesitate to kill. Hesitation will get you killed.'

'We have badges now.'

'Yeah, and officially we're cops, but make no mistake, Karlton, we are still executioners. A policeman's main job is to prevent harm to others. Most of them go twenty years and never draw their gun in the line of duty, no matter what you see on television.' I laid shirts on top of bras and underwear in the drawer. 'Our main job is to kill people; that's not what cops do.'

'We don't kill people, we kill monsters.'

I smiled, but knew it was bitter. 'Pretty to think so.'

'What does that mean?'

'How old are you?'

'Twenty-four, why?'

I smiled, and it still didn't feel happy. 'When I was your age I believed they were monsters, too.'

'How old are you?'

'Thirty.'

'You're only six years older than me, Blake.'

'Cop years are like dog years, Karlton, multiply by seven.'

'What?' she asked.

'I may only be six years older than you chronologically, but in dog years I'm forty-two years older.'

She frowned at me. 'What the hell is that even supposed to mean?'

'It means, how many vampires have you executed?'

'Four,' she said, and it was a little defensive.

'Hunted them down and killed them, or morgue stakings where they're chained to a gurney and unconscious while you do it?'

'Morgue, why?'

'Talk to me after you've killed some of them awake, while they're begging for their lives.'

'They beg for their lives? I thought they'd just attack.'

'Not always; sometimes they're scared and they beg, just like anybody else.'

'But they're vampires, they're monsters.'

'According to the law we uphold they're legal citizens of this country, not monsters.'

She studied my face. I don't know what she saw there, or wanted to see, but she finally frowned. I think a blank face wasn't what she'd been hoping to see. 'So you really do believe that they're people.'

I nodded.

'You believe they're people, but you still kill them.'

I nodded again.

'If you really believe that, then it would be like me killing Joe Blow down the block. It would be like me putting a stake through a regular person's heart.'

'Yeah,' I said.

She frowned and turned back to unpacking. 'I don't know if I could do my job if I thought of them as people.'

'It does seem a conflict of interest,' I said. I began debating on where to put the weapons I'd want easy access to, just in case. Knowing that the Harlequin might be planning to try to kidnap or kill me made me more than normally interested in being well armed.

'Can I say something without you taking it wrong?' she asked, and sat on the edge of her bed.

I stopped with one gun and two knives laid out on the bed. 'Probably not, but say it anyway.'

She frowned again, putting that little pucker between her eyes.

If she didn't stop frowning so much she'd have lines there before too many years. 'I don't want to get off on the wrong foot with you.'

I sighed. 'What I mean, Karlton, is anytime someone asks me, "Can I say something without you taking it wrong?" it usually means it will be something insulting. So say it, but I can't guarantee how I'll take it.'

She thought about that a minute, serious as a small child on the first day of school. 'Okay, I guess that was a stupid thing to say, but I want to know the answer enough to be stupid.'

'Then ask,' I said.

'We had some of the other vampire executioners come and give lectures. One of them said you'd been one of the best before you got seduced by the master vampire of your city. He says that women are more likely to be seduced by vampires than men, and you're proof of that.'

'It was Gerald Mallory, the vampire hunter assigned to Washington, DC, wasn't it?' I said.

'How did you know?'

'Mallory thinks I'm the whore of Babylon because I'm sleeping with vampires. He might forgive shapeshifters, but he hates vampires with a depth and breadth of hate that's frightening.'

'Frightening?' She made it a question with a upward lilt of her voice.

'I've seen him kill. He gets off on it. He's like a racist who has permission to hate and kill.'

'You say race because I'm black.'

'No, I say racist because it's the closest thing I can imagine to his attitude toward vampires. I'm not joking when I say after seeing him stake vampires that he scares me. He hates them so much, Karlton. He hates them without reason, or thought, or any room in his mind for a reason not to hate them. It consumes him, and people consumed by hate are crazy. It blinds them to the truth, and makes them hate anyone who doesn't agree with them.'

'He also says that you should always stake a vampire. He doesn't approve of using silver ammunition.'

'He's a stake and hammer man.' I knelt by my backpack and came up with the Mossberg 500 Bantam shotgun. 'This is my favorite for shooting them in their coffins. All you need to do is destroy the brain and the heart, but don't just shoot them in the head and chest and think you've got the job done. You need to make sure the brain is leaking out on the floor, or the head is completely detached from the body, and then you need to see some daylight through the chest. The older the vampire, the more completely you need to destroy the heart and head.'

'He said just staking the heart was enough.'

'If I see daylight through the chest and the heart is completely destroyed, you're probably okay, but if I have time I destroy the brain, too, just to be safe, and I want you to know that's safer in the field. I'd still go back and shoot them in the head after the heart was taken out in a field situation.'

'You mean on a hunt,' she said.

'Yeah.'

'This is my first hunt.'

In my head, I thought, *Well, fuck*. 'You mean you have never participated in a hunt?'

'No,' she said.

'I know you said you'd only done morgue stakings, but I thought you'd gone on at least one hunt as the junior marshal. You've never even seen a vampire hunted and killed in the field?'

'I can handle myself.'

I shook my head. 'Now I need to ask you something without *you* getting insulted,' I said.

She sat on the side of her bed. 'That's fair; what do you want to know?'

'This is a bad case, Karlton. It's not a hunt for a first-time field agent.'

'I know it's a bad one,' she said.

'No, you don't, not yet.' I sat on my bed and faced her. 'I want you to sign the warrant over to me, please.'

She was angry and didn't try to hide it. 'I can't. I'm the girl, and if I back down on this the other marshals will never trust me again.'

'It's not about being a girl, Karlton, it's about being new and inexperienced.'

'I'll have your back, Blake.'

'I'm not worried that you'll get me killed.'

She frowned again. 'Then what are you worried about?'

I looked into those dark brown eyes, that earnest face and said, 'I'm worried you'll get yourself killed.'

There was no more girl talk after that. We just got ready for bed. I went into the bathroom to get dressed. I had packed my weapons, but not my clothes. Nathaniel, the most domestic of us all, had. I was fine with the jeans, T-shirts, boots, and jogging shoes, but the pajamas, well, I'd be talking to him about the pajamas. It was a camisole and boy shorts except they were both black lace and stretchy fabric that fit like a second skin. There was enough lift to the fabric that the camisole actually supported my breasts enough for it to fit right. The skimpy pj's looked great on me, but were so not appropriate marshal jammies. But they were the most appropriate of what he'd packed. Soooo going to talk to him about that.

When I came out, Karlton said, 'Nice pajamas. Sorry to disappoint that you're not bunking with the boys.'

I didn't bother to glare at her. 'My boyfriend packed my clothes while I packed the weapons.'

'You let a man pack your clothes?'

'He's usually pretty good at it, but I think he picked the pajamas for what he wanted to see.'

She snorted. 'That's a man.'

I sighed. 'I guess so.'

The oversized T-shirt she was wearing had someone I didn't

recognize singing into a microphone stand. I slid between the covers, and the sheets were the cheap cotton that had been in every hotel or motel on this trip. I missed the silk sheets of Jean-Claude's bed, and the high-thread-count cotton of the bed that Micah and Nathaniel and I shared. I was sheet spoiled.

'Do you always sleep with that many weapons?'

'Yes.' It wasn't entirely true. I always slept with a gun close at hand, but I didn't normally sleep in the wrist sheaths with their slender silver-edged blades. They weren't that comfortable for sleeping in, but if the Harlequin were faster than normal vampires and shapeshifters, then there might not be time to reach under my pillow for a gun. The knife draw from the wrist sheaths was quicker, because any gun under my pillow either had the safety on or stayed in a holster, so either way it was a few seconds slower than just drawing the knives. I put the big knife that usually rode along my spine beside the bed, on top of the back-pack, so that I could reach it if I had to, though honestly if the two knives on me and the gun under my pillow didn't take care of the problem I'd be dead before I got the third blade, or the other guns. With that cheerful thought, I turned off the light on my side of the room.

The room was suddenly very dark, only a thin line of artificial light sliding between the slightly crooked curtains that led to the balcony, which was just a sort of walkway with a railing. The door led directly out into the night. Vampires couldn't come into the room without permission, but wereanimals could, and bespelled humans could, and . . . I was less than happy with the room, but it was cheap and I'd learned that if you were traveling on the government's dime they pinched their dimes; pennies didn't even figure into the equation.

Her voice came out of the less-than-perfect dark. 'Is Gerald Mallory right – are women more likely to be seduced by vampires than men?'

'No.'

'Then why are you the only marshal who's living with them?'

'Have you ever been in love?' I asked.

I couldn't see her face, but I felt her go still, and then the sheets rustled. 'Yes.'

'Did you plan on falling in love with him?'

The sheets moved again, and then she said, 'You don't plan love, it just happens.'

'Exactly,' I said.

Sheets sighed in the dark as she turned over. 'I get it. I have seen pictures of your Master of the City; he's pretty if you like white boys.' And she laughed.

It made me laugh, too. 'I guess so. Good night, Karlton.'

'Call me Laila; all the guys call me Karlton. I'd like to hear my name sometimes.'

'Okay. Good night, Laila.'

'Good night, Anita.'

I heard her roll over a couple more times, the sheets stretching and moving with her, and then her breathing evened out and she slept. Edward and I would play by the book until they consolidated the warrants, and then we'd try to take over the hunt; until then, we waited for a warrant to be reassigned. The trouble was, the only way it got reassigned was if one of the other marshals was too injured, or too dead, to finish the hunt. I lay awake in the dark, and thought, *Please, God, don't let her get killed.*

5

The dream came as it had most nights for a month. The details changed but the theme didn't. The theme was Haven, not as in a place of rest and peace, but as in the lover I'd killed. Some nights he died in my arms. Some nights we made love and then he bled to death on top of me. Some nights it was like a movie replay of how he'd actually died. Tonight's version was new, but after the other nightmares new didn't seem bad.

I was in a maze formed of black walls. They were slick and almost shiny, almost stone, almost mirrors, so that the ghost of myself wavered in the black surfaces. I had hopes that this was just a regular nightmare until I heard his voice. Haven called me somewhere in the maze: 'Anita, I'm coming, Anita.' Great, he was hunting me tonight. Sometimes turnabout is so not fair play.

I was dressed in jeans with a belt and buckle, T-shirt, jogging shoes, but no weapons. This just got better and better.

'I can smell you, Anita. I can smell all that sweet skin.'

I started moving in the black maze, away from his voice. I thought about needing a weapon. I thought about my Browning BDM and it was in my hand. This was a dream. I could change some of it – normally I could break free of dreams, but something about the ones with Haven seemed to trap me. I think guilt made me stay to see the horrors.

I started moving faster, taking left turns only. All mazes had the same premise: One direction would lead out and one would lead to the center of the maze. I don't know why I chose left; why not? I just prayed that it led out and not deeper into the blackness. But it was a nightmare, and you never really win in nightmares. No, they're all about losing over and over again.

The center of the maze was a huge square space with a fountain in the middle of it. The fountain was all black squares and quietly pulsing water; as the center of a scary night-dark maze it wasn't bad. It could have been worse; and then, of course, worse stepped out of an opening on the other side. Worse was six feet and a little more of slender, muscled handsome. Haven's hair was still short, gelled into spikes on top of his head, all of it done in shades of blue as if some artful hairdresser had pretended that blue could be a real hair color and have highlights. The hair made his pale blue eyes look more blue than they actually were, I think; it was hard to tell since the hair was always so close to his eyes. The hair and the Sesame Street tattoos on his shoulders were what had made me nickname him 'Cookie Monster'.

'What do you want, Haven?'

'What I always wanted: you,' he said.

'You can't have me.'

'Here I can. Here there's just me.'

'Fuck you.'

'Let's.'

'You're dead. You're dead. I killed you.'

'I remember.'

'You're dead, you don't remember. You're just my guilt visiting every night.'

'Am I?' he asked, and something about the way he said it made me ask, 'What else could you be?'

Other figures stepped from the entrances around the square. Figures in white masks and black cloaks: Harlequin. I raised the gun and pointed it vaguely; there were too many of them, and I wasn't that fast, not even in dreams.

Movement made me glance at Haven; he was wearing a black

cloak and held a white mask in his hand. 'We're coming,' he said, 'wake up.'

I woke staring at the dark ceiling, pulse thudding, throat almost closed around it, and then I heard it. The door, not the knob, but the brush of someone against it, like the first tentative touch. I drew my gun from underneath the pillow and tried to think how to warn Laila without them hearing me. They were either vampires or wereanimals; they'd hear any whisper. Then I realized they'd heard the change in my heartbeat; they knew I was awake.

I had time to say, 'Laila, they're here!' The door opened as she sat up in bed but didn't reach for a weapon. Shit. There was no one in the doorway. It stretched pale and empty, filled with night and the artificial lights of the parking lot beyond. Then I heard it, a creak of board, and knew something was crawling on the floor, hidden from me by Laila's bed.

She had her gun in her hand now, and whispered, 'What is it? Why is the door open?'

I started to say, 'It's by you, on the floor,' but one minute she was on the bed with her gun and the next a black shape whirled over her and she was gone. I'd seen the speed of lycanthropes and vampires, but all I saw was the cloak like a black sheet and it dragged her over on the other side of the bed with it. It wasn't just fast, it was as if the thing, whatever it was, was formed of the blackness of the cloth and nothing more. Fuck, that couldn't be real. Had it mind-fucked me? If the answer was yes, I was about to lose in real life and not just in nightmare.

'Yell for help and we kill her,' a voice said on the other side of the bed. It was male and growly; I was betting shapeshifter of some kind.

'How do I know she's still alive?'

'Do you think I could kill her that quickly?' the voice asked.

'Yes,' I said.

He laughed. 'Say something, girl.'

There was a moment of silence, then a small pained sound, and Laila said, 'I'm alive.'

'Are you hurt?' I asked.

'No.'

'Oh, I'm sad that you think I haven't hurt you yet. The next thing I do to you, you won't doubt that you're hurt.'

'Leave her alone.'

'We will if you give us what we want.'

'What do you want?' I asked. I had the gun pointed in the direction of the voice, but there was nothing to shoot at. If I was patient maybe there would be; nothing is faster than a bullet.

'You,' and it was such a direct echo from my dream that it startled me.

'What do you mean, you want me? How? Why?'

'Does it matter? If you don't come with us, I'll kill your friend.'

'Don't do it—' Laila said, and was cut off abruptly, and this time the pain sound was a little louder.

'Ask her if she's hurt again,' the growling voice said, and he sounded eager.

I'd heard that tone before in voices; I knew that they liked causing pain, so I did what he asked so he wouldn't hurt her again to make the point.

'Laila, are you hurt?'

Her voice was shaky. 'Yes.'

'What did you do to her?'

'Nothing permanent, yet,' he said.

'She'll heal?' I asked, and as in the dream I pointed my gun toward the voice, but also at the open door. Most of the Harlequin traveled in pairs or more. But with their speed I wouldn't have time to shoot twice. I'd need a target and a decision before I'd really had time to decide anything.

'Yes,' he said.

'What do you mean you want me? Sexually?' I was almost hopeful on that one; it wasn't a fate worse than death and it certainly wasn't a fate worse than having Laila murdered while I listened to her die.

'We're not allowed,' he said, and he sounded sad.

'You're not allowed to have sex?'

'Just not with you.'

That was interesting. 'Then what do you want with me?'

'My master is outside. Simply put down your weapon and walk out the door to him. I will release the girl and follow you.'

Laila said, 'Don't do it, Anita!' She yelled it, and then she screamed for real. Edward and the other marshal were next door. Help was coming.

The cloak rose up, and I saw the white mask, but Laila was held in front of him like a shield. Her eyes were fluttered back in her head, but she was alive. I raised the gun barrel higher so I'd hit the white mask and miss her. Then he was gone; I swear that he moved so fast Laila simply stayed in the air where he'd held her, and he was through the door and gone before she began to fall.

Edward shouted, 'Anita!'

'I'm okay, did you see that?'

'I saw something,' he called back.

I kept an eye on the doorway as I searched for Laila's pulse. Edward was in the doorway: shirtless, boxers, with a gun in each hand. I let him watch for bad guys and looked down at Laila. Her arm was broken at the wrist and maybe higher up. There was blood, too, and it wasn't from the arm. Fuck.

I heard the other marshal go back toward the room. 'I'll call for an ambulance, and then will someone tell me what the hell just happened?'

Edward kept watch out into the night, but said, 'Her warrant is vacated. I guess we have our warrant of execution.'

'I didn't want it this way,' I said.

'She's alive, Anita. It could have gone the other way.'

He was right. I knew he was right, so why did I feel so shitty? 'I don't know where the blood is coming from, but somewhere on her back. I don't want to move her, but there's too much blood. We need to find the wound and put pressure on it. If she bleeds out, nothing else matters.'

He knelt down to help but kept his side toward the door so he could still see movement. 'We can hunt them now, Anita, our way.'

He helped me lift her and try to keep her neck from moving. It probably wasn't a spinal injury, but back wounds can be tricky, and cautious was better than being wrong. He helped me lift her just enough so I could search for the wound. But it wasn't just a wound, it was several. I found at least three. 'Shit!' I said.

'What's wrong?' he asked.

'It's multiple wounds, which means it wasn't a blade. He used claws.'

'Powerful enough shapeshifter to change just his hands,' Edward said.

'Yes.'

'They're all going to be that powerful,' he said.

'I know.' I got towels from the bathroom to press against the wounds. 'These are punctures. If they're deep, her chances of catching lycanthropy are higher.'

'You'll have to tell the EMTs when they get here.'

'I know.' I pressed the towels against the wound and tried to stop the bleeding. Edward kept holding her up and trying to keep her neck from moving. It was the best we could do until the medics got here.

'What's our way?' I asked.

'What?' he asked.

'You said we'd be able to hunt them our way now. What's our way?'

'Violent, and very, very final.'

I looked at him over Laila's unconscious body. My hands were already soaked with her blood. I was kneeling in it. 'Did you see the speed of the thing?'

'Incredible.'

'How do we kill that speed?'

'Wound it, then chop it up.' He sounded eager.

'I'm scared, Edward.'

He looked at me, his eyes empty and cold as a winter's moon. 'I'm not.' I guess he meant it to be comforting, and I guess maybe it was.

6

One of the good things about wearing the tight, tiny jammies was that no blood had gotten on them. Edward had had to give up his boxers to go into a baggie for the lab. They had let him put on shorts and a T-shirt since his room wasn't a crime scene. Until the techs were done, my room was off limits. But neither of us had gotten to clean off the blood yet. My jammies were blood free, but the rest of me wasn't. I had blood on my legs from the knees down, and on my arms nearly to the elbow on one side. Forensic techs had taken samples of the blood on little swabs but hadn't let me clean up yet. The blood was drying and had that crinkly feeling to it like it always did, as if I could feel it adhering to my skin. I was never sure if that was a sensory illusion or if I could really feel it drying. Either way, I could feel the blood almost catching on my skin every time I moved just right. I wanted a shower. They had given me a blanket to hold around my shoulders in the chill of the night air, but the cement of the open balcony area was damn cold under bare feet. It was also awkward holding my gun in one hand while trying to hold the blanket in place. Detective Lorenzo had offered to let me put my gun in Edward's room since the crime scene techs weren't in there, but I'd declined. The Harlequin had tried to kidnap me tonight; I wanted a gun.

Detective Lorenzo was taller than me, but only an inch or so taller than Edward, about five-nine. His hair was thick, and though cut short it had waves to it. He'd have had to shave his head to not have waves, so that, though short, his hair would never be neat. His eyes were a dark, even brown, his face open and friendly, and cute in that boy-next-door way. He was probably thirty because of the detective shield, but he didn't look it. There was some bulk under the suit that let me know either he had naturally good shoulders or he hit the gym, or maybe both. He'd been one of the detectives called to the crime scene before everyone was certain it was part of an ongoing federal investigation. Technically the Marshals Service could have kept him out of things, but most of us tried not to alienate the local police if we could help it. The preternatural branch especially ended up being alone a lot in the field. We relied on local police more than most other federal officers, even the rest of the Marshals Service. One of the nicknames among other cops for the preternatural branch was 'lone wolf.' On the radio they'd say, 'We've got a lone wolf on site.' I wondered how the nickname worked when there were this many of us. Can you say 'lone wolves' and not sound silly?

Marshal Raborn was taller than all of us, and the fact that he carried a few extra pounds gave him some weight to back it up. He seemed to try to fill the room with his physical presence as if he were a much larger man than he was, or maybe his pissy attitude just seemed to take up more space.

'How did you know it was claws that cut Karlton if you didn't see them?'

'Once I felt multiple wounds, I knew it had to be. If he'd used a blade, I'd have seen his arm moving as he drew it out to stab her again. His arm was stationary. He never had the range of movement to use a knife like that. Claws come out like switchblades; just hold them against the skin and they stab.'

'Only if they shift form first,' Raborn said.

'I told you, the really powerful lycanthropes can shift just their hands, so it's just claws springing out.'

'That's not possible. They have to shift into at least wolfman form to have claws.'

'I never said it was a werewolf, Raborn.'

'*Wolfman* is what we call all the shapeshifters in half-man form, Anita,' Edward said. He was trying to use his Ted voice, but there was too much of the real Edward leaking through, so it came out cold.

'He was covered head to toe,' Marshal Tilford said. 'He could have been in wolfman form.'

I glanced at Tilford. He was about the same height as Edward and Lorenzo; we were having an average height day on the crime scene, at least for the men. Tilford's hair, what little there was of it, was cut very short and close to his head. He was carrying a little more weight around the middle than Raborn, which meant if he didn't hit the gym soon he'd fail his physical retest. The preternatural branch had to test with the HRU, Hostage Rescue Unit, which was the marshals' equivalent of SWAT. But it was a new requirement since an investigation late last year had ended with fault laid on lack of physical fitness on the officer's part as a major contributing factor to his injuries and the deaths of two civilians.

I must have looked at him too long, or maybe my anger at Raborn was still in my eyes, because Tilford said, 'Hey, I'm just saying what I saw.'

'He was too human-shaped even under the costume. If he'd been in half-man form, there would have been differences in his legs, his arms; the shape isn't perfectly human even covered up like that,' I said.

'And how would you know that?' Raborn asked.

I gave him glare for glare. 'Experience.'

'I'll just bet you have experience with wolfmen.' His voice was low and angry, and disdainful.

I don't know what I would have said, but Lorenzo broke in and said, 'The news crews are filming us. Maybe stepping inside Marshal Forrester and Tilford's room would be a good idea?' He smiled while he said it, kept his voice mild and placating. He was trying to smooth things down. Good someone was.

'Blake here likes publicity, don't you, Blake?' Raborn asked.

I started to say something, but Edward touched my shoulder. It was enough. I shut up and went into the open door of their room. Everybody else followed. Edward shut the door behind us.

'What changes in his body would have been there if he'd been in wolfman form?' Tilford asked.

'The legs are sort of longer, but crooked, almost like the knee joint is wrong, and the femur and tibia are both longer. The mask wouldn't have fit that flat to his face. There's more muzzle, for lack of a better word.'

Tilford nodded, as if he were filing it all away for later use. I hoped he was. We needed more of the marshals to know as much as possible about what we hunted. Lorenzo was actually writing it down in a little notebook.

'You should give a lecture next time we have training. This would be good stuff to know out in the field,' Tilford said.

'I'm always happy to share information,' I said.

'Well, aren't you just the center of attention anytime a roomful of men shows up,' Raborn said.

'Jealous?' I asked.

'Of what, the men?'

'You're jealous of something. If it's not the men, then what the fuck is it?'

'Are you calling me a homosexual?'

Edward touched my shoulder, more firmly this time, and moved me back so he could step between us. He was probably one of the few people in the world that I would have let move me back.

'Let's all calm down.' He had found Ted's good-ol'-boy voice again. It was a voice to make you agree to anything, or at least not mind disagreeing.

We were saved by Raborn's radio. He was called to the crime scene to deal with something. The tension in the room dropped by a ton when he left, and it wasn't just me who felt the relief. It showed on Lorenzo and Tilford both.

'What is his problem with you?' Lorenzo asked.

'I have no idea,' I said, and finally let myself sit down on the edge of the bed, careful to keep the blanket between me and the sheets.

'It feels like you have history,' Tilford said.

'I swear to you that I've never met Raborn.'

'Maybe you have a friend in common, or an enemy,' Lorenzo said.

That made me look at him. 'That's a good idea, Lorenzo; I'll see if I've ever pissed off anyone Raborn's close to.'

'Hey, I'm not just another pretty face,' he said, and grinned.

It made me smile, too, which I needed. Men often make women smile or laugh when they don't know what else to do. It's not a bad survival skill in a relationship.

There was more talking, but we didn't learn anything new. I persisted with the crime scene techs until I got permission to use Edward and Tilford's shower. Edward lent me a T-shirt and a pair of boxers with a drawstring to put on after I had the blood washed off. Yeah, it would have been more attractive with just the overly long T-shirt on, but I wasn't going for cute, I was going for professional, and it's just hard to be professional without pants on. It would be hours, maybe even morning, before I was allowed into my room to get my own clothes. I wanted my clothes, but honestly, I wanted my weapons more. Edward had offered me my choice of several dangerous things from his arsenal. I took a second gun with extra clips, because he didn't have any extra clips that fit my Browning BDM. He didn't have any holsters that fit me, or fit the waistband of the boxers, so I was left carrying the guns around the room, but I still felt better, if a little like I should be trying to juggle.

We finally got to sleep after the hospital had confirmed that Karlton was going to be okay. Though they'd have to wait on the lycanthropy test to see if she was clean. My room was still off limits, but I could sleep for a couple of hours while they finished processing everything if I wanted to. I probably wouldn't have, but Edward stepped in and played mother hen.

'I'll need a new room,' I said.

'You'll be in our room,' he said.

I raised eyebrows at that.

'I can get another room,' Tilford said, and fought for blank face.

'No, you as a chaperone is a good idea,' Edward said, and again his Ted voice was sliding away.

'So you're just going to sleep together, I mean . . .' Tilford looked embarrassed.

'We're not lovers,' I said.

Tilford looked even more uncomfortable. 'I didn't say otherwise.'

'I know the rumor mill has me screwing most of the men I'm close to, Tilford; it's okay.'

'I'm not sure I'm comfortable, or if regulations even allow us to sleep in here with a woman,' he said.

'Karlton is lucky to be alive. I'm not risking Anita. She stays with me tonight. If you aren't comfortable with that, then you do need another room,' Edward said. He didn't even try to be Ted; it was just Edward stating facts.

'I'll check and see if they'll even let us stay with a woman in the room they're paying for,' Tilford said.

'We can pay for our own room,' Edward said.

Tilford checked, and sometimes mixed-sex marshals were forced to share a room by finances. Raborn threw a fit and all but accused me of seducing both Tilford and Edward, but he stopped just short of anything I could really bitch about or that would get him into trouble with anyone listening. He was too senior a man on the scene to sweat much.

In the end Tilford opted not to share the room with us, something about his wife not allowing it. By that time I was so tired my eyes burned, and I just didn't give a damn. Edward was supposed to take Tilford's bed, and I was taking his, farther from the door, but the moment the door was locked behind us, he said, 'Help me move the bed in front of the window.' We put the second mattress and bedspring up against the big and only window.

'It won't keep them out,' I said.

'It will slow them down,' he said, 'and give us time to shoot.'

I nodded. 'Agreed.' I looked at the bare bed frame. 'You know this leaves us with one bed.'

'It's for a couple of hours.' He frowned. 'Or are you saying that you'll need to feed the *ardeur* when you wake up?'

I took the question seriously. 'I've gotten better at controlling it. I'll need solid food, protein. Staying fed physically helps control all the other hungers.'

'Good,' he said, and began to lay his guns on the bedside table.

'How am I ever going to reach a handgun on the floor?' I asked, as I climbed onto the far side of the bed by the wall.

He handed me a P90 carbine, though *submachine gun* was always what I wanted to say when I saw one. 'Try this.'

'My MP5 is in the other room,' I said as I checked out the feel of the new gun. I'd shot one, in fact this one, but only at the shooting range with Edward. It was a sweet gun, but the MP5 was a nice gun, too. I put the bigger gun on the side of the bed, practiced rolling over, and I could reach it better than the handgun.

Then came that awkward moment when we were actually supposed to get into a twin bed together. I slept with and had sex with a dozen men on a regular basis, but suddenly it was awkward. Edward and I weren't lovers, and never would be. We were friends and damn near family.

I sat up on my side of the bed by the wall. 'Am I the only one who feels a little awkward here?'

'Yes,' he said, and sat down on his side of the bed. He grinned at me suddenly, that smile that was all that was left of a younger man before his life went hard and cold. 'You know, you may be a succubus and a living vampire, but part of you will always be the small-town girl who isn't sure she should be doing all this.'

I scowled at him. 'Should I be insulted?'

'No, it's part of your charm that no matter how many men you have in your life, you never quite get comfortable with it.'

I scowled harder. 'Why is it charming?'

He shrugged. 'Not sure, but it's very you.'

I frowned at him. 'And being all mysterious and vague is very you.'

The grin faded a little, to almost his normal smile. It was a colder smile.

I had a thought. 'What would you have done if I'd said that I'd need to feed the *ardeur* when I woke up?'

He lay down, spilling the sheet over him. I already had the sheet over me. He turned and looked at me with the lamp still on. 'Dealt with it.'

'What does that mean?'

'It means we would have dealt with it.'

'Edward . . .'

'Let it go, Anita,' he said, and then he reached up and turned off the light. And just as he was one of the few people in the world that I would let back me up, he was one of the few that I would let drop this particular topic. He was right; we'd deal with it, the way we dealt with everything else.

I lay on my back in the dark. He was doing the same. 'Edward,' I asked.

'Hmm,' he said.

'Are you a side sleeper, or a back sleeper?'

'Back.'

'I'm a side sleeper, so no spooning, I guess.'

'What?'

I laughed and turned over on my side. 'Good night, Edward.'

'Good night, Anita.'

We slept.

7

I woke to country music and my arm flung over someone's stomach. That someone was wearing a T-shirt; no one I slept with wore clothes to bed. I felt that someone move as he rose up and said, 'Yes, morning.'

The moment I heard his voice I knew it was Edward, and the night came flooding back. Without rising up, I said, 'Who is it? Is it another murder?'

'It's Donna,' he said.

That made me lift my head and blink at him. It also made me take my arm off his stomach and scootch a little back from him so we weren't touching, as if his fiancée could see as well as hear us.

'It's Anita,' he said.

Donna's voice was suddenly loud enough for me to hear it. 'What's she doing waking up beside you?'

'There was only one bed.'

I buried my face in the pillow. That was so not the answer he should have given.

'Hold on,' he said, and he used his phone to take a picture of the mattress and box springs against the window. 'I'm sending you a picture that shows what happened to the other bed.'

'This better be good,' she said, voice still loud with anger.

I glanced at Edward's calm face as he listened to her angry breathing. A few minutes later she asked, 'Why is the bed in front of the window?'

'So that if the vampires and wereanimals we're hunting tried to break in, the bed would slow them down enough for us to start shooting.'

'What happened?' she asked, but her voice was already calmer.

'Anita and another marshal were attacked last night. The other woman is in the hospital. I didn't trust anyone else to guard Anita but me.'

'Of course not, you're the best at what you do.' Her voice got soft enough I couldn't hear her side of the conversation.

Edward handed the phone toward me, saying, 'Donna wants to talk to you.'

I shook my head vigorously, *No*.

He gave me the hard look, which let me know I wasn't going to win this fight. I took the phone carefully and tried for cheerful, or at least not nervous, as I said, 'Hey, Donna.'

'Are you all right?'

'I'm fine.'

'How badly was the other marshal hurt?'

'She'll live. She'll heal, but we're still waiting to find out if she's got lycanthropy.'

'It was a shapeshifter?' And I could hear the fear in her voice.

I cursed myself for being careless. Donna's first husband had been murdered in front of her by a werewolf. Peter, who was then only eight, had picked up his father's dropped gun and killed the werewolf, saving both his mother and his little sister. Peter was seventeen now, and in a lot of ways he seemed more Edward's son than Donna's.

'Yeah, it was, but we're okay. I mean, the other marshal isn't, but she was new on the job, and . . .'

'How new?'

'It was her first real hunt.'

'I'm so sorry.'

'Yeah, me, too.'

'Take care of Edward for me and the kids.'

'You know I will.'

'I know you'll bring him home to us safe, and he'll do the same for you.'

To that the only thing I could say was, 'We will.' She wanted to talk to Edward then, so I handed the phone back to him. I also went into the bathroom to do morning stuff and give them some privacy. Since when did Donna and he talk every morning? But hey, it wasn't my relationship.

When I came back out he'd hung up. He looked at me. I looked at him. 'That went way better than I thought,' I said.

'Donna trusts you.'

'She trusts me to keep you alive. She doesn't trust me with you.'

'She doesn't trust any woman with me. She's a little insecure in that area.'

I frowned at him. 'You give her reason to be.'

'No, insecure people don't need an excuse to distrust. It's just what they do.'

'I couldn't live like that,' I said.

He smiled at me. 'You're polyamorous, which means many loves?'

'I've never actually called myself that.'

He gave me a look. 'You're living with multiple men, and sleeping with more, and everyone knows about it – that's about as poly as you can get, Anita.'

I wanted to argue, but couldn't. I shrugged. 'Fine.'

'None of your men can be insecure or they couldn't be poly with you.'

I laughed. 'Oh, no, don't believe that there's no insecurity. There is. The hardest part about having this many loves in my life is the emotional upkeep. Trust me, we all have our issues.'

He looked at me, studying me for a moment.

'What?'

'I guess I just thought that you had to be completely secure to be in a relationship like that.'

'No one is completely secure, Edward.'

'Not even your Master of the City?'

'No, not even Jean-Claude,' I said.

He looked thoughtful, then stood up and took his shirt off. 'Are you getting dressed?' I asked.

'Yes.'

'Do I go in the bathroom, or do you?'

He frowned at me. 'Why?'

'I'm not comfortable with you dressing in front of me.'

He gave a half-laugh. I think I'd surprised him. 'You live with shapeshifters, and they go around nude all the time.'

'Seeing my friends and lovers nude is fine, but seeing you nude, no.'

He studied my face. 'It really would bother you.'

'Yes.'

He frowned again. 'Why?'

'If I'm having sex with someone it's okay to see them nude, but if sex isn't an option, then no nudity.'

He laughed, abrupt and surprised. 'You're still a prude, and you always will be.'

'It wouldn't bother you to strip in front of me?'

'No, why should it?'

I sighed. 'Fine, I'm a prude. I'll go into the bathroom while you dress.'

'No, I'll dress in the bathroom.' He was still smiling, his face shining with the remains of his laughter, as he gathered up his clothes.

'Glad I could amuse you after less than two hours of sleep,' I said, arms crossed under my breasts in his oversized T-shirt.

'I guess you're right,' he said, as he walked past me. 'Everyone has their issues.'

I had no idea what to say to that, so I didn't try. He went into the bathroom to get dressed, and I realized all my clothes were still in the other room. I hoped forensics would let me back in; otherwise I was going to have to send Edward shopping for clothes for me. Edward had a lot of talents, but I was betting that shopping for women's clothing wasn't one of them.

8

The good news was that forensics cleared my room enough for me to get dressed and get my weapons. The bad news was that the powers that be gave Karlton's vacated warrant to another new marshal who had about as much experience. Ironically, his last name was even Newman. It was a little too heavy-handed on the whole fate thing for my taste.

Sadly, Raborn was still the go-to man in the field. I didn't have a lot of faith that he'd listen to me, but when it went bad, and it would, I wanted my protest on record. 'Nothing personal to Newman, but he's exactly what his name says, Raborn. He's new. What I saw last night would make me afraid to just take fresh meat on the hunt, but to put the fresh meat in charge is dangerous both to him and to the rest of us.'

Raborn leaned his shoulder against a tree on the edge of the parking lot. His arms were folded across his chest, which made his shirt bunch and emphasized that he had enough stomach that his arms were sort of resting on it. It wasn't a flattering look, but maybe I was prejudiced.

He looked at Edward, who was at my side, where he'd pretty much plastered himself all day. He'd gone from fellow marshal to bodyguard head space after last night's 'incident'. The other police seemed to take it for devotion after the sex they assumed we'd had the night before. No one had said anything directly. It was the little eye flicks, the expressions, the soft voices that quieted as we walked up. Fuck them all, or rather, not fuck any of them.

'What do you think, Forrester?' Raborn asked.

'Now, Raborn,' Edward said in his good-ol'-boy Ted voice, 'you know that no other operation like this would have a rookie in charge. Veteran marshals won't follow him, or trust him. No reflection on Newman, but it's not just us that have a problem with it.'

Raborn sighed enough that his stomach rose up and down. He unfolded his arms and spit onto the parking lot, as if it had all left a bad taste in his mouth. 'You aren't the first marshals to come to talk to me. Hell, the local PD has asked for a more senior marshal to be in charge of the hunt.'

'Then why is Newman still in charge?' I asked.

His eyes narrowed when he looked at me; just because he agreed with me at this point didn't mean he liked me any better. 'Tilford is in charge of the other warrant, so he's partnering Newman.'

'I know that Tilford requested that the other warrant go to Ted or me,' I said.

Raborn nodded. 'He did, and it was duly noted.'

'Why give the other warrant to a rookie?' Edward asked again. 'Especially, why give the senior warrant to a rookie so that he can be in charge of the operation?'

'It's the older warrant, and new regulations say that the oldest warrant of execution on a joined case becomes senior officer.'

'It's a bad rule,' I said.

Raborn just nodded. 'But it's still the rule.'

'It's the same killers, they're both the same warrant,' Edward said.

'Used to be, you'd be right, but you got too many marshals in your branch getting their toes stepped on, so they changed it.'

'They're wanting to phase us old-timers out,' Edward said.

'What do you mean?' I asked.

'They think the new marshals will be easier to handle, but first they have to prove the newbies can do the job.'

'Stupid,' I said.

'Politics in the field always is,' he said.

'It wouldn't be so bad if Newman would let Tilford lead, but he's not. He's taking that I'm-in-charge-so-I-have-to-be-in-charge attitude. He's never been on a real hunt. At least Tilford has, not many, but I'll take some experience over none,' I said.

Raborn tried to frown at me, but in the end he just shrugged. 'Agreed.'

It was the first thing he'd ever simply agreed to with me. It made me hopeful. 'What can we do to keep this from going pear-shaped?' I asked.

'Try your powers of persuasion on him, Blake. I hear you can convince most men to do just about anything you want 'em to do.' He looked at Edward then, and it wasn't a friendly look. More a guy look, and I wondered if there was just a touch of sexual jealousy there. It wasn't that Raborn wanted to sleep with me, but there is a type of man who feels if a woman is sleeping around he shouldn't be left out. It's almost not personal to the woman; it's just a guy thing.

'You sound jealous, Raborn,' I said. I've found a direct assault is best on shit like this.

'So you admit it.'

'Accuse me of something and maybe I will admit it, but don't make snide remarks and tiptoe around the question; just fucking ask, or don't.'

He glared at me and Edward. 'Fine, you want me to ask, fine! Did you fuck Forrester last night?'

'No,' I said.

'Bullshit,' he said.

'We shared a room so he could keep me alive and safe, because I trust him to do that more than any other person on the planet. But you and every other son of a bitch here is going to believe what they believe, and there's not a damn thing I can do about it. I learned a long time ago that I can't prove a negative.'

'What the hell does that even mean?'

'It means I can't prove that I didn't sleep with someone. It's easier to prove you did something than that you didn't. You know that from court cases, every cop does, but cops love rumors, they fucking love 'em, so either way, believe what you want, but if you're not going to believe the truth, don't ask.' I finished the last sentence pretty much up in his face, as much as the height difference would allow. I was perilously close to touching him, and hadn't realized it. I was angry, that fine burning anger that made the tips of my fingers tingle. It was disproportionate to the situation.

I took a step back, took a few deep even breaths, and said, 'I need some air.'

'You're outside,' he said.

'I need away from you, then,' I said, and I walked away. Why was I this angry? And down low in my body, lower than a gut, deeper than anything a surgeon would ever reach with a scalpel, I felt something stir. My beasts, the animals I carried inside me, were moving, responding to my rage. I couldn't afford to lose control of myself like that. I didn't actually shift form, but I still carried the beasts inside me, and they could still try to tear their way out of the prison of my body. I had almost gotten to the point where it didn't happen, but now I felt the beginnings of it, and realized I'd skipped everything but coffee. Feeding the physical body helped control all the hungers, the beasts, the *ardeur*, and the anger, because I'd learned to feed off that, too. It was something Jean-Claude, my supposed master, couldn't do. I needed to eat something, and soon.

Edward caught up to me. 'Why'd he get to you like that?'

'I forgot to eat real food. I need protein and I need it now.'

'Beasts?'

'Yes.'

'We'll get breakfast,' he said. He walked toward the car we were sharing, and I followed him. We'd have to make it quick and unhealthy, going through some kind of drive-up, but anything would help.

9

I was eating my Egg McMuffin as Edward drove. He'd gotten the breakfast burrito, which always puzzled me, but hey, it wasn't my stomach. He'd eaten his before he put the car in gear. He still had that guy and cop ability to inhale food because you might not get to finish it otherwise. I'd never mastered it. If I'd been a regular cop I'd have starved by now.

'I know the food helps,' he said, as he watched the road and drove carefully, precisely, as he did most things, 'but you need to feed the *ardeur* soon, or am I wrong?'

'You're not wrong,' I said, between bites.

'You could go into any bar in the city and find someone.'

'No,' I said.

'You complicate your life, Anita,' he said, as he turned onto the street that the motel was on.

'I just can't do casual. I don't think I ever will.'

'I thought the *ardeur* wiped out all that, and you just had sex.'

'It can, but it can also be addictive, and some people are more susceptible than others.'

'You mean like drugs – some people get addicted quicker than others.'

'Exactly. I'd hate to pick some stranger and he turns out to be one of those. He'd be addicted to something he might never be able to find again, and I'd feel guilty, and have to take him home with me like a stray puppy.'

'You would, too,' Edward said, like he found it a character flaw.

'You wouldn't feel guilty, would you?'

'You mean could I fuck someone, addict them to the *ardeur*, and just walk away?'

'Yes,' I said.

'Yes,' he said.

'You're one of my closest friends, but I totally don't understand that.'

'I know.' He pulled into the parking lot with all the other police cars.

I finished the last bite of my breakfast and took another sip of Coke, because coffee tasted bad with Egg McMuffin. I wiped my hands on napkins.

He turned off the engine but didn't get out. I waited.

'You're not as ruthless as I am, but you kill as easily as I do.'

'Thanks,' I said, because I knew it was a compliment.

He gave me a small smile, I think to acknowledge that I was one of the few people on the planet who would have known it was a compliment.

'But if anything goes wrong, I know you'll see Donna and the kids right.'

'You know I will, but it's not like you to be this morbid, Edward. You have a premonition?' I asked, and I was serious, because cops get those sometimes. A lot of them are a little bit psychic; it's one of the ways they stay alive.

'It's Peter. He needs me or someone like me to finish training him.'

'You know I still don't approve of you training him to follow in the family business,' I said.

'Being a marshal, you mean?'

'No games, Edward, not between us,' I said.

He nodded. 'He wants me to take him out of the country on a job when he turns eighteen, if I think he's ready.'

'Will he be ready?' I asked.

He pursed his lips and then nodded. 'I think so.'

'You sound sad about that.'

He nodded again. 'You know how it is on hunts like that, Anita. Being good isn't enough.'

'You have to be lucky, too,' I said.

'I'm afraid that I'll be so worried about him I won't be careful enough.'

'You're afraid if you take him that you'll get yourself killed protecting him and once you die, he'll die, too,' I said.

'Yes,' he said, and turned in the seat to look at me. His face was very serious, not blank, not angry, not threatening, just serious.

'Don't take him,' I said.

'I can't back out on him now, Anita. It would destroy him.'

I frowned at him, sipped my Coke, and tried to think. 'What do you want me to say?'

'I'm about to ask a favor, one that I don't have the right to ask.'

That surprised me, and it must have shown on my face. 'What could you possibly ask that you don't have the right to ask?'

'Come with me on Peter's first hunt.'

I blinked at him. I thought about a lot of things, but finally said, 'When?'

'Next year, probably fall.'

I nodded. 'Just like deer season,' I said.

'Yeah.'

I nodded again. 'I'll probably have to bring some of the bodyguards for me, and you know that I don't approve of what you're doing with Peter.'

'But you'll still come,' he said.

'Yes, I'll still come.'

'I know that if you die, you risk pulling everyone you're metaphysically tied to down to the grave with you, everyone you love, and you'll still come.'

I sighed. 'I should talk to them first, to be honest, and I will, but we can't keep each other from living our lives; then we become prisoners, and none of us want that.' I started putting all the trash in the little bag. 'Besides, I think Jean-Claude is powerful enough to keep everyone alive. But if I'm going to risk all that out of the country, then we have to defeat the Mother of All Darkness and the Harlequin before next fall. I can't risk dying and letting her win.'

He nodded. 'Okay, I help you solve your problem first and then you help me with mine.'

'Agreed.'

He smiled, and it was a mixture of Edward's fierceness and Ted's good ol' boy. 'I get to help you kill the oldest vampire on the planet who is just spirit, so we'll need magic to kill her.'

'She may not be killable. We may only be able to trap her magically, but honestly no one's come up with anything that will work.'

'So I help you do the impossible, and then you come on a much more mundane kill with me and Peter.'

'I know you'll pick something tame for Peter's first hunt, so yeah, that about sums it up. You help me kill the unkillable, hunt and slaughter the most fearsome warriors and assassins known to either vampire or shapeshifter, and then I'll help you do something much easier.' I smiled, I couldn't help it.

He shook his head. 'It isn't the killing that will be hard with Peter, it's the emotional stuff.'

'How's he doing?' I asked.

'He's my son,' he said, but he didn't sound happy about it.

'You mean he's a ruthless, cold-blooded killer?'

'No, I mean he wants to be.'

'Worse,' I said.

'Much worse,' he said.

'He's killed before when he needed to. He's saved my life and risked his own. He's a good man.'

'He's a boy.'

'Anyone who can stand shoulder to shoulder with me when

the monsters are trying to kill us, and not flinch, isn't a boy, Edward. He's just young, and time will fix that.'

'I hope so,' Edward said.

I realized then what the real problem was. 'You don't want to see him die.'

'I don't want to get him killed.'

'You won't get him killed, Edward.'

'How can you be so sure?'

'I know that you won't take him unless you think his skills are up to the job. I know how good you are at training people for this; you helped train me. He's got good instincts and he's a shooter. He doesn't hesitate. He's brave as hell.'

He looked at me. 'You like him.'

'We talk on the phone at least once a month, sometimes twice. He's a good kid.'

'You called him a man earlier.'

I smiled. 'When he's shooting, he's a man; on the phone, he still sounds like a kid.'

'He still has a crush on you.'

I nodded. 'I've noticed.'

'It used to bother you that he liked you.'

'A little, but he needs a friend he can talk to about the stuff that the two of you are doing to train him up.'

'I didn't know he talked to you about that.'

'I decided I'd rather know what you're doing with Peter than have to guess.'

He looked at me. I looked back. We had one of those guy moments. He knew I didn't approve, but I'd still support him and Peter. The silence said it for us, all that and more. 'What do you think of his training?'

'I think that you're a scary son of a bitch, and he's lucky to have you in his life.'

Edward looked down at the steering wheel, his hands sliding over it, as if he just needed something to do with them. 'Thank you for that.'

'It's just the truth,' I said.

He looked up, that serious, almost sorrowful look still in his blue eyes. 'Let's get out and find Newman and try to reason with him.'

'Reason how?' I asked.

Edward gave me Ted's grin, but it was his own words, 'I'm a scary son of a bitch, let's see if I can spook him.'

I grinned. 'I like it. Scare him into giving up the lead.'

'Tilford will listen to us; Newman won't.'

'Let's go scare the rookie,' I said.

He grinned. 'Let's.'

10

Newman was tall, as in over six feet tall, but slender, in that way that's all genetics. He was probably one of those men who had trouble putting muscle over an otherwise athletic frame. He ran his fingers through his short brown hair and put his hat back on, setting it on his head like he wasn't used to it yet. I wasn't sure if he thought the cowboy hat made him look older, or if it had been a gift. Either way, it was new and hadn't been broken in yet. It wasn't like Edward's hat that was creased and loved by his hands and head. This was a new, white hat. At least Edward's was sort of off-white.

'I appreciate the concern, really, I do, but I think I have a plan,' Newman said.

'We're just trying to help out,' Edward said in his best Ted voice. He'd quickly realized that he'd get further with charm than scare tactics. Since I didn't really have a lot of charm that worked with men I wasn't trying to date, I let Edward do the talking. I rarely got in trouble letting Edward do the persuading.

'I do appreciate that,' Newman said, but he somehow implied in his down-home tone that he knew exactly what we'd been trying to do and he was having none of it. He was young, but he wasn't stupid, and there was a quiet toughness to him that it was hard not to like. But the Harlequin wouldn't care about his toughness, or his down-home charm, or the fact that he reminded me of a younger version of Ted. Not a younger version of Edward, but of Ted, if Ted had been really who Edward was, which was sort of weird, and made my head hurt just a little.

'What's your plan?' I asked.

His brown eyes flicked to me, then back to Edward, then back to me. It was almost like he didn't quite know what to do with me. He struck me as someone who'd been raised that women were to be taken care of, and here I stood all petite and feminine looking, but decked out in guns, knives, and a badge. Would I have puzzled him less if I'd been taller?

'Dogs. We're going to track 'em.'

It was a good idea, but . . . Edward and I exchanged a look. Newman frowned, because he'd caught the look. 'What? What did I miss?'

I gave a small nod, and Edward said in his pleasant Ted voice, 'Well, now, Newman, did you find dogs that are trained to trail shapeshifters?'

Newman frowned harder. 'They just have to follow the scent,' he said.

'Most dogs won't track shapeshifters,' I said.

He frowned harder, which made him look even younger, like a serious five year old who just happened to tower over me. 'Why not?'

'They're afraid of them,' I said.

'What do you mean?' he asked.

Edward smiled, and it was a good smile, not condescending at all, just cheerful and sharing information. 'Dogs get a whiff of a shapeshifter, especially one that's partially or completely form shifted, and they're afraid of 'em.'

I explained, 'Dogs can be around humans who shift form, but there's something about once the change takes place that freaks out most dogs unless they've been trained to it.'

'Why would that make a difference to a hound? They track any scent.'

I glanced at Edward, but he just kept smiling at Newman.

'The dogs are afraid, Newman. They're just afraid of them, that's all.'

'But why?' he asked.

'Have you ever seen a shapeshifter in animal or half-man form?' I asked.

'I've seen pictures, film.'

I sighed, and said, 'They didn't even bring in a shapeshifter to shift in front of your class?'

'It's too dangerous,' he said.

'Okay, why is it too dangerous?' I asked, and I had his full eye contact now. He wasn't worried about me being petite or a woman, he just wanted to understand.

'Because once they shift they have to eat living flesh. They'll kill anything near them.'

I shook my head. 'Not true, not even close to true of most shapeshifters.'

'The books and instructors say it is.'

'It's true of the newly infected shapeshifters. They can wake as ravening beasts and have complete blackouts as people for the first few full moons, but after that almost all of them regain themselves. They just happen to turn furry once a month, but they become the people they were.'

He shook his head, frowning and so serious. 'Not what we saw on the films.'

'I'll bet money they were newbies, the newly turned lycanthropes. They can be just animals.'

'You're telling me that what I saw in class isn't what they are, that they're more people than monsters?'

'Newman, I live with two shapeshifters. Do you really think I could do that if they tried to kill me every time they changed form?'

He frowned harder. 'So that rumor is true?'

'Some of the rumors are true, most aren't, but that's true. Trust me, the men that I love have never tried to hurt me in any form.'

'So this shapeshifter from last night should be like a person in a fur suit,' he said.

I shook my head. 'Not what I said.'

'You're saying on one hand they're just furry people and on the other that the dogs are so afraid of them they won't track them. You can't have it both ways, Marshal Blake; either they're monsters or they're people.'

'Tell that to the BTK killer,' I said. 'He was a churchgoer, raised two kids, married, and resisted the urge to kill for decades. He was a person, but he was a monster, too.'

'But dogs will track a serial killer,' Newman said.

Edward tried. 'Newman, it's a good idea, but if he was even partially shapeshifted, and he had to be to hurt Marshal Karlton, then the dogs will be too afraid to track him. Did you ask for dogs trained on tracking shapeshifters?'

'I asked for the best dog we had nearby.'

I shrugged. 'It doesn't matter; the chance of having a shifter-trained dog is almost nil. It's a seriously specialized training.'

'Why?' Newman asked.

I was already tired of him asking that. 'Because, Newman, shapeshifters, even the nice legal citizens, don't like training dogs designed to be able to hunt them down so people can kill them on sight.'

Newman blinked at me. 'I don't understand.'

I was tired of it, and him. 'I know you don't.'

'Explain it to me, then.'

'I don't think I can. Some things you just have to learn in the field.'

'I'm a fast learner,' he said, and he sounded a little defiant.

'I hope so, Newman, I really hope so.'

'What's that supposed to mean?'

Great, I'd behaved myself and he was still getting upset with me. 'It means that I had to watch last night while this shifter tortured and sliced up Marshal Karlton. He used her as a human shield so I couldn't shoot him, and then he moved faster than any shapeshifter I've ever seen. All I could do was hold pressure on her wounds and try to keep her from bleeding to death and pray that moving her so I could keep her from bleeding out hadn't just injured her spine and crippled her for life. It didn't, thank God, but I didn't know that last night, and a whole spine does no damn good if you bleed to death first.' I was up in his face as I finished, and though the closest to glaring into his face I could get was the middle of his chest, he flinched and backed away from me.

I just turned and walked away. My anger crawled over me and through me. The beasts in their hidden place inside me swirled so that I had a moment where things twisted, a hint of the claws to come pawing at my gut. It made me hesitate as I walked.

Edward called, 'You okay?'

'Sure, yeah, fine.' I kept walking, but I needed to feed the *ardeur*. I probably needed to feed before we started tracking the shapeshifter, but since the dog wasn't going to track it, I had time. I also had an idea. I'd go visit the local weretigers and see if they'd tell me things they wouldn't tell the other marshals. They probably would, and I knew one of them would. Alex was the son of the local clan queen, my lover, and my red tiger to call. I'd tell the other marshals I was trying to gather information, and I would, but it was a booty call. A booty call to keep me from being torn apart by my beasts.

11

Raborn stopped us on the way to the car. 'Where are you two going?'

'To see if I can find a clue,' I said.

'So you'll miss the hunt just because they wouldn't give you the warrant?' he said.

'We'll be back for the hunt,' Edward said, and went around to the driver's side of the car, which left me with Raborn. Perfect.

'I heard a lot of rumors about you, Blake, but I never heard that you'd leave before the monster was dead. Everyone said you were tough.'

'I am tough,' I said. 'You let the dogs do their best, but they won't find these things, not today, not just with dogs.'

'How can you be sure of that?'

Edward leaned over and pushed the door open as a sort of hint that I needed to get in now. 'Call it experience,' I said, and climbed in the open door. He was still frowning at us as we drove off.

I had Alex Pinn's cell number and I'd called it, but he didn't answer it. A man I didn't know answered it. 'Alex's phone, whom may I say is calling?' It sounded way too formal, and I was betting an assistant of some kind.

'This is Anita Blake, to whom am I speaking?'

Edward glanced at me as he pulled out onto the highway, but he didn't ask questions he knew I'd explain later.

'Then, this is the phone of Li Da of the Red Clan, son of Queen Cho Chun. Why are you calling our prince?'

'I think that's private between Alex and me.'

'You are not alone?' He made it a question.

'No.'

'Can the person with you not be trusted?'

'He can be, but I share as few secrets of the clan with outsiders as I can.'

The man was silent for a moment, then said, 'That is wise.'

'I do my best. What is your name?'

'Why?'

'Because I'm talking to you and it's polite to know someone's name when you address them.'

He hesitated and then said, 'You can call me Donny.'

'Call you Donny,' I said.

'It will do until we see how much you can be trusted.'

'Okay, Donny, where's Alex and why are you answering his phone?'

'Li Da is with our queen. She knew you would call him.'

'She did, did she?'

'Queen Cho Chun said you would not be able to resist the call of each other, and she was correct.'

I didn't know what to say to that. I was trying to feed the *ardeur*, basically a metaphysical booty call, but from the moment I'd accidentally tied Alex to me, his mother had been pushing for it to be more. She'd have preferred he settle down with a nice little weretigress, but she wanted me to choose among the clans and make Alex my official tiger king, which would make the red clan the top cat in the world of weretigers. I had no intention of doing that for a lot of reasons, but one of the main ones was that neither Alex nor I wanted it. Not to mention that Jean-Claude and all the other men in my life would probably get pissy if I ever actually married anyone, especially if that one wasn't any of them. But I'd found that all the clan queens were pushy bitches, and serious as a heart attack about bloodlines, power, and marriage.

'Look, Donny, Alex is your clan prince, that's true, but he's also my tiger to call.'

'Come to our meeting place, and if you can call him away from our queen's side then he is yours, but if you cannot then you are not the Mistress of Tigers.'

I swore softly under my breath. 'Are you all aware that I'm in your city trying to solve murders? I'm trying to save the lives of other weretigers.'

'None of the dead are clan tigers; they are all survivors of an attack. Their deaths are unfortunate, but not clan business.'

'Do you understand that if they finish up the lone tigers that aren't part of a clan, they may turn on the clans themselves?'

'We can defend ourselves, Anita Blake.'

'Pretty to think so, but no tiger clan has faced these guys in hundreds, if not thousands of years. They wiped out all of you guys in your homeland, all the weretigers regardless of clan color.'

'Legend says we were unprepared. We will not be this time.'

I listened to the certainty in his voice and knew it was a mistake, but I also knew that nothing I could say over the phone would change his mind. I even knew that it wasn't his mind I had to change; it was Queen Cho Chun that I needed to convince. This was her certainty, her arrogance.

'Fine, Donny, just tell me where to meet and we'll go from there, but I really do need to see Alex sooner rather than later.'

'You would feed on our prince as if he were the lowest prostitute on the street. We do not approve of how you treat him.'

Again, I knew it was the queen talking, but I let it go. Donny was a good little mouthpiece, and arguing with the help never changed any boss's mind, so I didn't try.

'That's between Alex and me,' I said.

'What affects our prince affects the clan.'

I was beginning to see why Alex had stayed the hell away from his clan for years before I met him. He was a reporter, and a good one. He'd done an amazing piece on the war in Afghanistan that had won a Peabody, which was a very big deal if you were a journalist. He was also in deep cover pretending to be human. He wore brown contacts to hide his yellow-gold eyes with their rim of orange red, like the sun rimmed in fire. He was pure clan; his eyes and hair proved that. The hair he passed off as a funky dye job, but the eyes, he had to hide those.

'Fine, I am the Mistress of Tigers, I am the first vampire in a thousand years to be able to use that title, and I do not argue with underlings, Donny. Tell me where to meet Alex and his mom, or I will call him to me across the city, but bear in mind that I'm not real precise when I do a roll call for tigers. I could end up with every unmated male in your clan coming to me, and then how would they pretend to be human?'

'You cannot do that.'

'Do you mean I can't, or I shouldn't?'

He was silent for a moment, and then he said, 'We felt your call when you bound our prince to you. I know you can do what you say . . . Mistress, but I would ask you not to do it.'

'It's not my first choice, Donny, I just want some alone time with my red tiger to call, that's all.'

His breath came out heavy, and then he said, 'I will give you the address to meet our guards. They will escort you in to see the queen and prince.'

'Great.' I opened my phone up so I could jot the address down as a note, and said, 'I'm ready to write it down, shoot.'

He told me. I typed it in, and then the phone call was over. Donny didn't seem to like me. Fine with me, I wasn't here to win any popularity contests.

I gave Edward the address and he started heading that way. He seemed to know Seattle a lot better than a man on his first visit. I'd asked him if he was familiar with the city, but he'd just smiled that mysterious smile of his and not answered. Mr Secret.

'Could you do what you threatened to do? Could you call all their unmated males to you like some sort of succubus Pied Piper?'

I thought about it, then finally said, 'I'm not sure; maybe. The tigers tell me I put out a call to all the unmated males in the country when I first hit this power, and that was accidental. The clans managed to keep the men from getting on buses and planes and coming to me, but that was an accidental call. If I did it for real and really meant it, I don't know if they could stop them. I also don't know how bespelled they'd be when they got to me, and if they'd all expect sex.' I laughed, but it was a nervous laugh. 'The red clan numbers in the hundreds. I'm good, but I'm not that good.'

'Then best not put out the welcome mat,' he said, as he turned onto a narrow side street.

'It was a threat, Edward. I make a lot of threats I hope I don't have to carry out.'

'I don't,' he said.

'I know, you mean every threat.'

He turned and looked at me as he waited for the light to turn green. Sunglasses hid his eyes, but I knew his face well enough to know the whole look. It was his cold stare, the I-could-kill-you-and-not-blink look.

'Save the scary for someone else, Edward.'

'I can't let you go in there without me unless I trust them to keep you from getting kidnapped by Marmee Noir.'

I sighed. 'I figured you'd say that. You have to promise me that nothing you see or learn today will ever be used against them on a hunt.'

He frowned at me. 'I hate it when you do this.'

'The light's green,' I said, just as the car behind us honked.

He drove forward, but said, 'If I don't promise, you'll go in without me.'

'Yep.'

'Damn it,' he said softly.

'Yep,' I said.

'I promise,' he said.

I smiled at him. 'I knew you would.'

'Don't push it,' he said, and he sounded genuinely angry. But he'd work through it, and once he promised, he'd keep his word. The red clan was safe from Edward, and I was safe because he was keeping me that way. Now, if I could just get through the interview with my would-be mother-in-law, the day would be perfect.

12

There were two guards at the door; they introduced themselves as Donny and Ethan. Donny was tall and perfectly bald, and he had eyes the color of orange fire. The red clan had the most trouble passing for human because of the eyes. They had tiger eyes that looked like tiger eyes, not just odd-colored human eyes. In public they wore sunglasses or colored contacts. The irony was that though all the clans disdained the survivors of attacks, the survivors looked more human in human form than the 'pureblood' tigers. In fact, it was a mark of the purity of their bloodline that they had tiger eyes and hair the same color as their tiger form, even as babies.

For eyes that dark you usually needed brown contacts to hide the color, but the bodyguard standing next to Donny had soft gray eyes, the color of kitten fur. His hair was a blond so pale it was almost white, and it had what looked like gray highlights in it, though saying soft gray could be highlights sounded wrong. There was one streak of dark, deep red, from his forehead to the back of his skull. His hair was short, but had enough wave to it that he was forced to style it on top, so that it looked like he was ready for a night out on the club with his choppy waved hair and his excellent dye job. He wasn't as tall as Donny's six-foot frame, and he didn't have the shoulder spread either. He looked almost delicate beside Donny, but it was Ethan who had a shoulder holster with a Glock in it, extra ammo on the other side of the holster from the gun, and the muscle tone in his lower arms that comes from a little bit of weights, but mostly some kind of athletic something. Just from the way he held himself, I was betting martial arts of some kind.

Edward touched my arm. It startled me. I'd been staring at Ethan. That made me realize that I really needed to see Alex sooner rather than later. A vampire with an animal to call is often attracted to that type of animal. Jean-Claude found it very peaceful to pet wolves, and that was his animal to call. I realized it wasn't just the sex from home I'd missed; I was missing the touch and interaction of the shapeshifters I was drawn to, like tigers. The fact that I thought Ethan was cuter than Donny went against the way most dominant weretigresses pick mates. They tended to like the ones with the tiger eyes, but there was some-thing . . . interesting about Ethan, or maybe I was just that hungry.

I took a deep breath, and that didn't help because they both smelled like tiger. But Donny smelled like red tiger, and Ethan smelled like more. It made me move toward him, sniff the air near him, try to clear my nose of Donny's closer, warmer scent.

'Anita,' Edward said, his voice sharp, 'you need to find Mr Pinn.'

I nodded and forced myself to step back from Ethan. 'You're right, absolutely right.' I spoke without looking at either of the weretigers. 'Take me to Alex.'

'We can't take you before our queen armed like that.' It actu-ally made me look at what we were wearing. Since neither of us was on an active warrant, the US Marshals Windbreakers hid most of our dangerous toys. I only had my Browning BDM, my Smith & Wesson M&P9c, extra ammo, two wrist sheaths with blades, and the big knife down my spine. The shoulder holster was specially made so the spine sheath attached to it, the handle hidden under my hair as long as I wore a jacket. If I wasn't wearing the big knife I'd started carrying the Browning at the small of my back where the M&P was now. Edward had two handguns and some blades, too.

'We don't have any submachine guns on us; we're packing light,' I said.

Donny studied my face, and then he blinked first. He also frowned. 'You're being honest.'

'I try,' I said.

'But the point remains, you cannot go before Queen Cho Chun armed.'

'Great,' I said, 'I don't want to see her anyway. All I want right now is Alex.'

'Prince Li Da,' Donny said.

'Fine, all I want right now is Li Da.'

'Prince Li Da,' Donny said.

I shook my head. 'Nope, I am Mistress of Tigers, so he's not my prince. He's Alex, or he's Li Da, but he's not Prince anything to me.'

'That is arrogant,' Donny said.

'No, it's not, it's just true, and I don't technically have to stand here and dick around with you or Ethan here. I can just lay down the law and say, "Bring him to me."'

'Queen Cho Chun would have the skin off my back if I let you get away with such insolence.'

I glanced at Ethan to see if Donny was exaggerating. Something in those soft, gray kitten eyes let me know that Donny was speaking the truth. Interesting; it didn't work that way in Vegas with the white tigers.

I turned back to Donny. 'She'd flay your back for just following my orders?'

'She is queen. We wait at her pleasure.'

I shook my head. I was back to staring at Ethan. I was oddly fascinated with the shape of his mouth. His upper lip was so deeply imprinted that it was almost like a dimple above the lips instead of under them.

'Anita,' Edward said. He moved in front of Ethan, blocking my view of the man. 'You need to feed.'

I nodded. 'You are absolutely right.' I turned back to Donny.

'Either Alex comes to me now, or I do what I said I'd do on the phone: I call him to me. You and Ethan are right here beside me and trust me, with vampire powers, proximity counts. I don't like you that well, Donny, nothing personal, but I like Ethan. My tiger likes him. If I call Alex, chances are he'll never get here before I've fed on Ethan, and maybe you. Is that really what your queen wanted, or did she just want you to put me in my place?'

'It is not my place to speak for our queen. She knows what she intended; I do not.'

'I'm going to count to ten and then I'm going to call Alex, but I'm not lying about the possible effect on you and Ethan here.'

Donny said, 'Ethan?'

'She smells of the truth,' he said. I couldn't see much more than a shoulder around the edge of Edward's body. I fought the urge to move so I could see more of him. It wasn't good that I was this fascinated with a stranger. God, didn't I have enough lovers in my life?

That Donny couldn't be certain if I smelled or felt like I was telling the truth meant he wasn't a very powerful weretiger. It also meant that he'd been guessing when he said I was telling the truth about our weapons. But now that it was important, he was willing to swallow his pride and let the more powerful weretiger answer the question. That was interesting.

'I will go and ask our queen what she wishes me to do.'

'Can't you just call her?' I asked.

'Some questions must be asked in person.' He gave a small half-bow to me. I wondered if he even realized he'd done it. He strode off down the corridor.

I called after him. 'Are you leaving Ethan here?'

'He is a guard; he will do his duty.'

'Even knowing that if you don't get back in time I'll feed on him, you'll still leave him here?' I said.

'He is a good guard, but he is not pure.'

'What does the fact that he's mixed tiger heritage have to do with anything?' I asked.

Ethan answered, 'He means I'm not worth protecting.'

Edward turned so that we could both look at the other man. 'Not worth protecting from what?' I asked.

Ethan shrugged. 'Much of anything, but in this case, you. You stole away the loyalty of some of the few remaining pure red tigers when they visited you in St Louis; that's why I'm guarding you, because if you bewitch me it won't damage the clan. It won't cost them more pure-blooded red babies.' He said it with only the slightest edge of bitterness in his voice.

'That's cold,' I said.

'That's the truth,' Ethan said.

I looked at Donny standing there watching us. 'So you leave him here to guard us or be the sacrificial lamb, and you don't much care which.'

Donny glanced at me, then at Ethan, and even at Edward. 'I will go tell Queen Cho Chun what you have demanded.' His eyes flicked to me, then to Ethan, and I realized Donny was nervous. I think my stating so bluntly that he was leaving Ethan to be food had bothered him a little. A lot of people can do awful things as long as they don't have to look at it too clearly. Lying to yourself doesn't work if the truth is clear enough.

He turned without another word and walked away. His black clothing melded into the dark corridor within a few yards. They needed more light down here.

We were left standing in the dim corridor in a strangely thick silence. I felt my red tiger stir like a streak of fire called to life from cold wood. It made me close my eyes, take a deep breath, but that was a mistake, because I'd moved closer to Ethan without meaning to, and he didn't just smell like red tiger. White tiger came out of the shadows where the beasts lived inside me. I knew there were no shadows inside me, or tall ancient trees, that it was just the landscape my mind created to help me cope with the beasts being inside me.

I was standing in front of Ethan staring up into those soft, gray eyes.

'Step back, Anita,' Edward said. I felt his hand hover over my shoulder.

I said, 'Don't touch me right now, Edward.'

He didn't argue, just dropped his hand. I felt the heat of it get farther away when he stepped back. 'Is the *ardeur* rising?'

'It's trying to, but it's more . . .' I stepped in close to Ethan. A good guard would have moved back, but he didn't. I was careful not to touch him, but my face was just above his bare arm, just above the skin; I breathed in the scent of him, deep.

Then another scent and my blue tigress rose and began to pace with the others.

'I thought we had the only blue tiger male alive today, but that's where the gray curls and eyes come from. The white tiger paled you out, but you're blue.'

'My grandmother was blue, but you do have the only pure blue tiger male. I'm so mixed up, I'm no color.'

'You're not just red, or blue, or even white, you're . . .' I didn't say it out loud, because the Harlequin were trying to kill all the gold tigers; so far they'd missed them, but here was one that held a touch of that rich, golden power.

'I'm what?' he asked, and just looking up into his face I was almost certain he didn't know that he held some of that precious bloodline. Interesting.

'How many forms do you have?' It came out as a whisper, with my mouth almost touching the skin of his arm.

'Three,' he said, and his voice was already deepening. I couldn't tell if it was tiger, or just male reaction.

I wanted to ask, 'Not four?' but I didn't. The weretigers intermarried for genetic diversity, and most of them just looked like one side of their heritage or another.

At home I had Domino, who shifted to black and white, but physically his hair was black and white, showing the mix. If the human form showed just one, then one was what the tiger seemed to have. I'd never met another tiger who could do three colors, let alone four, but there was still that sweet scent of golden power. The gold tiger in me gave a soft, whuffing purr. I tried to think reasonably, but I didn't feel reasonable. My skin felt heavy with need; things low in my body tightened. The reaction staggered me. Ethan reached out, took my arm, just instinct. Someone almost falls and you try to catch them. I could feel his hand through my jacket like heat and weight, as if his human shape were already only just something to hold all that power.

'Get out, Edward,' I said in a strangled voice.

'What?'

'Go back, see how the hunt's going, but you can't be here.'

'You're going to lose control.'

'I think so,' I said.

'Anita—'

'Go, now, Edward, please, just go.' I was worried about my friend, but my eyes were all for the man in front of me. I stared up into those gray eyes and knew now that it was the color of his tiger. This close I could see the differences between human eyes and the tiger's in his face. His arms had slid around me, drawing me in against his body; my arms were already around his waist.

'You want me?' He sounded surprised.

'Yes,' I said, and four different tigers began to trot up the long dark space inside me. I buried my face against his T-shirt and the chest underneath. He smelled like hot, red flame and the air after a lightning storm when it's clean and fresh, and under that was candy. He smelled like cotton candy, sugary, sweet, something that would melt on your tongue. I'd found that all the gold tigers smelled like something sweet to me, under the sweet smell of candy was another sweet scent. Clover – white clover on a hot summer's day – was what his blue tiger smelled like. Cynric at home smelled like a whole garden in high summer, so apparently blue tigers smelled like green, growing things. Four of my tigers stared up at me, their lips drawn back, to take in the scent of his skin, as deeply as we could breathe it in. They gave a chorus of growling purrs that rumbled up through my body as if my bones were a tuning fork for the beginning of some deep, bass song. It made my knees go weak. Ethan caught me, which pushed our bodies that last inch together. I could feel that his body was hard and eager already. The sensation of it drew a small noise from me. 'Yes, I want you.' And the *ardeur* rose up in me like a wave, but this time the tigers inside me weren't fighting it; their power mingled with the *ardeur*, and I realized something I hadn't before. I had some of the same power as the old Master of Tigers, but the *ardeur* had turned it into something else, something warmer, kinder, more alive. That aliveness spilled up my skin and over his, so that he cried out, wordless, eyes closing, back bowing, arms tightening around me to simply keep him standing.

'So much power,' he whispered.

I had a moment to wonder if this was just the *ardeur* feeding, or if I would accidentally bind him to me metaphysically. I didn't need more men in my life, not permanently. The thought helped me push the *ardeur* away, just a little, so I could have another thought. Ethan didn't deserve to be bound to me forever, not by accident. I didn't want to take his free will. I didn't want to trap him, or me.

I was able to climb back into the driver's seat of my own head. Ethan stared down at me. 'What's wrong? The power's fading.'

'Something is wrong with this feeding, Ethan. It's different.'

'What?'

'There's a chance that it won't just be the *ardeur*. That I'll bind you to me as my tiger to call.'

'Like Alex?' he asked.

I nodded, staring up at him, searching his face. He was handsome in a guy sort of way, cheekbones high, but thin-faced, so the shape was a soft rectangle. He had a dimple in his chin.

'Alex still has his life, his job; you haven't hurt him.'

'I don't always know how deep the binding will be, Ethan.

Do you understand that? Do you understand that I can't predict what will happen?'

He blinked down at me, trying to fight free of the pheromones on the air. He swallowed hard and then said, 'You're giving me a chance to back out.'

'Yes.'

'What's the worst thing that could happen?'

'You could be a bride, as in Dracula's brides. No real will of your own.' I stopped holding him so tight and tried to give us a little physical space to think. Ethan's arms tightened against my back. 'You can't want that for yourself.'

'The red clan breeds with other clans. If the child looks like the other clan, it's sent to them to be raised; if it looks like red clan, it stays here with us. But if the baby doesn't look like either clan, then it stays with the mother, not because she wants it, but because the other clan won't take it.'

I kept one arm around his waist but raised the other so I could touch his hair. I touched the white and gray of it, and last I stroked the dark, rich streak of red in his bangs, pulling on it just a little. It made me smile up at him, and that made him smile at me.

'You're beautiful, don't let anyone tell you different,' I said.

His smile widened. 'The clan females won't have sex with me because they don't want to bring an impure child into the world. I even had a vasectomy three years ago, so I couldn't get anyone pregnant. I thought that would make me safe enough for the clan females to want me, but they still saw me as impure, as if just my touch would make them less pure-blooded.'

'I'm so sorry that they've been stupid, Ethan.'

He smiled, a little sad around the edges. 'Me, too.'

Domino back home was a half-black and half-white tiger. He'd been security for the white clan, but just as alone as Ethan was; at least with Domino the white clan had found him in foster care and adopted him. They hadn't bargained for his birth and then treated him badly. It seemed somehow worse.

I smiled at him. 'Since I don't want to get pregnant by anyone, it's a plus for me. Your lycanthropy already protects you from any disease, so with me on the birth control, too, we're about as safe as we can get.'

'Our lycanthropy,' Ethan said.

'What?'

'You're a panwere, right? You just don't change shape, so our lycanthropy protects us from any other disease but the lycanthropy.'

I frowned, because I hadn't really thought about it like that. 'I don't know; since I can carry multiple strains of lycanthropy, I'm not a hundred percent sure I can't catch other diseases.'

He nodded. 'That's true, so you still have to worry about STDs.'

'If I'm with humans,' I said.

'Are you ever with humans?'

'No, but I bet you do just fine with the human women,' I said.

He smiled, and it was almost shy. 'I tried dating humans, but I can't tell them what I am, and you can't hide it forever.'

'No,' I said, 'you can't.'

'It's like denying what I am, who I am. It's almost lonelier than not having anyone in my arms.'

I nodded. 'I had a boyfriend, a fiancé who wanted me to do the white picket fence – so not my gig.'

He grinned at me. 'I can feel that you want me.' He leaned over me, sniffing against the side of my face. 'I can still smell the scent of red, and white, and blue . . . and something else I've never smelled before. You smell sweet and . . . Why do I see gold in my head? A gold tiger.'

'Because part of you is gold.'

'That's not possible,' he said.

'I can smell the truth on your skin.'

He drew in a deep breath.

'Gods, you smell like home.'

'I was told that gold tigers don't look for home.'

He shook his head. 'Then they must have already found it, because everyone looks for home in someone.' He whispered it as he turned his face against mine and put his lips on my cheek. It was almost a kiss, but not quite. His breath was warm against my skin.

My pulse was thick in my throat, my body tingling with his nearness. 'Do you understand what could happen to you?' I tried to sound reasonable, but it came out as a hoarse whisper.

'I think so.'

'We just have to wait for Alex, and then we can think about it. You can have time to think about it.'

His hand cupped the side of my face, sliding his fingers into my hair. He kissed me, ever so softly on the other side of my face. 'I don't want to think.'

I closed my eyes as he rubbed his face against mine, like a cat scent-marking, his hand tightened in my hair enough that I made a small noise for him. 'What do you want?'

'I want to go home,' he whispered.

I drew away enough to look into his eyes; they'd already gone soft, half-focused. His lips were parted, and his lower lip was wet as if he'd licked it. The *ardeur* pushed at me; the tigers slapped at me, raking their claws down the inside of my body so that I half-crumpled in his arms. He caught me, held me, his face all concern. 'Are you all right?'

I nodded. I was, but I wouldn't be if I fought too much longer. I thought about Alex, and I felt him, he was coming, but I felt his irritation with his mother; she'd delayed him. He was too far away, I couldn't hold out . . . I smelled Ethan's skin and was honest with myself: I didn't want to hold out. Yes, it was the *ardeur*, yes, it was the tigers inside me, but it was also his loneliness. I'd been lonely for years; I knew what it was like to be different and have no one love you for it.

'Are you all right?' he asked again, his hands on my arms now, as if he were afraid I'd fall.

'I will be,' I said.

'What can I do?'

I drew back from the *ardeur*, shoved the tigers down, and knew it wouldn't last. 'I need you to understand that I can't control all of this. I don't know how much of your free will you'll lose when we do this. I need you to really understand that, Ethan.'

His gray eyes were very serious as he looked down at me. 'I understand.'

'Do you?' I asked.

'No, but for the look in your face just a few minutes ago, for the smell of your skin, for that taste of belonging . . . Don't leave me here alone.'

I thought at Alex. I thought, too late, *Stay away*, and then I stopped fighting. Stopped fighting the *ardeur*, stopped fighting the tigers, and stopped fighting myself. I gave myself to the moment and the man in my arms.

13

It took time to disarm each of us. My concern for my weapons helped chase back the *ardeur* enough that other issues came up – like the fact that the small room Ethan had kicked open was the machinery room. It was bare and concrete floored. I was down to my bra and jeans with a pile of weapons at my feet when I laughed and said, 'Where can we have sex that we won't lose skin doing it?'

Ethan peeled his shirt over his head and dropped it on his own pile of weapons. I would have tried to find someplace more comfortable to have sex, but seeing him shirtless distracted me. The fine muscles I'd seen in his arms hadn't quite prepared me for how very nice he looked out of the shirt. There was always that moment when you got the clothes off for the very first time. It never grew old for me, that wonder of the first time, from the clothes coming off, to the first touch, the first kiss. Everyone kept telling me that with this many people in my life, and bed, I'd get jaded, but I never did. It was always fresh wonder, and Ethan standing there shirtless helped me chase back the *ardeur* even more, or maybe I just had more control of it now. But whatever the reason, I moved toward him, my hand outstretched so that I could run my fingers down the smooth, muscled grace of his chest. I had other men in my life who were more muscled, had more bulk, but Ethan's level of muscle was just dandy. I ran my hand over the smooth swell of his chest, avoiding the nipples for now, because I actually wanted to caress him before we raised the *ardeur* too far again.

I ran my hand over the smooth ridges of his stomach. 'Hmm, a six-pack, that takes work.'

His breath came out in a shuddering sigh, from just that innocent caress. 'All I am to my clan is muscle, so I have to be the best muscle I can be.'

I curved my hands on either side of his waist, following along all that lean, hardworking muscle. Such a small touch, but it made him close his eyes and sigh. That reaction alone let me know just how long it had been since someone touched him. It made me sad for him. And then I felt something in the hallway, something hot and powerful, and angry . . . I turned back and went for my gun in its holster, but like Ethan's gun it was under my shirt. I was on one knee, my shirt still in the air as I raised my gun up to aim at the door. Ethan was going for his gun, but he wouldn't reach it in time.

14

My finger was starting to pull the trigger as the door burst open, and I had a second to see that it was Alex in human form. If I'd been truly human I'd have shot him, but I had the reflexes to stop in time and aim the gun at the ceiling, though a moment later I wasn't sure I'd made the right choice.

I had a heartbeat to see him, a second to have that moment of frozen, crystal-hard vision, when adrenaline and violence slow everything down as if you have all the time in the world to do something, to see it coming. It's an illusion — if you see the same moment later on film, it's all so fast. But it let me see bits of things so clearly and the rest was lost. Alex's dark red hair was shorter than last time I'd seen him, almost shaved. He flashed yellow tiger eyes at me, his human face set in a snarl of rage as he rushed in a blur of speed and power at Ethan, who had his gun in his hand, but no time to aim, and if he had, would he have shot his prince?

Alex's body hit Ethan's and sent the other man back against the machinery behind us. Metal snapped, and groaned, as it broke underneath them. A harsh, coughing roar came out of Alex's human throat as he snarled into Ethan's face.

I was yelling, 'Alex! No! Alex! No! Stop!' I aimed the gun at him, and moved with it aimed so that I had a clear head shot while he snarled into Ethan's face. I had the shot, but I couldn't take it. I'd kill Alex at this distance, and he was my tiger to call, which meant when he died, I might die too, and so might everyone that I was metaphysically tied to. Fuck!

I holstered the gun and let it fall to the floor, and went to them. I had the angle now and could see that one of the metal pipes had pierced Ethan's side. There was blood all over that nice upper body. Fuck! I couldn't risk shooting Alex, but I wouldn't stand there and watch him tear Ethan apart either. I went back to my pile of weapons for a blade. But I'd forgotten what Ethan was, all he was to his clan: muscle.

His fist moved in a pale blur and Alex staggered back, blood flying from his face. Alex fell to the floor, catching himself on one hand. Ethan began to drag himself down the pipe. The sight of it twisted my stomach; God, it had to hurt. His power rolled off him in waves, and three of my tigers loved the taste of it, the heat of it, the disaster of it, because just watching Ethan force his body down that pipe in his side, I knew that when he got off that pipe the fight would be on.

I stepped between them, which if I'd meant to fight either of them would have been stupid, but I wasn't planning on slugging it out with either of them. I didn't so much drop my metaphysical shields as just find the anger that always seemed to be bubbling right below the surface of me. Feeding on sex was Jean-Claude's vampire line, the line that descended from Belle Morte, Beautiful Death, but anger, that was mine. The anger came to me as if it were a warm shower to touch and caress my skin. It felt so good to feed on it, to draw in all that rage. I had a moment of feeling that I had a choice whether to swallow it, or use it to be angry myself. That was new; usually it was just food. I 'ate' the anger, letting it soak into me.

Alex stared up at me, still on the floor, on his knees, one arm braced. 'What just happened?' he asked. His energy had completely changed; he felt normal, felt like himself.

'I ate your anger. Why are you so pissed?'

'I have no idea.'

Movement made me look back at Ethan. He shuddered with

the pipe halfway out of his side. That one movement let me know how hurt he was. Yes, he'd heal if it wasn't silver, but that didn't stop having a pipe shoved through your side from hurting like hell. I couldn't imagine trying to drag my body down it. I was thinking about it too hard, and my stomach clenched with nausea.

'What do you mean you have no idea, Alex?' I asked.

'I don't know,' he said. He looked up at me, and then called out, 'George, come help us.' I turned and found another guard in the white T-shirt and khaki pants that passed as their uniform. His short, thick hair was the traditional deep, almost-black red, his eyes like orange and yellow pinwheels of fire. There was a slight gold tinge that just added to the exotic effect that some of the reds had.

'My prince,' he said, and literally dropped to one knee, his fist coming back to touch his chest. I raised an eyebrow at that, because I'd never seen anything that formal at any of the other clans. It was like medieval formal.

'Help Ethan.'

'As my prince wills,' George said, and stood.

I heard a gasp of pain behind me, and the sound of a body falling. I turned to find Ethan on the floor, on his knees, his hands catching him from falling. His skin was almost gray and beaded with sweat from the pain and shock. But even as I watched, the blood flow was lessening. His body was beginning to heal itself. A wave of relief that I hadn't known I needed swept through me. It wasn't that Ethan meant that much to me yet, but getting him killed for plain stupid jealousy would have just been so unfair.

George, the guard, was only partway to Ethan when the anger came back. One minute Alex was standing, wiping the blood off his face, his usual calm self, and the next he was snarling and hit the wounded man twice before Ethan could defend himself. They came up off the floor in a snarling, pounding mass.

I tried to eat the rage again, but it was as if I slid off it. I couldn't reach the anger. Something was blocking me. The men began to beat on each other in a snarling, pounding mass.

I turned to the guard. 'Stop them.'

'If my prince wishes to discipline him, it is not my place to interfere.'

'Seriously?' I asked.

George gave a little smile, shrugged, and said, 'Seriously, I'm not crossing the Red Queen just for Ethan.'

'You are a useless piece of shit,' I said.

He frowned at me. '"Off with your head" isn't just for *Alice in Wonderland*'s Red Queen, Anita Blake.'

I had a second to think about the fact that this Red Queen beheaded her guards for disobedience, and then the fight took all our attention. If Ethan had been well, he'd have just kicked Alex's ass; it showed in the fact that he was beginning to win even as hurt as he was. Alex was strong, fast, in good shape, but his day job was as a reporter. He had a chance to hit the gym and probably even took some kind of fighting class, but Ethan did nothing but train. He did nothing but make himself a better fighting machine, and as his body began to knit together, he began to hit back with more force, block more of Alex's blows. It was the difference between an amateur and a professional in a fight; unless the amateur gets lucky early, he will lose.

Alex took another hit to the face and it spun him around. He tried to turn back, but Ethan kicked out and took his knee. I heard the meaty pop of it. Alex screamed and went down. Ethan kicked him in the face. Blood sprayed, and the screaming stopped. Alex fell to the floor unconscious. If he'd been human I'd have worried about a broken neck, but he wasn't human; no one in the room was, not really. And yeah, I included myself on that list.

Ethan turned toward us, his breathing harsh. His chest rose and fell with it. The sick sweat had turned into just sweat. He wiped at the blood still on his side, and the wound was almost closed.

The guard beside me drew his gun and pointed it at him. 'You know the punishment for hurting any of the queen's family.'

'In a battle over a female, that rule doesn't count,' Ethan said, his voice barely showing his breathing. He was already recovering, controlling his body.

I saw George's hand tense, and I reacted, not really expecting to get there in time, but I did. I swept his hand and the gun to the ceiling. The shot was thunder in the small room. The echoes were deafening.

He relaxed his arm against my hand, not trying to lower the gun. It made me look away from the center of his body to his face. I saw his lips work and heard his voice distant with the ringing in my ears: 'You're faster than I thought.' Then he tensed, and I had less than the blink of an eye to know that his other hand was coming for me. There wasn't even time for me to see it, let alone judge where it would land; there was just him tensing and the feel of his body moving.

His arm slammed across the side of my body. It was just a straight arm into my waist, but it raised me a few inches off my feet and sent me falling. Years on the mat in judo helped me fall as well as I could, taking most of the momentum with a slap of my hands and arms on the rough floor. Even then, I had a moment of blinking and being half-stunned on the floor. Another shot rang out, sharp, and hurting, like a blow to my ears. My brain was screaming, *Get up, get up, or you'll die!* I got up.

15

I got to my feet in time for a third shot to whirr over my head and make me crouch back down. Ethan got the gun away from George as I watched, but George punched him at the same time, and the gun went spinning across the floor. A knife flashed in George's other hand as I moved toward the fallen gun. I had it up and aimed it at the fight, but they were too fast. Ethan was fast, but George was faster, not fast enough to cut him, but fast enough that it was all Ethan could do to keep George from cutting him. They moved in a blur, circling and punching, and using their knees against each other's lower bodies, because they were too close in to use the whole leg to kick. I couldn't get a clean shot. Every time I thought I had it, Ethan was in my way.

I realized that George was purposefully moving Ethan around so he spoiled my shot, which meant that George was even better. I realized he had openings to punch Ethan, and I knew he had the strength to knock him back, but if he did that then he wouldn't have Ethan as a shield against the gun. He could have won the fight, but he needed Ethan in front of him, and close to him. Fuck, but he was good.

Did Ethan think he was holding his own, or did he understand what the other man was doing? I heard footsteps running in the hallway. I hoped it was help coming.

'I'm not here to hurt you, Anita Blake,' George said in a voice that showed no strain.

I ignored him and waited for a shot to open up.

Ethan stopped trying to fight and let George cut his arm. It gave him an opening to push back and let himself fall to the floor and give me a clear shot. I aimed at George's center and squeezed the trigger, but he was already moving, impossibly fast, a blur that I tried to follow with my hands and the gun as I fired. The gun was a Glock 21, which was a .45ACP, and it took my hands up toward the ceiling so that by the time I had the gun back down and ready to aim again he was through the door and out of sight.

I said, 'Motherfucker!' and got to my feet, gun held up, elbows bent, so if I had another shot I would be able to take it. But the hallway was a mass of people in white T-shirts and khaki pants. Most of them had the same short, dark red hair, so that there was no target to aim at, or there were too many.

Some of the figures were on the ground, white shirts blossoming crimson with blood. I prayed that one of them was George, but somehow I knew he wouldn't be.

I felt movement behind me and started to bring the gun around, but Ethan said, 'It's me.' I stopped in midmotion, telling the beating of my pulse in my throat that of course it was Ethan; no one else in the room was conscious. That made me think about Alex, and wonder why his being hurt hadn't hurt me. I'd taken damage when some of my other animals to call had been hurt, so why hadn't it hurt me?

I glanced behind to see that Alex was still motionless on the floor. I'd check on him after I knew what had happened to the bad guy.

Ethan moved in front of me, and I realized he'd taken the time to get his weapons. His T-shirt was untucked so that it didn't all fit back as neatly as it had started, but shoulder holsters chafe without a shirt. I had time to see that his wound was bleeding freely and starting to get all over his white shirt, as he put me at his back and did what a good guard will do: be a meat shield. When all else fails, that's the last duty of any bodyguard, to literally put his body between you and harm.

I started to say I didn't need it, but honestly, I couldn't have held my own against the other man as long as Ethan had. I could admit that he was not only stronger than I was, but better at slugging it out. I didn't like it, but I admitted it in my head, and I let him wade out into the fight in the hallway first. Did it hurt my pride? Yes. Was my pride worth dying for? No.

But when I started moving out behind him from the doorway, Ethan put a hand back and stopped me. 'Wait,' he said. There was a time when I wouldn't have listened, but the speed . . . the speed at the end had been too fast even for a shapeshifter. He'd been as fast as the masked shapeshifter who had injured Karlton. He wasn't tall enough, but he was fast enough. He had to be one of the Harlequin. I still wasn't certain if I'd hit him, or if he truly had been faster than a speeding bullet. It had all happened too damned fast.

I picked out words from the babble of voices in the hallway: 'He was too fast . . . dead . . . help me stop the bleeding . . . it's too late, he's dead . . . get the doctor.'

Ethan motioned that I could move forward. I pointed the gun down at the floor, but kept it in a two-handed grip. There were two men down in a pool of blood. A guard with yellow hair was holding his hands on one man's throat, trying to stop the bleeding, but blood gushed out from between his fingers. I'd known shapeshifters powerful enough to heal a wound like that, and I'd seen one die from an almost identical wound. He'd been killed by one of the Harlequin's animals to call, too. Were they trained to go for the throat?

The other fallen guard had less blood on him, but his eyes were already set in death. It looked like a stab straight to the heart. There was no recovery from a silver blade through the heart for a lycanthrope. He'd been dead the moment the blade slid home. Two other men were down with knife wounds, and a third was mobile but bleeding like Ethan.

George had fought his way through them in a matter of moments: two dead, three wounded, five if you counted Alex and Ethan. He did all that to a group of trained bodyguards who were also shapeshifters. Apparently the Harlequin were going to live up to their reputation. They were scary good.

There was nothing I could do for anyone out here, so I said, 'Ethan, I'm going to check on Alex.'

'Good idea,' and he followed behind me. One of the other guards asked, 'What's wrong with the prince? Is he hurt?'

'He's hurt,' Ethan said.

'Did George do it?' the man asked.

I answered before Ethan could. 'Let's just see how hurt Alex is.' I didn't want to get bogged down in details, and I also didn't want to see Ethan hurt before I could explain that it was the Harlequin that had made Alex attack and forced Ethan to defend himself. It was too complicated to explain with two of their men dead and more wounded. Complicated could wait until after everyone calmed down.

Alex was sitting up as we walked toward him. Ethan got to him first and dropped to one knee as George had done, hand going to his chest. 'My Prince, forgive me.'

Alex looked at him and then at me. 'It's okay; I would have killed you if you hadn't fought back. The rage was . . . like nothing I've ever felt.' He held out his hand to the other man. 'Help me up, and we'll call it even.'

This was the reasonable Alex I remembered. Ethan helped him stand up. There was bruising on Alex's face where the other man had kicked him, but it was as if the injury were days old instead of only minutes. If Alex had been a more powerful shapeshifter, there wouldn't have been any mark by now.

The other guard with us asked, 'What is Ethan apologizing for?'

I asked, 'Do you know where the rage was coming from?'

'It was like a dark voice in my head,' Alex said.

The guard blinked orange eyes at us, running fingers through his short orange-red hair. 'I feel like I'm missing something.'

I looked at Alex. 'I know there are real vampires that feed on emotion. I've met one that fed on fear and could also cause it to rise in people just by thinking at them.'

'Handy to be able to make your own food,' Alex said.

I nodded.

'You think this was a vampire?' Ethan asked.

'I know that the weretiger who ran out of here was one of the people that we're hunting. That speed, that level of weapons work, it was them.'

'You mean George was a spy,' the new guard said.

'First, what's your name, and second, how long has George been here?'

He smiled. 'I'm Ben, and a couple of months.'

I thought about that. 'They put him in here almost as soon as she woke up.'

'What?' Ben asked.

I shook my head. 'Just thinking out loud.' They'd put a spy in here as soon as the Mother of All Darkness woke.

'They put him here near me,' Alex said. 'They knew eventually you'd come visiting.'

'His paperwork checked out,' Ben said.

'Some of these guys have been master spies for a thousand years or more,' I said. 'They're good at what they do.'

'He cut through us as if we were human,' Ben said.

'Did I hit him with the last shot?' I asked.

Ben frowned; I think he was trying to replay the fight in his head. 'He had blood on his T-shirt, here.' He touched the left side of the chest, shoulder area. 'Was it Ethan's blood?'

'I never touched him,' Ethan said.

'Then, yes, you shot him.'

I grinned and felt that it was a fierce baring of teeth. 'Please tell me all your guns are loaded with silver shot,' I said.

'Of course,' Ben said. 'Silver will kill a human or a shapeshifter; lead only stops humans.'

'Then he's hurt,' Alex said. 'Silver makes even the strongest of us have to heal human-slow.'

'You were faster than he planned for,' Ethan said. 'He said so. Most of the guards would have missed that last shot. You did it with an unfamiliar gun, against someone faster than anyone I've ever seen.' Ethan gave me an admiring look that wasn't about sex, but about that guy moment when they realize you are not just another pretty face, but maybe, just maybe you can be cute, petite, and one of the guys all at the same time.

'I'll call Ted and let him know that the bad guys are trying to find me.'

'Why did he say that he hadn't come to hurt you?' Ethan said.

'I think he hoped I wouldn't shoot him.'

Ethan gave me a look. 'He could have been lying.'

'Yeah, but the other one last night that cut up the marshal said the same thing. They want me alive.'

'Why?' Ethan asked.

I shook my head. I didn't know Ethan well enough to answer that question, but I knew now that the Mother of All Darkness wanted me alive. There was only one reason she wanted me that way: so she could take over my body and make it hers. George had said he wasn't here to hurt me. He was lying. He wanted to kidnap me and feed me to the Dark Mother of them all. So she could use my body to live again. Not hurting me? Yeah, right. George was a lying bag of shit.

16

The weretigers' doctors and medics descended on the hallway not long after that. They took the more critically injured and left the dead to be carried away. Both the wounded and the dead were carried farther into the underground where they had their hospital area. We had one in the underground back home in St Louis, too. They patched up the knife wound on Ethan's arm. It was shallow and long; if the knife hadn't been silver-edged he'd have healed it already. Edward reported the disaster of the tracking dogs after he heard my report about the Harlequin spy. The dog had been as useless as we'd said, but he was more concerned about what had happened to me than about the case.

Alex went with most of the guards to report to his mother, the queen. They left two on the door of the room where we'd managed to wreck half the machinery that handled ventilation to their underground lair. A repair person was coming to look at it later. Business was being handled once the wounded and the dead were tended to, because no matter how much blood is spilled, you still need your air circulation to work. The mundane aspects of life keep needing attention no matter what else is happening. If you live through the disaster you still need to get groceries, do laundry. That's one of the hardest things to understand when you first get involved in violence. That once it's over the world goes on, and you have to go along with it.

Edward was adamant about talking to Ethan and me in private.

Once the door was closed, he let Ethan see just how unhappy he was with him. He was up in Ethan's face. 'I thought you were supposed to be good at your job.'

'I am,' Ethan said, and that first trickling heat began to fill the room. He'd been patient, but no one's patience is limitless, not even Ethan's, apparently.

'Edward, this wasn't his fault. This wasn't anyone's fault.'

Edward turned on me, hands in fists, eyes paled to that cold color of blue like a winter sky. I'd never seen him upset like this; he was usually one of the most controlled people I knew.

'I trusted your safety to him, Anita. I left you in his hands, literally.' He was up in my face now, and the height difference made him loom a little over me. He was one of those men who weren't that tall, but could really loom when they wanted to, and he wanted to. 'The only reason you're not dead is that he had orders to take you alive, Anita.'

I realized something and did the girl thing and said it out loud. 'You really do care that much about me.'

That stopped him in midword. Made him close his mouth and just look down at me, shaking his head. 'What?'

'Sorry, had a girl moment.'

He frowned at me.

'It's just that I've been in danger before. I've had people try to kill me before and you were somewhere else when they tried. You've never gotten this upset.'

He turned around, hands on hips. I think he was trying to regain control of himself. It wasn't like Edward to lose it. I had a thought: Was it the vampire? Was he that good, even in daylight, to spread anger like this?

'Edward, are you wearing your holy item?'

That made him turn around and face me. 'What?'

'Are you wearing a holy item?'

He gave me a very Edward look, like I should know better. 'You know I don't wear one.'

'You've seen my cross glow. You know blessed holy water

works. I've never understood why you don't wear something.'

'Holy water works because a priest blesses it; a cross works only if the wearer has faith in God. I don't.'

I let the theological discussion wait for another day. 'The vampire caused Alex to be filled with rage and try to kill Ethan. Now you're as angry about something like this as I've ever seen you, and you're angry at Ethan again.'

I had a thought: What if I wasn't the only one who had figured out that Ethan carried some of the gold bloodline? What if while George was here waiting for me to show up for the last two months, he smelled the gold on Ethan? What if today hadn't just been about capturing me, but about killing Ethan? Was that too twisty-turny, or was it just devious enough for the Harlequin?

Edward was studying my face. 'You've thought of something.'

I looked into his very calm, very Edward face. But it was Ethan who said, 'This isn't like the anger that was in the Prince. That didn't go away.'

I nodded. I didn't say out loud that it had to be a change of heart toward me on Edward's part. Once I'd believed that if he had to he'd kill me – he might miss me, but he'd do it. Now, I realized maybe he wouldn't. Maybe he was finally emotionally attached to me in a very un-Edward-like way.

If Edward had known that Ethan was part gold tiger, I'd have just said my thinking out loud, but he didn't know. I was thinking that the fewer people who knew, the better, but if the Harlequin knew, then Ethan wasn't safe. Of course, maybe it had just been coincidence that he was the guard who was with me when Alex attacked me. I frowned and rubbed my forehead. I was giving myself a headache.

'I think I'm overthinking this.'

'Overthinking what?' Ethan asked.

I looked from him to Edward. We were alone. Alex had gone with the guards to tell the queen what had happened. They'd left some guards outside the door of the room we were in, but only Ethan was in the room with us, mainly because Edward had insisted he needed to talk to Ethan.

'Okay, I'm thinking that maybe Alex attacking you wasn't just to make you kill each other so I'd be alone and easier to snatch. I think maybe George saw a way to kill two birds with one stone.'

Ethan frowned at me. 'I don't understand.'

I told them both what I'd smelled from Ethan's skin. He gave me an incredulous look. 'If I were part gold I'd have the power to command the other colors, and I so do not have that.'

Edward was looking at me. 'Anita is the Mistress of Tigers; if she says you smell like the golden tigers, then you do.' He looked at the other man.

'I have three tiger forms, three.' He actually held up three fingers. 'Red, blue, and white, that's it. No gold.' He folded the fingers down into a fist. 'I can't be.'

'All I can tell you is that you carry the strain. I've never smelled a weretiger that smelled of four different colors, so I can't tell you why you don't have three shapes to go with it, but I can tell you it's there.'

'You think that George sensed it, too, and when he had a chance to kill Ethan and not get caught, he took it,' Edward said.

'Maybe,' I said.

'If that's true,' Ethan said, 'then I'm dead. They are the greatest warriors, greatest assassins and spies that ever lived. I am so dead.'

He seemed oddly calm about it.

Edward and I exchanged a glance. I saw the slight frown of disapproval around his eyes, which let me know he wasn't sure it was a good idea, but that he wasn't going to say no, because he wasn't sure it was a bad idea either.

'Then you stay with us, with me.'

Ethan raised eyebrows at that. 'How does that keep me safe?'

Edward and I looked at him.

Ethan smiled, quick and surprised. 'Are you saying that the two of you are better than all of us?'

I shrugged, not always the most comfortable thing in the shoulder holster. It made me have to resettle the straps with a shoulder movement that looked like what it was, adjusting a strap on a holster that wasn't quite comfy.

'I think it's more that Ted and I trust each other more than we trust a bunch of men we don't know.'

'What she said.'

'You're human,' Ethan said. 'You saw what just one of these people did to a hallway full of weretigers. They're trained guards, Anita.'

'They're not as well trained as you are,' I said.

He shrugged, and had to do his own version of resettling the straps; without his own marshal Windbreaker it was very obvious. 'The other guards wouldn't agree with you.'

'You held your own with George. Hand to hand with him armed with a gun and a blade, and you kept him at bay.'

'He was toying with me, Anita. He was keeping me enough in the fight so my body was blocking your shot.'

'When did you figure that out?' I asked.

'When he had an opening for the knife and didn't take it.'

'If you hadn't sacrificed your arm to his knife and thrown yourself backward, I'd have never been able to shoot him.'

Edward motioned at the bandage on Ethan's arm. 'So you let him cut you, knowing it was a silver blade, and threw yourself back onto the floor so Anita could shoot him?'

Ethan nodded.

Edward gave a small smile. 'You trusted her to shoot him before he could fall on you and finish you.'

Ethan nodded again.

Edward studied the other man. 'You trusted that George was more worried about Anita shooting him than about killing you?'

'Yes,' Ethan said, and he was frowning now.

'Why?' Edward asked.

'Why what?'

'Why would you trust Anita that much? You'd just met her.'

Ethan frowned. He seemed to think about it for a moment or two. 'Her reputation, and the fact that one of the greatest fighters to ever walk the face of the earth was so worried about her. He was convinced that she would not only shoot him, but kill him. He was way more worried about her than me.'

'So you trusted that the bad guy had researched Anita, and if he was scared of her, then you'd trust her to be scary?'

Ethan thought about that for another moment or two. Then he nodded. 'I guess so.'

'You decided all that in the middle of a fight,' Edward said.

'While healing a wound in his side,' I said.

Edward looked at me. 'What?'

'When the bad guy made Alex go crazy with rage, he shoved Ethan into the machinery.'

'I got that,' Edward said.

'Did you also get that one of the broken pipes got shoved through Ethan's side?'

Edward raised eyebrows just a little at that. 'No.'

'He dragged himself off the pipe while I was trying to calm Alex.'

'Dragged himself off the pipe?' Edward said.

'Yep.'

Edward looked back at Ethan, and it was a considering look. He finally gave a small nod. 'That'll do.'

I smiled, because I knew what that meant.

Ethan frowned at both of us. 'What'll do?'

'You,' I said.

He frowned harder. 'What?'

'You've passed inspection,' I said.

Ethan looked at Edward. 'His inspection?'

'Our inspection,' Edward said.

He looked from one to the other of us. 'You guys have worked together a long time.'

We glanced at each other and then back to Ethan. We both said, 'Yes.'

17

Edward's phone rang. When it wasn't Donna, apparently his ringtone was an old-fashioned ring. Good to know. 'Forrester here.'

I heard a man's voice like a rumble over the phone. I wondered if Ethan could actually hear the other side of the conversation.

Edward went straight into his Ted voice, all cheerful and aw-shucks. 'Tilford, that's good thinkin' if ya got a good enough psychic.'

Ethan raised eyebrows at the change in Edward's voice, but it wasn't just his voice. Edward stood a little differently; his facial expressions matched the voice. There was more than one reason that he'd been so good at undercover work. He wasn't just good at killing people; he was, in his way, as good at hiding among his prey as the Harlequin.

'Really, Morrigan Williams.'

The moment I heard the name, my stomach tried to drop into my feet. She was a very good psychic. A little too good if you were keeping as many secrets as Edward and I were.

'So Morrigan Williams was here visiting. You lucked out, Tilford.' Edward grinned at the phone as if Tilford could see him. He could do the Ted voice without the whole body and face going with it, but he tended to stay in character if we were with more law enforcement, as if he were more concerned about not dropping the act when he knew he'd be 'Ted' for a long time.

He'd mentioned the name twice so I'd be sure to get the point. Neither of us would want to be spending much time near her. She was entirely too good, and her specialty was things that dealt with death. She specialized in serial killer cases and other violent death. Violence spoke to her psychically, the way it drew Edward and me in real life.

Edward got off the phone. The moment he was off, his face began to close down, go from smiling Ted to blank and serious. His blue eyes were cold when they looked at me. 'You heard.'

'Neither you nor I can be anywhere near her,' I said.

'Why? She helps the police solve cases and talks to ghosts. Why should that be a problem for you guys?' Ethan asked.

'I've had psychics tell me that I'm covered in death. That my energy was so stained with all I'd done that they couldn't be near me. They were gifted, but like most psychics they got impressions more than anything else. From all accounts Morrigan Williams gets much more detail.'

'You're afraid she'll see something about you two and tell the other policemen,' Ethan said.

'Yes,' I said.

'She's that good?' He made it a question.

'If her reputation is deserved, yes,' I said.

'Can you avoid her?' Ethan asked.

I liked that. We'd told him the situation and he went straight to testing for a solution. 'I don't know.'

'Tilford has her at the first murder site now.'

'You mean the first murder site in this city,' I said.

Edward nodded. 'You're right, it's not even close to the first, but yeah, he's at the softball field.'

'That was fast,' I said.

'Apparently, she contacted the police. She was told that she could help them find what they seek.'

'That sounds like the regular psychic stuff,' Ethan said.

'True,' I said. I looked at Edward. 'Maybe her reputation isn't deserved.'

'Maybe,' he said. We looked at each other for a minute.

'What does Tilford want us to do?'

'He's got a feeling that she'll give them a direction to hunt in, so he wants us back to help finish the hunt.'

'That's a lot of faith,' I said.

'I think Tilford trusts you and me at his back more than Newman.'

I grinned. 'Well, who wouldn't?'

'Is Newman bad at the job?' Ethan asked.

'No,' I said.

'We don't know yet,' Edward said.

'He is literally the new man on the team,' I said.

'So untried commodity,' Ethan said.

'He's fresh out of the training and he's never been on a real vampire hunt.'

'I wouldn't want him at my back either,' Ethan said, 'or at least not just him.'

'We can't leave Tilford hanging just because the psychic may see something she shouldn't,' I said.

Edward nodded. 'I know.'

'What are you going to do?' Ethan said.

'We're going to the crime scene,' I said.

'What will you do about the Williams lady?'

'We'll try to stay at a distance,' I said.

'Will that help?'

Edward said, 'Will it?'

I thought about it. 'She'll be in the middle of experiencing a very violent crime scene. If she's like most psychics, especially the good ones, she'll be overwhelmed with violent images and really bad emotions. She probably won't be able to tell our stuff from the crime.'

'Probably,' Edward said.

'*Probably* is the best I got unless you want to leave Tilford to hunt these guys without us.'

Edward sighed. 'No.'

'Then we go,' I said.

He nodded.

Ethan asked, 'Do you really think I'm in danger?'

I looked at Edward. He motioned at me. 'I'm not sure.'

'He can't go to the crime scene with us,' Edward said, 'so he's safer staying here, just farther into the underground where they'd have to fight their way in.'

'If I knew for sure he was a target, then I might disagree, but I think it's the best we got.'

We all agreed. I made sure that the two guards on the door outside walked Ethan back away from the entrance. One of the guards asked, 'What about you guys? You're only human. He's not.'

'George is carrying my bullet in his side, not anyone else's. I think I did okay.'

'He moved through us like we were standing still,' the guard said, and his eyes looked haunted. 'None of the rest of us could touch him. You did better than just okay, and you know it.'

'Thanks,' I said.

He motioned to Ethan, and the three of them walked down the corridor. I unholstered the Browning and put a round in the chamber.

Edward looked at me.

'I shot him because I had the gun out and aimed. If I'd had to draw first, I'd have missed.'

Edward didn't argue, he just got out his Glock and jacked up a round, ready to fire. 'Any other advice?' he asked.

The fact that he asked me was very high praise. 'I appreciate your asking, but no.'

'Let's go see if Morrigan is as good as her rep, and if Raborn will really let Tilford order a full-blown hunt on the basis of a psychic's vision.'

'I'm betting he won't,' I said.

'I'm betting you're right,' Edward said.

'Which is another reason Tilford wants us there. If Raborn doesn't sign off on it, then we'll be going in with just the marshals with us and some of the locals.'

'Yep,' Edward said, already sliding back into his Ted persona. He started up the tunnel, and I fell in beside him. We walked out with our guns drawn and ready to fire. There were no bad guys waiting for us, but I didn't feel weird about having my gun out and ready, I just felt safer.

When we got to the SUV we put on the full gear for monster hunting, including the vest, which I hated the most. It hampered movement and it wouldn't stop either a vampire or a wereanimal. They'd peel it off us like getting a turtle out of its shell, but regulations stated that the vest was part of the outfit. I had to change out my holsters to accommodate the vest, so that I could still get to the Browning, but the Smith & Wesson had to move even more to a front cross draw. Only the knives got to stay put.

'Hate the vest,' I said.

'Think of it like an air bag on your car.'

I looked at him. 'You wearing yours more often?'

'Some.'

And just like that I knew Edward had changed. Or was it me? I was harder to hurt and healed almost anything short of a death blow and Edward didn't. He was more fragile than I was; it seemed so wrong.

'What?' he asked.

'Nothing.' And, in the end, there really was nothing to say but it made me sad.

18

Edward's phone rang. He slipped it from his pocket. 'Forrester here.'

I heard the murmur of a man's voice on the other end but couldn't tell more than that. Edward made little *um* noises, and then finally said, 'We're ten minutes out. Wait for us.'

He listened some more and then turned to me, phone still to his ear. 'The psychic has pinpointed the vampires as very close to the first kill site here. Close enough to find them and stake them before full dark. Some of the other police are pushing Newman to be a man and go into the woods before we get there. Apparently the fact that they think we're fucking has cost both you and me credibility.'

'They're going in with SWAT, then?' I said.

'They didn't think the vampires would be in the woods. They didn't put out a full call, and by the time they get out here to the middle of Bumfuck, Nowhere, it'll be dark.'

'The vampires are still asleep, but the wereanimals aren't. There is at least one wereanimal near the vampires, maybe more, I'll guarantee that.'

Edward handed me the phone and started driving fast enough to make the narrow tree-lined road exciting, but not in a good way. I held on to the oh-shit handle and hoped it didn't earn its nickname.

Tilford said, 'Why are you so sure that the wereanimals are near the vampires?'

'Because they are their animals to call, which means their main job is to help their vampire masters. If the vampires are just buried in the leaves in a wood, then no way would their wereanimals leave them totally unguarded during daylight hours. A large animal could uproot them and expose them to sunlight. It's just too dangerous to leave a vampire alone like that. You saw how fast he was, Tilford. Do you really want to go into the woods around here with only a handful of marshals and local PD?'

'No,' he said.

'Then don't,' I said.

'You know if the rest of them go in, I can't stay behind.'

'Don't let them bully Newman, then; protect him, damn it, and protect the rest of them even if it's from themselves.'

'The other marshals don't think you and Forrester being here will make that much difference. They'd rather not lose the daylight.'

'Do you believe that less than ten minutes will make that big a difference?' I asked. Edward took a curve and with the phone in one hand I had to brace my leg and hold on to the handle very tightly. I muttered 'Jesus' under my breath.

'What's wrong?' Tilford asked.

'Ted's trying to cut down on our arrival time. We'll be there really soon if we don't go off the road.'

'We won't go off the road,' Edward said, eyes still on the road as he hit the gas harder, and I tried to pretend I believed him.

'I'd rather have you both with us, but neither of you is exactly everyone's favorite person right now.'

'Because everyone thinks we slept together?'

'I didn't say that,' he said.

'Ted said that's why he lost his street cred with some of the marshals. I know my rep was already trashed.'

'I'm sorry,' he said, which meant it was the truth.

'They're just jealous,' I said. I fought not to make one of those girly squeak noises as the side of the SUV brushed tree limbs on the side of the road.

'What?' Tilford asked.

'Either they want to know why I won't sleep with them, or they hate the fact that I fucked someone and I still kill more monsters than they do.'

'I don't think the first, but the second, maybe.'

'It's a guy thing, Tilford; it's not that they really want to sleep with me, it's just if one guy is, then why not them? It's just a fucking stupid guy thing.'

He was quiet for a few breaths. 'We're going in.'

'We're almost there, I swear.'

'If the thing that hurt Karlton is in there, the two of you won't make that big a difference, Blake.'

'You'd be surprised,' I said.

'What can you do that we can't?'

I didn't know what to say to that, but finally settled on, 'I can sense wereanimals and vampires sometimes.'

'So can the psychic,' he said.

'But can she shoot them?' I asked.

He gave a small chuckle. 'Probably not. We're going in.'

'Tilford, please wait.'

Edward half-yelled, 'We're almost there!' The SUV skittered around a corner and then Edward slammed on the brakes so hard that only my braced leg and the desperate grip on the oh-shit handle kept me from kissing the dashboard.

'What the fuck, Ed . . . Ted?'

'What's wrong?' Tilford asked.

'There's a truck in the middle of the road,' I said.

'A wreck?' Tilford asked.

The truck was upside down, the cab partially crushed, some of the windows broken as if it had flipped. 'Yeah.'

'Any injured?'

Edward and I kept staring at the truck. 'No one we can see,' I said.

'If there's injuries we can have one of the locals call it in,' Tilford said.

Edward's hand was on the door handle, but he wasn't getting out. I touched his arm. 'We'll call you back,' I said, and handed Edward his phone. He put it away, and we looked at the wreck, and then we both started looking around at the trees so close to the road.

'The truck doesn't look right,' I said.

'There isn't room to flip a truck that size on this road,' Edward said. 'It should be in the trees, maybe on its side, but there's no way to flip it.'

'Yeah,' I said.

I undid my seatbelt. Edward's was already undone. I moved the MP5 around on its sling so it was in my hands and ready. Edward had his FN P90 in his hands. But he dropped one hand off to sort of caress the M4 where it sat against his leg.

'Debating between guns?' I asked, as I scanned the trees on my side.

'The P90 from the car, but once we hit the woods I'll switch to the M4.' I knew without turning around that he was scanning his side of the road.

'Mine's still at the gun shop being modified,' I said. All I could see was trees, lots of trees.

'I'd have done it for you,' he said.

'You're in New Mexico; it's a little far to go for gun repair,' I said.

'I thought you said it was being modified, not repaired.'

'Yeah.'

'You getting the specs I suggested?' he asked; his voice had gone very quiet.

'Yeah,' I said, and my voice was doing the same thing. We were talking, but we were also listening. You always did that, even though with wereanimals our most likely bad guy we'd probably never hear them coming. You still strain for it, and try to listen; all the while your eyes are almost hurting because you're looking so hard. I tried to let my gaze relax and just look for movement, just look for anything that didn't look like trees. I needed a shape that was out of place.

'I don't see anything,' Edward said, finally.

'Me either,' I said.

'Did they do this to keep us from going in with the other marshals, or is this an ambush just for us?' he asked.

'I don't know.'

'Three choices,' he said.

I kept scanning the trees. The shadows were thick in them. We were maybe an hour and a half from full dark. I said, 'We get out and hike to join the hunt, or we stay put, or we back up and get out of here.'

'Yep,' he said, and I didn't have to turn around to know he was scanning his section as hard as I was scanning mine.

'Can't just stay put,' I said.

'No,' he said.

'Either they're going to jump us the minute we get away from our truck, or they'll wait until we start hiking through the woods toward the other marshals.'

'That's what I'd do,' he said.

'Shit,' I said.

'There are moments when I hate the fact we carry badges,' he said.

'Because otherwise we could just back up and try to leave,' I said.

'Something like that,' he said.

I had a thought. 'What if we back up like we are leaving?'

'You mean that if they think we're running, it will force them to show themselves.'

'Yeah,' I said.

'Good idea.' I felt him turn in the seat, but he said, 'I'd rather you drive and I shoot, actually.'

'I would have had us in the ditch two or three times, Edward. I can shoot, but you're a better driver. The question is, are we actually driving, or is it all about shooting?'

'Are you admitting I'm a better shot?'

'From a distance, with a rifle, you are.'

'Belt yourself in; this isn't about distance, and we may need to drive.'

I did what he said, and was now trying to keep my attention on the entire area. Which wasn't possible, but Edward had to drive, so I'd do my best. I actually put one knee in the seat, raising myself up and trying to steady myself as I scanned the road, the woods on either side.

'Behind us, Anita, make sure they don't cut us off.'

I did what he said, but I said, 'We're not really leaving, right?'

'We have to make it look good,' he said.

I couldn't argue with that, but I didn't want to leave our fellow police on their own in the shadow-filled woods. I did my best to keep an eye on everything as he backed up, at a speed that I wouldn't have even attempted on this road, especially going backward. I put a hand on the headrest to steady myself and the MP5, because it would be a bitch to fall and accidentally shoot Edward. I'd never tried to aim and keep watch on this much area, while the vehicle I was in was speeding backward down a narrow road. My pulse was in my throat, and a little voice screamed in my head, *There's too much. I can't keep an eye on it all.* I shoved the doubts away and held on, and just had to believe that if the time came I'd be able to shoot the bad guys.

I saw movement to the right, but to aim I had to come to my knees in the seat. The seatbelt was around my legs and officially useless. I prayed that Edward wouldn't have to slam on the brakes, and wrapped one arm around the headrest to help steady me and the gun. Whatever I'd seen was gone. There was nothing but trees, and the road, and a fallen tree in the middle of the road. It took me a blink to realize what I'd seen, and then I yelled, 'Tree in the road!'

Edward slammed on the brakes. I clung to the seat desperately, no longer worried about shooting, just about not going through the windshield. The car skidded to a stop and we had that second of breathless silence while the blood roared in our ears, and the body feels too full of blood, as if the adrenaline makes everything feel like more.

Edward said, 'That wasn't there five minutes ago.'

'I know,' I said. I was back to aiming the gun again, trying to find something to shoot. 'We're boxed in, now what?' I asked, cheek snugged up against the MP5.

'It's an ambush,' Edward said. 'The best cover we have is the car, so we stay put. We make them force us out into the open.'

I undid my seatbelt so it didn't tangle my legs as I sat back down. 'They've used swords up to this point; let's hope they don't go all modern on our asses.'

'Agreed.' He got his phone out as he continued to scan the area. He answered my look. 'I'm calling Tilford, because if this is a trap for you then it's a trap for all of us, and you're the only one they want alive.'

I realized he was right; they wanted me alive, and that was that. 'Shit, Edward.'

'Yeah.' He spoke into his phone, 'Tilford, it's a trap. They've blocked the road that leads out.'

I heard Tilford's voice a little louder this time, but still couldn't quite make out the words.

'Wrecked a truck and pulled a dead tree across the road.' Edward listened and made small noises, and then he turned to me. 'They've found a vampire dressed in full gear complete with mask. Newman has already staked him and they're about to decapitate him.'

I shook my head. 'They wouldn't have left their masters alone and unprotected, Edward. They may want me, but not enough to risk their masters' death.'

'Tilford, check the teeth,' Edward said.

Almost a yell from Tilford, but Edward said, 'If there's modern dentistry, then it's not the vamps we're looking for.'

I thought about that. 'Not necessarily,' I said. 'Chipped teeth might still happen, I don't know for sure, but no cavities. Check for cavities.'

Edward repeated that. We waited for Tilford to do it. We kept the guns ready, but the lack of movement and the growing shadows were beginning to get on my nerves. I realized that they had us boxed in; all they had to do was wait for nightfall.

'Shit,' I said.

'What?' Edward asked me.

'They're waiting for dark.'

He nodded, and then spoke to Tilford. 'Four modern cavities; then it may be a vampire but it's not one of the ones we're looking for. It's a decoy, Tilford.'

Edward hung up, and then said, 'Tilford believes us.'

'What about the rest of them?'

'Not sure.'

'Edward, we can't just sit here until it gets dark — then we'll have not just the one or two wereanimals but both of their vampire masters. The odds are better now.'

'Are we heading to the other marshals?'

'More guns are better,' I said.

'They only want you alive, Anita. The rest of us are just hostages, or collateral damage.'

'If I go in the opposite direction of everyone else, they may not attack anyone but me.'

'You can't fight them all by yourself, and you can't walk out of here after full dark.'

I took a deep breath in and let it out slow. 'I know.'

He studied my face for a moment. 'Where you go, I go.'

'Yeah, but what about everyone else? Do we move toward them, or away? Do we hope the bad guys follow us, or risk that they'll go to the other cops without us there to help them, and either slaughter them or take them as hostages to make me do what they want like they did with Karlton?'

'You're overthinking this,' he said.

'Okay, then tell me what to think.'

I watched his eyes go distant, cold, and knew he'd shoved all the emotion away so he could make his decision based on nothing but facts. It was a nifty trick if you could pull it off. I'd never managed to be as dispassionate as Edward.

'I think they'll follow you. So we lead them away.'

'Okay,' I said.

'We have to kill the wereanimals before the vampires rise,' he said.

'I know.'

'We have just over an hour before they rise.'

'I know,' I said.

We had a moment to look at each other and have a thousand things pass between us. There were no words, no need for them. Edward put his hand on the door handle; I did the same on my side. Edward counted down, 'One, two, three.' We got out.

19

I went around the SUV, walking sideways and sort of backward so I could watch my side of the woods. I was fighting to keep my eyes soft-focused, looking for movement only, shapes that were out of place. Edward's hand found my back, and I knew without turning around that he was looking forward, probably with the FN P90 in one hand. The M4 was a two-handed gun. We eased into the woods like that with him forward, me watching our backs. The smell of pine was everywhere, the needles shifting under my jogging shoes. Movement across the road. I must have tensed, because Edward whispered, 'What?'

'They're coming.' They were black shapes in the trees. If they'd been willing to lose the long black cloaks they could have blended in better, but there was something about the way the cloth moved that wasn't tree, or animal, but just out of place.

'How many?'

'Two.'

They were like those shapes you see from the corners of your eyes; if you looked directly at them, they wouldn't be there, but looking obliquely they were always there, flitting through the trees as if the cloaks floated on their own. I got a flash of white from one of their masks, and that let me know that the next flash would be close enough for a target.

Edward whispered beside me, 'See it.'

I breathed out, lower than a whisper, 'Left.'

'Right,' and the word was less than a sound, as if he breathed it out. He moved a little away from me so his muzzle blast wouldn't be too close to me, or mine to him.

I saw the white flash of mask just before they broke cover, and I fired. I knew I missed, because there was no hesitation in their speed. I aimed lower as my target got to the trees on their side of the road. Even with all the time in the world to make the shot, I still missed the main body mass. The blurring speed hesitated and he dived behind the SUV's side, putting the engine block between us.

The other Harlequin was around the edge of the truck and coming for the trees. Edward shot again, but the figure never hesitated. 'Missed,' he said.

I turned and got ahead of the figure. It was more luck than skill, but I took the shot. The figure went down and tumbled into the side of the ditch, so that all I could see was a dark pile of cloth almost lost in shadow.

'They're too fast,' Edward said, as he went toward the fallen figure. I moved toward the SUV, tensed to fire at anything that peeked around the truck. Nothing moved. There wasn't even a sense of movement. It hadn't been a kill shot, I knew that. I stayed far enough away from the underside of the vehicle that someone under it couldn't grab me. I kept the MP5 snugged up against my shoulder, tensed and ready to shoot. I was inches away from rounding the last edge of the hood and having a clean visual when Edward fired behind me. It made me jump, and then he made a noise. I hurried the last few inches around the truck before I let myself look behind me. There was no one hiding behind the truck. I knew I'd hit him, but he wasn't there.

I turned, muttering, 'Shit,' under my breath. I couldn't see over the top of the SUV. I rushed around the front of it, gun still at my shoulder. Edward was on the ground shooting up at the figure above him. I had time to register that he wasn't shooting him in the chest, but the legs, and I knew why I had no body in the road. Vests. They were wearing bulletproof vests. Shit. But one thing I knew was that even if a bullet didn't go through, it still hurt, so I aimed at the middle body mass, using the shots to force him back away from Edward. The shots staggered him, and then he was moving away from Edward, away from me into the trees, but he wasn't moving in that blur of speed. He was fast, but not super-fast. He wasn't much faster than human. Edward rolled onto his stomach and kept shooting. The Harlequin started using the trees for cover. He was hurt. Good.

I felt something behind me, and threw myself toward the ground before I'd finished turning around. I hit the ground harder than I wanted, but I was aiming up, and got one shot off before my eyes registered the masked figure in front of me. The shot went wild, and then he was simply gone, moving in that blur of speed that I'd seen at the hotel.

There were more shots from across the road and men yelling. The other police had joined the party. I turned onto my stomach and found the slight curve of the ditch blocking my view. I had to get to one knee before I could look into the trees and the shadows that were filling them up. There was nothing to shoot at; they were out of sight, but one was wounded. The question was, how hurt was he?

Edward was on his feet; I climbed up the other side of the ditch to stay by his side. He had his gun up and ready and was moving in that shuffling, bent-legged walk that most of the special forces and especially SWAT used. It was supposed to help you move well, but keep you as steady as possible for shooting. I'd never been trained, but I'd grown up in the woods, and hunting. I knew how to move in trees.

I heard the other police behind us, crashing through the trees like a herd of elephants. I knew they weren't actually that loud, but they seemed thunderous behind us, so that the noise seemed to make it even harder to search the shadowed trees for the Harlequin, as if the noise masked everything. I fought the urge to turn and yell at them to be quiet.

'Cover me,' Edward said.

I moved until I was almost over him, looking out into the ever thickening shadows as he knelt down. 'Blood,' he said.

I glanced at him, still trying to keep a peripheral sense of the trees and the growing darkness under the trees. There was more light on the road behind us, but here in the thick trees night would come early.

'You wounded them?' This from Tilford, as he came up on the other side of Edward. He had his own M4 pointed out into the trees.

I said, 'Yes.'

Edward said, 'We follow the blood trail.'

'It'll be dark soon,' Tilford said.

Edward stood up. 'It will.'

Newman was with us now. 'I've never seen anything move that fast.'

'We need them dead before full dark,' I said, and was already moving through the trees.

'Why?' Newman asked.

'Because the vampires will rise,' Edward said.

'How do you know there will be vampires?' Newman asked.

Tilford answered, 'Wereanimals don't wear masks and cloaks. They don't sneak around. They just attack. The only thing that makes them behave like this is a vampire master. Night means we get to meet their masters, and I'd rather the shifters be dead before we have the vampires to deal with.'

Edward and I exchanged a quick look. We both thought better of Tilford in that moment. I said, 'What he said.'

We followed the blood trail in the ever-growing dark. We followed the fresh blood even though every molecule in my body was screaming for me to run. Run before dark. Run before the vampires came. Run. But I didn't run, and neither did the other marshals. We followed the trail, because that was our job. We followed the trail because if they got away and killed more people, none of us wanted to look down at the body and explain why we'd let shadows and maybe a threat of vampires scare us off. We were US Marshals. We hunted and killed the monsters. We did not run from them.

20

It got dark enough that Edward and Tilford turned on the flash-lights that were attached to the barrels of their M4s. It was a mixed blessing. It allowed us to follow the blood trail but ruined our night vision. I finally kept my gaze away from the lights. One of us needed to be able to see what the deepening shadows might hold. Following the blood trail was important, but if the Harlequin that were bleeding found us first, there'd be more blood, and some of it would likely be ours. Was that pessimistic, or realistic? I had trouble telling sometimes.

Newman followed me ahead into the creeping gloom. 'Do you see something?'

'Not yet.'

'Saving your night vision from the lights?'

That made me glance at him. 'Yes, how'd you know?'

'I was raised in the country. I'm okay in the dark most nights.'

'Me, too,' I said.

'Country girl?'

'Something like that.'

'I'd have pegged you for a city girl,' he said. All the time we talked we looked out into the coming dark, searching the trees for movement. He had his gun at his shoulder just like I did. I was beginning to like Newman and I didn't want to, because I'd liked Karlton and now she was in the hospital breathing with help. The shapeshifter had collapsed one of her lungs. They were waiting to see if her body would heal it without operating. If she had caught some version of lycanthropy then she'd heal as good as new, so they waited. The waiting meant they thought her blood tests were going to come back contaminated with the virus. With deep puncture wounds, lycanthropy was usually a given.

'I'm a city girl now,' I said.

Edward came to us, the light pointed at the ground, and finally turned it off before he got to us. Even that much light for that small an amount of time seemed to make the thick twilight thicker.

One look at his face and I asked, 'What's wrong?'

'The blood pattern has changed. One of them is carrying the other, and he's running with him. He's been running through the woods while we crawled after them; that's why we haven't heard them.'

'They're gone,' I said.

'Good as,' he said, and there was still enough light for me to see how disgusted he was with it all.

'If we can't trail them, then Tilford is right – we need to get out of here before full dark.'

'We don't have enough people to move the truck, Anita.'

'We can move the tree,' I said, 'and we can all fit in our SUV.'

He nodded. 'Done.'

Tilford didn't argue, and Newman didn't try to argue with the three of us. He was learning. If we could keep him alive, maybe he'd actually be good at the job.

21

The tree was an old deadfall. It wasn't as heavy as a fresh tree would have been, but it was heavy enough, and big enough that the four of us had to think about how best to use the muscle we had available.

Tilford keep glancing up as well as out into the trees, while we decided where best to grab hold. 'Why do you keep looking up?' Newman asked.

'Sometimes they fly,' Tilford said.

Edward and I just nodded.

Newman started glancing up, too. He was a quick study; I hoped he didn't die. And the moment I thought it again, I realized I was being morbid. Crap.

We put Tilford and Newman at the front of the tree, and Edward and I took the back. That part was bigger, a little heavier, but there was less of it to shove across the road. Edward counted, 'One, two, three,' and they pulled, and we shoved. I'd never really tried to use every bit of the new strength I'd gained through vampire marks and lycanthropy. I tried now. Our end of the tree moved, really moved, and it startled me and Edward. He slipped in the leaves a little. I slipped forward and scraped my arm on a jagged root. It was sharp, and immediate, and I knew it was going to bleed before I felt the first trickle. I cursed under my breath.

'How bad?' Edward asked.

'Keep shoving,' I said.

He took that to mean it wasn't bad, and we shoved. The tree trunk was onto the road completely now. I felt the vampires wake like a jolt down my spine. It was still light enough that they couldn't come for us, not yet, but we were minutes away. I dug my feet in, put my shoulder down, and prayed. I prayed that if I had any super-strength, I would use it now. I prayed, 'God, if I can move this tree, let me move it now.'

I breathed out in a yell, the way you do sometimes in the gym when you're lifting something heavy, something that you're not sure you can move. But it moved. Edward put his shoulder beside mine, and the other men pulled, and the tree moved. I yelled again, and the tree slid across the road as if it were on wheels. It just gave. I fell to my knees, because I hadn't expected it to move like that.

'Anita . . .' Edward started to help me up.

'Car, start it now.' I said.

He didn't argue with me. He just did what I said. I liked that. I moved my gun around on its strap so it was in my hands and ready.

Tilford crashed through the trees on the other side of the road, with Newman behind him. I pointed at the car, and my right arm glistened with blood, black in the moonlight. 'Car, now!'

'They're coming,' Tilford said.

'I know,' I said. I got to my feet. The SUV roared to life. The three of us ran for the car. I felt the night fall around us like something warm and thick and velvet. I pushed the thought away that it felt like Her. I was just scared, just freaked. It wasn't Marmee Noir. It was just nerves.

I felt the vampires, felt them freed of the last bit of daytime paralysis. I felt them like distant thunder trembling along my skin, rushing toward us through the trees. It made me run, and I was suddenly ahead of the men. Like moving the tree, I didn't run human-slow.

I was the first one to the door. I opened it and turned, looking past the other two men, searching the dark shapes of the trees for something that wasn't trees.

I yelled, 'Hurry, damn it!'

Newman slipped and went down, face first into the gravel. Tilford opened the door on the other side, saying, 'I'm in.'

I heard him shut the door. I saw Newman scramble on all fours as he got to his feet. There was blood on his face. He'd fallen hard, but I kept an eye behind him, above him. They were coming. Moving like wind that never stirred a leaf, or brushed a twig, like a silent movable storm that was coming just for us.

I yelled, 'Newman!'

I moved at the last minute so I was farther away from the open door but he could go straight into the car without fouling my line of sight. He fell into the car.

Edward yelled, 'Get in!' I realized he had his window down and the barrel of his gun searching the darkness. Windows would mess up the first few shots. He knew we weren't going to get out of here without a fight; so did I.

I put my back against the open door, searching the woods, trying to hear something above the engine's thrum. I thought, *Where are they?* And just like that, I could feel them on the other side of the road. They were just inside the tree line, hiding in the shadows and the night.

I breathed, 'Shit.' I climbed into the truck, shutting the rear door behind me. I had time to say, 'Drive!' Edward put it into gear and started backing up at speed. I made Newman move over so I could try for a seatbelt as the SUV slithered across the gravel. I knew right where they were; I felt them standing there watching us drive away. Why were they just watching? My pulse was in my throat. I was suddenly more afraid than I had been a second before.

'They aren't chasing us, Edward. They're just watching from the trees.'

'You saw them?' Newman asked.

I ignored him.

'Why are they just watching?' Tilford yelled from the front passenger seat.

'I don't know.' I slid the buckle of the seatbelt home just as Edward found the four-way with its stop signs. He turned the big SUV in a circle of flying gravel. He got us facing the right way around and hit the gas. The car jumped forward. He had a moment where I could feel him fighting to keep us on the road, and then we were speeding away from them.

Almost at the edge of even my night vision, two figures stepped out from the trees. They stood and watched us go.

'That's them, isn't it?' Newman asked.

I nodded, watching the two figures as if afraid to look away, for fear of what would happen if I took my eyes off them. It was silly, almost superstitious, but I watched them stand there until even I couldn't see through the thickening dark.

'Why didn't they chase us?' he asked.

'I don't know,' I said.

'I don't care why,' Tilford said, and he turned around in the front seat so he could see us both, 'I'm just glad they didn't.'

'They didn't need to chase us. They blocked the road again,' Edward said.

We all looked, and this time it looked like they'd pulled up half a dozen trees and formed a wall. 'That took time,' Tilford said, 'and more manpower than we thought they had.'

Edward slowed the car. 'Tilford, you're driving.'

'What?' Tilford asked.

'Anita, cover me. Newman, help her.' He was already climbing out from behind the wheel. Tilford cursed under his breath as he fought to slip behind the wheel before Edward was completely out from behind it. The SUV swayed, but we stayed on the road.

Edward was climbing past us and into the far back. 'What are you going to do?' I asked.

'Shoot them if they get too close. Shoot anything that moves around that barrier.' He was rummaging around in the back in some of the weapons that were too big or too cumbersome to carry easily. It always scared me when Edward started getting into his big stuff. The last time it had been a flamethrower, and he'd damn near burned a house down with us in it. But I did what he asked. I rolled down a window and divided my attention between the barrier on the road and the way we'd just come.

Tilford had stopped the car. 'What do you want me to do?'

'Move forward, slowly,' Edward said. His upper body was mostly below the back of the seat.

I did my best to ignore him and do my part of the plan. Edward had a plan, and I didn't, so he was in charge until either he ran out of plan, or the plan turned out to be too crazy. Though right that second, I couldn't think of anything crazy enough to make me say no.

Newman said, 'Holy Jesus!'

It made me glance back at Edward. For a blink, I thought it was just a bigger gun, and then I forgot to watch the dark or hunt for vampires. I took a few seconds to stare at what he had in his hands.

'Is that . . .' I said.

'Light anti-tank weapon,' he said.

'It's a LAW,' I said.

'Yes,' he said. He rolled back over the seat so he was kneeling between Newman and me. 'Open the sunroof,' he said.

'If you had this, why didn't you use it on the tree?' I asked.

'It's the last one I have,' he said.

'Last one,' Newman said. 'How many did you have?'

'Three.'

I said, 'Don't argue, just open the door. Watch the road edge and the sky and be ready to jump back in when Tilford guns it.'

'Why not just aim through the windows?'

'Because we can't watch the sky as well from the window.'

'But . . .'

'Just do it,' Edward said.

Newman glanced at me, then at Edward, and opened his door. I did the same on my side. When I was standing with one foot on the ground and the other on the running board, MP5 snugged at my shoulder, I said 'Edward.'

'Anita?'

'Do it.'

I heard him slithering up through the sunroof. I just trusted that he was halfway through the sunroof.

Tilford asked, 'Do you want me to start easing up toward the roadblock?'

'No,' Edward said, 'we don't know what they put in the pile; better farther away until it blows.'

I kept staring out at the moonlight and trees as I said, 'What could they put in the pile to make it dangerous?'

'Ask me later,' Edward said. I heard him move again. Enough that it made me glance back to find that he was standing on the headrests on the front seats, as if height were important.

I got a glimpse of Newman staring, too, and pointed at my eyes, and at him, and back out into the night. He went back to looking sort of guilty, as if I hadn't been doing the same damn thing. I went back to glancing up at the star-filled sky, and then down at the trees. Nothing moved but the wind. It made the leaves shudder and gave that sound that always makes me think of Halloween, as if the leaves are skittering across the ground like little mice. Normally I like the sound, but tonight it was distracting, and the leaf movement made me jumpy.

Newman shot into the dark. It made me jump. Newman yelled out, 'Sorry.'

'Nothing there, Newman,' Edward said.

'I said, sorry.'

'Get a grip, rookie,' I called.

Tilford spoke from the front. 'We all shoot at shadows when we're new, Blake.'

He was right, but I'd apologize to Newman later if I needed to. I went back to watching my own windy section of trees, and dark sky, and road. They came onto the road behind us, two of them in the same long black cloaks and white masks. It made them anonymous, impossible to tell if they were new Harlequin or ones we'd seen before. The only thing I was almost certain of was that they weren't the ones Edward and I had wounded in the woods. These two moved in a slow, athletic glide. The moment they moved, I knew they were wereanimals and not vampires. Vamps move like people, just more graceful.

I called, 'Newman, watch in front. I've got the shifters behind us,' I said.

There was a *whoosh* like the world's biggest bottle rocket overhead. The heat pushed at the back of me, so that I flinched and dropped to one knee, turning as I did it to bring the MP5 up to aim at the Harlequin behind us. The explosion from in front of us made me flinch again and want to turn that way, but I had to trust Newman to handle anything in that direction. I knew there were two Harlequin behind us, and I knew I was fast enough to wound them; I didn't know the same of Newman.

But there was only one thing in the road now. It was on fire, a blazing, burning shape, so bright that it chased back the dark in fire shadows, as it crouched on the road.

I heard Newman say, 'Holy Jesus.'

It made me glance behind me to the roadblock that wasn't there anymore. The road was clear. Tilford yelled, 'Blake, get in!'

I got to my feet, the gun aimed back at the figure in the road. I realized he wasn't crouching; he was trying to shift form. I stood on the running board, one hand on the handle by the roof, the other pointing the gun at the burning mass in the road. Did he think shifting form would help him heal, or put out the fire? Or maybe it was all he could think to do. Then he started to scream. It was a low growl of a scream as if a human throat and some large growling animal were both screaming at once. It was the kind of sound that would haunt your nightmares, or cause them. I'd seen vampires burn 'alive', but never a wereanimal. Vampires burn faster and more completely than humans do, but wereanimals are just people that heal almost anything. Anything but fire.

The SUV jumped forward. I grabbed the inside edge of the roof, one foot on the running board, the other on the door edge. My free hand aimed the MP5 out at the trees as they began to rush by. The open door brushed the trees and swung in on me. I used my knee to keep it riding just out from me. Edward was still at the sunroof. I wasn't sure if Newman was in or out. Tilford was driving. I knew as much as I could. The car picked up speed. It bounced hard, and I was almost airborne. I couldn't stay like this. I slipped into the open door and closed it behind me and hit the button for the window to rise. I had a moment to see Newman securely inside the car on his side. Edward slipped out of the sunroof and hit the button to close it. Then he yelled, 'Anita!'

I was aiming at the window before I saw anything to shoot at. There was a gleam of silver, but it wasn't at my closing window, it was at Tilford's open one. I fired, and the bullet went past his head and into something dark at the end of that gleam of sword, because that was what it was, a sword, a fucking sword.

The shot was thunderous in the car, too small a space to be shooting without ear protection. I was deaf for a moment, but the figure fell and didn't come back. The sword stayed like an exclamation point in Tilford's shoulder and the seat. He was pinned.

Edward crawled over the seat and took the wheel. 'Stay on the gas, Tilford.' He took Edward at his word because the car leapt forward as if he'd buried his foot to the floorboard. Edward steered one-handed, the other keeping the gun up and ready, though he had to watch the road, which left Newman and me to watch everything else. Fuck.

There was a noise from the roof, soft. I wasn't even sure why I heard it over the engine and the ringing in my ears. It was almost as if I'd been listening for that soft slither of a sound. 'They're on the roof,' I said.

Newman didn't react, so I said, 'Newman, one of them is on the roof.'

He gave me wide, startled eyes. It was hard to tell in the dark, but he looked pale. The pulse in his throat looked like it was trying to jump out of his skin. He was scared, and I didn't blame him. If I'd had time I'd have been scared, too.

I was looking up at the sunroof when someone looked down at me. I had time to register that there was no mask. It was just dark eyes in a pale face: vampire. I was firing up into the face before I had time to really 'see' everything. The face slipped away, but I didn't think I'd hit it.

Newman fired up into the roof after I did, but he kept his finger on the trigger so that the car was an echo chamber for the bullets, and the hot casings spilled on me. Most of them hit my jacket, but one found the back of my hand and there was nothing to shoot at now.

I grabbed his hand, yelling because I was too deaf to know how loud to talk to be heard. 'Stop! You're wasting ammo!'

He looked at me, eyes wild, showing too much white, like a horse about to bolt. I aimed his gun a little down. I could feel air through the holes he'd punched in the roof. 'Ease down. Save your ammo.' I was probably still yelling, but he stared at me as if either he couldn't hear me over the ringing in his own ears, or he couldn't understand me through the fear. Sometimes when you're afraid enough, the sound of your own blood in your ears is all you can hear. I remembered those days.

I got him to nod at me, and then I turned to look at the front seat. Edward and Tilford were driving like a team. We went through the smoking remains of the roadblock so fast I had only the barest glimpse of the charred remnants.

I saw the flashing lights in the distance, down the road, before I realized I'd been hearing sirens for a while. My hearing was not happy with all the shooting in the car. I wondered if everyone else was as deafened as I was.

I probably yelled, because I had no way to gauge my own voice, 'Who called backup?'

Newman yelled back, 'I did.'

It wouldn't have occurred to Edward and me to call for help. We'd been lone wolves too damn long. For once I was very glad the rookie had done a rookie thing; he'd followed procedure and called for backup. The Harlequin were invested in remaining secret. We were safe, for now.

We began to slow down. Edward's voice echoed thin and distant in my head, as he yelled, 'Tilford, Tilford!'

Shit! I slipped my seatbelt as the car slowed to a stop and reached around the seat to Tilford's shoulder with the sword still sticking out of him. I knew better than to try to take the sword out; that was a job for a doctor, but the bleeding, I could do something about that. I took off the Windbreaker and it was only as I slipped it over my arm that I remembered I was hurt, too. The jacket scraped over the wound, and the pain let me know I was hurt. The fact that I'd started to feel the pain let me know that the adrenaline and endorphins from the emergency were beginning to fade.

Edward brought us safely to a stop. He put the SUV in park. The cars and sirens barreled down on us, the sirens still not as loud as they should have been.

I realized that my blood was all over the jacket, though. I turned to Newman and pantomimed him giving me his jacket. I looked at my hands and they had my blood on them, too. I carried lycanthropy in my blood. I didn't change shape, but that didn't mean that if my blood got in Tilford's bloodstream that he wouldn't. I couldn't risk it if there were other blood-free hands to hold the wound.

I changed places with Newman and managed to direct him how to hold his jacket and hands around the sword. He moved the blade by accident and Tilford passed out.

Newman mumbled/yelled apologies. I waved them away. The first cars were parked, and marshals, uniforms, detectives, emergency personnel of all kinds were spilling out toward us. There'd be an ambulance in there somewhere.

22

Tilford came to as the EMTs were trying to shift him from the car to the stretcher. He grabbed Edward's arm. 'Warrant, my warrant, it's yours. It's yours, Forrester.'

Edward nodded and patted his hand. 'I'll get the bastards for you, Tilford.'

'I know you will,' he said. He kept hold of Edward as they got him on the stretcher, and Edward didn't fight it, he just stayed at his side on the way to the ambulance. Newman came to join me beside the SUV as I blinked out at the swirl of lights and police. Raborn was suddenly in front of us. 'What the hell happened, Blake?'

I blinked at him. An EMT pushed between us. 'Back up, can't you see they're both hurt?' I blinked into her pale eyes. Her blond hair was pulled back in a ponytail. She started shining a light into Newman's eyes. His thin face was a mask of blood. Apparently some of the gravel had cut his forehead so the blood had just rained down from there.

Raborn pushed into my face, trying to use his height to intimidate me. He should have known better by now. 'Talk to me, Blake.'

'The serial killers that we've been chasing across the country were here and tried to ambush us. We were better armed than they planned for, so we got away.'

'Why would they ambush you?' This was Detective Lorenzo,

who was in the group of cops. I hadn't seen him in the dark with the flashing lights. It was like looking at strobes, or maybe I was shockier than I realized.

'When we catch them, we'll ask,' I said.

Another EMT reached around Raborn. 'You're bleeding.'

I looked down at the arm he was looking at, but it didn't seem very important. I knew it was my arm, and when he touched the wound it hurt. The little sharp spark of pain helped clear my head a little. That let me know that with the adrenaline leaving, the soft edge of shock and relief had set in; now that the emergency was over, my body was trying to shut down a little.

Raborn backed up enough so the medic could look at it, but he hovered over the guy's shoulder. 'Are they still out there?'

'Far as I know,' I said.

The EMT reached for my arm. I pulled out of reach. 'Let me at least look at it, that's a lot of blood.'

'I'm a carrier for lycanthropy.'

He hesitated. 'I need to double-glove then.'

'That's why I said something.'

'I'll be right back,' he said, and went at a half-run toward the ambulance.

'If they're still out there, we need to get them,' Raborn said.

I nodded. 'Yep, we do.' In my head I thought, *It's a bad idea.* Out loud, I said, 'They're faster, stronger, see better in the dark, and smell almost as well as most dogs, and they have swords at the very least.'

'Are you saying we shouldn't go after them?' Raborn asked.

'No, I just want everyone who goes into those woods to know what we're up against, that's all.'

'If that was a pep talk, you suck at it,' Lorenzo said, and he was smiling.

I didn't smile back. I don't know what my face looked like, but it wasn't a smile, and whatever he saw in my eyes made his wilt around the edges.

'Marshal Forrester and I wounded two of them. One bad

enough that he's being carried by the other. There's another one that was on fire, but I don't know if he's dead.'

'On fire, how'd he get on fire?' Raborn asked.

'Backwash,' I said.

'What?'

Newman was batting the female EMT away from his face. 'Forrester used a rocket launcher.'

'What?' Raborn asked.

'He used a LAW,' I said, 'Forrester did.'

'Is that what scorched the back of the car?' A woman's voice, and I got a vague impression of her in the back of the group, tall, dark-haired, thin-faced.

'Yeah,' I said.

The EMT with the dark hair was back now with another color of glove on top of the first one. He said, 'Excuse me, but I need to look at her wound.' He looked at Raborn until he stepped back. The EMT unfolded my arm, and only then did I realize my right hand was in a fist.

'What did this to your arm?' the EMT asked.

'Tree limb, root,' I said.

'What?' he asked.

'I slipped and cut myself on a dry tree branch,' I said.

'It must have been one hell of a tree.'

'Yeah.'

'Both of you come with us to the ambulance so we have more light to work,' the blonde said.

'I'm fine,' Newman said.

I just started letting the man lead me toward the ambulance. Raborn called, 'I heard you were tough, Blake.'

I turned, looked at him. 'The days when someone like you could make me feel like a wimp because I let the medics work on me is long past, Raborn.'

'What's that mean?'

'It means that whatever I needed to prove to myself, I did it years ago, and your opinion of me doesn't matter.'

Newman's body reacted as if someone had poked him, as if something about what I'd said mattered, or surprised him. In the swirling color of lights I watched his face debate. Should he go with me to the ambulance or stay with the guys and tough it out?

I also wanted to talk to Edward in semiprivacy away from Raborn and the rest, and he was still by the ambulances. Besides, what I'd said was absolutely true. I had nothing to prove to anyone anymore. I knew how tough, how brave, how good I was at my job. Raborn could go to hell, and I'd actually matured enough that I didn't have to tell him that last part out loud. It was plenty satisfying to simply walk away.

Raborn's voice rose as he said, 'You going to be a girl about this, Newman, or a man?'

I turned around, still walking, and yelled. 'Yeah, Newman, be a man, keep bleeding until you pass out in the middle of the woods with shapeshifters and vampires after your ass.' Then I went back to following the dark-haired EMT.

The light that spilled out from the ambulance seemed terribly bright and totally screwed my night vision, but Matt, the EMT, needed the light.

The blonde EMT came to join us, muttering under her breath. I caught, 'Stupid . . . men. Scalp wounds bleed . . .'

Matt had cleaned my arm and was squinting at it as if he either needed glasses he wasn't wearing, or would soon. 'Julie, can you look at this?'

The blonde, Julie, stopped cursing the stupidity of men under her breath and just joined him in staring at my arm. She was careful not to touch me, since she hadn't double-gloved, but she let his fingers do the walking. When he spread the edges of the wound, I protested. 'That hurts,' I said.

'Sorry,' he said, but didn't look up from the wound.

'How long ago did you say this happened?' Julie asked.

'An hour, less,' I said.

'No way,' she said.

Matt finally met my eyes. He was frowning. 'I'd say this was hours, maybe a day old, at least.'

'I told you I carry lycanthropy. It means I heal faster than human-normal.'

'It's healing so fast it's going to heal crooked. Stitches would have kept it from doing that,' Matt said.

'Crooked?' I asked.

'It's going to scar more,' Julie said, 'than if a doctor had stitched it for you.'

I looked down at my arm. It was a long, jagged cut, almost like angry lightning going from elbow to almost wrist. 'Nothing to be done about it now,' I said.

'Actually if you go to the hospital they can cut it open again, and then sew it up. We just had a seminar on preternatural patients. Lycanthropes can heal so fast that they scar more, or even get their muscles bunched up so the wound gives them pain almost like arthritis.' Matt said it staring down at my arm, as if it were a sort of show-and-tell.

'Is there a time limit for when I need to come in and get this done?'

'Sooner is better, at the rate you're healing,' he said, poking at the wound again.

'Please, stop poking it,' I said.

He looked up a little startled. 'I'm sorry; it's just the first wound like this I've seen since the seminar.'

'Matt's a big one for theory in the field,' his partner said.

I looked at her, nodding. 'I usually heal without scarring now.'

'Well, this is going to scar,' she said.

I looked at it and believed them, but wasn't sure why it was happening. I thought about it, and then realized I'd absorbed anger when I visited the red tigers, but I hadn't fed the *ardeur*. The anger had taken the edge off my hunger, but it hadn't really refueled me. I wasn't healing as well as normal, which explained why the tree limb had hurt me so badly in the first place, as well as the scarring. I could go longer between feedings. I could control it, but apparently this was the price. I healed better than a pure human, but not as well as I could heal. That wasn't good when hunting the Harlequin. Shit.

I tried to imagine what Raborn would say if I actually did take time out for a nookie break. It didn't even bear thinking about; I couldn't stop for sex, not until we finished hunting through the woods. Well, fuck, or rather no fuck. Damn it, I was tired of getting punished for not having sex. It was sort of the horror movie cliché turned on its ear; only the slutty survived, not the virginal.

I couldn't explain any of this to the EMTs, or anyone else here but Edward. Always before with the *ardeur* it had consumed me, forced me to feed, but now I had enough control that I could delay it. The angry purple and red wound on my arm showed me the price for controlling the *ardeur*. Staring down at the wound, I realized that I had started counting on healing and being harder to hurt. I tried to remember the last time I'd been hurt by accident like this, and I couldn't remember. My stomach clenched tight and it wasn't hunger – that wasn't where the *ardeur*'s hunger hit me – it was fear. If a tree limb could do this to me, then what about a sword, or a bullet? Shit.

'You okay?' EMT Julie asked.

I nodded. 'Fine.'

'You really need to go to the hospital and let a doctor open the wound and then stitch it back up,' she said.

'I know,' I said.

She frowned at me. 'But you're not going to do it, are you?' She sounded disgusted with me, I really couldn't blame her.

'I can't let them go into the woods without me.'

'You know, the marshals around here do just fine when you're not in town. They hunt vampires and beasts, and they do a good job. Let them do their jobs and let us do ours and take you to the hospital.'

Matt pulled at the edges of the wound. 'Stop that,' I said.

'Sorry, but it's almost like one of those fast-forward films of flowers, you know, where you watch them bloom. I swear I can almost see your skin knitting together. It's so cool.'

Julie hit him on the shoulder, and it must have been harder than it looked, because he said, 'Ow!'

'She's a live patient, Matt, not a cadaver in class.'

He blinked up at me, and then looked embarrassed. 'I'm sorry, I just . . .'

'It's okay. Just patch me up so I can finish this hunt.'

'You're being totally stupid,' Julie said.

'Not as stupid as Marshal Newman. He's still bleeding.'

'He's going to keep bleeding until he passes out, too,' she said, and the disgust was thick in her voice.

'Probably,' I said. 'At least I'm letting you bandage me up.'

'Your wound will be closed by the time you finish this hunt. You're not losing more blood.'

'Then just wrap it up so I don't keep hitting the wound on things.'

She frowned, but got gauze and started wrapping my arm.

'Make sure none of it gets in the wound,' I said.

She looked at me. 'I know my job.'

'I don't mean to imply otherwise, but if I'm healing as fast as you think I am, sometimes the body can heal around the cloth.'

They both looked at me. Matt said, 'You mean the body will actually knit closed with some of the bandages inside?'

'I've seen it happen,' I said.

'To you?' he asked.

'No, a friend who was a werewolf.'

Matt's face glowed with eagerness. I could almost feel the questions bubbling to the surface.

'You're wrapped up. Sign here, so we can say we tried to take you to the hospital in case something goes wrong with your arm, which it will.'

I signed, and hopped off the back of the ambulance. 'Sorry I'm being a pain in your ass.'

'When the tall guy passes out in the woods, try to keep things from eating him,' she said.

'I'll try,' I said, and I would, but with my arm beginning to ache from the rapid healing, I wouldn't try too hard. Newman had let Raborn talk him out of even a bandage. I'd been green, but never that green. Maybe it was a guy thing and I'd never understand that level of stupid, or maybe mine was a girl thing. My arm began to twitch, the muscles fighting against each other as they knit together. I hadn't had that happen since I first got lycanthropy in my bloodstream. Shit. Maybe Newman wasn't being any stupider than I was. I guess I would try to keep him from getting eaten. Damn it.

23

Newman passed out, but I made sure nothing ate him. We were deep in the trees by the time he went down. He'd done well to make it this far. I stayed by him in the wind-kissed trees with the other police working their long line of searching, but I could see the other stretch of road, and I was pretty certain that there were no monsters to find. The Harlequin had fled. Either they were still trying to stay secret enough to avoid this many cops, or they hadn't expected Edward to be packing a rocket and they'd retreated to rethink their plans. I think they'd underestimated both of us, hell, all of us. I looked down at Newman where he lay on the ground. Detective Lorenzo was holding his inner suit jacket on Newman's wound, trying to slow the blood down. He'd put his outer jacket back on so it still read *Police*, but also it was cold. My hands were numb with it. Weren't cold summer nights an oxymoron?

Lorenzo's partner, Detective Jane Stavros, was helping me guard the two men, both the unconscious one and the one who had his head down tending the wounded one.

The police Windbreaker swam on Detective Stavros's thin frame. The pantsuit that was showing was cheap, black, and too large for her. She was at least five-ten in her sensible and ugly black lace-up shoes. If she'd been dressed better I might have thought she was a professional model, but she had dieted too much for her bone structure, so she looked starved, and she'd dieted away all her curves so she was built like a man. Her straight brunette hair was back in a loose ponytail. Some women on the job try to dress like the men, to fit in, to pretend that they aren't women. I hadn't seen any woman who had been on the job long enough to get a detective's shield carry it to this extreme. Maybe she was a newly minted detective; sometimes that can throw you back to old issues. But it wasn't just the men's clothing; it was that she was sloppy, as if she'd rolled out of bed and put on someone else's clothes by mistake. Nothing fit her right, as if she were wearing someone else's skin.

But she held her gun like she knew what she was doing, and she watched the darkness and her partner's back. She hadn't done anything to make me think less of her except buy into the whole guy thing a little too much, and who was I to bitch about that? But there was almost a starved feeling to her, as if she'd never had enough. Enough food, enough love, enough anything worth having. An air of jaded tiredness and wariness hung over her like a dark cloud. It was an interesting mix of that ten-year blasé that cops get, and the nervousness that usually goes away by then, as if she'd seen it all, but instead of being bored it had spooked her.

Edward had gone ahead with the line, because we wanted one of us with the group; besides, my right arm wasn't very happy with me. My right arm, my main shooting arm, was twitching so badly from the overly rapid healing that I couldn't have used it to shoot anything. Moments like these were why I practiced everything left-handed. I wasn't as good on the left as I was on the right, but I was still better than average, and it would have to do. I'd forgotten how much it hurt to have the muscles fighting against each other, as if my arm were at war with itself. A little sex would have kept it from happening, but I'd been stubborn, and the red tiger Harlequin had interfered, but I should never have left off feeding for days. It was stupid, but until Seattle there hadn't been anyone in town for me to feed on. Okay, no one I was willing to feed on. I was paying for my rule of no strangers now. My arm was twitching so badly it could no longer help me hold the MP5 in place for shooting.

'What's wrong with your arm?' she asked.

'I'm healing faster than the muscles can keep up.'

She gave me a disbelieving glance. There was enough predawn light for me to see her expression now.

Lorenzo said, 'You're hurt more than you let on, Blake.'

I shrugged, and just concentrated on breathing through the pain of my arm being at war with itself.

It was Raborn who tramped back through the trees, 'They're not here, Blake.'

'Probably not,' I said.

He put his gun over one shoulder so the barrel was pointed up at the sky. 'That kind of twitching means you've damaged nerves. You need to go to the hospital when they take Newman.'

'You bully Newman into passing out, but me you'll send to the hospital? Why, so you can say, "See, she's just a wimpy girl"?'

I watched Raborn's expression by the cold, white light of dawn, but I couldn't decipher it. He looked down at my arm. It was shivering, a continuous dance of muscles. The pain was mind-numbing and only pride kept me from making small noises, or bigger screams.

'I didn't know you were this hurt, Blake.'

'You didn't ask,' I said.

'The EMTs are almost here; go with Newman to the hospital. No one will think less of you.'

'I told you, Raborn, I don't care what you think of me.'

Now I could read his look; it was angry. 'You just won't give an inch, will you?'

Edward came up behind Raborn and said, 'It's not her best thing.'

Raborn moved so he could see all of us. 'She might get along better if she were a little more flexible.'

Edward nodded, smiling his Ted smile, as he tipped his hat

back from his forehead, his P90 pointed one-handed at the ground. 'She might, but if she were more flexible she'd be screaming from the pain, instead of watching the woods, doing her job.'

Raborn seemed to think about that for a second, then just shook his head. 'All you old-time hunters are stubborn bastards.'

I smiled at that. Raborn had to have me by at least a couple of decades, but I was an old-time hunter. Then my muscles tried to form a fist inside my arm and tear their way out. The pain broke me out in a light, sick sweat.

'You just went pale,' Stavros said.

I nodded, not trusting what my voice would sound like.

Matt and Julie, our EMTs from earlier, were carrying a stretcher sideways through the trees. Apparently they'd had to wait for us all. I'd actually expected the shift to have changed or something.

Edward said, 'We've searched the woods. They're not here.'

'Tell your partner here to go to the hospital,' Raborn said.

He gave Ted's smile again and just shook his head. 'I'll take Anita where she lets me take her, but I doubt that will include the hospital.'

'There's stubborn and there's stupid,' Raborn said, 'but she's your partner.' He walked away from all of us, apparently too disgusted to stick around and see who went to the hospital.

Stavros looked at me, gun pointed at the pale light of the sky. 'Too-rapid healing causes pain? I thought it just healed if you had lycanthropy.'

'It can,' I said, in a voice that was thin with strain, 'but sometimes it does this.'

'Is the healing worth it?' she asked.

I nodded. 'Yeah.'

The EMTs were here. Edward and I walked Newman to the ambulance. Edward also talked to me about the arm and the muscle twitching. 'If it scarred that badly and you were human, I'd be worried you'd lose mobility.'

'That's what they said about my left arm and the scar tissue at the bend, but as long as I hit the weights regularly I'm fine.'

He stepped on top of the log, not over. When you're in the woods long enough you step on logs, not over, in case of snakes. It just becomes automatic so you can look before you step.

'The new one is a longer scar and involves more muscles and tendons.'

'What are you wanting me to do?'

'See if the doctors can do anything for it.'

'The EMTs said they'd cut it open and stitch it to keep it from scarring.'

'If you do that, then you can feed the *ardeur* and it'll be all better.'

I gave him an unfriendly look as we followed the stretcher onto the road, and the morning light was suddenly more serious without the trees blocking it.

'I don't like stitches,' I said.

He grinned at me. 'No one does.'

'If I wimp out you'll never let me live this down, will you?'

He grinned wider and shook his head. 'Not if you lose mobility in the arm, and get us killed because of it.' The grin faded, and his eyes went serious. 'I'll hold your hand.'

I glared at him. 'Oh, that'll make it all better.'

'I don't offer to hold hands with the other marshals.'

We had a moment of looking at each other, a moment of years of guarding each other's backs, of being friends. I nodded. 'Thanks.'

He smiled, but his eyes were still too serious for it. 'You're welcome, but save the thanks until after you finish cursing me.'

'Why will I curse you?'

'The rapid healing means drugs go through your body faster than normal, right?'

My arm chose that moment to spasm so hard it almost dropped me to my knees. Edward had to catch me, or I would have fallen. When I could talk, I said, 'Yeah.'

'Is this the worst injury you've had since you got lycanthropy?'

'Without preternatural healing, yeah,' I said. My voice still sounded breathy.

'So you don't know if painkillers still work for you, or if like all lycanthropes drugs run through your system too fast.'

I stared up at him. I was already sweating and pale; I couldn't pale anymore without passing out. 'Fuck,' I said.

'See, I told you you'd curse.'

Edward drove me in the SUV with its new scorch marks on the back. We followed the ambulance to the hospital, where we'd find out if painkillers still worked for me. I was betting they didn't. Fuck.

24

They gave me a local directly into my arm, and then Dr Fields cut open the scar. Apparently he'd attended the same seminar as Matt, the EMT, so it was Dr Fields's first time seeing if the theory worked in practice. He was very honest about it. 'I'm not a hundred percent certain it will leave you scar free, but it will probably make the muscle and tendon issue better.'

'So we could do all this and I could still scar and still have some mobility loss,' I said.

'Yes.'

I think I started to get off the examining table, but Edward was there, and he put his hand on my shoulder. He just shook his head. Damn it. Edward made me lie back down and held my hand like he said he would. Double damn it. An hour later, I was cut open, and the local had worked for that. It wasn't pleasant, and the shots were a bitch, and I really hated feeling my skin part under the scalpel, but it was nothing to feeling my skin being tugged into place with a needle and stitches. That was always a creepy feeling even if it didn't exactly hurt. Matt, the EMT, had forgone sleep to watch, and so had a lot of other doctors and interns. No one had seen the practical application of the theory and they wanted to, though everyone was in face shields and full gear just in case blood spread. It was technically contagious, though my variety seemed not to be up to this point. I was medical miracle enough to excite the med students all to hell.

Fields and I had already discussed that it needed to be the kind of stitches that dissolved, just in case my body tried to grow over the stitches. 'You heal that well?' he'd asked.

'I've seen other people with lycanthropy do it. I'd rather not risk your having to operate on me to remove stitches below my skin.'

He'd just agreed.

We were about halfway through the stitches when the local began to wear off. 'Painkiller is wearing off,' I said.

'We'd have to wait for the shots to take effect again, and you're healing, Ms Blake. I might have to cut more of the wound again and start over, or I can stitch ahead of the healing.'

Edward said, 'Anita, look at me.'

I turned and he was on the side opposite the doctor. He gave me calm eyes and I nodded. 'Do it,' I said.

I held on to Edward's hand, gave him some of the best eye contact I'd given anyone in a while, and Dr Fields tried to stitch me up ahead of my body's healing. Even with the *ardeur* days from being fed I was healing too fast for normal medical help. Fuck.

Edward talked low to me. He whispered about the case, tried to get me to think about work. It worked for a while, and then the painkiller was all gone and I was still being stitched up. I couldn't think about work. He talked about his family, about what Donna was doing with her metaphysical shop, about Peter in school and in martial arts. He was working on his second black belt. Becca and her musical theater, and the fact that he was still taking her to dance class twice a week, that amused me enough for me to say, 'I want to see you sitting with all the suburban moms in the waiting area.'

He'd smiled Ted's smile for me. 'Come visit us and you can help me pick Becca up from class.'

'Deal,' I said, and then I just concentrated on not screaming.

'It's okay to yell,' Dr Fields said.

I shook my head.

Edward answered for me. 'If she screams once, she'll keep screaming; best not to start.'

Fields looked at Edward for a blink or two, and then went back to racing my skin up the cut. He had to tell me that he was finished. My arm was one mass of pain. It was on fire, or . . . I had no words for it. It fucking hurt from the start of the wound to the bottom, and past to my fingertips. I was nauseated with it all. I had only two goals: not to scream, and not to throw up.

Fields gave us some pills. 'This should put her out for a little bit, let her body catch up with the damage.'

'How long?' Edward asked.

'An hour – two, if we're lucky.'

'Thanks, doc,' he said. He took the pills, but I didn't see what he did with them. The world had narrowed down to the piece of floor I was staring at. I was concentrating on my breathing, on just being and trying to ride the pain, or at least endure it.

'We'll get a chair to take her to the door,' someone said.

I didn't say I didn't need one; I was afraid if I opened my mouth I'd lose the food I hadn't eaten today. When I didn't argue, neither did Edward. So I left the hospital in a wheelchair, pushed by one of the many medical personnel who had watched my treatment. It turned out to be a male nurse who tried to be chatty, and turned out to have all sorts of questions about lycanthropy. I didn't have any answers, not right then.

Edward made me take one of the pills before he put me in the SUV. I didn't argue. I couldn't remember what Dr Fields had said the pills were, but whatever they were they were strong, because the last thing I heard before I fell asleep, or passed out, was the purr of the engine, and Edward at the wheel.

When I woke I was in a bed, in another generic hotel room with Edward handing me another pill and water. I started to protest, and he said, 'Take it,' in that tone of voice that said I could take it voluntarily or he could make me take it. Of all the people I knew, I knew Edward would do exactly what he threatened, which would be undignified if I couldn't stop him from force-feeding me a pill, so I took it without an argument and sleep rolled over me before I could really feel how much my arm hurt, which was probably a good thing.

I didn't so much wake as become aware that there was a man wrapped around me. For a moment, I cuddled his arm closer around my waist, wrapping him around me like a favorite coat, and then the extra closeness let me know he was nude, and since the only man I knew in the room when I went to sleep was Edward, that was a problem. My eyes were suddenly wide open, and my whole body tensed.

The sleepy voice behind me mumbled, 'You smell good.'

I didn't recognize the voice. Good news, bad news; good news, Edward wasn't naked in bed with me, so that awkward moment had passed, but bad news, I had a naked stranger in bed with me. What the hell?

I tried to scoot away, but the arm tightened, and he drew me into the bow of his body, his head bending over and nuzzling the top of my head. I propped myself up on my elbow, turning so I could see who was cuddling me. White-blond hair with a streak of deep, dark red, and then soft, gray eyes blinked up at me. As Ethan raised his face up, I could see more of the gray highlights in all that pale hair, and all of it was a mass of little curls in a sleepy disarray.

He kept his eyes rolled upward so he could watch my face as he kissed my back. It reminded me of the way you never let your gaze leave your opponent in the fight ring, because they'll beat your ass if you do. He laid that well-shaped mouth, with its deep dimples above and below his lips, against my skin, and watched my face. It was as if he expected me to be angry at him.

I frowned. 'Where's Edward?'

'He's off with the police.'

I tensed, and again his arm tightened around me. 'Was there another killing?'

'He doesn't discuss ongoing police investigations with civilians.'

'You're quoting him,' I said.

He nodded, and again he laid a soft kiss on my bare back. He kept his eyes upward, as if he really were afraid I'd hurt him. 'What did you do that you feel guilty about?' I asked.

He blinked at me, and moved his mouth far enough back so he could speak. 'I don't feel guilty.'

'You look it.'

'You look and feel angry; I'm trying not to piss you off more. Tell me what expression you want on my face and I'll try to give it to you.'

I smiled, a little, and sighed.

'Well, at least you're not angry,' he said.

I realized I was propped up on my wounded arm. I looked down at it. The wound was a yellow and pink line of scabs. It looked days old. 'How long have I slept?'

'Not that long,' he said.

I sat up, and he just let me go so I could do it. I kept one hand on the sheet, so I covered my breasts at least a little bit. From the way the wound looked, I knew we'd been sleeping naked for days, but I hadn't known we were naked and I hadn't been asked about it, so I preferred to be covered. It was just one of my little peculiarities, and I'd stopped fighting it.

I held my arm out to him as he lay back against the bed. 'This is really close to healed and I wasn't healing like normal. This is days of healing.'

One of his arms was spread out behind me, so if I lay back I'd be able to cuddle in against him. I wasn't sure I was going to be cuddling anybody. I wanted answers. 'It's been a day, just a day. Alex and I have been taking turns sleeping with you so that our energy helped you heal.'

'If a wereanimal of the same flavor sleeps with any of us, we heal faster, yeah.' I frowned. 'Wait, with a whole clan of weretigers, why is it just one of you at a time? I'd heal faster if I had two of you sharing your energy.'

'The Red Queen will not risk more of her males with you.

You've had only two of us near you and we're both smitten.'

'Smitten?' I said.

He smiled, and nodded. 'Yes, smitten.' He rubbed the back of his head against the pillow, and the movement went down his spine, so that he writhed in pieces, as if someone were petting his back, until the writhing vanished under the sheet that was still pooled at his hips.

I seemed strangely fascinated with the way the covers were angled across his hips. His legs trembled under the sheet as the writhing spilled out the last of his body. The movement pulled the sheet a little lower over his hips, so that one side of the covers showed almost all of his hip, but only on the one side. The covers were pinned under his other hip, so they were held in place.

He gave a small deep chuckle. It made me look at his face and ask, 'What?'

'I love the way you look at me.'

I frowned at him.

'What did I say that was wrong?'

I frowned a little harder, and then just shook my head. I made myself look away from him, pulling my knees to my chest, so the front of me was covered, though it left the back of my body completely bare, but nothing was perfect.

'May I touch your back?'

I almost said no automatically, and then made myself be reasonable. I was going to have to feed the *ardeur*. I couldn't afford to be this hurt again. The Harlequin were in town. I needed all the metaphysical help I could get. If Alex wasn't here, then Ethan was going to have to be food. But I so didn't want to add a new person to my life. Yes, hopefully he wouldn't be coming home with me, but still . . .

'Oh,' he said, 'your friend left this for you.' He stretched out one arm, and the nightstand between the two beds in yet another generic hotel room was so close he didn't have to move his body at all, just his arm. He handed me a folded piece of white paper.

I unfolded the paper and recognized Edward's precise printing.

He almost always printed. The message was short and direct. 'No more fast food. Eat a good meal. I need you at my back, Ted.' The 'Ted' was an actual signature, small and strangely sloppy. When he signed 'Edward' it was neater; his two personas had different signatures as if they were each real people.

I reread the note. Edward acted like I just needed a good steak dinner as opposed to fast-food burgers. It wasn't like that; it wasn't like that at all. But Edward was out there without me. He was out there hunting the Harlequin without me at his back. What would I say to Donna and the kids if he died because I wasn't there? What would I say to myself? Fuck.

'Was it bad news?' Ethan asked.

I glanced at him. 'You didn't peek at the note?'

'It's not my note,' he said.

'It wasn't sealed, just folded over, and you didn't peek?'

He frowned and said, 'No, it's not my note.'

I looked at him. I'd been attracted to him from the moment I met him, or my tigers had, or hell, I didn't know anymore, maybe it was all me. Maybe the beasts just opened up things that were already there? Who the hell knew? Sex with this man wasn't a fate worse than death. Was it sex with a stranger that bothered me, or just sex in general, or both? I was betting both. I looked away from Ethan, stared at the pale wall with its copy-of-a-copy painting beside the dresser and its TV. I'd try it, and if it felt too weird, I'd say stop, and wait for Alex; at least I'd already slept with him.

'Yes, you can touch my back,' I said, but couldn't make my voice sound completely happy about it.

But Ethan took me at my word, not my tone. His fingers trailed down my back and kept going until he was tracing the edge of my butt.

'That is not my back,' I said.

He drew his hand away from me. 'I'm sorry,' he said, softly.

'No, it's not you, it's me. I always have a problem with having to have sex.'

He sat up, drawing the covers over his lap so he stayed covered.

It meant I had to hold on to the covers to stay as covered as I was, but I appreciated the attempt at modesty on his part. 'I can call Alex. He's working, but you can ask him how soon he could be here.'

I looked at his face, so careful, so . . . hurt. I remembered then, a little late, that he'd spent his life not being wanted by the women of his clan. Shit. I sighed, and said, 'I can't explain all my issues right now, but just give me a minute. I do want you. I am attracted to you. I just didn't expect to wake up beside you before we'd even had sex. I didn't expect to miss out on the crime fighting while I had to heal.'

I hugged my knees to my chest. 'I'd gotten used to the extra healing that I get with the metaphysics. I thought the super healing was because of the lycanthropy and the vampire marks; I didn't realize it was tied this much to the *ardeur*.'

'And that bothers you?' he said.

I nodded. 'Yeah.'

'Why?' he asked.

'I can go days without feeding the *ardeur* now. I was so happy and it was going to make being a US Marshal so much easier, but now I know the price of not feeding. When I'm hunting bad guys I need the extra healing, so that means I still have to feed regularly. Do you know how hard that is on an active warrant of execution out of state?'

'No, but I can imagine.' I could feel some tension go out of him, so that he was just sitting on the bed, not waiting to get up and call Alex.

'May I touch the back of your body?' he asked, 'and did you hear the difference in what I asked?'

I thought about it for a second, trying to work out why I was getting in my way so badly. Finally, I said, 'Yes, and yes.'

He touched my back again, but this time I tensed. 'It really bothers you that you have to feed so often.'

'Yes,' I said, and hugged my knees a little tighter. 'It's almost impossible to do the out-of-state warrants.'

He laid his hand on my shoulder, not petting, more comforting. 'But you can go days without feeding if you have to, and from what you're saying, that wasn't true before.'

I thought about it. 'No, I mean, you're right.'

He scooted on the bed so he was sitting behind me. I fought the tension in my shoulders, not liking his being where I couldn't see him. I'd slept nude in a bed with him for hours. He'd already proven he was willing to risk his life to keep me safe. He'd trusted my ability with a gun enough to take a knife wound and throw himself on the mercy of a Harlequin. What more did I want from him?

He put his hands on my shoulders. 'You're still tense. What can I do to help?'

'Help me do years of therapy in the next five minutes,' I said.

'I don't understand,' he said, and I didn't have to see his face; I could hear the puzzlement in his voice.

I shook my head and hugged my knees harder. 'Ignore me.'

'I don't want to ignore you,' he said, and his voice was moving closer. He moved my hair to one side, and I felt the heat of his body hesitate before he laid his lips against my back. When I didn't protest, he kissed me, and when I didn't complain about that he kissed me again, a little lower on my back. The bed moved as he kissed his way, ever so gently, down my back. I began to relax a little more with each kiss, my arms unclenching, letting my spine straighten so that I was sitting up straight by the time he reached the end of my spine.

He rolled his tongue in small circles at the base of my spine until I shivered for him, and then he plunged his tongue downward, tracing between my cheeks. It brought a surprised sound from me. He bit me, gently, on one cheek.

I whispered, 'God.'

'I take it you liked that,' he said, voice already growing deeper.

What was I supposed to do, lie? 'Yes,' I said my voice a little shaky.

He bit me again, a little harder, but still not hard. I half-rolled, half-fell onto my side. He bit farther down my cheek, harder yet. It made me shiver again, my breath catching in my throat. He touched my thigh, lifted, and I opened my legs for him. He set his teeth in the last bit of cheek, before he got to other things. He bit me this time, hard enough that it made me gasp and try to sit up, but his hands were on my thighs, and ass, and sitting up wasn't happening. I was suddenly staring down my body to find his face between my thighs, looking up at me.

'Too hard?' he asked. The side of his face rested on my thigh, his other hand wrapped around my other thigh, holding my leg wide and up.

'A little,' I said, and my voice was breathy.

'Do you like teeth everywhere?' He was strangely serious with his face on my thigh. But considering what his face was so close to, it was a serious question.

'No, not everywhere.'

He smiled, a quick flex of his mouth, making the dimples even deeper. 'Then no more teeth.'

Honestly, a little biting along the inner thighs was nice, and if it was done right a little teeth in more intimate places could work for me, but I didn't know Ethan that well. Erring on the side of caution seemed like a good idea for the first time.

'No more teeth down there,' I said.

'Anything else you don't want me to do?'

I thought about it. He stretched my leg out and let part of it rest lower down on his side, while he used my other thigh as a pillow. It was all strangely casual.

'Let's try not to mark me where I'll have to explain it to the other cops.'

'But I can mark you where they can't see?'

'Depends on the mark, but if I'm in the right head space I like to come away with marks.'

'What can I do to get you in the right head space?'

'You like to leave marks?' I asked.

'Only if you enjoy it.'

'What do you enjoy?' I asked. The mood of sex and seduction was easing into something more normal.

He smiled and it was almost shy. That seemed the wrong word when a man had his head resting on my thigh and was looking at the most intimate parts of my body, but it was still the truth.

'Tell me,' I said.

He frowned up at me, and said, 'You really want to know.'

'Of course I do.'

He rubbed his hand over the outside of my thigh, more petting it than anything. 'Why "of course"?'

'I want you to enjoy yourself, too.'

He grinned, wide and sudden, his gray eyes filling with something close to laughter. 'Oh, I'll enjoy myself. I want to make sure you enjoy yourself.'

'Why?' I said.

'If you enjoy yourself, then there's a better chance you'll want to be with me again.'

It was perfect boy logic. 'But I still want to know what you enjoy, Ethan.'

He looked perplexed. 'I like sex with girls.'

That made me smile. 'I think we have that covered.'

He grinned again, and then again that shy look came over his face. 'I want to touch as much of you as you'll let me. I want as much of you on as much of me as I can get. I want to do as much as you'll let me do.' The shy look gave way to something much sadder.

'Once I feed the *ardeur* we'll lose a lot of control.'

'I don't want to lose control too soon,' he said. 'I want it to last.'

I nodded. 'I do need to feed and get back to crime solving, but . . . How long has it been for you?'

He shook his head, rubbing his cheek against my thigh. 'I don't want to say, it makes me sound like mercy sex.'

I rubbed my foot along his hip, and let him see in my face how amazing he looked cuddled down there. I still hadn't seen all of him bare of the covers, but if everything else was half as nice as what I had seen, it would be worth seeing. I let him see that I saw him. I saw him as beautiful. I saw him as desirable, and I realized that the *ardeur* wasn't just about sex anymore. It was more and more about giving people their heart's desire. Ethan wanted what a lot of people wanted: to be wanted. We all want to be desired. I did my best to let him see that I did.

His face showed a soft wonder, as if no one had looked at him like that in a very long time. I held my hand out to him.

'I thought I was doing this first,' he said.

'Trust me, I want you to go down on me, but first I want to kiss and cuddle. Once you do me orally I'm just going to want you to fuck me.'

His eyes went wide, and he shivered.

'What?' I asked.

'The way you talk.'

'Something wrong with the way I talk?'

'No,' he said, 'it's great. It's just . . . perfect.' He went up on all fours to crawl up toward my head, and I was able to see him completely nude for the very first time. All the talk had made him soft again, so that that flat, ridged stomach was edged by the soft, dangling bits of him. It made me, as it usually did, want to go down on him while he was still soft and I could fit all of him in my mouth without working at it.

His face was over mine when he said, 'You watch my bits the way some men watch breasts.'

I blushed, I couldn't help it. I glared up at him with his knees between my spread thighs, a hand on either side of my shoulders, both of us buck naked. I tried for dignity and promptly failed. He was smiling that big dimpled smile of his that I already knew was his really pleased smile.

'I didn't expect you to blush.'

I kept glaring at him while the blush faded. I tried to fold my arms across my chest but with bare breasts my cup size, it just didn't work.

He lay down beside me, propped on his side, and watched my face. 'I expected a lot of things from you, Anita, but not this.'

'What? That I'd blush?'

'That, and you're so . . .' He touched my hair where it lay on the bed, gently, as if he weren't sure I'd let him do it. When I didn't protest he touched my cheek. 'Sweet,' he said.

'I am not sweet,' I said.

He smiled. 'Endearing?'

I frowned at him.

He laughed.

'You haven't known me long enough to be that amused.' But I was smiling slightly as I said it.

'You're just not what I expected.'

'What did you expect?'

'Someone harder, harsher.' He looked down my body. 'You are beautiful.'

I shrugged.

'You are,' he said.

'Thanks, you're not so bad yourself.'

He grinned. 'You are not your reputation.'

'What does that mean?'

'It means that rumors say you're this great seductress. That you eat little weretigers for breakfast and possess their bodies first and then their hearts.'

'I told you that feeding the *ardeur* could make me own you lock, stock, and heart.'

'You did.'

'I wasn't lying, Ethan,' I said, and I searched his face, tried to see if he really understood what could happen to him. He was so lonely. He so wanted to be wanted and to belong to someone. The *ardeur* would give him what he wanted, but the price of belonging to someone was that you belonged to them.

'I have almost a dozen lovers at home, Ethan. If the *ardeur* binds you to me then you get in line, and Jean-Claude, Nathaniel, Micah, some of the others are always at the head of the line.'

'How often do you make love to the men who aren't at the top of the list?'

I touched his chest, running my hand over the muscled swell of his pectoral. He was so lean that all the muscles showed. He was almost too lean, but not quite; it just looked like his body type.

He pressed his hand over mine, holding it still against his chest. 'How often?'

'I don't keep count.'

'Average?'

'Three days a week, I guess.'

He laughed a surprised sound. It made me look at his face. 'That's a lot better than I'm getting now.'

'That's if you're okay with being in the bed with other men and me. Since there's so many we do a lot of group scenes. It helps everyone get more turns.'

'And you're the only girl for all of them?'

I thought about that. 'No, a couple of them have other lovers.'

'And you're all right with that?'

It was my turn to look surprised at him. 'Are you kidding? There's only so much time in the day, so a helping hand is great, especially for the men that I'm not in love with.'

He nodded. 'So, I could have a girlfriend if I found someone who would have me?'

'I'd encourage it.'

'Because you wouldn't be in love with me.'

'But you might be in love with me, do you understand that?'

His face was solemn again. 'I do.'

'And you still want to feed me?'

He raised my hand up and laid a gentle kiss on my palm. 'You've already given me more physical contact than I've had from a woman in two years.'

I couldn't keep the surprise and the near horror off my face. 'Dear God, Ethan, not even sleeping in big naked kitty piles?'

'I am an outcast, Anita, barely tolerated. I will be their muscle until the day something faster and stronger than I am kills me. It is my only use to the red clan. You don't cuddle at night with someone you're sure is basically a meat shield.'

'That's harsh,' I said.

'It's my life.'

In my head I thought, *It's not much of a life.* 'If you come to St Louis there will be plenty of people to cuddle with, as long as you don't insist on it all being weretigers.'

He entwined his fingers with mine. 'You have such small hands.'

'They match the rest of me,' I said.

He smiled. 'Not all of you is small. Your breasts are amazing.'

'Yeah, yeah, my chest is all breasts.'

'No, breasts, and muscle. You're in amazing shape. You hit the gym like a guard.'

'I work out with our guards as often as I can.'

He gave me wide eyes. 'I've never heard of a royal that works out with the guards.'

'I'm not big on the whole royalty thing,' I said.

'Our queen thinks you show a lack of respect.'

'She's right,' I said.

'It's been wonderful sleeping next to a woman again. I hadn't realized how much I missed just holding someone in my arms.'

I realized that Ethan wasn't dominant enough to push the sex forward. I was going to have to be bolder, or we'd be talking for another hour. Talking was good, I liked that I could talk to him, but I needed to feed the *ardeur* and find Edward. He needed me at his back.

'Kiss me,' I said.

'What?' he asked.

'Kiss me.'

He looked uncertain then, nervous.

'Has it been two years since you kissed a girl?'

He nodded, and he wouldn't meet my eyes.

I reached up with the hand he wasn't holding and touched his face, made him look at me. 'Has it been two years since you've done anything with a girl?'

'Yes.' He whispered it.

I smiled at him, trying to make it gentle. 'You're going to be good at it.'

'How can you tell?'

'You're a wereanimal, so that makes you a sensualist, and I've seen you fight. You know how to use your body; that translates to the bedroom.'

'I've known fighters who weren't good in the bedroom.'

'They had issues,' I said.

'How do you know that I don't have issues?'

'Everyone has issues,' I said, 'but if the issues are too much I'll let the *ardeur* free and it takes away all the doubts.'

'I didn't think I'd be this nervous,' he said, and he let go of my hand and just looked at me.

'It's okay to be nervous,' I said.

'Are you nervous?' he asked.

I smiled at him. 'I was, but I'm not now.'

'Why not?' he asked.

'Because you're more nervous than I am.'

'That doesn't make any sense. Why shouldn't that make you more nervous? Why don't you think I'm a pussy for being nervous?'

'You called me sweet earlier; I'll return the compliment.'

'Sweet isn't what a woman wants from a man.'

'Oh, I think you'll find that a lot of women rate sweetness in a man pretty damn high.'

'Do you?'

I smiled up at him. 'Kiss me, Ethan, just kiss me, and we'll go from there.'

'Why not feed the *ardeur* and take all the doubts?'

'Because I'd like some of what we do to just be us, and not the metaphysics.'

'Why?' he asked.

'Because I'd rather ease you into your first sex in two years than pounce on you like a starving wolf.'

'Pounce on me?' He gave me a look as if he didn't think I could pounce on him.

'Oh, yeah,' I said, 'I could totally pounce on you.'

He smiled, flashing those dimples. 'Bet you couldn't.'

'If you mean arm-wrestle you and win, you're right. I'd lose, but pouncing isn't about strength.'

'What is it about?' he asked.

'Sex,' I said.

He frowned at me. 'I do not think pouncing means the same thing to you that it means to me, then.'

I grinned at him. 'Probably not, but you want me to have sex with you, right?'

'Very much.'

'Then I'll win, because you want to me to pounce on you.'

He flashed those dimples again. 'You're saying that I'll let you win.'

I reached up, sliding my hands over his shoulders, drawing him down toward me. 'I'm saying that it's a win–win.' My hands slid down his back as he came closer.

His face was so close I couldn't focus on it, as he said, 'I like to win.'

'So do I,' I said. I whispered it against his lips.

Then he kissed me, tentative at first, as if he weren't quite sure what to do, and then a sound escaped his throat. A sound full of longing, eagerness, and he remembered how to kiss. He remembered how to kiss, and how to have eager hands run down my body while he did it. We kissed until we had to break just to catch our breath, and broke apart laughing.

We laughed until he moved his hips just a little and I could feel that he was hard and eager now. It made me look down at him and there was nothing soft now. He was very hard, long and smooth, and wide. 'You're beautiful,' I said.

'I've never had a woman say that to my penis before.'

I looked at his face. 'Then they were fools, and I like men. I like everything about them.'

'Most women seem a little afraid of us.'

I shook my head. 'I'm not afraid.'

'No,' he said, and his voice was growing deeper, 'you're not.' He drew out of my arms and slid lower on my body. 'I want to taste you. I want to look up your body and watch your eyes roll back into your head, and then I want inside you.'

Just staring down at him, watching that eager darkness fill his eyes, tightened things low in my body. I tried to get in my way; tried to keep myself from enjoying the moment, but the *ardeur* was just there behind my eyes, inside my head, my heart, my gut, and it wanted him. The beasts inside me seemed strangely sluggish. The weretigers in all their colors that had been so eager for him earlier flicked a tail tip at me, opened lazy eyes the color of fire, and three different shades of blue: pale sky blue, the gray-blue of a cloudy day, and blue with that golden edge of dawn to it. All three of the tigresses concerned with the man who was kissing his way down my hip seemed almost sleepy, content, as if they'd already fed, or just woken from a nap. Apparently, the drugs they'd given me for pain really had worked. I'd remember to get the name of the drug so I could share it with the other wereanimals. Any painkiller that actually worked for lycanthropes would be a real godsend.

The tigers were content to let the *ardeur* feed, while they watched like some huge version of sleepy housecats. Or maybe it had just been so long since I'd fed the *ardeur* that even the beasts inside me knew it had to come first. Maybe they hadn't liked the physical cage of my body being so badly injured either. How do you know what a tiger thinks?

Ethan snuggled down between my legs, kissing slowly on the very inner edge of my thigh, each kiss getting him closer and closer to things that were so intimate. Again, I tried to get in my own way; what was I doing letting a stranger go down on me? But his mouth moved from my thigh to other things, and that one caress of lips and tongue bowed my spine, threw my head back against the pillow, made my hands grab onto the sheets.

His mouth was so warm, his tongue licking around and over me, tracing the edges of every fold, exploring every part of me, so that it wasn't just about hunting for that magic button and the orgasm, but truly about exploring and tasting me. He'd told me exactly what he wanted, and now he was doing it. It wasn't just that it felt amazing, but the sheer joy he took in it. Some men, like some women, do oral sex like a duty, but some truly enjoy it. Take pleasure in every part of the act, enjoying, relishing every lick, every suck, every bit of writhing they can get from their partner. Ethan was one of those lovers. But then he'd had years to fantasize, and now that the fantasy was true, he was going to suck every bit of enjoyment out of it he could.

He sucked on that one sweet spot, and drew me over the edge, spilling that heavy, delicious, weight between my legs up and over me. It bowed my spine so that my upper body half rose from the bed like someone was pulling me upward on a string like a puppet lost to pleasure. My body fell back against the bed, writhing and jerking like the strings had been cut and I could only dance brokenly, joyously on the bed. I was boneless, helpless with pleasure, eyes fluttered closed so that I was blind.

The bed moved around me and I knew, vaguely, that he was crawling upward across my body, but it wasn't until I felt him long and hard, brushing against the delicate bits that he'd just finished sucking that I cried out again, my body writhing, eyes opening wide, staring up at him. He brushed the tip of him across that spot again; it made me writhe again and stare down between our bodies to find his hand around himself, using his own body as a toy to brush against me, and begin to roll the tip of him over and over on that spot.

There were already little jerks of preorgasm coming as he rubbed himself against me. The question was, would I go before he did? I wanted him inside me before that happened. I wanted to feel him put what was brushing against the smallest bit of me deep inside me.

I tried to find words to say that, to be able to articulate around the growing weight and warmth that was already building again between my legs.

His voice came breathy with strain, 'I can't hold out. I'm too close.'

I managed to gasp, 'Inside, inside me.'

He looked at me, gray eyes a little too wide, and just nodded. He used his hand to guide himself lower, and I felt him begin to push inside me. 'Gods, so tight, so wet, so warm.' I wanted to say that sometimes after oral sex I seemed to tighten, but I had no words outside my head as he pushed the head of himself inside me. It felt too good for words. It felt too good for thinking.

I cried out for him, 'God!'

'I'm not in yet,' he said, 'try not to move that much, please.' The *please* was strangled, his voice deeper, eager, as if more of his body wanted inside than just the part that was sliding inside me.

I tried to do what he asked. I tried not to move, but parts of me were moving that were even more involuntary than the rest of me. 'Gods, you're spasming around me.'

'Inside, just shove inside me,' I managed to say.

'I don't want to hurt you.'

'You won't, I promise.'

He shook his head and tried to stay with his careful push, but I'd had enough, or the *ardeur* had, or both. I unleashed that passion, that tidal wave of want and need. One moment he was being careful, the next his eyes went so wide I could see the whites of his eyes, and then he shoved himself inside me in one long push of his hips. It made me scream his name to the ceiling, and when he started to thrust in and out of me, finding a nearly desperate rhythm as he fought his body, my body, and the *ardeur* so that it would last, my body writhed.

'Ethan!' My nails dug into the bed, because I needed something to anchor me, to anchor us, as he rode above me, and I felt him fill up every inch of me.

'Gods!' He yelled it, in a voice gone low and growling.

I looked up at him and watched his gray eyes shift above me. They'd been tiger eyes, but now they were tiger eyes the color of amber and morning sky. I knew that color.

His hips thrust one more time so deep that it did dance that line between overwhelming pleasure and almost pain, but it brought me, too, so that we rode the orgasm together, and I fed. I fed on his body between my legs; I fed on him spilling himself inside me; I fed on my nails raking down his arms, as he stayed propped above me, and then his body convulsed again, thrusting deep, tearing screams from both our throats, and with the second release his body gave. The human body above me spilled outward in a rain of thick, hot liquid, and the body between my legs was golden furred with stripes of dark amber framing that face with its hazel-blue eyes.

He growled my name. 'Anita, what have you done to me?'

I ran my hands down the light, dry fur of his arms; it was unbelievably soft. 'Brought you home,' I said.

He collapsed on top of me, and I had to push at the last minute so this larger, heavier upper body didn't press me into the bed. He was still deep inside me, bigger there in this form, too. It made me turn my body, so that we were on our sides, one of my legs over his thigh. I couldn't move well enough to wrap myself around his hips yet.

I think he tried to pull out of me, but he wasn't used to the new size, and he'd just had sex, and just done a violent shapeshift that had left him exhausted. He blinked at me. 'This isn't me.'

'I smelled gold on you the first time we met,' I said, and my voice was hoarse.

'Impossible.' He managed to put one furred hand on my side so he could see the golden fur against my skin. He was growing softer with the wonder of it all, or the exhaustion, or the shock, and was able to spill out of me. The movement made us both writhe. When we could talk again, he said, 'No one has four forms.'

'You do,' I said, and laid my hand against the swell of his pectorals. They'd been nice in human form, but everything got bigger in the beast-man form. He looked like a bodybuilder in this body. It made me wonder what some of the other wereanimals at home who were serious bodybuilders must look like in beast-man form. It was unusual to have sex in half-form, so I didn't usually get this close.

'What are you thinking?' he asked.

I moved my gaze from his chest to his face, that strangely attractive mix of human and cat. I said the only thing that I could say in that moment. 'That you are beautiful.'

It made him do that cat grin, drawing back to flash teeth that could have torn me to bits. He drew me into his arms, his fur the driest thing in the bed. I'd never understood why the liquid from the shapeshift gets everything else wet and leaves the fur dry. 'I'll get you all messy,' I said.

'It's my mess,' he whispered, and he drew me into the warm, dry, circle of his body, while I was still covered in the thick, cooling liquid. He hugged me to him, and I had to snuggle down to find that point where I could rest under his arm, against his chest, against his stomach, and vaguely against the rest of him, but it wasn't about sex now, it was about comfort. He held me to him, held me close, and began to shake. It took me a moment to realize Ethan was crying.

I petted the fur and muscle of him, so tall now, so strong, able to tear me limb from limb without a thought, but all that big body clung to me. He clung to me and cried and I held him, my hands petting him, soothing him. I didn't ask why he was crying; it didn't matter what sorrow he was weeping out against my body, against the damp sheets, it only mattered that I held him and told him that it would be all right.

25

Before I could go off crime solving I had to shower. I was covered nearly head to foot in thick, clear goop. I'd learned from past experience that it dried fast and became very tacky, very quickly. I didn't even want to put clean clothes over the mess of it, let alone explain to the other cops what it was, and why I was covered in it, which was why I was in the shower when Ethan knocked on the door of the bathroom.

'Anita,' he called; his deeper voice must have been lost in the rush of water the first time, because he said my name again, and knocked louder. 'Anita!'

I turned off the water, grabbed a towel to wipe my face, and got my Smith & Wesson from the little shelf in the back of the shower. That shelf's supposed to keep soap from getting wet while you shower, but my soap could take its chances; some of the smaller handguns actually fit just fine there.

'What's wrong?' I asked, towel in one hand, gun in the other. Depending on his answer I'd know if I had time to wrap my hair up.

'There's a marshal at the door. I can't answer the door like this.'

He was still in half-man form, and he was absolutely right. Wereanimals were legal citizens with a health issue, but to police they were a walking, talking public safety hazard. Some cops would shoot first and let God and the paperwork sort it all out later.

I called, 'I'm coming.' I put the gun back on the shelf so I could wrap my hair up in the towel. Then I got the second towel and wrapped it around my body. I didn't take time to dry much either. I did not want some overzealous fellow marshal to get a glimpse of a weretiger through a drape edge and think he had to save me. Having someone shoot Ethan, or my having to shoot another cop to save him, would have all kinds of suck on it.

With the towel secured, and my left hand on top of it just in case, I was as decent as I was going to get without taking time to throw on clothes. My modesty wasn't worth Ethan getting shot.

I was toweled and gunned as I came out of the bathroom. 'Get in the bathroom,' I said.

He blinked those blue and gold eyes at me. 'Am I hiding?'

'No, just out of sight until I explain that you're a good guy to the other marshal.'

Ethan did that cat smile again, a drawing back from the teeth. 'Am I a good guy?'

I took the time to smile at him, as someone knocked very solidly on the door. 'Of course you are.' I used the gun to motion him toward the bathroom. He did what I wanted, bending down to get under the doorway. As the door closed behind him, I went to the door. I called out, 'Who is it?'

'Anita, it's Bernardo Spotted-Horse.'

That stopped me for a second. The last time I'd seen Bernardo had been in Las Vegas when he, Edward, and another marshal were after a preternatural serial killer. He was using his real and only name as a marshal, but before he got a badge he'd worked with Edward as a mercenary, bounty hunter, and assassin.

I unlocked the door, gun at my side, and opened the door. The towel chose that moment to begin to slip off me, so I was grabbing for it as the door swung inward.

'Now this is the way for a woman to open the door,' Bernardo said.

I glared up at him. I had the towel hugged to my breasts, and no nipple was showing, but way more flesh than I'd planned was on display.

He grinned down at me. With the wraparound sunglasses still on he looked model perfect, if you were into tall, dark, and handsome. I'd once thought he was American Indian *GQ* gorgeous, but the attitude was way more *Playgirl*. His nearly waist-length hair spilled around his shoulders, a black so dark that it had blue highlights in the sunshine that slanted across the cement upper story. His wide-shouldered upper body was encased in a black leather jacket that fit like a second skin and emphasized the black jeans that damn near outlined his lower body and ended in midcalf boots.

'I was in the shower,' I said.

'I can see that.' The grin was not his usual come-hither smile, it was just pure delight.

'Oh, stop it,' I said, 'and give me a second to refasten the towel.'

'Tease,' he said.

I frowned at him and ducked behind the partially open door to secure the towel again. When it was as secure as I could make it, I opened the door and ushered him inside. 'You were wearing nothing but a sheet the first time I saw you,' I said.

He entered the room close to the wall, eyes searching the room as he took his sunglasses off. His eyes were as pure a brown as my own. He nodded. 'I'd have come across the moment I met you, so it wasn't false advertising on my part. But unless you've changed a great deal you aren't going to offer me that much hospitality.' His eyes were searching the room, taking in the details. Ethan had stripped the far bed down to its mattress. He must have done it while I was in the bathroom, but he'd been right to do it, unless we wanted to owe the motel a new mattress.

I knew that Bernardo had taken in the stripped bed, the pile of bedding. Hell, sometimes you can smell sex in a room if it's recent enough. He looked at me, face softening to something more serious. 'I saw a shadow a lot taller than you through the drapes. Why are you hiding him?'

'I thought it was one of the local marshals,' I said.

'You're a big girl, why hide?' he asked. He gave me a very direct look. When we'd first met years ago he'd played the handsome flirt and hidden that there was a good mind to go with the great body. Smart is way more dangerous than cute when you're hiding things.

I called out, 'Ethan, it's all right, you can come out.' I made sure to watch Bernardo's face. His eyes widened, just a bit. He made one of those, well, faces, as in, *Well, I didn't expect that.* He tried to cover that I had shocked him, or at least surprised him, by sliding the earpiece of his sunglasses into a pocket on his chest. He busied himself unzipping his jacket.

I glanced behind me to find that Ethan had stopped about halfway across the small room. The sunlight streaming through the big window was barely filtered by the thin curtains; no wonder Bernardo had seen a shadow from outside. But now Ethan was half revealed in that bright filtered light, and half in the room's dimness, as if he stood in the midst of trees and sunlight streaming through leaves. It was almost as if even standing in the bland motel room, an echo of jungle and wildness touched that shining yellow and gold fur. He was also at least six-six, maybe six-eight in this form. Bernardo was six-one and used to being tall. He had his left hand sort of half behind the swell of his ass, and I knew that the short, stylish jacket was short for a reason. He was carrying his main gun at the small of his back. In a short jacket he could be warm and still do a quick draw. Winter concealed carry was always a fight between staying warm and not getting yourself killed because you couldn't get to your weapons in time.

'Ease down, Bernardo, he's okay.' I held my hand out to Ethan.

He shook his head. 'He's armed, and he's scared of me. I'll stay farther away.'

I glared at Bernardo. 'Stand down, Bernardo. He's my' – what word should I use? – 'lover. It's okay.'

'Edward said that you were with a local weretiger. He said you were feeding the *ardeur*.'

'Then why is your hand still on your gun?' I asked.

'Because from the smell and look of the bed he just changed shape recently, which means he's hungry. You're his lover, he likes you; he doesn't know me.'

'New shapeshifters are compelled to eat right after the change. That stops being true as they get more practice. Do you really think I'd be alone with a shapeshifter so new that he'd lose control like that?'

'You're like me, Anita; you don't always make good decisions when you find new tail.'

'I don't like that phrase. None of my lovers are just "new tail."'

He shrugged, hand still touching his gun. 'Fine, but when we see someone we want to sleep with, we don't always think it through first.'

Was he right about me? He was certainly right about the *ardeur* picking quick and hard, and not always the best choices. I had more control now, but . . . If he was right, he was right, and I had to let it go.

'And, Anita, this is a small room, and honestly if I didn't trust you, I'd have my gun out and pointed at your blond friend. Pointed, aimed, and ready to shoot would be my only chance against something as fast as a lycanthrope in a room this small, Anita.'

I nodded. 'I know that.'

'Then why are you bitching that I'm touching my gun?'

It was a good point. I shrugged, which made the towel begin to slip again. I caught it earlier this time, so I was still covered. 'Fine. Ethan, this is Marshal Bernardo Spotted-Horse.'

Ethan waved a hand that was big enough to palm Bernardo's skull. I guess in the end there was nothing I could do to make Bernardo comfortable with the big weretiger in the small room, and then I realized something else. Ethan was naked. He was like most wereanimals and not bothered by nudity, but in this shape he wouldn't fit in any clothes he'd brought for his under-six-feet human form. Well, maybe the boxers?

But a lot of men had problems with other men being nude, especially if they were well endowed. There was always a measuring stick in a man's mind when it came to certain things. Who was taller, and who was, um, well, bigger.

I tried to look at Ethan in this form from a guy's point of view, and realized there might be more than one reason that a human male might be intimidated.

I looked back at Bernardo, and it was my turn to grin. 'Is the nudity bothering you? I mean, Ethan's?'

Bernardo shook his head, but his eyes sort of flickered downward.

My grin got broader. 'Of all the human men I've seen nude, Bernardo, you are the last person I thought would be intimidated by size.' I laughed, I couldn't help it.

'Are you saying that he's as big in human form as I am in this form?' Ethan asked. Most men wouldn't have asked that blandly.

I glanced back at Bernardo. 'From what I remember, yeah.'

Bernardo gave me a mild version of his sexy smile, but it never reached his eyes. They were all wary, and worried about the most dangerous thing in the room. He'd flirt, but not until he was sure of the weretiger. The way he was acting, I wasn't certain there was a way for him to be comfortable around the weretiger in half-man form.

'Is he an old lover of yours?' Ethan asked.

'No,' I said, and my face was still soft with the fading laugh.

'Then how do you know how well endowed he is?' Ethan asked.

I looked at him. 'Are you jealous?'

The cat face frowned, but there was a very human intelligence through those eyes. 'I think so, and I'm sorry. I know that doesn't work for you, and it doesn't work in the red clan. The women totally get to pick the men, so I can't even say it's my culture.'

He spread those big hands that I knew with a flick of his muscles could reveal claws big enough to slice me open. 'It's just that it's been a long time, and the thought of sharing this soon hurts a little.'

I went to him, and was out of hands. I put the gun on the edge of the bare mattress and turned back to the towering, furred figure. I'd learned a long time ago that being physically intimidating didn't keep you from getting your feelings hurt. Everyone's heart is the same size.

I hugged him one-armed, until his arms wrapped around me, holding me close enough that the press of our bodies would hold the towel in place. I hugged him with both arms then, letting my hands play in the soft, thick fur of his back. He leaned down over me, bending more and more of that tall upper body over me until he could press his face against the top of my head. He huffed against my hair; it was something a lot of cats did, sort of halfway between a breath going out and in, and a soft sound that was used for talking to kittens or favorite people. It was a good, caring sound. I hugged him tighter, rubbing my cheek against the warmth of him. The fur was thinner on the front of him so that I could touch his skin through the silky fur. He was so warm.

'Thank you,' he said, as he stood up straighter. Something about the hugging and moving made the towel begin to slide down, but all Bernardo was seeing was my bare back. He could see that. I kept hugging the big weretiger, and looked up until I could meet those blue and gold eyes. 'You're welcome, and thank you for stripping the bed.'

'We'd have ruined the mattress otherwise.'

'I know, but thanks for thinking of it anyway. I like men who are domestically inclined.' I grinned at him, but he was still too serious. I tried again. 'I do want you, and I'm inviting you now to come to St Louis when this case is over.'

He smiled that flash of frightening teeth, but I'd been around enough beast forms to see the delight in his face, and the happiness in his eyes was unmistakable. He picked me up, sudden, unexpected, and effortless. He lifted me so he could look into my face. There are no lips to kiss in beast form, but I'd been dating lycanthropes for a while, and I knew to put my face against his and let him rub his furred cheeks on one side of my face and then the other. I returned the gesture, and put my arms around his shoulders. I realized the towel was no longer covering me. I had a choice of ruining the moment for modesty's sake, or not worrying about the fact that Bernardo was seeing my bare ass. I decided not to worry, and let the joy in Ethan's face be all the covering I needed. In the end, if you can make somebody that happy, what's a little flashing between friends?

26

We wrapped Ethan's new golden self in the last of the bedspreads, and had him fold all that size into the backseat of Bernardo's rental car. While still in the room, Ethan had said, 'I could be waiting for you when you get back.'

'I'll be gone for hours, maybe until morning,' I said.

'I'd wait.'

I smiled at him. 'If the bad guys weren't killing weretigers, then I'd say yes, but I don't want you here by yourself.'

'You don't think I can take care of myself?'

Watching for male ego, I said, 'You need to eat now that you've changed forms. Though I don't like anyone else knowing you have a gold form, the only safe-ish place I can think to take you is back to the red clan.'

'But not forever,' he said, and even through the gold and the pointy fangs meant for meat-rending, he was unsure, almost afraid.

'I promise, Ethan, it's not forever, but I gotta go catch bad guys now.'

So he hid in the backseat, and I called Alex so someone would be there at the entrance to meet him. Alex was actually about to go into a press conference for his day job as a reporter, but he promised that two guards would be there, and they'd take care of Ethan for me. 'I'm the prince of the clan, Anita; they'll do what I say.'

'Unless your mother the queen disagrees,' I said.

He laughed. 'Well, there is that.'

But there were two guards waiting to take Ethan into the underground and help hold all the weapons that didn't fit on his taller man form. They raised eyebrows at glimpses of his fur through the bedspread.

I told them, 'No one else knows, and I want to keep it that way.'

'We have to tell our queen,' one of the guards said.

'And if I tell you not to, what then?'

They looked at each other. 'You are a little queen, but you won't kill us for keeping secrets from you; she might.'

'If Ethan gets hurt because you let others know he has a third color form, and I think it's your fault, do you really think I won't kill you?'

'So, his safety is our safety?'

'Yeah, something like that.'

'I can take care of myself, Anita, you know that,' Ethan said.

'Against anyone but the bad guys we're chasing, I'd agree, but you saw him tear up a dozen of you guys in seconds. I want you safe.'

He wrapped me in the bedspread and the warm muscle and fur of his body. 'I've never had a woman care about me like that.'

I didn't say that I was more worried about losing one of the few goldens we had who wasn't part of the bloodline the good Harlequin had hidden away, genetic diversity and all that, and that I didn't love him yet. I let him believe what he needed to believe so I could go back Edward up with the other cops. I didn't have time to discuss love and lust and the difference with Ethan. Those conversations were always long ones.

Bernardo drove me through a fast-food drive-up. Not the healthiest, but I needed meat; burgers would do. It would help delay the next need to feed, and I wanted to delay that and still keep my healing ability. I had a faint scar on my right arm, and it was my own damn fault for not taking care of my metaphysical business. It was while we were in line waiting to pick up the order that Bernardo said, 'Before we meet up with Edward, I have to tell you something. He made me promise.'

'That's ominous,' I said, looking at him.

He smoothed his big, dark hands around the wheel, and that one gesture looked like a nervous gesture. Not good.

'What the hell is it?' I asked.

He took off his sunglasses, and took a deep breath. 'I'm not the only one Edward called in to help watch his back while you were hurt.'

I had a moment of not understanding, and then I got it. 'Jesus, not Olaf.'

Bernardo looked at me with eyes as dark a brown as my own. 'Yeah, he called in the big guy.'

I sat back in the seat and would have folded my arms over my chest, but there were too many weapons and the vest in the way. 'Shit,' I said, and the one word had a lot of feeling to it.

Olaf was also Marshal Otto Jefferies, an alias that allowed him to work for the armed forces on special projects sometimes, and the name on his US Marshal badge. He'd never broken the law on US soil to my knowledge, but in other countries, under his real name, he had. He earned his money as a mercenary and assassin, but his hobby was killing women. He'd kill and torture men, too, but usually only if necessary for work. Small, dark-haired women were his victims of choice, and I was very aware that I fit his victim profile. He'd made me aware of it the first time we met.

'Why did he invite Olaf to come play?' I asked.

'He didn't know how long you'd be out of commission. He needed backup, and since he has one of the warrants of execution he got to call in anyone he wanted. If he can't have you, he wants us.' There was a certain unhappiness to Bernardo's voice.

'You sound jealous,' I said.

He frowned at me as he eased the car up in line behind the other cars in the drive-up. 'Maybe it's a little hard on the ego for Olaf and me that he prefers you to us. You've never been military. You've never been a lot of things that the three of us have been, and yet Edward prefers you as his main backup.'

'You mean because I'm not a big, strong man, you feel slighted that Edward likes me better?' I let my tone speak for my view of that particular attitude.

Bernardo gave me a flat look. His face was still handsome, but there was now something in the eyes that might once have made me nervous. I was way past being nervous from hard looks. Hard looks couldn't hurt me, and it wasn't close to the hardest look he was capable of anyway. He didn't mean it.

'You know that's not what I mean.'

'Isn't it?' I asked, and gave him flat look for flat look.

I watched something slide through his eyes, and then he smiled. 'Well, I'll be damned.'

'Probably,' I said, 'but what did you just think of?'

He gave me a quizzical look, shook his head as if to chase the puzzlement away, and said, 'It is exactly that. I thought I was a little more evolved, but you're right. I'm this big, macho guy, with all this training that you don't have, and Edward would rather have you at his back than me. Edward is better at judging men and what they're capable of than anyone I've ever met except this one sergeant.' He shook his head again. 'Never mind, but my point is that if Edward believes you're better than me, or Olaf, at this job, then he must be right. It does hurt my ego that you sit there all itty-bitty and cute as hell, and you must be more dangerous than I will ever be. Yeah, that fucking bothers me.'

I smiled, I couldn't help it. It was so terribly honest. Most men wouldn't have said it out loud, even if they'd thought it. It made me wonder how much therapy Bernardo had had, but I didn't say that part out loud. What I said was, 'I'm flattered that Edward thinks I'm that good, because I know just how good you and Olaf are, well, when he's not distracted by the whole serial killer thing. But you're good, when you're not distracted by a woman.'

'I just dragged you out of someone's bed so you could hunt bad guys, Anita; don't throw stones at my hobbies.'

'I had to feed the *ardeur*, you know that.'

'Yeah, but after a while it doesn't matter why you do something, Anita, only that you do it, and you are as into sex as I am now.'

I started to try to argue, but we were at the window to pay. I handed him money, and he tried to hand it to the teenage girl at the window. She didn't take the money because she was staring at Bernardo.

He flashed her that dazzling smile and folded the money into her much smaller hand. He folded her fingers around the money, managing to half-hold her hand as he did it. It made her blush, and she stammered as she took the money and tried to count change back. I was betting that the change would be wrong; she was too flustered to count.

She handed him back some bills and coins. He handed them to me. I started unfolding it all and counting change against the receipt in my hand.

'Is this your girlfriend?' she asked.

'No, we just work together,' he said, smiling.

The blush had begun to fade, and now it climbed up her neck and face again. 'I get off at five o'clock.'

'Sorry, babe, but you're way too young for me, and I've gotta work anyway.'

'I'm eighteen,' she said.

I doubted that. Apparently, Bernardo did, too.

'You got ID that proves that?' he said.

She dropped her eyes, and finally shook her head. The car behind us honked. A man with a badge that said *Manager* came into her little cubicle. She mumbled, 'Please drive to the next window, sir.' He was talking to her about her conduct as we drove forward to the suddenly empty line in front of us. The other cars had gotten their food and left while he was flirting.

'You have to be really careful with the younger women,' he

said. 'They'll lie about being over eighteen and it's never them that gets in trouble. Police always believe that the young, innocent girl was taken advantage of. I had one sixteen year old who kept sending me lingerie shots of herself. In some states my receiving that kind of shit in my email could get me up on child pornography charges.'

'What'd you do?'

'I turned her in to the cops. Told them I was concerned that she'd send this stuff to someone who wasn't as moral as I was and get herself hurt.'

'You didn't,' I said.

'Oh, yeah I did. The girls think it's a game, or something, but it's not them that goes to jail. I don't like them that young anyway.' Then he looked at me, and the moment I saw the look I knew whatever he said next would be some kind of teasing, and I wouldn't like it. 'But you do, don't you?'

'I do what?' I asked.

'Like them that young, or is it just a rumor that you've got that weretiger, Sydney, or something, from Vegas living with you now?'

'His name's Cynric, and it's not a rumor.'

'Sixteen is too young even for me, Anita.' But he smiled as he said it, enjoying being able to be morally superior. 'And he was a young sixteen, Anita, what little I remember of him.'

What was I supposed to say, that I hadn't meant to have sex with Cynric? That we'd been possessed by the biggest, baddest vampire of them all, Marmee Noir? It was true, but after a while the explanations just sounded hollow, because I kept having to make them.

'He's seventeen, and he's legal, and he's in St Louis because he's the only male blue tiger alive today that we can find. He's on the Harle— bad vampire's hit list.'

Then I realized that wasn't true anymore. Ethan was blue, and he was all grown up. Could I send Cynric home to Vegas? And if I could, should I? He was already my blue tiger to call, but

Alex was my red and he didn't live in the same state. Of course, the Harlequin might kill him to hurt me. Shit.

'So you're keeping Cynric safe,' Bernardo said.

'Trying to.'

'By fucking him?'

I glared at him. 'Thanks a lot, Bernardo.'

He grinned at me as he pulled out onto the main street.

I glared at him as I unwrapped my burger. I so didn't want to try to eat while we had this conversation, but I did want to have food in me before we got to Edward and Olaf. I definitely didn't want to see Olaf on an empty stomach. I'd need all the strength I could muster.

I tried to decide if I should be angry with him for real, and if I did get angry, why was I angry? Because I felt guilty about Cynric, and that made me defensive about him. I ate my burger without tasting it, and wondered, not for the first time, what the hell to do about Cynric.

'That's it?' Bernardo said. 'That's all you're going to say to me? You used to be easier to bait.'

I drank some Coke and picked up a French fry. 'Were you trying to pick a fight?'

He smiled. 'Not a real fight, but it's fun to get you riled up.'

I ate the French fry, knowing it was all grease and salt, but then that was what made it taste so good. Why did so many things that were bad for you taste so good?

He glanced at me, then back to the road. 'Either you really like the kid, or he bothers you for real.'

I sighed, eating my yummy fry and trying not to hunch in the passenger seat. I so didn't want to have this conversation with Bernardo, but then he'd met Cynric the same time I did.

'You met him when I did, Bernardo. He was a virgin, because the white clan is like all the clans, it's all about purity of blood-line, and their queen tiger, Bibiana, likes her men to be monogamous.'

'It's because she holds her husband to the big *M*, and she can't ask the head vampire of Vegas to do something she doesn't make her tigers do.'

'Yeah,' I said, 'and also teenagers don't always have the control with their first orgasm not to shift and eat their partner.'

'How's Blue Boy's control?' he asked.

I shrugged, very deliberately not looking at him. 'It's good, and don't call him that. He has a name.'

'Cynric doesn't sound like a real name for a teenage guy,' Bernardo said.

'He goes by a short version of his name.'

'Rick?' he asked.

I shook my head.

'Rick's the only thing short for his name,' Bernardo said.

'Nope.'

He started merging into traffic. It probably meant we were going to exit soon. I hadn't been paying enough attention to where we were, and I wasn't familiar enough with the city.

'What does he call himself, then?'

I mumbled something.

'What?'

'Sin, okay, he likes Sin.'

Bernardo laughed out loud, head back, mouth wide, face alight with it.

'Yeah, yeah, enjoy it, laughing boy,' I said.

When he could talk, he said, 'It's just too good, Anita. Too easy.'

'I tried to talk him out of it, but his cousin Roderic goes by Rick, so he thinks of it as taken.'

He gave that low male chuckle. 'Sin, you're screwing a seventeen year old that's named Sin. Oh, man, when I met you, you were like the virgin queen, so untouchable, and now—'

'Just stop, okay, I feel bad enough.'

He glanced at me as he waited for the traffic to let him exit. 'Why feel bad about it? So he's young, so what?'

'You said it yourself, he was a young sixteen. I took his virginity, Bernardo.'

'You were mind-fucked by Mommie Darkest at the time, and so was Cynric.'

'So were about four other weretigers. Your first time shouldn't be in a vampire-induced orgy, but his was.'

'It wasn't your fault, Anita. I was in Vegas. You're lucky to have lived through it, and so were the weretigers.'

I shrugged. I put the rest of the food in the bag. My stomach was in a hard knot, and food just didn't sound good right then.

'Well, they're not living through it this time.'

'It's not your fault that Mommie Darkest is making the bad vamps hunt weretigers.'

'Maybe,' I said.

'Oh, can the Catholic guilt.'

'What does that mean?' I asked, glaring at him.

'It means that you do what you have to do, and you try to enjoy it along the way. It's what we all do.'

'You were the one who teased me about Cynric,' I said.

'That was because you were supposed to tell me to go to hell like you always do. You weren't supposed to actually let it bother you. If I'd realized you felt this bad about doing him, I'd have left it alone.'

'Thanks, I guess,' I said, and I stared out the window as he wove the car through the narrow streets.

'Why do you feel so bad about this one?'

'He's seventeen,' I said.

'So, he'll be eighteen next year.'

'He's a senior in high school, Bernardo. Jean-Claude is his legal guardian and had to enroll him in school. He comes home with homework and shit, and then he wants to cuddle and have sex. It weirds me the fuck out.'

He was quiet as he wove through the progressively narrower streets. 'You haven't even asked where we're going.'

'To Edward,' I said.

'Yeah, but we're not going to the police station, and you haven't asked why.' He glanced at me. 'You're a control freak. Why aren't you asking?'

I thought about the question, and finally said, 'I don't know. I don't seem to care. I mean, I trust you, I trust Edward, and I even trust Olaf to do the job. I just don't trust him with me.'

'You shouldn't,' he said.

'Okay, are we going to a new crime scene, or what?' I asked.

'You ask, but not like you care, as if it doesn't matter at all. Things matter to you, Anita; it's one of your charms and irritations.' He smiled, but I didn't feel the need to smile back.

'I think I'm homesick. I think I'm tired of chasing bad guys. Did Edward tell you his idea that Marmee Noir is killing the tigers so that I'll be away from St Louis and all our people? The last one of her guards that talked to me said that she wants me alive. It's what saved us twice, I think. She doesn't want me dead.'

'He mentioned some of it. Could she really possess your body?'

'She thinks she can.'

'What do you think?' he asked.

'I think she might be able to.'

'That would scare the hell out of me.'

I nodded. 'Trust me, Bernardo, I'm scared.'

'You don't seem scared. You seem distracted.'

'Maybe I don't know how to be scared. Maybe that's what the distraction is,' I said.

'Whatever it is, you need to get your head in the game, Anita. We need you. Edward needs you, and you sure as hell want to bring your A-game when you meet Olaf.'

'He still want me to be his serial killer girlfriend?' I asked.

'He still thinks you *are* his serial killer girlfriend.'

'Great,' I said.

'You haven't even asked if it's a new crime scene.'

I looked at him, startled at last. 'They've never killed twice in one city.'

'No, they haven't.'

I scowled at him. 'Stop the games, Bernardo. Tell me where we're going and why the mystery.'

'Edward called Jean Claude.'

I know my face looked as surprised as I felt. 'Why?'

'Because he found a way for you to have bodyguards, and he thinks they can help us find these bastards.'

That Edward approved that strongly of the guards Jean-Claude had working for us showed the best stamp of approval I could imagine. I knew they were good, but that Edward agreed with me was both cool and interesting.

'So we're going to meet them,' I said.

'Yeah, but first Olaf and you get to say hi.'

'Why?' I said.

'Because Olaf thinks you have a relationship with him, and if you meet him first and privately, he can keep that illusion. Edward's afraid of what Olaf will do if he realizes that you aren't ever going to be his girlfriend.'

'I am not meeting privately with Serial Killer Guy.'

'Edward and I will be there,' he said. He'd found an empty space and was parallel parking like a pro, smooth, no hesitation.

'You live in the city,' I said.

He killed the engine and turned to me. 'Why, because I can parallel park?'

I nodded. 'A city where that's the only parking you get to use most of the time, or you grew up where that was the only parking.'

'Don't profile me, Anita.'

'Sorry, can't I just be impressed with your parking skills?'

He seemed to think about that for a minute, then shrugged. 'Then just say "Good job" or something, don't speculate.'

I nodded. 'Okay, great job of parallel parking. I suck at it.'

'Country girl,' he said.

'Most of my life,' I said.

'I told you more of my background the first time I met you than most people ever know. I think I thought the whole foster-care-system sob story would soften you up, but nothing makes you soft, not like that.'

'I'll quote Raquel Welch: "There aren't any hard women; only soft men."'

'Lie,' he said.

'In the normal world it's pretty true,' I said.

He grinned sudden and bright in his tanned face. 'Since when does either of us live in the normal world?'

That made me laugh. I shrugged. 'Never.'

We got out of the car so I could meet Olaf and convince him he still had a chance in hell of ever getting in my pants. Sometimes you lie because the alternative is too awful to think about. Edward, Bernardo, and I all feared what Olaf would do if he ever lost hope of me having sex with him. I think we all knew that if he gave up all hope of my dating him voluntarily, he'd go for something less voluntary. Something that included chains and torture. Someday I'd have to kill Olaf, but hopefully today wasn't that day. Hopefully.

27

The building was an old Victorian house that had been divided into apartments. The one that Bernardo led me to was empty, all pale empty walls, and that slightly sharp smell of fresh paint. Bernardo went in first, his broad shoulders and back blocking most of my view. Edward walked into view, face grim, and then they both stepped aside so I could see Olaf.

He stood at the far side of the room, to one side of the bay window. He was watching the street, or watching something. The ten-foot ceilings made him seem shorter than he was, but he was only bare inches from seven feet. In the heeled boots he probably was seven feet. He was the tallest person I'd ever personally known. But unlike a lot of really tall people, he had some bulk to him. It was hard to see in the black jeans and black leather jacket, but I knew there were muscles under the clothes. His head was as smooth and free of hair as ever. Since he had to shave twice a day to stay clean-shaven, I always wondered if he shaved his head, too, but I never asked him. It never seemed important once he looked at me.

Two things startled me when he turned around. One, he was wearing a white T-shirt when all I'd ever seen him in was black. Two, he had a narrow black Vandyke beard and mustache. The color matched the eyebrows that arched thick and graceful over his deep-set eyes. He was too tall, but I could admit that he was attractive until you got to the eyes. The truth of what he was always stared back from those eyes, at least to me. I knew that other women seemed not to see it, but he never hid his eyes from me. When I first met him it had been because he wanted me afraid of him, and later I think he, like Edward, enjoyed that I was one person he didn't have to hide the truth from. I knew who and what he was, and hadn't run screaming. I might be the only woman he'd ever met more than once who knew the truth and still managed to have some sort of 'normal' relationship with him. Maybe that was part of his attraction to me. I knew.

'So is this the good Olaf, via *South Park*, or the evil Olaf as in the old *Star Trek*,' I said.

He smiled; he actually smiled, though it left his dark, dark eyes almost untouched. They were black to begin with, so it was hard to make them shine. The well-trimmed facial hair framed his lips nicely. It reminded me of one of our vampires, Requiem, who was now second banana to the Master, or rather, Mistress, of Philadelphia, and her main squeeze.

'You like it?'

That he asked my opinion, any woman's opinion, was real progress for him. He'd been one of the most misogynistic men I'd ever met a few years back, and I met a lot of them. It was progress, so I answered as if he weren't scary.

'Yeah, I do.' I realized I did. It added definition to his strangely bare face. Most of the men in my life were like Bernardo, all shoulder-length or longer hair.

He moved toward me, still smiling. He moved like he did most things, in a graceful lope. For such a big man he was surprisingly graceful; if I hadn't thought he'd take it wrong, I'd have asked if he had ever had dance training, but I doubted that would fit his ideal of macho.

He stopped about halfway to me. I wasn't sure what was going on until Edward touched my arm. I looked at him, and he gave me a look. Oh, I remembered this part. Olaf saw it as weakness to come to me. That he'd met me even halfway was again a lot of progress.

I started walking toward him. The sixty-four-thousand-dollar question was, what was I supposed to do once I got there?

I offered him my hand, even though the last time I'd done that he'd done the double-hand grab up my arm and reminded me of the one and only kiss we'd had, over a body that we'd just cut up. It had been a bad vampire and we had needed to take its heart and head, but he'd acted as if the blood on both of us were an aphrodisiac.

A handshake was still the most neutral thing I could think to offer. He wrapped his big hand around my much smaller one and pulled me into one of those guy hugs. You know, the handshake that turns into a sort of one-shoulder, one-arm hug. But it was unexpected. I went with it, but . . . it would have worked better if there hadn't been two feet of height difference. It was meant to bring me in against his shoulder, but I ended up pressed to the front of his body with my entire head below his chest, so sort of his upper stomach/chest area. God, he was big.

I had enough guy friends that I'd automatically put my arm around him for the hug, like body memory. His much bigger arm was around me, and what was supposed to be a quick, manly, I'm-not-gay hug turned into more. His arm tightened around me, keeping me against his body. My right hand was in his, his arm behind my back, my left arm around his surprisingly slender waist.

The moment his arm tightened, I tensed against him, my mind going over my options. He'd feel me let go with my left arm, so any weapon reaching was going to be telegraphed big-time.

He held me against him, his arm pressing me close. I was tensed, my heart thudding, pulse racing, waiting for him to do something creepy, and then I realized he was holding me. He was just holding me. Of all the things Olaf could have done, that surprised me most. He let go of my right hand and just hugged me. He just held me close. It was so unexpected that I was at a loss, but my right arm was between our bodies, so that did two things to help my comfort level: It let me keep enough distance that we weren't pressed completely against each other, and I could touch the butt of the Smith & Wesson in the shoulder holster. His arms tightened across my back almost too tightly; he let me feel how terribly strong he was. He wasn't shapeshifter strong, but you don't have to be able to bench-press a car to hurt someone. There was enough strength in his grip to let me know that he could hurt me. I wasn't sure if he was doing it on purpose, or was simply that unaccustomed to hugging people.

I erred on the side of caution. I snuggled against him with my left arm and body, making that little wriggling motion that girls and some smaller men make. I was hoping it would distract him from the fact that I was using my right hand to draw the gun from its shoulder holster at the same time.

'You just drew your gun,' he said, in that deep voice that matched the big body.

I fought not to tense as I pressed the gun against the side of his body. 'Yes.'

I felt him bend over me, and then he kissed me on top of the head. Again, so unexpected that I didn't know what to do. I mean I couldn't shoot him for kissing the top of my head and giving me a hug. It was too hysterical. But this new, more tender Olaf puzzled the hell out of me.

'I've held many women in my arms, but you're the first who's managed to draw a weapon.'

It was a little hard to be tough talking into his stomach, but having the Smith & Wesson shoved into his side helped. 'They didn't understand what you were.'

He spoke with his chin resting on my hair. 'They understood in the end, Anita.'

'But not until it was too late,' I said, and I didn't feel silly pushing the gun into the hard muscle of his side. It felt safer.

Edward spoke from behind me. 'She will kill you, if you give her a reason.'

Olaf rose up enough to look at him more comfortably, but he was still holding me. 'I know she will shoot me, if I give her cause.'

'Then let her go.'

'It is the possibility of danger that makes us both enjoy her, in our own ways.'

'You and I do not think of her the same way,' Edward said, and his voice was growing colder. I knew that voice. It was headed to the tone he used when he killed.

I wanted to tell Olaf to let me go, but I'd seen him move. He was fast, not shapeshifter fast, but close. I thought I was fast enough to get enough distance that he couldn't try for my gun, but I might not be fast enough, and then I'd have to shoot him to keep my gun and to keep him off me. It seemed almost stupid to be thinking of that while he was still hugging me so normally, or as normally as I'd ever seen him interact with me.

'I'm stepping back now, Olaf,' I said, and started moving out of the hug, though I kept the gun barrel hard against his body. That would be the last thing I moved.

I thought he'd fight me, but he didn't. He hadn't done anything I'd expected him to do since I stepped into the room. Then the gun was the only thing touching him. I wasn't looking at the center of his body like they teach you in boxing; I was more looking to one side. It was like being in the woods and looking for movement among the leaves; you see more by not looking.

The gun barrel left the side of his body but was still pointed at his center mass. I felt him move almost before he did it. I couldn't have told you what moved, or what clued me, but I knew what he was going to do. He tried to disarm me and if I'd been human-slow, he'd have done it. He was that fast, that good.

I moved to one side, let his hand pass by my gun, my arm, my side, and hit his wrist with the butt of my gun as he missed me. I could have kicked his knee and dislocated it, but he was supposed to be on our side. I didn't want him crippled for the hunt. When he wasn't being all serial killer weird, he was a good man in a fight.

He came back at me with his other hand, and I had the gun pointed at his heart, and one of the sheath knives pressed to his groin.

Edward yelled, 'Enough!'

I froze, Olaf's life in my hands twice. 'If he behaves, so will I.'

'You're faster than I remember,' Olaf said.

'Funny, that's what the weretiger spy said.'

'I told you she's faster,' Edward said.

'I needed to see it for myself,' Olaf said. I could feel the weight of his gaze, but I didn't look away from my two targets. He could stare all he wanted to; I had my priorities.

I spoke low and carefully, afraid my tense muscles would drive the knife a little into his flesh. If I ever stabbed him in the groin I knew it would have to be a killing blow, not an accident. 'If you keep testing my limits, Olaf, one of us will get hurt.'

'I will step back if you lower the weapons,' he said.

'I'll lower the weapons if you step back.'

'We are at an impasse then.'

Edward said, 'I'm behind you, Anita. I'm going to step between you both, and you will both back the fuck up.' He came into my view, and then he did what he said he'd do, and began to step between us.

I let him back me up, and so did Olaf. We stood staring at each other. With Edward between us I was finally willing to look up into Olaf's face, and what I saw there wasn't comforting. He was excited: his eyes alight with it, his mouth half parted. He'd enjoyed being close to me, and the danger, or maybe he'd enjoyed something I didn't even understand, but calling him a sick fuck seemed counterproductive to us working together, so I just thought it really hard.

'Now,' Edward said, glaring from one to the other of us, 'we're going to meet Anita's backup and go hunt bad guys, not each other.'

'I will need a side trip,' Olaf said.

'Why?' Edward asked.

Bernardo answered from near the door, where he'd moved, apparently, when Olaf and I started our dance. 'Hospital emergency room. She broke his wrist.'

Edward and I both looked at Olaf, and at his wrist. It wasn't at an odd angle, so it wasn't a bad break, but he was holding it still, and a little stiff against his side.

'Is it broken?' Edward asked.

'Yes,' he said.

'How bad?' Edward asked.

'Not too bad.'

'Will you be able to use a gun?'

'It's why we all practice left-handed, isn't it?' Olaf said. Which meant no.

'Fuck,' I said.

'You didn't mean to break his wrist, did you?' Edward asked, looking at me.

I shook my head.

'I saw in the woods how much faster you are. I think you're stronger than you realize, too. I'd be careful how hard I hit people if I were you.' The look on his face was so not happy with me. I couldn't blame him. I'd just crippled one of his backups, and one of our most dangerous marshals. And I hadn't done it on purpose. I lived with, trained with, sparred with, hunted, and killed shapeshifters and vampires. When was the last time I'd worked out with someone who was human? I couldn't remember. Shit.

'I'll take him to the hospital,' Bernardo said, 'but what do we put on the paperwork?'

'Tell them it was a lover's quarrel,' Olaf said.

'Over my dead body,' I said.

'Eventually,' he said.

'Don't be a sick fuck, Olaf,' I said.

'I know what I am, Anita,' he said. 'It's you who keeps fighting the truth.'

'What truth is that?' I asked.

'Don't do this,' Edward said, and I wasn't sure which of us he was talking to.

'You hunt and kill just like I do, like we all do. There is no one in this room who is not a murderer.'

'Yeah, tell me something I don't know,' and my voice showed the truth of it.

I had the satisfaction of Olaf looking surprised. 'Then what makes you different from me?'

'I don't enjoy killing; you do.'

'If that is the only difference between us, Anita, then we should date.'

I shook my head and stepped back. 'Take him to the hospital, Bernardo; get him a cast, get him a pill, get him fixed, just get him out of here.'

Bernardo looked at Edward. He nodded and said, 'Do it. Call me from the hospital and let me know how bad it is.'

Bernardo left, shaking his head. Olaf said, 'I owe you for this, Anita.'

'Is that a threat?' I asked.

'Of course it is,' Edward said. 'Now you get the fuck out of here. You' – he pointed at me – 'stop talking to him.'

We did what Edward said. The question was, how long could I work with Olaf and not talk to him, and what would he see as payback for the wrist? Had I finally made him stop thinking of me as his girlfriend and just as a victim, or had some weird rivalry set in? Either choice was a bad one. Multiple choice should have at least one right answer, but some people only come with wrong answers. Some people are like rigged tests where you can only fail. One way or the other, I was going to fail with Olaf and one of us was going to die. Great; the Harlequin were trying to capture me, Mommie Darkest wanted to destroy my soul and take over my body, and now one of the people on our side wanted to either fuck me, kill me, or a combination of both. Could things get any worse? Wait, don't answer that, I know the answer.

The answer is always yes. It can always get worse. Right now the Harlequin hadn't captured me, Mommie Darkest hadn't possessed me, and Olaf and I were both still alive and hadn't fucked each other; when I looked at it that way, it wasn't a half bad day.

28

We were all set to go hunt the bad guys our way, with muscle from home to back us, and then we both got phone calls. We were called into the office to explain ourselves. I'd never been called by any marshal brass to explain myself before. When I asked Edward if it was a first for him, too, he just nodded. We were actually going to ignore the calls, but some police officers in marked cars showed up with orders to escort us to the 'meeting'.

'Who'd you piss off while I was unconscious?' I asked Edward.

'To my knowledge, I haven't done anything to anyone.'

'I was unconscious, so it couldn't have been me.'

He shrugged, and we got in his SUV to follow the nice officers to talk to our superior officer. Technically, we could have refused, but it would have put the uniformed officers in a really awkward spot. We tried to leave my homeboys out of it. Edward and I would go down to talk to the other marshals, and my guys could settle into their hotel rooms. But the uniforms had orders to bring in Marshals Forrester and Blake and the illegal backup. The moment they said it that way, we got a clue as to why we were being called to explain ourselves.

It was Marshal Raborn who had tattled on us to Teacher. It wasn't his warrant, so it wasn't his business. But just because it wasn't Raborn's warrant didn't mean he wasn't being a pain in our ass. He'd made enough fuss that we were back at the local marshal offices discussing things, rather than trying to track down the killers. My 'illegal' backup was out in the hallway like high school kids waiting for their turn to get yelled at by the principal. It was a colossal waste of time and resources. Night would fall, the vampires would rise, and we were stuck playing departmental politics. Perfect.

'You can't just let her bring in a bunch of hired muscle and say they represent the Marshals Service,' Raborn said. He was talking to his immediate supervisor, Marshal Rita Clark. She was tall for a woman, but not as tall as Raborn's six feet. She was in better shape, though; there was no extra weight on her lean frame. Her brown hair was cut just above the shoulders in a careless mass of curls that was less a hairstyle and more just the way the curl worked that morning. Sun had tanned her brown and given her lines around the eyes and mouth, but they suited her, as if every smile or laugh she'd ever had was there on her face, so you just knew that she would rather laugh than frown. But the look in her gray eyes let us all know that though she preferred to laugh, she didn't have to. The fact that she was Raborn's boss was nice. One of the things I liked about the Marshals Service was that the normal branch had more women than any other law enforcement unit in the country. They had also been one of the first to allow women to join them. I liked that a lot.

She said, 'Marshal Forrester ran their names by us before Marshal Blake's backup landed. We've done background checks on all of them. They don't have criminal records, and technically under the new law it wouldn't matter anyway.'

'It should matter,' Raborn said, and he was standing again, pacing to the side of her office, which was enough bigger than his that he had room to pace, if he was careful.

'Perhaps,' she said, watching him pace, 'but the way the law is written, it doesn't.' She looked from his nervous, angry pacing to Edward and me in the chairs in front of her desk. Edward gave her the good-ol'-boy Ted smile. I gave her calm, patient face. If I were a boss, who would I like better, the angry man pacing in the corner like a problem about to happen, or the two calm, smiling people who seemed reasonable? I knew what my vote would be, and looking into Marshal Clark's serious gray eyes I was betting she would agree with me.

Raborn came to lean his hands on her desk and sort of loom over her. I watched her eyes narrow so the smile lines deepened. If I'd had that look aimed at me by someone who could fuck up my day, I might have backed off. 'Look at them out there; they are thugs, or worse. Just because they've never been convicted of a crime doesn't make them innocent.'

I fought the urge to look out in the hallway where my backup was lingering. I knew what they looked like, and *innocent* wasn't a word that anyone would have used to describe them.

'First, Raborn, that is exactly what innocence means under the law, you should know that.' Her voice was going quieter with each word, but the heat in each syllable was notching up. Again, I would have seen the warning signs and acted accordingly, but Raborn seemed past that. He'd let his anger take him to a place that his ass might have trouble getting out of, or maybe I just didn't understand the normal branch of the service whose badge I carried.

She put her elbows on the arms of her chair, her hands like a double fist in front of her lips. 'Second, get the fuck off my desk.' Oh, I did understand the normal branch of the service. It worked just like all the others.

He startled, visibly, back straightening, as if he'd just realized he had touched her desk. He didn't know me well enough to hate me this much personally, but he had enough of a problem with me that he was hurting his career. What the hell was going on?

She stood, slowly, carefully, and at five-eight she was tall enough in her boots to back him up a little. She managed to loom and seem much taller just by her presence. I've been told I can do the same thing, but it was nifty watching it from the other end.

'Marshal Blake is within her rights as a US Marshal of the preternatural branch to deputize people she believes will aid her in executing her warrant in the most efficient and lifesaving manner possible.'

'The law was written for emergency situations in the field,' Raborn said, 'when a marshal doesn't have access to other marshals for backup. It was never intended to allow us to pick and choose whom we deputize for a given job when there are enough marshals to get the job done.'

'There were three branches of the government last I checked, Raborn. We're the branch that carries out the law as written and given to us. If the legislative and judicial branches decide at a later date that the law as written needs to be changed, they'll change it, and then you can come bitch to me about Marshal Blake's choice in deputies, but until then, we will uphold the law as written and act within its confines. Is that clear, Marshal Raborn?'

A hint of red was creeping up his neck – not a blush, more an angry flush, I thought. Through tight lips he said, 'Yes, ma'am.'

She looked at us, 'You two go do your job.' She looked back at Raborn. 'You get the fuck out of my office and stay the fuck out of their way.'

Edward and I stood, and did as we were told. Raborn hesitated behind us. I heard him intake a breath and wondered if he was going to keep pushing, but it was no longer my problem. Clark had backed me, and that was good enough.

My backup was waiting in the hallway outside the office. The other people with badges watched them covertly and were probably just as unhappy as Raborn, but they were smart enough to let it go. You could pick out which of my backup was ex-military. They stood a little straighter, as if fighting not to come to attention as we stepped up. Bobby Lee had grown thinner and somewhere the sun had turned his blond hair paler and tanned him deep brown, darker than most blonds could get. His brown eyes watched me from behind gold-framed glasses. He was older than the rest of us, but it only showed in fine lines around his eyes, an extra line here and there on his face. He'd always been tall and fairly lean, but he'd been out of the country on some secret assignment for the wererats for a long time, and wherever he'd been, it had carved him down. There was a look in his eyes now, almost a flinching, as if whatever he'd seen, or done, had worn the inside down as much as the outside.

'Well, darlin', are we staying, or going?' His soft southern accent was deeper than it had been before. I didn't believe it was because he'd been somewhere the accent existed, more like it was a piece of home they couldn't take from him.

I didn't even tell him not to call me *darlin'*; it was nothing personal, and he seemed to need all his down-home charm like a shield against whatever had taken the shine from his eyes.

'Staying,' I said.

He smiled, and gave a small nod. Lisandro, tall, dark, handsome, with his black hair in a ponytail trailing down his shoulders, stepped up beside him. He wasn't quite as pretty as Bernardo, but he was ballparking. He looked like the proverbial Hispanic leading man. He was married and had two kids. He coached their soccer teams. We'd had sex together once for a sort of emergency feed to keep Marmee Noir from doing bad things. To keep his wife from trying to kill us both, we'd agreed it would never happen again. Actually, we just pretended it hadn't. Worked for me. 'Why is Raborn against you?'

'I honestly have no idea.'

Lisandro gave me a look.

I smiled. 'I'm not lying, I just met the man.' I turned to Edward beside me. 'Tell him.'

'He took an instant dislike to Anita.'

'Maybe it's just being a woman and being better at the job than he is,' Socrates said. His skin was the color of coffee with a little cream added. Hair was short, clipped close to his head, just long enough on top that he could style it, but today he'd chosen not to, so that the hair formed tiny little curls. It looked . . . cuter than his usual, but he'd actually explained that this was natural, and cops didn't like you styling your hair on the job. He was an ex-cop, so he'd know. He wasn't as tall as the other two men, less than six feet by a few inches. He tended to round his shoulders, slumping a little, as if he'd gotten his height early in life and never lost the habit of trying to hide it, even though he wasn't the tallest kid in the room anymore.

'You think it's as simple as that? Raborn is a misogynist?'

He grinned at me, filling his dark brown eyes with that spark he could get. 'That's a big word just to say he doesn't think much of women.'

I grinned back, and shrugged. 'Hey, I'm not just another pretty face. I have a vocabulary.'

'You gotta watch the big words there, ma'am, we humble bodyguards don't know what you're talking about,' Ares said.

I turned to him. He was just under six feet, blond and brown-eyed. He'd lost the desert tan he'd come to us with. He'd been out of military on medical discharge for a while, but he still couldn't quite lose the *ma'am* and *sir*, or the shoulders-back, spine-straight stance. He'd tried letting his hair grow out, but finally he'd cut it short again, keeping the top long, but his hair was as straight as Socrates' was curly, so the longish top spilled a little over and to one side of his face. He had a habit of pushing it away from his face, as if it bugged him. I was betting next trip to the barbershop he'd be evenly short. Socrates had tried to help him style it when the top was longer so it was in sort of anime spikes, but that just wasn't Ares. If he hadn't caught lycanthropy, he'd have probably been lifetime Army.

But the real anime hair was Nicky's. He was white-bread enough to have yellow-blond hair, shaved short on the sides, but long on top so it spilled out over one half of his face, in a long triangle of straight blond hair. With Ares right beside him it was more apparent that there was some body or wave to Nicky's hair. Ares' was straight as the proverbial board. Nicky's overly long fall of hair had a sort of curve to it. It made the two of them look like they were going out to a club, or to an anime festival, but Ares dyed his hair so he could remind himself he wasn't in the military anymore, and Nicky grew his out to hide that he was missing an eye.

The woman who raised him, who was technically his mother, had taken his eye when he was fourteen because he tried to say no to her sexual abuse. Women are less likely to be active abusers, but when they are, it's usually more violent. Nicky's childhood had been bad. He had one lovely blue eye, but the other was just a smooth empty socket of scar tissue. The hair hid it completely, and managed to look like a fashion statement at the same time. The hair might have made people take him less than seriously, but he was six feet even, and the body that went with the rest of him made certain that anyone who knew what they were looking at wouldn't underestimate Nicky. All the guards lifted weights as part of their training, but either Nicky hit them harder or genetics made him bulk up, because even in jeans, T-shirt, and a light jacket, the swelling of his shoulders and biceps showed. He wasn't the tallest guy waiting for me in the hallway, but he was the biggest.

'Hey,' he said softly.

I smiled at him. 'Hey.' That was it, not the most romantic, but there was more emotion in those little words than in anything I'd said to anyone else. Nicky was my lover, and my Bride, in that Dracula, Prince of Darkness way. It made us closer than just dating ever would have. Thanks to my having to have private time with Olaf, and then uniformed cops arriving on the scene, I hadn't gotten to really greet him. It had been a wave, and a hi, and oh, cops.

Domino stepped away from the wall so I had to look at him. I think I'd left Nicky and Domino for last because they distracted me. Domino's hair was black and white curls, mostly black today, with just a few white, which meant that the last couple of times he'd shapeshifted he'd done black tiger. His hair tended to reflect

whether he'd last shifted into his white tiger or black tiger form.
I wondered if Ethan's hair would change color with his shift.
Domino had sunglasses that hid his eyes, because his eyes were
always tiger eyes. They were deep reddish orange with spirals
of gold through them, which was actually more black tiger than
white genetically. He was only about an inch shorter than Nicky,
but he tended to like boots with heels, so that added a couple of
inches. Nicky was more a jogging-shoe kind of guy, but then he
wasn't insecure about his height, not in the least. Domino wasn't
insecure either, he just liked boots. He was one of my tigers to
call. It was a different bond than with Nicky; Domino had free
will. He could argue with me, fight, and tell me I was wrong.
Nicky could do those things to a point, but if I gave him a direct
order he'd do it. Domino followed my orders, but he had a
choice.

With the jacket on, Domino looked much less muscled than
I knew he was, but then clothes can hide a lot of good things,
and I knew that what lay under his clothes was very good.

I was in the midst of giving Domino the smile he deserved
when Ares said, 'I feel ignored.'

I glanced at him. 'Sorry.'

He grinned at me and took a breath to say something, but his
eyes went behind me. Everyone looked behind me and it wasn't
entirely friendly. I turned to find Raborn coming up behind us.
He'd closed the door to Clark's office and she was on the phone.

'What do you want, Raborn?' I asked.

'Who's in charge of the muscle?' he asked, and he made sure
his tone was offensive.

Nicky shoved a thumb in my direction. 'Anita is.'

Raborn gave him a look that said clearly, *I don't believe you.*

'It disappoints me, too,' Ares said with a grin, 'but she's it.'

'What does "it" mean?' Raborn asked.

'The boss, the big cheese, the head honcho, or honchette,'
Ares said. 'She's it.'

'Why would you listen to her?'

Ares looked at me. 'Do we have to explain ourselves to him?'

'No,' I said, 'we don't.'

Ares gave Raborn a big grin that filled his olive-green eyes with glee. 'You heard her.'

'You all fucking her?' Raborn asked.

I felt Edward tense beside me. 'That was over the line, pardner.' His Ted voice was a little strained around the edges. But it was the other men who were scary in that moment. They went quiet, but it was the quiet that a predator will use when it hunkers down in the long grass beside the trail. It was a tense, waiting quiet, and the energy coming off all of them raised the hair on my arms and tickled down my spine.

'Easy, guys,' I said.

'He doesn't get to talk to you like that,' Domino said in a low voice.

'No, he doesn't,' I said. I sighed and looked up at Raborn. 'Do you want me to bring you up on sexual harassment charges?'

'Since when is the truth grounds for harassment?' he asked. His eyes were angry, defiant. I thought in that moment that Socrates was right; it was the fact that I was a woman. Cops usually thought policewomen were only two things: bitches or sluts. I had a reputation for both.

I stood there and thought of several replies, none of them helpful. Raborn said, 'So it's true then?'

I let out a breath, and smiled at him. 'Actually, I'm fucking' – I pointed to Nicky and he stepped forward – 'and' – I pointed at Domino, who moved up to join Nicky. 'I forget anyone?' I asked gazing down the line.

Most of them shook their heads, faces very serious. Bobby Lee just stared at Raborn; it was not a good look, or rather it was a very good look if your sense of self-preservation was low.

'See, Raborn, I'm only fucking two of them. Does that make you feel any better?'

He blushed, except the color spread past his hairline and didn't stay red. He was turning a sort of purple. Either it was the darkest blush I'd ever seen, or he was just that angry. Either way, the reaction was sweet and insulting.

'Any other questions?' I asked him.

He glared at me, and then Clark's voice came from behind us. I guess she'd finished her phone call and opened the door quietly enough that Raborn and I didn't hear her. 'Marshal Raborn, I need you to drive to Oregon for me, right now.'

He glanced back at her, and then moved so he could keep an eye on both her and us, which meant he wasn't as stupid as he seemed. 'We have a serial killer in Seattle and you're sending me on some trumped-up errand?'

'As your superior I'm telling you that you are driving to the far side of Oregon today; if you question my orders again, I'll find something for you to do on the far side of Alaska, is that clear?'

'Why?'

'Because I'm tired of your attitude and because I can. One more word and I promise you that you will be seeing so much real estate that by the time you drive back this case will be over.'

He closed his mouth tight, lips thinned with anger. The flush that had been fading began to darken again. If it was blood pressure, eventually he was going to stroke out if he didn't learn to control himself. He just nodded.

She handed him a piece of paper. 'This is where I want you to drive and what I want you to pick up for me.'

His eyes barely flickered over it before he turned on his heel and marched off. I think he didn't trust himself to keep quiet if he stayed near us all.

Clark looked at me and Edward, but finally settled on me. 'Bringing in lovers as deputies won't help your reputation, Blake.'

I sighed. 'I know, Marshal Clark, but neither of them is just a pretty package. They'll be an asset to the case, or we wouldn't have flown them in.'

'They better be more than a booty call, Blake. No offense, gentlemen.'

'None taken,' Nicky said.

Domino just looked at her.

It was her turn to sigh. 'Prove to me that they're more than just pretty, or muscle. Prove to me that they can help us catch these things.'

'Things?' I made it a question.

'Whatever is killing the weretigers isn't human. Whatever injured Marshal Karlton wasn't human either. What my marshals chased in the woods with you was sure as hell not human. We have a body in the morgue that is charred halfway between human and animal form. Nothing on this case is human, so until I have another word for them, they're things, perps, monsters. Now get out there and do something useful.' She went back into her office, and we started moving down the hallway like we had a purpose.

'Raborn is going to be trouble,' Lisandro said.

'He'll try,' I said.

'How do we stop him?' Domino asked.

Edward said, 'Execute the warrant; be so good at the job that he can't come back at Anita.'

'The job is to kill . . .' Ares hesitated, trying not to say *the Harlequin*. 'The killers, right?'

'Yep,' I said.

Ares smiled, a flash of teeth in his delicate face. 'We'll be good at the job.'

The rest of them just nodded. I realized in that moment we were a pack, a pride, we were a unit. We were – us. And for the first time since I understood that it was the Harlequin killing the weretigers, I felt . . . hopeful.

29

Edward was at my right as we walked across the parking lot. Nicky came up on my left. His fingertips brushed mine. I had time to squeeze his fingers before Edward said, 'We've got company.'

Nicky dropped back a step like a good bodyguard. I knew without looking that Domino was at my back; I could feel him like heat behind me. I was aware of the other men the way I was aware of my surroundings, or men in general, but not the way I was with the other two; they were mine in ways the others were not.

Marshal Newman was leaning against our rental car. He had a nice, noticeable bandage on his forehead. He looked a little pale in the sunlight, so that the few freckles he had stood out against his skin. I hadn't noticed them last night, or was it two nights ago? I honestly didn't know what day it was. Newman's short brown hair looked as if he hadn't bothered to comb it since he got out of the hospital. He leaned that tall, lanky body on the side of the rental and watched us.

When we were close enough, Edward called out, 'How's the head?' He was back to his happy Ted voice like a new person was walking around in his skin. I was used to it, but sometimes it still creeped me.

'Fine,' Newman said, pushing himself to his feet.

We let it go at that, but Edward and I both knew Newman

wasn't fine. He was functioning, he was well enough to work, but his head probably ached like a son of a bitch. We'd all have given the same answer. He was fine.

'But Karlton isn't,' he said.

It took me a moment to realize that the last thing I'd heard about Laila Karlton had been waiting to hear back from the tests. 'They told me she was going to pull through just fine,' I said.

Newman nodded. 'Physically she's well.'

'Ah,' I said, and I looked down for a moment gathering my thoughts. 'So she's positive for lycanthropy.'

'Yeah,' Newman said.

'What kind?' I asked.

He looked startled. 'Does it matter?'

I nodded. 'Yeah.'

Some of the men around me said, 'Oh, yeah . . . Very much.'

Newman looked around at the men. 'So you guys really are all lycanthropes?'

'They are,' I said, and Newman looked back at me.

'I didn't ask what kind of lycanthrope she's going to be; I didn't know it would matter that much.'

'It matters for a lot of reasons,' I said.

It was Socrates who stepped up and asked, 'I heard about what happened to the marshal. How is she taking the news?'

Newman looked at the other man and just shook his head.

'How bad?' Socrates asked.

Newman's hands clenched around the hat he was still carrying. 'I think if her family weren't here she'd eat her gun.'

'Shit,' I said. I looked at Edward. 'What's the plan now that we have backup?'

'We go back to the last place they attacked us and use one of your friends here to track them.'

'You mean use them like I got to use werewolves to track that one serial killer in St Louis?' It had worked so well, I'd hoped that it would become more standard for police around the country. I mean, it was like having a tracking dog that could talk to you, but the prejudice against shapeshifters was too deeply ingrained. You could bring a shifter to a crime scene, but you couldn't bring them in animal form, and in human form their noses weren't much better at tracking than a normal human being.

He nodded.

'Cool, but the odds of actually finding them close enough to track are pretty remote after all this time,' I said.

'They are, but it's still a plan.'

'I don't have a better idea,' I said. I thought about it and then said, 'You take some of the men with you, track the bad guys. If you actually find a workable trail, call me.'

'Why won't you be with us?'

'I'm going to the hospital to talk to Karlton. I need to let her know that her life isn't over.'

Edward moved me a little away from Newman so we could talk privately. 'Since when do you have to hold the other marshals' hands?'

'Since Micah became the head of the Furry Coalition, and I saw what a difference it can make to have another shapeshifter to talk to when you first find out. Having someone on the other side say, "Look, I've got it and I'm doing okay." It helps.'

'You feel responsible for what happened to her,' he said.

I shrugged. 'A little, but I know it will help to talk to me and some of the guards.'

He studied my face. 'I don't like splitting up.'

'Me either, but I'll have good men with me, and so will you. I'll check on Olaf, too. I didn't mean to break him.'

'I didn't think he'd try you, and that was my fault.'

'What made him feel the need to try his luck with me like that? It was worse than last time.'

'I think it was the rumors about all the men, and that you're as fast and strong as a lycanthrope.'

'A combination of boyfriend and work jealousy,' I said.

'Yes.'

I shook my head. 'Has he decided that I'm not his little serial killer pinup now?'

'I don't know.'

I rolled my eyes at him. 'Great, just what we needed on this case.'

'Olaf came into town asking about the rumors of new men in your life. He asked specifically about Cynric.'

'Why especially Sin?' I asked.

Edward looked at me. 'Sin?'

'He's seventeen, and Cynric sucks as a name for a teenager.'

'But Sin?' Edward asked.

I shrugged again. 'If he were a different kind of kid he'd be a pale person in black, writing death poetry. I'm not real happy with the nickname either. But what is it about Cynric that bothers Olaf?'

'I think it's the age.'

'Because he's a teenager, or the age difference between him and me?'

Edward said, 'Your guess is as good as mine. He wouldn't talk about it, but he asked more questions about Cynric. He wanted to know if the rumor that you'd moved a teenage boy in with you as a lover was true.'

'He asked it like that?' I asked.

Edward seemed to think about it, and then nodded. 'He asked, "Is it true Anita has a teenage boy living with her?" I said it was, and then he asked, "Is he truly her lover?" Again, I said yes.'

'Has he ever asked about any other specific lovers before?' I asked.

'No, just if you had as many lovers as the rumors say you do; to that, I said, no one could be fucking that many men.'

'You didn't want to tell him how many men I was sleeping with,' I said.

'Part of Olaf's hatred of women comes from thinking they're all manipulative whores. You weren't having sex with anyone when he met you, so that helped him not have issues with you.

I thought it was probably good to leave numbers of lovers vague.'

I couldn't really argue with his reasoning, but . . . 'Do you think I've gone over some magic line in Olaf's mind? Am I not his girlfriend anymore, but just another whore that he'll want to kidnap, torture, rape, and kill?'

Edward took off his sunglasses and rubbed his eyes with finger and thumb. He shook his head. 'I don't know, Anita, honestly I just don't know.'

'Well, crap, that could complicate things,' I said.

'And you broke his wrist, so he's going to be trying to prove that you're not better at this job than he is; almost any man would.'

'I didn't mean to make it worse, Edward.'

'I know.' He looked at me, his blue eyes pale and tired under the shade of his cowboy hat. I still couldn't get used to the fact that 'Ted' wore a cowboy hat and Edward didn't. Edward didn't like hats. He put his sunglasses at the back of his shirt, rather than the front. They were less in the way for shooting back there.

'What do you want me to do about him?'

'Hell, Anita, I don't know. If he's decided you're just another whore, then you can never, ever work with him again. And he may try to go after you for real.'

'You mean make me one of his victims,' I said.

'Yes.'

We looked at each other. 'So I don't check on him at the hospital when I talk to Karlton?'

He shook his head, took off his hat, and ran his hands through his hair. He put the hat back on and moved it until it was back at the same comfortable angle it started at. He was being Ted more than himself the last few years; maybe Edward liked hats, too, now?

'I don't like you being at the hospital at all with Olaf there, Anita.'

'You're not asking me to skip the talk with Karlton, are you?'

He shook his head. 'I know better.'

'Because I can't let fear of Olaf prevent me from doing my job.'

'Holding Karlton's hand isn't your job, Anita.'

'No, but I don't want Micah in this city with the Harle—shit, *them* here. He'd be a hostage, or a target.'

'Agreed,' Edward said.

'Then that leaves me to do it.'

'I know you'll be careful.'

'Like a virgin on her wedding night,' I said.

He smiled, but it left his blue eyes untouched. He reached back and unhooked his sunglasses from the back of his shirt. He slid the glasses over his eyes so I couldn't see how cold and unhappy they were. 'I don't want to kill Olaf until after he's helped us catch these bastards.'

It was perfectly him to say he didn't want to kill him until after, not that he didn't want to kill Olaf, but just not now, not before the big man had been useful on the case.

'You do your bleeding-heart routine for Karlton. I'll try to send Newman with you, and you try to leave both of them at the hospital.'

'He wasn't useless in the woods, Edward.'

'No, but he's new, fresh out of training, which means he won't bend the rules like we do.'

'No one bends the rules like we do,' I said.

'Not true, a lot of the old-time marshals do it.'

I thought about it and nodded. 'Fair enough.'

'If you count Bernardo and Olaf with us, then no one is as ruthless about bending the rules than we are,' he said.

I grinned. 'I'll include them.'

He smiled again. I wondered if his eyes were smiling behind the dark glasses. 'I'll go try to track the big, bad vampires while you waste time at the hospital.' He started walking away from me.

'Edward,' I said.

He spoke without turning around. 'Sorry, I'm sorry, but until

I know what Olaf's intentions are toward you, Anita, I don't like you away from me.'

I touched his arm, made him look at me. 'Are you really more frightened by the idea of Olaf kidnapping me than the . . . Those Who Shan't Be Named?'

He took in a lot of air, let it out slow, and then nodded.

'They'll try to let the Wicked Bitch of the World possess my body, Edward. I'll be worse than dead.'

'But they won't torture you first, and I trust you to be strong enough psychically that you'll still be in there, which means we might be able to get you back. If Olaf takes you, Anita, there won't be anything left to save. You have no idea what he does to his victims.'

'And you do?' I asked.

He nodded. He looked pale through his summer tan.

'You've seen it in person?'

He nodded, again. 'We'd finished a job, and we were all celebrating. We'd gone to a brothel, and I didn't know Olaf's rule that he waits until after a job to indulge.'

'What happened?' I asked.

'Another customer was drunk and went in the wrong room, and started screaming. The sound stopped abruptly. All of us who weren't drunk came out of our rooms, armed; you just knew the sound of screams being cut off like that.'

'Yeah,' I said.

'The man who had screamed was dead in the doorway. The girl was tied to the bed.'

'She was dead?' I asked.

'No.' He said it softly.

I gave him wide eyes.

'We thought she was dead, but she wasn't. I wished she were dead when we found them. I would have killed him, but he was standing there pointing a gun at me, at all of us. He bargained with us.'

'Bargained how?'

'We could all die, or we could we all live. We lived.'

'Why would you ever work with him again after that?' I asked.

'There aren't that many people as good as I am, Anita. He's one of them. Besides, part of the bargain was that he'd never indulge himself again, if he was working with me.'

'So you made a deal to dance with the devil to keep him from killing more women?'

'Yes.'

'Was Bernardo there?'

'No, he's never seen Olaf's work in person. He'd never work with him again if he had.'

'Because he spooks easier than you do,' I said.

'Easier than either of us,' Edward said.

I took the compliment. 'What do you want me to do?'

'If you even suspect that Olaf has decided you're his next victim, kill him. Don't wait for a clean shot, don't wait to be sure, don't wait for no witness, don't wait at all, just kill him. Promise me, Anita.' He reached out and grabbed my arm, holding tight. 'Promise me.'

I could see my reflection in his dark glasses. I said the only thing I could say: 'I promise.'

30

Laila Karlton looked small in the hospital bed. Her face was very round and with her hair around her face in tight waves, she looked five, an earnest, sad five. The looking small and young could have been because the three men on either side of her were big guys. All three were at least six-four and built big and solid. The two younger men were muscular and fit, their barrel chests fitting into trim waists. The older of the younger men had a flat stomach that promised a real six-pack under the T-shirt. The younger one was softer in every way; though he hit the gym, he didn't hit it as hard as his brother did. The oldest man looked like a slightly aged version of the younger men. It had to be Karlton's father and football-playing brothers.

Once I saw the mountain of men in the room, I was glad that I'd left Nicky and Lisandro out in the hallway. Socrates and I were enough to add to the crowd.

'Anita,' Laila said, and her large brown eyes were suddenly shinier, as if tears were threatening. Jesus, all I'd done was come into the room.

'Hey, Laila,' I said, and went toward the bed.

'This is my dad and my brothers.'

'I remember you talking about them, and you vastly under-estimated how damn big they all are.' That made everyone smile, which was what I'd hoped for, but I honestly did feel a little dwarfed by the three men. One at a time, fine, but all three were like a crowd of buildings that moved and held out their hands as Laila introduced us.

Her father was Wade Karlton, the older brother was Robert, and the younger was Emmet. Laila called him Em, immediately, as if his whole name were M, but Robert she always called by his full name.

'And this is Russell Jones,' I said, motioning Socrates forward from where he'd waited by the door. Russell was his real name, not the nickname he'd been given when he joined the werehyena group in St Louis. Their Oba, or leader, gave them names, usually from Greek philosophers or mythological characters. A lot of animal groups had naming conventions for some reason.

Everyone shook hands, but Laila looked a question at me. 'Russell used to be a cop,' I said.

She looked from him to me. 'Used to be?'

'Until a gangbanger turned out to be a shapeshifter and cut me up.'

She gave him wide eyes, and again there was that shimmer of unshed tears. 'You're a . . .' She just stopped.

'Shapeshifter,' he finished for her.

I felt the three men around me tense, as if his saying it out loud either made it more real or made them feel insecure. They were big guys, used to being big, strong guys, but though Socrates was inches smaller in both height and shoulder width, he was suddenly someone they had to take into account. Shapeshifter meant that you couldn't just look at him and get a good sense of his physical capabilities. Size wasn't everything now; it was probably not a thought the Karlton men had to think very often. And then I felt something in their posture, something that made me glance up to see their faces. They looked angry, and the younger brother couldn't hide that there was fear underneath that anger.

'Jesus, people, you act like Russell is going to shift on the spot and go on a rampage.'

The brothers looked at me and were a little embarrassed, but the father kept his anger and his cool. 'It's nothing personal to Mr Jones, but he is contaminated with something that turns him into an animal.' I was beginning to realize where some of the problems were coming from for Laila.

I smiled at him. 'Mr Karlton, may I speak with you out in the hallway?'

He looked at Socrates. 'I'm not comfortable leaving my children with Mr Jones.'

'Mr Jones works with me,' I said. 'He's here to help me catch the person who hurt Laila.'

'It takes a monster to catch a monster,' Wade Karlton said.

'Daddy,' Laila said, 'he's just like me. He's a cop who got attacked on the job. Do you think I'm a monster, too?'

Wade turned and looked at her, his face stricken. 'No, baby, I'd never think that about you.'

'Yes, you do, you won't even hold my hand.'

He reached out toward her but stopped in midmotion. The pain showed on his face, but he couldn't make himself touch his daughter. The younger brother, Em, took her hand in both of his, holding her hand up against his body. He glared at his father. His eyes were shiny now, too.

Robert, the older brother, laid his hand on her leg under the sheets, because that was what he could reach. He wouldn't look at anyone, and I caught the shine of tears as he turned away.

'Mr Karlton, you need to talk with me out in the hall, now. Russell will talk to Laila.'

'I can't leave my boys with him.'

That was it, I'd been nice. 'Your boys, as if Laila isn't your girl anymore. She's not dead, Mr Karlton, she's just a shapeshifter. She won't even change until next month's full moon. She's still your daughter. She's still everything she ever was.'

'But not a US Marshal.' This from Laila.

I turned and looked at her. The first tear trickled down her cheek. 'They're gonna take my badge.'

'Did they say that?' I asked.

She frowned a little. 'No, but you know the rules.'

'For regular cops, yes, but for the preternatural branch of the service, they're a little more flexible.'

'You don't change shape, Anita, that's why they haven't taken yours.'

'Maybe, but I know that until you shift they absolutely cannot take your badge, not without a fight.'

She looked at me. Her younger brother was looking at me now. Robert was wiping at his face with his free hand, the other still on his sister; I think he was too emotional to look at anyone just then.

'You're a shapeshifter, too?' Em asked.

'No, but I carry lycanthropy. My blood tests come back with it, I just don't shift.'

'You'll shift,' Wade said, 'you all do.'

'I've been like this for two years now. I carry it, it helps me heal, be stronger, but I don't change shape.'

'Can Laila not change shape?' Em asked.

I shrugged. 'She probably will, but until the week of her first full moon she won't be a danger to anyone.'

'You don't know that,' Wade said.

I looked up at him, and it was good that I'd had lots of practice staring way up at very tall people and being tough while I did it. I let him see the anger in my eyes, because I was angry with him. He was making a terrible situation even worse for his daughter. Fathers weren't supposed to make things worse.

'I do know that,' I said. 'I've lived with two shapeshifters for years now.'

'They gave it to you,' he said, and his tone made it sound liked the bubonic plague or AIDS.

'No, they didn't. I actually got cut up by a bad guy and a shapeshifter who waded into a fight to save me. The bad guy didn't mean to contaminate me, he meant to kill me.'

Socrates came up behind me, and I got to see Wade Karlton flinch a little. 'My sister felt the same way you do when I got hurt. I haven't seen my nephews, or her, in five years. Mama and the rest of us miss them.'

Wade looked at Socrates. 'You mean you miss your family.'

'No, Mama invited me to the first Thanksgiving after I was hurt. When my sister saw me, she took her kids and left, said she'd never be there if I was there. Said I wasn't safe, said I was an animal. Mama takes a dim view of anyone badmouthing her children, so I see my family every holiday. I'm the oldest of five. I've seen every nephew and niece as a newborn, and been at all the birthday parties, ball games, school plays that I can manage. My one sister stopped coming because she thought I'd be there. Then two years ago her oldest got involved with a gang, and I went down there and helped get him out of it, because gang-bangers are just as scared of wereanimals as you are. I made sure the boy got himself straightened out. Last semester he was on the honor roll and it looks like he's got a shot at a football scholarship to a good college.'

Wade looked at Socrates, and I couldn't quite read the look, but apparently Socrates could, because he said, 'His father was bigger than me, built more like your boys and you.' Socrates grinned, sudden and happy in his dark face. 'I've seen defensive lines just give up, once he hits them just once.'

'You play ball in high school?'

'In high school. I wasn't big enough or good enough for college ball, but John is; he's what his father could have been if he'd had someone to keep him out of the gangs.'

'You knew his father?'

Socrates nodded. 'Went to high school with him, but the gangs and the drugs got him.'

The two men looked at each other. I just tried to be quiet and invisible between them, because this moment wasn't about me, it was just them.

'I coach a city school; we lose a lot of kids.'

'Too many,' Socrates said.

'Does your nephew play locally?'

'No, they're in Detroit.'

'What's his name?'

Socrates told him.

It was Em who said, 'I know him. We were at football camp together. He was the only guy as big as me, and as fast.'

Wade nodded. 'I remember him. What schools is he being scouted by?' And just like that, they started talking football, and there was no more us vs. them, it was just guys and sports. I'd never been so happy to listen to people talk about sports in my life.

Socrates moved Wade and Em off to one side to talk football and colleges. Robert moved up and took Laila's hand. I came to the other side and put my hand over hers where it lay on the sheets. She looked a little startled. We didn't know each other that well.

'I don't wanna go steady or anything,' I said, 'but I want you to know that there's nothing wrong with you. You're good, Laila.'

She shook her head, and moved her hand so she could hold my hand. The tears began to trickle down her face. 'I'm not good. I'm going to lose my badge.'

'I told you, they can't take it yet.'

'But they will.'

'Maybe,' I said, 'probably. I won't lie to you; if you keep your badge you'll be the first full lycanthrope to ever manage it, but right now you are a US Marshal of the preternatural branch, and thanks to having lycanthropy you're healed, right?'

She nodded. 'They kept me because they're trying to talk me into a government safe house where I won't be a danger to others.'

'Bullshit on the safe houses. They're about to lose a Supreme Court decision this year, for unlawful detainment among other things. You're not a danger to others, Laila.'

Her voice squeezed down, and she said, 'I will be.'

I shook her hand, made her look at me. 'Yeah, for the first few months, or even the first couple of years near the full moon you'll need your pack to make sure you're in a safe place, but that's part of what they do for new members.'

'My pack?'

'Your animal group. What flavor of wereanimal are you?' I asked.

'Flavor?' She blinked up at me, still crying.

'Kind of animal?'

'Wolf. I'm a werewolf.' She said it like she didn't quite believe it yet.

'Then *pack* is the right word. Different animal groups have different words for the group.'

'I know some of that from class,' she said.

'Yeah, you'll have a step up because you've studied werewolves.'

'Their crimes,' she said, and started crying again.

Her brother patted her arm while he was still holding her hand. He looked at me as if to say, *Do something*. I was strangely used to large, athletic men looking to me to fix things.

I shook her hand again, and when she didn't look up, I said, 'Laila, look at me.' She still didn't. 'Marshal Laila Karlton, look at me!' Maybe it was using the title, but she finally did what I wanted, and looked up at me with so much pain in her eyes, so much loss.

I had to swallow hard and realized there were tears underneath somewhere in me, too. There are always tears. 'Do you want to catch the man who did this to you?'

She frowned, and then nodded.

I held her hand tight for another moment, then let go and gave her the stern look she needed. 'Then get up, get dressed, get your gear, and let's go catch the bastard.'

'I can't . . .'

'You were stabbed four times, but thanks to the lycanthropy you're well. Hospital beds are for sick people; you're not sick.

Get the fuck up, get dressed, and help us catch the monster that tried to kill you.'

She looked startled.

Mr Karlton behind me said, 'Language,' as if it were automatic.

I didn't apologize, as earlier had been about him and Socrates, and now was about Laila and me. 'Do you want to catch the guy that did this to you?'

'Yes,' she said, her voice a little breathy.

'Then get up and let's do it.'

She looked at me, startled almost, and then the ghost of a smile touched her face. 'You mean it?'

'Hell yes, I mean it. Get dressed, we've got bad guys to catch.'

She grinned at me, sudden and wonderful with the tears still wet on her cheeks. Robert caught my attention across the bed, still holding his sister's hand. He mouthed, *Thank you.*

Some days it's not about catching the bad guys. Some days it's about helping the good guys feel better. It had taken me a few years to realize that the second part of the job was every bit as important as the first.

31

Socrates stayed with Laila to explain to her and her family what it might mean for her to be a werewolf. I went to get her clean clothes from the motel. Nicky was at my back and we were within sight of the big outer doors when someone called, 'Anita.' I knew that voice.

'Damn it,' I said under my breath, and turned around to see Olaf. He was striding toward me with Bernardo hurrying to catch up. There probably weren't many people that made six-foot-one Bernardo have to trot to keep up. The nurses watched Bernardo openly, admiring the view as he went past. They watched Olaf with sideways eye flicks, as if afraid to stare. Some of the looks were nervous – he was a very big guy – and some were the kind a woman gives an attractive man, just a little less bold than with Bernardo, as if even though they had no words for it, they sensed something different about Olaf. If they only knew his idea of sex, they'd have been running the other way, but like most serial killers he didn't look like a monster most of the time. He had that predator energy toned way down as he came toward us. He also had a bright blue wrist cast on his right arm. Fuck.

Nicky and Lisandro moved to either side of me, and a little ahead. It was to give us all room to maneuver and to put them first in line if it was a fight. They were my bodyguards in their day jobs, but hiding behind Edward was one thing; hiding behind anyone else might be enough to make Olaf put me in the girl box, and once he thought of me as just another girl who needed men to protect her, I would become just another potential victim in his eyes.

I did what I had to do: I stepped in front of them. Nicky didn't argue, just stepped back and let me lead. Domino hesitated, but with Nicky moved back, I was up even with him, so it was good enough. I wasn't cowering behind either of them.

But Lisandro saw what I'd done, and he gave me that extra step in front. He and Nicky were secure in their manhood; they'd let me stand in front, because neither of them had anything left to prove to anyone. I liked that about both of them.

I wasn't so sure of the big man standing in front of us. He should have been as secure as they were, but he wasn't. It wasn't just being a shapeshifter that made them secure, or Olaf insecure. I stood there staring at the big man, and knew if he'd really been my friend there were questions I'd have asked him, but we weren't friends. Real friends trust that you won't kidnap, torture, and rape them, and I really didn't know that about Olaf. It put a real crimp in the idea of being buddies with him.

Bernardo had caught up, and said, his words a little too fast, 'Is someone else in the hospital?' He was standing so he faced us both but was still vaguely in the middle of us, without actually crossing that line.

'We're here visiting Marshal Karlton,' I said, but kept my attention on Olaf.

'The one that's got lycanthropy,' Bernardo said.

'Yeah,' I said.

Olaf just stared at me with those dark deep-set eyes like two caves in his face, with a glimmer in his eyes like a distant light in the dark.

'How's she dealing with losing her badge?' Bernardo asked, and there was a hint that he really cared about that question.

All the preternatural branch marshals lived with the idea that we could be next. When you hunted shapeshifters, death was just one of the things you risked.

'They can't technically take her badge yet,' I said.

Bernardo frowned. 'Most marshals give it up when they come back positive.'

'But they don't have to,' I said.

It was Olaf who said, 'You told her to come hunting with us.' His voice was lower than normal, a rumbling in his chest, as if some emotion were dragging his voice down.

'Yep,' I said, and fought the urge to put my hand nearer any of my weapons. He hadn't done a damn thing to threaten me. He was just standing there, looking at me. For him, it wasn't even a bad look, just intense.

'I do not want another woman on this hunt, only you.'

'It's not your call who comes. The warrants are mine and Edward's. He's got Newman with him now.'

'The boy has to learn,' Olaf said, 'but the girl will be a were-wolf in a month's time. Training her is a waste of effort.'

He was right, as far as it went. 'She needs this, Otto,' I said, remembering just in time that his official name was Otto Jefferies. Marshal Otto Jefferies.

'She will slow us down,' he said. He kept staring at me, but it was eye contact. I couldn't accuse him of staring at my breasts or anything. I normally like eye contact, I give great eye contact, but there was something about Olaf's attention that made holding his gaze feel like work, as if his eyes were weight that I had to hold up just to stay standing there. If he'd been a vampire I'd have accused him of doing some vampire mind shit that I hadn't heard of, but it wasn't that. It was just him. Just the weight of his personality and our growing shared history. Shit.

'Maybe, but she's still coming.'

'Why?' he asked, and I think it was a real question. A real attempt to understand what I was doing and why, so it deserved a real answer.

'This has really shaken her confidence, and she feels like a monster already. Her father wouldn't even touch her hand, as if just that would contaminate him.' I shook my head and didn't try to keep the anger off my face.

'Why do you care about her? She is a stranger to you.'

'I'm not sure I can explain it to you,' I said.

'Once I would have thought you meant I was too stupid to understand, but I know you do not think me stupid.'

'No,' I said, 'I never think that.'

'Then explain to me why you care.'

'We're supposed to take care of each other, Otto.' I spread my hands wide, almost a shrug, showing that I just didn't know how to say it better than that.

'If they are an asset in the field, you want them healthy so they can give you backup. That is common sense, but the new marshal will not be helpful. She is traumatized, and that slows most people down. She will make bad decisions.'

'You don't know that,' I said.

He gave an arrogant smile. 'I do know that.'

'You don't know Karlton. You don't what she'll be like in the field now.'

'She is a woman. She will be weak.'

I suddenly had no trouble meeting his eyes, at all. Anger makes so many things easier. 'Do I point out the obvious?' I asked.

'If you like,' he said.

'It wasn't a man who broke your wrist.'

Bernardo stepped a little more between us, so we both looked at him. 'Let's take this outside.'

'Why?' I asked.

He leaned in close enough that his long, straight hair spilled up against mine. I had a whiff of expensive cologne, something spiced and musky, but just a hint, not too much, and you had to be close to notice it. Unlike some men who seemed to bathe in it. No matter how nice the cologne, if the man put too much on it smelled horrible; Bernardo didn't smell horrible.

He whispered, 'What you just said doesn't match the story we told the emergency room staff.'

Oh. Out loud I said, 'Sorry, yeah, let's take it outside.'

We all moved for the big doors and the outside world. A woman in a white coat with her short brown hair in a tiny pony-tail got my attention. It took me a second to recognize her from when I got stitched up. She was one of the interns. I couldn't think of anything she needed from me, but I stopped like you're supposed to; I was girl enough not to keep walking.

The men stopped with me, waiting. She seemed a little flustered at that, and motioned me away from them. I wondered if she was going to ask me more questions about my healing abilities, or even ask to see the wound. I'd had other medical professionals ask to see injuries that they'd helped treat.

She was only a little taller than me, maybe five-five, though I glanced down as she leaned in, and saw she was wearing at least two-inch heels on her low boots.

'Marshal Forrester had a wife and family, but how about the other marshals with you?'

I didn't try to explain that he wasn't legally married to Donna. They'd been living together longer than Micah, Nathaniel, and me, and only a couple of years less than Jean-Claude and I had been dating.

'The one with his hair back in a ponytail is married with kids.' I hesitated about Nicky. Technically he was free to sleep with other women. I wasn't monogamous, so it seemed unfair to make him cleave only unto me, but he was here to feed the *ardeur* and guard my back, so I said, 'The blond is with me.'

'Lucky you,' she said.

I smiled automatically. 'Thanks. To my knowledge neither Marshal Spotted-Horse nor Marshal Jefferies has a girlfriend.' Then I realized I was talking to a petite dark-haired woman. The hair was a little less dark than he preferred, but she was close enough to his victim profile for me to think of it. If I thought of it, so might he. Crap.

'Oh, sorry, Marshal Jefferies, the tall guy, is involved with someone. It's new, I keep forgetting.'

'How new?' she asked.

I smiled. 'Trust me, what was your name again?'

'Reed, Patience Reed.'

I crooked an eyebrow at that.

She laughed, and it was a good laugh, happy, light. She seemed younger just from the sound of it. 'I know it's a terrible name for a doctor.' She rolled her eyes, and again I thought, young, innocent. So, had to keep her away from Olaf.

I smiled, and pushed it all the way up into my eyes, so she wouldn't see me worry. 'Patience is pretty funny for a doctor. Anyway, Olaf is pretty serious about the new woman in his life, but Bernardo is free and clear for dating.'

'Bernardo, is that his name?' She looked behind me as she said it, and I was pretty sure without turning around that she was looking at him.

'Yep, Bernardo Spotted-Horse.'

'He's Native American?' she asked.

'Yep.'

She looked away hastily and blushed just a touch. I was betting that Bernardo had favored her with one of his killer smiles. The one that made the drive-through girl tell him what time she got off work.

Patience Reed said, 'He's almost too beautiful to ask out.'

'You should ask him out,' I said.

'You think he'd go out for coffee, or drinks?'

I nodded. 'I don't know if any of us are going to have time to socialize much, but you should give him your number or something. We might have some down time, you never know.'

'Oh, I couldn't just ask him like that.' Then her eyes narrowed at something behind me. It made me glance back to find a couple of nurses talking to Bernardo. He was smiling and talking to them.

'I'd give him your number before they do,' I said.

Patience began to walk very purposefully toward the growing crowd. She moved up to join the circle around Bernardo. The hesitation was gone as she pushed her way through the now three other women. Lisandro was fending off an admirer by raising his left hand and showing off his wedding ring, which meant she'd gotten pushy. God she was fast, from zero to making him flash the wedding band in less than five minutes.

Nicky was against the other wall being charming with a blonde pretty enough that even I thought words like *beautiful*. She was a little short on curves, but when they're almost six feet tall a lot of women seem to lose curves, as if it all goes to those long, long legs. I was almost sure the blond curls spilling over her pale blue scrubs were her natural color. I was betting on blue eyes to match the scrubs.

Nicky turned as I came closer. One minute he was smiling and flirting with the blonde and the next he was focused on me. He wasn't rude, and even introduced us. 'Anita, this is Michelle.'

I smiled and did my best to be friendly. She didn't disappoint me on the eyes, flashing big, soft blue ones at me, but the look in the eyes wasn't soft. She'd had all his attention, or so she thought, and then I walk up, and it was like the sun turning away to shine on someone else. I knew Nicky could be charming. He'd told me once that his ability to flirt had helped him do better undercover work, and even get information from women by seduction. Pillow talk was supposed to be very good for gathering intelligence. Most of the time he didn't bother flirting with the female shapeshifters and vampires at home. He'd explained that he could have fuck buddies among them, but they all knew he was mine, and he preferred me to them. Harsh, but now I saw it for myself. Even I had thought he was genuinely interested in the blonde. Had he been, or had it all been an act?

He smiled at me, and though we didn't touch each other, not even to take hands, we were just together. I wasn't sure how to explain it, but one minute he was giving off signals that he was available and the next he was aware of me and he was just no longer on the market. The blonde's eyes flicked from one to the other of us. She had a moment of letting it show on her face that she wasn't used to losing out to other women once she'd started trying for a man.

I smiled, not quite sure how to react. I tried to keep it friendly, but it was as if she felt cheated somehow. Nicky had been giving all the signs of flirting and saying yes to at least coffee, if not more, and then it was suddenly turned off, gone, and he made his allegiance to me very clear. He'd flirt, he might even do more if he got the chance and I was okay with it, but he was mine. There were other women who would have been angry about him flirting, and maybe I would have been a little jealous if he'd kept flirting, but he'd reacted instantly to me, and made it clear, subtly, that he wasn't really on the market. He was window shopping, when she wanted to buy.

Nathaniel, Jean-Claude, Asher, Dev, Jason, and Crispin all flirted more and even better than Nicky, but all of them but Jason did the same thing that Nicky did. Jason was just a close friend with benefits and had a steady girlfriend in another state, so it was good he didn't react that way. He wasn't mine. The fact that Damian did react that way was one of the bones of contention between him, me, and his steady in-town girlfriend, Cardinal. She hated me just a little because of it, and I didn't entirely blame her.

I totally did blame the blonde, Michelle, for disliking me so instantly. She'd talked to him for a few minutes; that was too quick to get possessive, but I'd noticed it with other strangers. I'd seen it before with Jean-Claude and Nathaniel and women at the clubs, but I'd thought it was because they were just both so damn beautiful. Nicky was handsome, yummy, but either I didn't see him the way others did, or it wasn't the level of pretty of the man in the situation but something else I was missing completely. I shrugged and let it go. So a strange woman was jealous that Nicky liked me better, not my problem.

Then I realized that we were a man down. Where was Olaf?

32

Olaf was outside, under a little covered area to one side of the hospital entrance. He was talking to a woman who was shorter than I was, in pink hospital scrubs. Her black hair curled over the shoulders of all that pink. Olaf was smiling, bending over so he could hear what she was saying. Whatever she said, it made him laugh. I'd never seen him laugh. It was a little unnerving, like seeing your dog sit up and try to hold a conversation with you. I mean, you know the dog communicates, but it's not supposed to speak the queen's English. I knew there had to be laughter in Olaf somewhere, but not this soft, smiling face. It changed his face, filled it with lines that seemed almost – kind. Either he really liked this woman, or he was a better actor than Edward.

He looked over her head at me, and for just a moment he let the laughter slip away. He let me see in those cavernous eyes that he did like her, he liked her lots, but not in a good way. He let me see in that strangely handsome face that he was thinking about her not without her clothes on, but eventually without her skin. He let me see the darkness in his eyes for a blink or two, and then the woman touched his arm, made him look back down at her. I realized that with the height difference she hadn't seen his eyes, hadn't seen what he'd shown me. Fuck.

She spared a glance back at us, as if wondering what had attracted his attention. She had that expression on her face that let me know she was looking at me as a potential rival, doing that girl thing that some women do of assessing who's the prettiest, who's a threat. Whatever she'd decided about me made her move just a bit closer to him and lay her small hand on his arm. She was marking territory. If I reacted badly, she'd know I was interested in him, too.

Olaf laid his big hand over hers, pressing it to his arm, and smiled down at her. The frightening look was gone, washed away in a terribly normal flirting. Shit.

'I thought he wasn't allowed to hunt anything but monsters on the job,' Nicky said.

'He's not,' I said.

'Then you better do something, because he's shopping for a victim.'

I sighed. 'Shit.' I moved toward them with Nicky at my back. The doors whooshed open behind us and Lisandro came hurrying up behind us. 'Anita, please don't do that again.'

I kept moving toward Olaf and the woman as I said, 'Do what?'

'Leave me alone with a beautiful woman who is obviously trying to pick me up.'

'You're a big boy,' I said. 'I thought you could handle it.'

'If I fall off the wagon again, my wife will divorce my ass. Help me avoid the temptation.'

I would have said it was ironic, his turning to me for help in avoiding the temptation of sex with other women, but we were up with Olaf and the woman. There wasn't time to worry about Lisandro's lack of logic.

Olaf looked at us, still smiling, the pleasant mask hiding everything but the faintest flash in his eyes. If you didn't know what you were looking at, you'd miss it, and how many women would be looking for serial killer sex in anyone's eyes?

The woman touched his arm again, but he didn't put his hand over hers this time. She noticed the lack of touch and looked at us all. She frowned at me, but seeing my US Marshal's jacket she both relaxed and frowned harder. Her hand tightened just a little, squeezing his arm. 'Do you have to go to work?'

'I told you I was here to hunt monsters.' He smiled while he said it, and lifted her hand off his arm, gently. He held her hand for a moment, lingering. 'This is Marshal Anita Blake and her deputies.'

The 'deputies' part wasn't exactly true, but it wasn't untrue either, so I ignored it and moved on. 'Hey,' I said, 'sorry, Marshal Jefferies, but we have to go hunt bad guys now.'

'So you just work together,' the woman said, her hand still in his. She seemed to take encouragement from the fact that he was still holding her hand.

I nodded, but he said, 'Only because she refuses to date me.'

The woman glanced back at him as if to see if he was kidding her. He kept his face very carefully full of wry humor, an expression I'd never seen on his face and a set of emotions that I didn't think he ever felt.

'Then she's a fool,' she said, and put her arm around his waist, and he cuddled her against him, tucking her up under his arm. She couldn't see his face anymore, and the charming humor was just gone; one minute he was a flirting man, the next he was Olaf. He let me see in his eyes, his face, that he wasn't thinking anything safe, sane, or consensual. He let the monster show in his face with no hiding. It stopped the breath in my throat, made me hesitate between one step and the next so that I almost stumbled. That one raw look let me know that Olaf hadn't changed at all; if anything he'd been hiding more from me.

Nicky touched my arm and kept me moving, whispering, 'Don't let him spook you; that's what he wants.'

I nodded and kept walking. He dropped his hand away and let me walk on my own, but he stayed beside me now. Lisandro trailed us both.

'We need to rejoin Marshal Forrester and the others now, Otto,' I said; my voice was calm, very calm, trailing down to that emptiness where it would have almost no inflection at all. I was one step away from going to that empty staticky place in my head where I used to go when I killed people. Lately, I didn't have to disassociate to pull the trigger. That probably should have worried me, but it didn't. Olaf worried me. One monster at a time, even if one of them is yourself.

'Time to go, Marshal Jefferies,' I said, my voice that low, careful, empty sound.

He was still holding the woman's hand. 'She wants to date me.'

She was looking from one to the other of us. 'Is something going on between you two?'

In unison, he said, 'Yes,' and I said, 'No.'

She tried to pull her hand out of his, but he held on. Without looking at her, he said, 'She has refused every offer from me.' He looked at the woman, and he dredged up one of those pretend smiles again.

She looked a little hesitant, and looked at me. 'You're not his ex-girlfriend?'

I shook my head. 'No.'

She smiled up at him. 'Great.' She even put her other hand on his arm, so she was holding on to him twice. It was sort of the girl version of the double-arm squeeze that some men use on women, except the guys always seemed aggressive and the woman just seemed like a victim clinging to his arm, or maybe the victim analogy was because I knew what he was.

'No,' I said, shaking my head, 'no.'

'You had your chance,' the woman said.

'What's your name?' I asked.

She looked unsure, but said, 'Karen, Karen Velazquez.'

'It won't help,' Olaf said.

'What won't help?' she asked.

'Giving him a name to personalize you,' I said.

'What?' Karen Velazquez asked, and she dropped the second hand from his arm.

Bernardo called out behind us. 'Hey, Otto, got a call for you from Forrester. You turn your phone off again?' His voice was all cheerful, and normal. It lay on the tension between us like oil on water. It covered, but it didn't change anything.

Bernardo kept walking up to us, as if the tension weren't thick enough to walk on. He was smiling and pleasant and again he stood halfway between us, but not exactly between us.

'We're supposed to join up with everybody. They found a clue.'

Edward would have called me first, I was ninety-nine percent certain of that, but I appreciated Bernardo trying to help get the woman away from Olaf. I didn't really think he'd hurt her here and now, but if he made a date with her there was only one kind of date that Olaf wanted from a woman. One with blood and death and things done that couldn't be repeated unless you liked the dead, and I had Olaf pegged for wanting his victims alive enough to feel pain or it was no fun.

Olaf raised Karen Velasquez's hand up and laid a kiss on it, but stared at me while he did it. She didn't seem to notice, just smiled, and was almost flustered in how pleased it made her.

'You are quite lovely, and I am eager to see you later.'

She nodded, grinning. 'Call me.'

He smiled. 'I will contact you.'

Bernardo said, 'Now, let's all go to the cars. Bad guys to catch.' He made a shooing gesture at all of us, and we began to go for the parking lot. The nurse called after Olaf, 'Call me.'

He waved at her, but his face was already emptying of that good humor and flirting. By the time we got to the cars his face was its usual self except for the new beard.

I took a breath, but Bernardo beat me to it. 'You know the deal, Olaf. If you do your hobby on American soil you lose everything. Your badge, both your jobs, everything, and Edward will kill you, so really everything.'

'He will try to kill me,' Olaf said.

I ignored the last comment, because Olaf had to make it, just like I'd have had to make it. We couldn't let anyone, not even

Edward, think he was automatically better. But the details of Olaf's deal were new to me. 'So, more people than just you, me, and Edward know what he is?'

'A few,' Bernardo said, 'but it all hinges on him not doing his serial killer thing here.'

I looked at Olaf. 'You must be really good at something for them to look the other way about the rest.'

'I am very good at many things.' He delivered the words almost flat; if it had been another man I think he'd have made it flirty, but Olaf didn't waste flirting on anyone but his victims, apparently. If he liked you for real, you got the real deal. Normally I preferred that in my men, but since the real deal was a sexually sadistic serial killer it was sort of a mixed blessing. Flattering, since I was pretty sure it was the most he'd ever shown himself to any woman, and scary as hell all at the same time. Flattering and frightening; that was Olaf all over.

'I believe that,' I said, and meant it.

'Do you?' He looked at me, and he seemed to truly be studying me, or trying to.

'Yes,' I said.

'It bothered you to see me with the woman.'

'You let me see in your face what you wanted to do to her, Olaf; of course that would bother me.'

'That bothered all of us,' Bernardo said.

Olaf looked up and I thought he was looking at Bernardo until he said, 'It didn't bother you, did it, Nick?'

'No,' Nicky said.

I turned and looked at Nicky, standing right beside me, face peaceful as it usually was. 'Do the two of you know each other?'

'Sort of,' Nicky said.

'Yes,' Olaf said.

I looked from one to the other of them. 'All right, talk to me. How do you know each other?'

Olaf said, 'I think we might wish to have the other men step away.'

'Why?' I asked.

'Plausible deniability,' Nicky said.

'What?' I asked.

Bernardo patted Lisandro on the shoulder. 'Let's give them some privacy.'

Lisandro looked from one to the other of us, and finally looked just at me. 'You tell me to give you some room and I'll do it, but only because Nicky is here. I won't leave you alone with Marshal Jefferies.'

Olaf gave Lisandro a long look. 'You will do what Anita tells you to do. I've seen it.'

Lisandro shook his head. 'I've seen you, too. I won't leave Anita alone with you, even if she orders me to.'

I started to say something, and Lisandro just turned to me and shook his head. 'We've all agreed, Anita, you don't get left with him.'

'And I have no say in it,' I said.

'No,' he said.

'He does not respect you,' Olaf said.

'I respect Anita, but you' – he pointed at the bigger man – 'you are not allowed to be alone with our boss.'

'If Anita truly leads, then it is up to her who is alone with her.'

'No, not on this,' Lisandro said.

Olaf looked at me. 'Will you let him rule you?'

The question was a trap. If I said any man 'ruled' me, it could turn me from serial killer girlfriend to serial killer victim for Olaf. As uncomfortable as it was for him to think of me as a girlfriend, it was a lot better than just being meat for him. I did not want to change categories in Olaf's twisted little fantasies.

'Lisandro doesn't rule me, no one does, but if you hadn't noticed, Edward doesn't leave us alone either.'

Olaf frowned. 'But if you wanted to be alone with me, he would allow it.'

'Oh, I got this one,' Bernardo said. He did that odd almost stepping between us again. We both looked at him. He said, 'No,

Edward won't. He's given me orders that if I let the two of you go off alone and something bad happens, he'll kill me.' He smiled while he said it, but it never reached his eyes. He was so not happy about it.

'You aren't responsible for me, Bernardo,' I said.

'I know that, but it doesn't matter, Edward meant it.'

'I'll talk to him,' I said.

He shrugged. 'You can try, but if the big guy here actually kills you, once Edward kills him, then we're all dead. Me, because he said he'd do it, and the rest of the men because they were your bodyguards and they failed. He'll kill us all, Anita, so do us a favor, stay alive; okay?'

I didn't know what to say to that. 'I'm a big girl. I can take care of myself.'

'Yep, you can,' Bernardo said, 'but Edward's grief if you die will be a terrible thing. It will hurt him, a lot, and men like him make sure they never grieve alone. He will spread his grief all over us, not because we failed, but because it'll give him something to focus on so he doesn't have to feel the pain.'

'What are you talking about?'

'If he blames all the men you brought with you and has to kill them all, plus me, it'll take time to kill us all, and there's always a chance we'll kill him before he gets us all. I'm good at staying alive and killing things, and the men with you are pretty damn good, too; it's a tall order even for Edward with us knowing he's coming.'

Nicky said, 'So, killing us all will give him a goal, things to do, so he doesn't have to feel.'

'Yeah,' Bernardo said.

'You've given this a lot of thought,' I said.

'When someone like Edward tells you that he'll kill you, you give it a lot of thought.'

I couldn't really argue with that.

'It's also a way to risk suicide without the suicide,' Nicky said.

'I think so,' Bernardo said.

'I don't think I'm important enough to Edward for all that. He wouldn't risk leaving Donna and the kids.'

'He'll do exactly what I just said, Anita. In the front of his head, no, that's not what he's thinking, but trust me, Anita, if you get dead, especially if he blames himself in any way, he will be a force of destruction looking for a place to be aimed. And he's blamed himself for introducing you to Olaf here from the get-go. If Olaf did to you what he's done to some of his other victims, Edward would drown the world in blood to try to erase those images.'

I didn't know what to say, but I wanted to protest. I wanted to say he was wrong, but a part of me asked, *What would I do if it were Edward tortured to death and I thought it was my fault?* I wouldn't kill tons of people, but anyone I thought was responsible for it – they'd be dead. I had more rules than Edward did, so if I felt that way about him, how much more would he do if it were me dead? Especially at Olaf's not-so-tender mercies? I didn't want Nicky and the boys dead, and I'd talk to Edward about that, and Bernardo. They didn't deserve that, but Olaf dead at Edward's hands, oh, hell yes. The thought that Edward would probably kill him slowly was like a warm, happy thought.

'I'll talk to him about you, all of you. I wouldn't want anyone else hurt just because I wasn't here.'

'You can talk to him,' Bernardo said, 'but it won't help. I've known Edward for years. I've seen him do things that he wouldn't do in front of you. Trust me; I'd rather have almost anyone else after my ass.'

Again, I didn't know what to say, so I just agreed. 'I wouldn't want Edward gunning for me, either.'

'All that, and you're going to concentrate on just that part?' Bernardo said.

I looked at him and shrugged. 'What else do you want me to say?'

'God, you really are a guy, I mean you look like a girl, but that is such a guy thing. You ignore all the emotional shit and grab onto that Edward is dangerous. Shit, Anita.'

'Are you always this much of a pussy?' Nicky said.

Bernardo glared at him and set his shoulders, moving slightly forward. People think that fights begin with frowns, or shouts, but they don't. They begin in much smaller body cues, the human version of dogs raising their hackles, but the dogs know what it means, and so do most men.

Nicky smiled, which was another way to egg the other man on. It was escalating the fight without most women realizing what he'd done, but I wasn't most women.

'Nicky,' I said, 'don't.'

He looked at me, his face trying for innocent and failing.

Bernardo moved a little closer, and I stepped between them. 'We are not fighting over stupid shit,' I said.

'You're not my boss, not yet,' Bernardo said.

'I don't know what you mean by the whole "not yet" comment, but I do know we are not wasting time having a pissing contest.'

'Bernardo's new,' Lisandro said. 'You haven't told Nicky that he can't fight him for real, and Nicky's been spoiling for a real fight for a while.'

'I don't know what you mean by a real fight. Nicky spars with the rest of the guards.'

'Sparring isn't real,' Lisandro said.

I turned and looked at Nicky. 'What have I missed?'

'Don't know what you mean,' Nicky said.

'Why would you want to fight Bernardo for real?'

Nicky just looked at me.

'Answer my question, Nicky.'

He frowned, sighed, and answered, because he had to; if I made it a direct question he had no choice but to answer me. 'I don't hurt people now because no one's paying me to do it, and you've told me I'm not allowed to kill anyone who belongs to you even if they start the fight. You've got some very tough people working for you. I could kill them, but if I can't kill them, they could hurt me, badly, so I don't fight.'

'You spar,' I said.

He looked out past the cars, as if he were counting to ten. 'It's not the same thing, Anita. It's so not the same thing.'

'Are you saying that you want to fight Bernardo so you can hurt or kill him?'

'I want to hurt someone, yeah.' His big hands folded into fists and a tightness ran across his shoulders and upper body like a coiled spring waiting for the switch to release all that pent-up power.

'Why?' I asked.

Nicky gave me a look that wasn't friendly. It was the look you see sometimes in the zoo from the beasts behind the bars. No matter how much land they have to run in, how many toys they have to play with, there's always one big cat that seems to remember running free, and knows no matter how big the cage is, it's still a cage, and he wants out. Nicky's lion filled his one good eye with amber, and then he blinked and it was back to his human color, but I knew it had been there, his lion peeking out from the cage that I'd forged for it; a cage that it, and Nicky, resented. How had I not seen it? I hadn't wanted to see it, hadn't wanted to understand that no matter how tame he seemed, Nicky was still the sociopath that I'd met a year ago. I hadn't changed him; I'd just broken him to my will. Crap.

Nicky hung his head enough that the long triangle of bangs spilled forward from his face, so that the scars over the other eye socket showed stark in the sunlight. He didn't actually like to show the scars much, so I knew he was just too upset to care. His entire body posture had changed, no longer belligerent, no longer violence waiting to happen, but something softer.

'You feel bad now, and I can feel it. You're a little sad. I know you feel bad for what you did to me, Anita. I don't want you to feel bad.' He raised his face and looked at me. There was something of pain in his face, a frowning effort to understand what he was feeling.

I reached out to him, and he moved closer so I could touch his face. He nestled his cheek against my small hand, and he let out a breath; something hard and unpleasant went out of him. He was my Nicky again, or what I'd begun to think of as mine. He pressed his hand against mine, pressing it closer against his face. 'God,' he whispered.

'That was creepy,' Bernardo said.

'You have tamed him like a pet cat,' Olaf said.

Nicky and I both turned to him, and the tension was just back in Nicky. His beast vibrated like heat down my hand and arm. He kept my hand pressed to his face as he glared at Olaf. It's hard to be tough when you're cuddling, but it didn't seem to occur to Nicky to let go of me, or maybe the desire to be near me was stronger than his desire to look tough?

'I heard you had reformed Nick, a good woman reforming a bad man, but it's not that at all. Nick had to make you feel better. He could not abide you being even a little sad.' Olaf looked at me, and there was something I'd never seen on his face before, a soft horror.

'Do the two of you know each other?' I asked again.

Nicky moved my hand from his face and held it. I wondered, had it bothered him that I hadn't touched him more when he first got to town? He was looking at Olaf; even as he began to rub his thumb across my knuckles, he was staring at the other man.

'*Of* each other, yes,' Nicky said.

'What does that mean?' I asked.

'It means,' Olaf said, 'that we know each other's work. Jacob's pride of werelions had a reputation in some circles for handling things that other mercenaries would not attempt. They were as good as their reputation until they came up against you, Anita.'

I wondered how much Olaf actually knew about what Nicky's people had tried to do last summer, and how badly they'd failed.

'Did you truly kill Silas with a blade?' Olaf asked, and that said he knew some real details.

Truth was I'd only hurt him with a blade, and then he'd knocked me unconscious and damn near killed me. I'd gotten another chance at him with a blade only after he got shot by somebody else. I don't know how much I would have shared, but Nicky answered for me. 'Yeah, she did.'

'Silas was good with a blade. That you killed him with one is impressive,' Olaf said.

I squeezed Nicky's hand; he squeezed back. Was he telling me to just agree? 'It wasn't as easy as it sounds,' I said. Nicky squeezed my hand again, and that was yes, enough. He didn't want me to overshare with Olaf. Probably the smart thing to do, so I did it; I could be taught.

'Then it must have been difficult indeed, because I worked once with Silas before he joined Jacob's lions. He would not have been an easy kill before he became a werelion. You are better than you have shown me.'

'Didn't Anita just break your wrist? How much better does she have to show you?' Lisandro said.

Olaf moved his head to look at the other man. He just looked at him, but apparently it was his signature cave-deep look. Lisandro gave him cold eyes back, and it was a stare that would have given a lot of people pause, but Olaf wasn't most people, and neither was Lisandro. 'Save the scary stares for the civilians.'

Someone's phone began to go off. It took me a few seconds to realize it was mine. The song was 'Bad to the Bone' by George Thorogood. I'd managed to figure out how to get the song 'Wild Boys' off as my main ring tone, but Nathaniel had chosen a lot of individual ring tones; I hadn't caught them all yet. Nicky didn't seem to want to let go of my hand so I could get the phone. That answered the question about whether it had bothered him that he hadn't had more attention when I first saw him.

'Yeah,' I said, when I finally answered the phone; I admit it was something of a snarl.

'Anita?' It was Edward's voice, but he made my name a question.

'Yeah, I'm here, I mean, it's me. What's up?'

'Is everything all right on your end?'

'Yes, yes, what's up?'

'Did you run into Jefferies at the emergency room?' he asked.

'Olaf has a wrist cast, but it's not really him that's causing the problem.' I walked away from the other men. Nicky trailed me. I started to tell him not to, but I wasn't sure if he and the other guards had decided I wasn't allowed to be alone, and I didn't want to argue, I just wanted to talk to Edward.

When the only person who could hear was Nicky, I spoke to Edward. 'Olaf was flirting with a nurse at the hospital. She's petite, long, dark hair, just his type.'

'She looks like you,' Nicky said. He moved closer to me, his broad shoulders probably hiding me from the view of the others.

I glanced up at him, and he was actually too close, so I had to step back a touch to focus on his face. 'No, she didn't,' I said.

'No, she didn't what?' Edward asked.

'Nicky says the nurse looked like me. I disagree.'

'Did Bernardo think she looked like you?' Edward asked.

'I don't know.'

Nicky moved close again, putting his hand on my shoulder. I started to move away from him, but two things stopped me. First, he seemed to need to touch me. Second, I'd almost totally ignored him when he got to town. Third, it felt good for his hand to be on my shoulder. It was like that with almost everyone who was tied to me metaphysically; it felt good to touch and be touched.

'If Bernardo says she looks like you, then she does.'

'I don't know what Bernardo thinks about it, but we already knew I fit his victim profile,' I said.

'You fit it, but not absolutely; if he was flirting with a nurse that looks a lot like you, Anita, that could mean things. Bad things.'

'It isn't good that he's looking to date a woman at all, Edward.' Nicky put his hand on my other shoulder. I stayed stiff for a moment, and then let myself sink in against the front of his body. The moment he felt me relax in against him, he relaxed even more, folding his big arms across my shoulders, going all the way across the front of my body. He could have wrapped me around a second time with all that muscle. I put my free hand over one of his arms, sliding it over the swell of his muscles.

'I don't give a damn about some stranger, Anita. Either he's flirting with this woman to see if it bothers you, or he's trying to find a substitute because you won't date him.'

'We can't let him date anyone, Edward. He doesn't date, he tortures and kills.' I rested my face against Nicky's arm, wishing that his jacket weren't in the way. It was leather, and a new jacket that I'd bought him to fit over the extra inches of muscles he'd put on since moving in with us, but even the soft leather wasn't as good as bare flesh would have been to me in that moment. Now that I'd given in to touching him, I wanted more skin contact; it was part of the problem with giving in to touching him at all, that once I started I didn't want to stop. Touching Domino would have been the same; almost anyone I had a metaphysical tie to would have been the same. I wondered if Ethan would affect me like that eventually, and I him.

'He says he's willing to date you,' Edward said.

'I know he wants to hurt me, Edward.'

'I don't mean date you like that.'

'You mean a date-date like dinner and a movie?' I asked.

'I don't know about dinner and a movie, but he would try something more normal than his usual.'

'He said that to you?'

'Yes.'

'I don't see you and Olaf sitting around and talking about girls.'

'I made sure he and I were clear on what he meant by dating you before I'd let him come as backup for me, Anita.'

'So what did he tell you?'

'He'd be willing to have vanilla sex with you.'

I tried to stand away from Nicky, but he curved his taller body over me, so I could stand more upright but he could still wrap himself around me. It felt warm and safe to have his arms around me, so good to have my body against the front of his, held so close. Close enough that I could feel the front of his body begin to swell. Sex had been part of the 'magic' that I'd used to bind Nicky to me, to steal his free will. He and his lion pride of mercenaries had kidnapped me and had been threatening to kill three of the men I loved. They'd almost killed me, and in the end they'd stripped me of every power I had except for one. I'd used that one power to make Nicky betray everyone and everything, so he'd help me save myself and the men I loved. Until Nicky I hadn't understood what I was doing, or what it would mean to the person I was doing it to, but with Nicky I hadn't been innocent. I let him hold me, not just because it felt good for him to do it, but because I did feel bad about what I'd done to him. Yes, he'd been a very bad man, but no one deserved to be mind-fucked until there was nothing left, not even a sociopath.

'Anita,' Edward said.

'Are you seriously saying you want me to have sex with Olaf? You can't be serious.'

Nicky tightened his arms around me, laying a kiss on the top of my head. I began to smooth my hand back and forth on his arm, outlining the muscles under the leather of his jacket.

'Do I want you to have sex with him? No.'

'Then what are you talking about?'

'I don't know.'

'You don't know, what does that mean? You always know what you mean.'

Nicky kissed my hair again. He tucked his body in tighter against mine, and just the feel of his body so hard, so thick against my ass, caught my breath in my throat, made me shiver against him, which made him wrap himself tighter around me, which made all the sensations more intense, which . . . 'Edward, sorry, just give me a minute.' I put the phone against my stomach and asked, 'Nicky, room, I need a little room. It's too distracting.'

'What's too distracting?' He whispered it against my hair and pressed himself a little tighter against the back of my body, giving a slight flex of his hips that made me have to try to step away from his body. He tried to hold on to me, tried to keep himself pressed against me, but I said, 'Let me go, Nicky.' And just like that he had to let me go, because I'd told him to do it.

I grabbed his hand in mine, and that small gesture earned me a smile that filled his face with such joy. It was so wrong that he reacted like that to me; you should only act like that around people you love. Nicky didn't love me, not in a way that should have brightened his face like that from a simple hand holding.

I put the phone back to my ear and tried to ignore Nicky and his too-happy face. 'I'm back, Edward.'

'You seem distracted, Anita. We have the . . . people that are killing the weretigers, and Olaf. You cannot be distracted and deal with either of them.'

'I'm on top of it, Edward.'

'Are you?'

Nicky pulled on my hand, drawing me a little closer. I moved my body to one side so that he couldn't draw us completely together. I couldn't afford to be distracted again so soon.

'Look, we're on our way to get fresh clothes for Karlton. Once she's suited up we'll join you in the field.'

'No, there's nothing out here. Your wererat trailed them to the edge of the woods and then nothing. We think they either flew or had a car waiting.'

'So the brilliant idea to use wereanimals to track the killers isn't so brilliant.'

Nicky moved closer to me. I kept the side of my body to the front of his. He leaned over and laid his face against the top of my head, resting against my hair as if it were a pillow.

'It was a good idea, Anita, and when we get a fresher crime scene we'll try again.'

'You're right, they'll kill again.'

'They will,' he agreed.

'I hate the idea of having to wait for another crime scene before we catch a break. It's like we want someone else to be killed.'

Nicky moved his head to lay a kiss against my hair.

'We'll meet you back at the motel while you're getting Karlton's clothes. You need to get rooms for the rest of your deputies.'

I leaned my forehead against Nicky's chest. 'How's Bobby Lee doing?' I asked, because I knew he was the one who'd shapeshifted to try to scent out the bad guys.

'He's passed out in the back of the car.'

'So he's already shapeshifted back to human form,' I said. Nicky put his arm across my back, trying to draw me in against his body again.

'Yes.'

I was out of hands to keep our bodies apart, so I turned my shoulder into his chest. His arm tried to turn me so that the fronts of our bodies would touch. I turned my body more firmly sideways to him. 'He'll be unconscious for at least four hours,' I said.

'Six to eight hours,' Edward said.

'Nope, Bobby Lee is a more powerful shapeshifter than that. He'll be four hours or less and then he'll wake.'

'Good to know.'

'Some of the other people with us don't have to pass out at all when they change form.' I was cuddling with one of them right that minute.

'That makes them very strong shapeshifters.'

'Yep,' I said. I let myself put my arm around Nicky's waist, and he tried to draw us into a complete hug, but I kept my body sideways, so that though we were hugging and the strong warmth of him wrapped around me, it wasn't as distracting as it could have been.

'You travel with some very big dogs, Anita.'

'I'm a big-dog sort of person,' I said. I looked up into Nicky's face. He kissed me on the forehead, lips so gentle.

'What are you doing, Anita?'

'Talking to you.'

'Your voice keeps changing, going soft.'

Nicky kissed my eyebrow, ever so gently. 'I'm not whispering, Edward.'

'I didn't say you were whispering. I said your voice keeps going soft, gentle. I didn't think Lisandro or Nicky had that effect on you.'

'Lisandro doesn't,' I said. Nicky kissed my eyelid, brushed his lips back and forth over my eyelashes. I raised my face up to him. He kissed my cheek, his breath hot against my skin.

'If Nicky distracts you this much, then you need to be careful, Anita.'

'I'll be careful,' I said, and it was almost a whisper, because Nicky's lips were just above mine.

'We'll see you at the motel, Anita,' Edward said.

'See you,' I whispered and hit the button so that when Nicky's lips touched mine I wasn't on the phone anymore. He kissed me. He kissed me gently at first, and then his arm tightened around me and I turned in his arms, against his body. We stopped holding hands and I finally let myself melt into his arms, his body, and his kiss. He kissed me hard and thoroughly, with lips, tongue, and finally teeth. He bit my lower lip, lightly. It drew a small sound from me, so that he bit a little harder, drawing my lip out and away.

I had to say, 'Enough.'

He let go of my lip, drawing back so he could see my face. He laughed when he looked down at me. 'We forgot your lipstick.'

I blinked at him, and realized he had red lipstick across his lips, and his smile showed lipstick on his teeth. I shook my head smiling, and reached up to touch his lips, trying to rub the scarlet off his mouth.

He laughed a low chuckle. 'Yours is worse.' He put his thumb under my lower lip and rubbed at the lipstick I couldn't see.

'I don't usually forget the lipstick,' I said, but I was laughing.

'You did miss me,' he said, and he looked entirely too pleased.

Lisandro called out, 'We can't keep him back forever.'

Nicky and I looked back at the other men. Lisandro and Bernardo were both in front of Olaf. Bernardo had his hands on Olaf's upper body, literally holding him back. Olaf wasn't trying to get past him very hard, but Bernardo's hands were definitely reminding Olaf to stay where he was, and Lisandro stood there like a sort of secondary defense in case Olaf really did try to get past Bernardo.

But it was the look on Olaf's face that was frightening. Rage was plain on his face, so much rage. 'He's jealous,' Nicky said.

'Yeah,' I said.

'He's more jealous of me.' I moved away from him, wondering if that would soften some of the emotion on Olaf's face. Nicky reached out, took my hand. 'Don't let him bully you, Anita. He'll take as much control of your life as you let him.'

I let Nicky keep my hand in his now, because he was right. I couldn't let Olaf's weird jealousy control me. What I didn't understand was why he was reacting so badly to Nicky, or had Olaf just reached another level of obsession with me, so that any interaction I had with other men was going to drive him nuts? That would be bad, but if it was just Nicky, then that was a different kind of bad.

I had no idea how to talk Olaf down from what I saw as an insane and undeserved jealousy. He wasn't my lover, wasn't a boyfriend, wasn't even my friend. He had no right to the anger on his face, no right to feel possessive of me, but how do you convince a seven-foot-tall psychopath serial killer that you're not his love bunny without him trying to kill you, or you having to kill him? I had no idea.

33

Bernardo split us up; he took Olaf, leaving Lisandro to drive Nicky and me. We managed to get into the cars and head to the motel without Olaf losing what was left of his control. In fact, he just suddenly went icily and completely calm. The total change in effect was more chilling than anything else he could have done, because the change of heart couldn't be real. It was like he'd taken all that rage and just locked it away, but I knew it was still in there. It was still in there and it would find a way out, and that way would be frightening.

Lisandro drove. I started to get in back with Nicky, but Lisandro said, 'Anita, sit up front with me.'

'Why?' I asked.

'You and Nicky got pretty distracted back there. It's part of what got the big guy so upset. He wanted to break you guys up.'

'Stop us from kissing, or hurt us?' I asked.

'I don't think Bernardo was sure which he meant to do; that's why he stopped him.'

'I appreciate you and Bernardo interceding for us,' I said.

'It was my job, and Bernardo is more afraid of Edward than he is of Olaf.'

'Thanks all the same,' I said.

'Just ride up front, that's thanks enough,' he said.

'Anita can sit in back with me,' Nicky said.

'I'm not driving around while the two of you make out,' he said.

'We're not getting in the back to make out, Lisandro.'

He just looked at me. 'So why does it matter if you ride up front?'

I opened my mouth, and then closed it. Why did it matter? Nicky brushed his fingers against mine, and it just seemed natural to fold my hand around his. I felt better, steadier. Ah, that was why it mattered. Could I promise that we wouldn't make out in the back seat? I thought I could. Could I promise we wouldn't touch each other? No, and why would it matter? What was so wrong with us touching each other? I shook my head. 'I'll sit up front.'

Nicky squeezed my hand. 'You're the boss, not him.'

'Yeah, but I can't promise him we won't let the touching get out of hand, Nicky. He's right about that.' I searched his face, and the only thing I saw there was need, almost hunger. This was the longest I'd ever been away from Nicky since he came to St Louis. I thought about it; was this the longest I'd ever been away from home since Jean-Claude and I had been dating? I stood there holding Nicky's hand and feeling it like an anchor in all this mess. If it had been Jean-Claude, or Micah, holding my hand, how much worse would the draw have been? Was I more than homesick? Was it more than just not feeding the *ardeur* that had caused the tree limb to hurt me so badly, and caused me to need sex to heal? Was it literally not being home with Jean-Claude and the other men that was affecting how well I healed?

I stood there holding Nicky's hand and feeling better than I'd felt in days, or was that just my imagination? I wasn't sure, and the fact that I couldn't tell said something, too. Shit.

'I'll sit in front because I want to touch you. It's like I'm more than just hungry for the *ardeur*, it's like the metaphysical tie is making you more touchable than normal.'

'What does that mean?' he asked.

'I don't know, but just let me sit up front and get to the hotel. We'll go from there.'

'I don't understand, Anita.'

'Neither do I,' I said, and we left it at that. But I sat up front with Lisandro, though when Nicky touched my shoulder, I put my hand up to his and we held hands all the way there.

34

Lisandro drove into the parking lot. I said, 'Park in front of the office. I've got to see if they have enough rooms for everyone.'

He didn't argue, just turned in the opposite direction from the rooms. Nicky leaned against the back of my seat, his hand still in mine, but now he could lean his face around the headrest and nuzzle the side of my face. I leaned in against that touch, as if I couldn't help myself, but I said, 'Car's still moving. You need your seatbelt on.'

He spoke low, mouth buried in my hair. 'We're going ten miles an hour, Anita. I'll be fine.'

I fought the urge to tell him to put it on anyway, because I was sort of fanatical about seatbelts staying on until a car came to a complete stop, but Nicky was right. Hell, as a shapeshifter he could go through the windshield full speed and survive. I had a moment to think, if my mother had been a shapeshifter she wouldn't have died when I was eight. I had one of those moments of clarity, and wondered if I dated only preternatural men because they would survive.

Lisandro found a parking space in front of the banked windows of the office area. I had to pull away from Nicky to get out of the car, but the moment we were both free of the car, he took my hand in his. It was my right hand and my main gun hand, but since he was right-handed, too, one of us was going to have to compromise their gun hand. I had to force myself to do what

I normally did automatically, which was to pull my hand out of his, and play a few minutes of who was going to complicate their ability to draw their weapon. I just knew it wasn't going to be me. It was one of the reasons that Nicky and I didn't hold hands much in public, because he was my bodyguard, among other things. The fact that we were both willing to have his right hand occupied, when we were out hunting dangerous things, was another clue that something was wrong with my need to touch and be near my metaphysical men. I promised myself to call Jean-Claude after he woke for the day and see if he had a clue.

But good idea or bad idea, Nicky and I followed Lisandro through the door to the office hand in hand. The moment we stepped inside, the rich, dark scent of coffee was everywhere. I realized I couldn't remember the last time I'd had coffee. How had I let that happen? It had been a busy day, but still . . . The desk clerk who had worried about losing his job at the crime scene turned from the full coffee carafe, smiling. His short, dark brown hair was neatly combed this time, and almost didn't match the oversized superhero T-shirt, jeans, and well-loved jogging shoes, as if his mother did his hair, but he dressed himself.

'Fresh coffee, if you want it?' he said, and pushed his silver-framed glasses up his nose in one of those automatic gestures people with glasses make.

'It smells like real coffee,' I said, pulling Nicky with me toward the tempting scent. Yes, we had bad guys to catch, but even crime fighters need coffee.

He grinned at me. 'Boss says I have to keep coffee in the pot all day. He doesn't say it has to be bad coffee.'

'I like the way you think,' I said.

He set out three cups and started pouring very dark, very rich coffee into them.

'You like coffee,' Lisandro said, from just behind us.

'None for me, thanks,' Nicky said.

The clerk, whose name completely escaped me, stopped in midpour, spilling a tiny bit down the side of the cup. 'Sorry.' He put the pot back on the coffeemaker and reached for napkins and wiped off the side of the second cup. 'I'm just glad some of you are drinking it. I hate wasting good coffee.'

Lisandro and I both took the cups. Nicky went back to being alert, as if someone might jump out of the walls and attack. He was right, though; he and I had to get a handle on whatever was making us be so touchy-feely, or I'd have to send him home. The real test would be if I was as bad around Domino, because he was the only other man from home who had a metaphysical tie to me. If it was both of them, then, well, that would mean something was wrong with the metaphysics, and that would be bad.

I breathed in the scent of the coffee, letting myself close my eyes for a moment and just enjoy it. I could tell by the smell alone that it wouldn't need sugar or cream, it was good just the way it was.

'How can I help you, Marshal?' the clerk said.

I opened my eyes and smiled. 'Sorry, got distracted by the coffee.'

He smiled back and shrugged thin shoulders. 'Glad I could make your day a little better. I'm so sorry about the other marshal getting hurt.'

'Thank you,' I said. 'We're actually here to get clothes from her room to take back to the hospital.'

'So she's okay?'

I shrugged and smiled noncommittally. I doubted the marshal service wanted the media to learn about Karlton being a were-wolf, and I knew Karlton didn't.

Lisandro said, 'We also need rooms.'

I nodded, and he was right to get me back on track. What the hell was wrong with me? I was losing focus in the middle of a case, that wasn't like me. Not to this degree anyway.

The clerk went behind the desk and said, 'How many people, and are they comfortable with sharing rooms?'

I started to answer, but Bernardo and Olaf came into the

office. Olaf was almost too tall for the drop ceiling. I had a moment to wonder how it would feel to be so tall that ceilings were too short. It was so not the problem I had.

'Fresh coffee,' the clerk called out cheerfully as he typed on his keyboard. 'How many rooms do you need?'

I counted in my head while I sipped the coffee. It was as good as it smelled; yum. 'Three, with two beds apiece.'

'Thanks, Ron,' Bernardo called out and went toward the coffee. It made me think better of Bernardo that he knew the clerk's name. If the clerk had been female I'd have expected it, but that he remembered the man's name to be friendly made me wonder if some of the flirting from Bernardo was just a level of social enjoyment that I didn't have with strangers.

'So, room for six,' Ron said, typing on the keyboard.

'Yeah.'

Olaf came to stand near the desk.

Ron gave him a nervous flick of eyes that seemed to take in the top of his bald head that was ever so close to the ceiling tiles. 'Coffee machine is over there.'

'No, thank you,' Olaf said, in that deep rumbling voice.

'He doesn't drink coffee or tea,' I said.

'Good to know,' Ron said, and his effort not to look all the way up to Olaf was almost painful.

'We just drink the blood of our enemies,' Nicky said.

Ron stopped in his typing and looked at Nicky. 'What?'

'He's teasing you,' I said, and glared at Nicky. The glare said, clearly, for him to stop it.

'We have two rooms upstairs near your original rooms, and one downstairs. Is that okay?'

'We need to be close to Anita's room,' Nicky said.

'Anita, oh, you mean Marshal Blake.'

'Yes,' Nicky said.

Ron typed some more. 'I'm sorry, that's the best we have until someone checks out.'

Lisandro was near the door, looking out and drinking the

yummy coffee. Bernardo trailed over to join us. He seemed to be enjoying the coffee, though he'd added enough cream to make it tan, probably added sugar, too. I thought about calling him a pussy, but decided it wasn't worth it, I'd actually started adding cream and sugar to some coffee myself. Never throw stones if you think they're going to come back and hit you.

A wave of dizziness rolled over me. I steadied myself against the desk and Nicky grabbed my arm. 'Are you all right?'

'Dizzy,' I said. My knees began to slide out from under me and the coffee spilled down the side of the desk. Nicky caught me. 'Anita!'

Lisandro collapsed. His empty coffee cup rolled across the floor. I thought, *Oh shit, the coffee*, but I couldn't seem to form the words out loud. I tried to reach for a gun, but I couldn't make my arms move enough. Nicky was holding all my weight in one arm, tucking me against his body, because he had his gun out; so did Olaf.

Bernardo collapsed to the floor with his gun in his hand. The damned coffee spilled about half of a cup into the worn carpet.

Ron, the clerk, was holding his hands out from his body, 'I didn't know—' Olaf shot him in the chest. The shot was like an explosion. I fought to focus through the dizzy, tilting world, and had a moment to see the door behind the desk open black and empty, but somehow I knew it wasn't empty. The black cloak and white mask were clear for a second as it moved in a blur so that it wasn't there when Olaf and Nicky fired.

I heard the bell on the door, and the last thing I saw before the dizziness ate the rest of the world was a blurring wave of black cloaks coming toward us. My last clear thought was, *Please, God, let that be the drug, and not their real speed.*

I heard Nicky yelling my name in the dark.

35

It was cold. Cold and hard. I was lying on something hard and cold, my cheek pressed to the rough chill of it. My hand spasmed and my hands were tied behind my back. My eyes opened wide, pulse shoved into my throat, heart thudding. I could see a darkly stained stone wall. I pulled at the ropes behind my back, but the rope was tight, biting into my wrists when I tugged on it. I moved my legs and realized my ankles were bound together, too. My boots protected my ankles, so the rope didn't bite into the skin, but they were tied just as tight. My heart was threatening to choke me, as if I needed to swallow it back down into my chest. I was so scared my skin ran cold with it, and it had nothing to do with the concrete floor.

I tried to think through the panic. Was there anyone to see me move? Had the movements been small enough that my captors hadn't noticed, or was I alone? There was nothing against the one wall I could see. The wall was water stained, which was probably one of the things that made the floor damp. I forced myself to notice things; there just wasn't a lot to notice. But taking the time to try had slowed my pulse, helped chase back the panic. I was tied up, but I wasn't hurt as far as I could tell. I'd come to in worse places, with lots worse happening to me.

I felt movement behind me. Maybe I heard it, but it was as if the air currents stirred behind me and I just knew that someone was behind me, and that they were close. I fought not to tense more than I already had, but it's almost impossible not to tense when you're tied up and you have no idea who or what is coming up behind you. Being completely helpless makes you tense.

'If you had just come with me and my master, things would have been so much simpler.' The deep growl of voice was the shapeshifter from the motel, the one that had stabbed Karlton and made her a werewolf. So at least I knew his flavor of shifter; that was something, not much, but something.

I swallowed and found my voice. 'Simpler for whom?'

'Whom, you say, whom, when I have you tied up on the floor, helpless.' I heard the brush of cloth now, and small noises that I couldn't have told you what they were exactly, but I'd have bet money that he was crawling on the floor toward me.

I felt the heat of him behind me, before the white mask and hood of his face peered over my shoulder. He leaned over my face so I could see that the eyes in the mask were pale green, and not human. He had wolf eyes in his human face, which might mean that the reason his voice was growly was because he'd spent too much time in animal form, either because he liked it, or because he'd been forced as punishment. The eyes usually changed first, and then the teeth, and then internal mouth and throat changes so the voice stayed deeper.

His eyes were so close to me that I could see the edges of them and knew he was frowning. 'You aren't afraid, and you're thinking something. What are you thinking that has helped you let go of your fear of just a moment before?'

I decided that truth didn't hurt. 'Who kept you in animal shape until your eyes stayed wolf even in human form?'

He growled at me, leaning that smooth, white mask close and closer until I couldn't focus on his green wolf eyes and all I could see was the white blur of the mask. My pulse sped up again; I couldn't help it. I was tied up and helpless, and he was looming over me. I wouldn't have wanted a human to do it, let alone a werewolf, though honestly that wasn't the part that bothered me. It was the white mask, and the speed I'd seen that first night. He was Harlequin, and being at their mercy, that bothered me.

I heard him draw in a deep breath behind the blur of mask. He pressed that smooth porcelain against my cheek and sniffed. 'Now you're afraid; good.'

He curled himself against the back of my body, pressing that cool, artificial face against mine. My vision was filled up with the blur of that white mask. One of his arms snaked across the front of my body, pressing us close together. He was enough taller than me that it was mostly his upper body that pressed so tight against the back of mine.

I fought to control my pulse, my heart rate. He wanted me to be afraid, and anything he wanted I didn't want to give him. My pulse quieted, heart rate going down. He growled in a low, heavy line that vibrated through his chest and neck along my body. It hit that back part of the brain that still remembers huddling around a fire with the night pressing close, and when that growl came out of the dark, you knew that something out there was going to kill you. I couldn't keep my heart from beating faster, couldn't keep it from sending my blood pumping hard and fast through my body. He growled harder, the vibration of it shivering down my spine, warning me that teeth and fangs came next after that sound.

I caught the faint musk of wolf like a half-remembered perfume, he was pressed so close. Something stirred inside me; a white shape rose in the dark of my mind. My wolf stood up inside me and shook her mostly white fur like any canine rising from a long nap.

He went very still beside me, and his voice was even deeper, so full of the growl that he'd been doing that it sounded like it would hurt for a human throat to talk like that. 'What is that?'

'You have a nose,' I said, in a voice that was only a little shaky. 'Use it.'

He drew in a deep rush of air, then let it trickle out slowly, the way some people let wine sit on their tongue. Swallowing the wine slowly, so they catch every nuance of it. My wolf sniffed the air back, as if she were catching his scent, too.

'Wolf; you can't be wolf,' he growled.

'Why not?' I asked, and it was almost a whisper because his face was close enough that much more than a whisper would be shouting.

'She wouldn't want your body if you were a werewolf,' he growled next to my face.

'Why not?' I asked, again.

'She can't control wolves.' I felt him tense. I don't think he was supposed to share that.

'Only cats,' I said.

'Yes.' The growl was beginning to fade a little, and it was more of a bass whisper, as if he didn't want to be overheard. The Harlequin had bugged all our businesses in St Louis once, so we were probably being listened to, if not watched, right this minute.

I did my best not to move my lips, and the whisper this time was more just breathing out. I didn't want them to hear us. 'The mother couldn't control you?' My wolf began to trot up that long, dark path inside me. It was my visual for an impossibility. It was impossible that there were animals inside me that wanted to come out through my skin, but they were still in there, so I 'saw' them as walking down a path, when there was no path, no space between me and them. In a very real way, they were me. Intellectually I knew that; to stay sane I visualized a path.

He sniffed harder, as if he would breathe me into him. He settled more of his body against the back of mine. My hands were in the way, so he couldn't spoon me completely, and he kept his face next to mine, so that the height difference put only his upper body against my hands. He had a long torso. I fought to keep my hands still where they lay pressed between the two of us. Cuddling was better than being threatened; I just had to not rush, and not do anything to make him remember he was here to scare me.

'No,' he whispered, and used his arm to pull me in tighter to his body.

I breathed, 'She forced you into wolf form.'

'She couldn't; my master forced me.'

I pressed my face into the smooth chill of the mask, letting it hide as much of my face as possible in case the camera could see my face. The scent of his wolf was stronger this way; it made my wolf trot faster up that invisible path. The light was better so that I could see her dark saddle in all that white fur, as she trotted through the light and shadow of the tall trees that lined the path. The trees, like the rest of the landscape, were no place I'd ever been.

I breathed in the scent of him, and down the long metaphysical cord, I smelled another wolf, several other wolves. I smelled my pack and they always smelled good to me, of pine trees and thick forest leaves.

He sniffed harder, hugged me tighter. 'You smell of more than just your wolf. You smell like pack. How can that be?'

'I'm the lupa of my pack, the bitch queen.'

He snarled behind his mask, drawing back enough that he could see my face. 'Liar!'

'If you're powerful enough to shift just your claws, you're powerful enough to smell a lie. I am the lupa of our pack; I swear it.'

'But you're human,' he growled, and it was almost a yell.

My wolf broke into an easy lope, almost a run, as if to prove the truth of what I'd said. But there were shadows in the dark around her, not us, as if I had called the ghosts of our pack. Their scents came with me, not the sight, but then for a wolf, smell is more real than sight. It's one of the reasons that wolves aren't bothered by hauntings, unless there's a scent to go with it. You can wail and moan all damn day, but if you don't smell like something, a wolf won't care.

I felt the loneliness in the man beside me. Not a loneliness of sex, or even love, but of not having another furry body to press side to side, tail to nose, as they slept. I'd been told that the *ardeur* was about lust, but my version was more about your heart's desire. What is it that you want, you really want? That part of me that carried the *ardeur* could see all the way through you to the truth. The man holding me didn't want sex, or even human love; he wanted a pack. He wanted to run in the moonlight with others of his kind, and hunt in a pack. No cat, not even a human one, would ever understand his loneliness.

'You're the only wolf,' I whispered.

'We had one other, but he left us.' The regret in his voice was like weeping without the tears.

'I know where he is,' I said. Jake was one of the Harlequin on our side.

'He's with you, we know that,' and this time his voice was a snarl, 'but he left us long before that. He betrayed us.'

'He did what wolves do,' I said. 'He took care of the pack, not just one wolf.'

'Tigers are not wolves!' He grabbed my arms, sat me up, shook me just a little; let me feel the strength in his hands.

'No,' I said, 'but he has wolves in St Louis. He has our pack. He's not alone.'

His fingers dug into my arms. The strength in them vibrated against my skin, as if he were fighting not to dig in farther, or maybe he was fighting not to send claws slicing through my flesh. Some people are grateful when you offer them what they want most, but some people are terrified of it. Because to gain your heart's desire you have to lose some part of your old life, your old self. To do that you have to have courage; without it, you can't make the leap. And if you don't make the leap, you have only three choices: You can hate yourself for not taking the chance, you can hate the person for whom you've sacrificed your happiness, or you can hate the one who offered you happiness, and blame them for your lack of courage, convince yourself it wasn't real. That way, you don't have to hate yourself. It's always easier to blame someone else.

I looked into his green wolf eyes and watched the fight. He growled, 'They said all you offered was sex.'

'They lied,' I said, softly. I let it be implied that maybe they'd lied about other things, too.

He let go of me as if I'd burned him, stood up, and went for the door in a swirl of black cape. He stopped at the door, and spoke without turning around. 'You have defeated me twice, Anita Blake. There is more magic to you than just being a succubus.'

'I never said otherwise.'

He opened the door, went out, and I heard a bolt shoot behind him. I was locked in, and still tied up, but I was sitting up, drug free, and alone. Alone wasn't bad.

36

The room was about the size of an average bedroom, but the walls were all stone, and the floor was concrete that looked like it had been poured too thick and never smoothed, so it had dried in odd shapes. Water stains discolored the wall nearest to where I'd come to, and in one corner the water stains had become a shallow standing puddle. No wonder I'd woken up cold. Were we underground? There was only one dim, bare bulb in the center of the room. The only furniture in the room was a large wooden table that looked solid and heavy, which was probably why it was still in the room; too heavy to take out. I actually looked back at the door and realized that the table must have been put together inside the room; otherwise how had it fit? I stopped trying to do the math of furniture moving, and looked at the only other things in the room: a pile of wooden boxes against the far wall with a stained tarp thrown carelessly over them, as if someone had started to cover them, but never quite finished. There might be something else under the tarp, but I'd have to inchworm my way over there, and I had no way of knowing if it was worth it. Besides, they were watching me. I doubted they would let me get close to anything that could cut through the ropes. I still might try to get closer to the boxes. They were the only thing I could see in the room that had any promise to them. Everything else was useless for cutting through the ropes, as far as I could see. I realized that once I'd have thought the room was dark, but I'd spent the last year and change living in the underground at the Circus of the Damned. The rooms were actually part of the cave system that ran under St Louis, so my idea of dim lighting had changed. My night vision had always been good, but I'd begun to wonder if all the animals I carried inside me had given me more than just superhuman strength and speed. My night vision was getting better.

I heard someone at the door. I hadn't moved anything but my head and body to look around the room, so I just sat there and waited for the door to open. I actually didn't have to scramble to hide anything, which was kind of disappointing.

It was another Harlequin in the black hooded cloak and white mask. He was taller than the werewolf, so someone new, or someone I'd seen briefly in the woods earlier with Edward. I wouldn't let myself hope that he'd save me; I would save myself, but it made me feel better that he was out there. I knew he'd move heaven and earth to find me, because I'd have done the same for him.

'We will need you to drop your shields for the Mother of Us All to possess your body.' His voice was completely human, no growl for him, and he sounded very reasonable, if you didn't listen to what he was saying.

'Then I don't think I want to drop my shields,' I said, and I sounded reasonable, too.

'We thought you might say that.' He turned with a swirl of black cloak, so that it blocked my view of the doorway for a moment. They all had to practice with the cloaks for those effects. When he stepped out of the doorway, letting his cloak fall to one side, three more Harlequin were standing there, carrying a man between them. Two of them held his arms, where they were chained behind his back; the third held his chained legs. Long black hair fell forward in a thick mass to obscure his face. My first thought was, Bernardo, but the energy hit me like a hot wave dancing over my skin: shapeshifter.

My heart was in my throat this time, because nothing good was about to happen. Fuck.

'If you change form we will shoot you,' the tall, reasonably voiced Harlequin said.

Lisandro, because that was who it had to be, made a muffled sound, and I knew before he raised his head and glared at me through the loose mass of his hair that he was gagged. His eyes had already gone from dark brown to black, the beginning of his shifting form.

The reasonable one drew a gun from behind his back.

'Don't!' I said.

'He was warned,' the Harlequin said, and put the gun barrel inches above Lisandro's left knee.

Lisandro glared at me, all that anger, all that energy in his eyes. There was no fear in them.

The Harlequin pulled the trigger and the shot was thunderous in the stone room. The echoes of it hit the walls and bounced everywhere, drowning out most of the sounds that Lisandro made. He didn't scream, but he couldn't be silent while the bullet ripped his knee apart. He also couldn't not struggle while the pain rode him, but the three Harlequin that held him acted as if his writhing were nothing, like they could have held him all night like that. When he quieted, and blood began to drip steadily from his leg onto the floor, the three holding him stared straight ahead like soldiers on parade. Their lack of reaction was almost as unnerving as the shooting.

The talkative Harlequin's voice was tinny, distant with the reverberations of the shot, 'That was a lead bullet; you'll heal almost instantly.' He drew a second gun from behind his back. It made me wonder what kind of holster he was wearing. 'This one has silver bullets in it; I'll cripple you with it, and then I'll kill you with it. We have other hostages, Lisandro. It is such a pretty name for so handsome a man.' The Harlequin looked at me. 'Don't you think he's handsome, Anita?'

'You know our names, what's yours?' I asked.

'We are the Harlequin, that is sufficient.'

'So I call you all Harlequin, like calling all dogs Rover? Come on, you've got to have names.'

'We are the Harlequin,' he repeated.

'Fine, Harley, what do you want?'

'You know Harley is not my name.'

'Tell me your name and I'll use it.'

'The Mother of Us All told us to give you no names.'

'Can't fuck me, can't give me your name, what else has she forbidden you to do with me?'

'I asked if you thought Lisandro was handsome; you ignored the question.'

'Yeah, he's cute. His wife thinks so, too.'

'Does that mean he's not one of your lovers? How disappointing.'

I swallowed hard, and when I looked at Lisandro his brown, human eyes met mine. I think he was thinking the same thing I was: Which answer would help us most? Would they hurt him more if they knew he was a lover, or less? If he wasn't a lover, would they just kill him? They had other hostages; who? Who, for the love of God?

Harley, for lack of a better name, stepped between us so we couldn't make eye contact. 'It is a simple question, Anita. Is he one of your lovers?'

'Honestly, I'm trying to decide what answer will make you the happiest.'

'The truth will make me happiest, Anita.'

I didn't like the way he kept using our first names, as if he knew us. I had never heard the voice, I'd have bet money on it. 'Would you believe yes, and no?'

He moved so I could see Lisandro again, and he put the barrel of one of his guns against his head. 'Perhaps I will simply kill him. I think you would be more cooperative after one of them dies.'

'Don't do it,' I said.

Lisandro told me with his eyes, *Don't do it. Whatever they want, don't do it.* I knew why they'd gagged him, because he'd have said all that out loud.

Harley spoke each word slowly, carefully. 'Is he one-of-your-lovers?' There was anger in each word now, the reasonable tone vanishing in the heat. 'If I smell a lie on you I will kill him, Anita.'

'We had sex once, but out of respect for his wife's wishes we've behaved since then. See, yes, and no, I wasn't lying.' I tried to quiet my pulse, but couldn't quite do it. I was telling the truth, but Harley seemed to want to hurt Lisandro, or maybe he just liked hurting people.

'His wife's wishes, what does that mean?' He still had the gun barrel pressed to the back of Lisandro's head. I did not want to have to watch his brains get blown out. I did not want to tell his wife and kids that I'd watched him die.

'It means that she told him that if he ever cheated on her again she'd leave him, and take the kids, or kill him, and me.'

He rubbed Lisandro's hair with the tip of the gun, almost like he was petting him with it. 'Do you think she meant that?'

'That she'd leave him and take their two kids? Yes.'

'No, Anita, the part about killing him and you. Did she mean that?'

I shrugged as far as I could with my hands bound behind my back. 'I don't know.'

He slid the barrel along the side of Lisandro's face. 'Oh, come, you must have an opinion of the woman.'

'I haven't met her,' I said.

'Interesting,' he said, and slid the gun barrel underneath Lisandro's chin. Lisandro jerked away, but Harley put the barrel more firmly under his chin, and forced his face up, until they could meet each other's gaze. 'Would your wife truly kill you both?'

Lisandro just glared at him.

'Oh, the gag, how silly of me, just nod. If you had sex with Anita again, would your wife kill you both?'

Lisandro just looked at him.

'Answer me, Lisandro.'

'Maybe he doesn't know either,' I said.

Harley looked at me. 'Don't help him.'

'I'm just saying that most married couples I know say things in anger they don't exactly mean, but I know she'll take his kids. He coaches their soccer teams. He wouldn't risk losing his kids.'

Harley used the gun barrel to force Lisandro's head back farther so that the angle of his neck was painful. 'Is that true, Lisandro? Do you value your family?'

This time Lisandro gave a tiny nod, as much as the angle of his neck would allow.

Harley moved the gun and let him put his head down. 'And do you value your bodyguard, Anita?'

Lisandro flashed me his dark, angry eyes again. Again, we were both wondering which answer would help us, and which one would hurt the most.

'He's my bodyguard; he's good at his job. I value anyone who's good at their job.' My words were calm, reasonable; the pulse in my neck didn't agree, but I was afraid of what was going to happen next. I couldn't find my calm on this one.

'Your words are those of an employer, but your fear is that for a friend. He is your lover, and your friend; yes?'

'I make friends easily,' I said.

Harley laughed then, and it was a good, full-chested deep chuckle. Under other circumstances it would have made me smile, at least, but with a gun in each hand, and Lisandro's blood still fresh on the floor, the laugh was unnerving. It didn't match what was happening. It's never good when the bad guy's reactions don't match normal human emotions. It means there's something wrong with them, and that they won't react like you expect. They become a sociopathic wild card. The kind of wild card that can get people hurt, or dead.

'You make friends easily, so we've heard.' His voice still held that edge of humor. 'Put Lisandro on the table.'

The three Harlequin carried him to the table. There was no blood trail from his wounded knee, it had already healed. They lifted him like a piece of luggage and laid him facedown on the table.

'Face up, please,' Harley said.

They flipped him over without a word or a hesitation. They never even exchanged a glance between them. What the hell was wrong with them? The Harlequin in the woods hadn't been like this; they'd been like Harley, like the red tiger Harlequin. Why were these three different?

Harley holstered his guns and came to loom over me. He had to be around six feet tall and from the ground he looked bigger, but they always did. I could see that his eyes were a soft gray. He knelt and picked me up in his arms, gently. He cradled me against his chest. It made me tense, for no reason other than that the gentleness was like the laughter; it didn't match.

But this close to him, I could smell the sweet pungent scent of leopard. My leopard rose like a darker shadow, to begin to pad up that long path inside me.

Harley stumbled in midstep, and I heard him sniff the air behind his mask. 'You smelled like wolf for your first captor, now you smell like leopard for me. I do not believe either is real. I think it is part of your sweet poisoned bait that lures the shapeshifters to you.' He was back to sounding oh so reasonable, but he leaned his face down toward me. I felt his chest rise in a long, deep breath, as if he wanted to catch the perfume of my leopard while he could.

My fear had made it good odds that one or more of my beasts would rise; the scent of his leopard had chosen who it would be. My leopard began to jog up the path.

Harley laid me, gently, on the table beside Lisandro. It had been a long time since I'd been laid flat on my back with my hands bound behind me; it wasn't any more comfortable than the last time I remembered it.

Harley whispered, 'If you shapeshift we will kill him.'

'I can't change form,' I said.

He rose up enough to study my face. 'You smell of the truth, but I smell your leopard. You can't be a wereleopard and not shapeshift.'

'I promise you that so far I haven't chosen an animal form.'

He stroked his black gloved hand through my hair. 'Is your hair as soft as all those curls look?'

'No,' I said.

He laughed again. 'You should have said yes; then I would have been tempted to take off a glove and discover the truth for myself.'

Touch increases all vampire powers. I wasn't sure this was a vampire power, but the fascination I seemed to have over them once they touched me was interesting. 'If you want to touch my hair, I can't stop you.'

His face was close enough that I could see the skin around his eyes crinkle upward, and knew he was smiling. 'Why do I want to take off my glove and touch your hair?'

I told him the truth. 'I don't know.'

'The compulsion is quite strong,' he said.

My leopard had stopped running, and seemed to be waiting for something, but I could feel her just below the surface of me like a diver waiting and counting the minutes before he can surface without getting the bends. You hold yourself suspended in the water, watching your bubbles rise, and waiting. The leopard had that feel to her, but there were no bubbles for her to watch, and leopards don't keep time, not like that.

'Touch me.' I whispered it.

He undid a snap on his sleeve and rolled the glove backward over his hand. The glove was a part of the shirt. He touched my hair, kneading his fingers through the curl. My leopard purred, stretching against his hand as if he touched her domed head, instead of my curls. I saw her in my mind's eye pushing her head against his hand like a big housecat, but then she slid herself down his arm, against his body. I had a moment of lying there on the table and feeling that other energy rub along the front of his body at the same time, like being in two places at one time.

His hand convulsed in my hair, his body shuddering under the brush of the leopard. It closed his eyes, bowed his neck backward, as if it felt unbelievably good.

He opened his eyes and gazed down at me. His eyes were deep gold leopard eyes. 'If you do that again, we'll shoot Lisandro again.'

'We'll all go deaf if you keep using the gun in this room,' I said, and my voice was amazingly matter-of-fact.

'Then we will use blades,' he said. He made a motion and I turned in time to see one of the silent Harlequin move in a blur of black. One minute standing still, the next a knife sticking into Lisandro's upper thigh. I had been looking right at him, and hadn't seen it all. God help me, they were fast.

Lisandro made a sharp muffled sound through his gag. His shoulders rose off the table as his body dealt with the pain of a huge-ass knife hilt-deep in his thigh.

'You said next time. I didn't do it again.'

He motioned again and I turned in time to see the same Harlequin wrap his hand around the hilt. 'Oh, shit,' I said. And he pulled the blade free in one quick pull. Blood welled out of the cut, staining his jeans farther up and on the opposite side from the knee injury. Lisandro looked at me, eyes wide enough to show too much white around the brown. The look was clear: *Stop that.*

'I didn't do anything,' I said, to that unsaid comment.

Harley motioned and one of the others went for the still-open door. It was like some kind of arcane sign language, or the small hand signals that special forces teams can use, but they weren't hand signals that I'd ever seen.

The remaining two Harlequin stepped up so one of them could

press hands down on Lisandro's shoulders, and the other had his legs. My heart was beating too fast, too hard.

'Don't hurt him anymore.'

Harley frowned down at me. He petted my hair again and ran his hand down the side of my face. 'Why does it feel so good to touch you?'

'I swear to you that I don't know, other than I'm the Nimir-ra for our local wereleopards.'

'You are human and vampire; you can't be Nimir-ra.' But even as he said it, his hand cupped the side of my face. His hand was very warm against my skin.

'As far as we know, I'm the first human Nimir-ra in the history of the pard,' I said. I snuggled my cheek against the heat of his hand. He jerked back as if I'd bitten him.

'Stay with them,' he said, and turned and left the room.

The two remaining Harlequin exchanged the first look between them that I'd seen. There was someone in there. Someone that maybe didn't know why they were suddenly alone with us, with me. 'What are your names?' I asked.

They glanced at me and then back at each other.

'Why did the Mother of All Darkness forbid you from telling me your names?'

They stared straight ahead, holding Lisandro in place on the table. If I were really a shapeshifter powerful enough to just shift my hands I could have gotten out of the ropes, easily, which was why Lisandro was in chains and I was in ropes. I tensed my stomach muscles and sat up on the table. The Harlequin didn't so much move as tense.

'Since you won't give me your names, I'll call you Thing One and Thing Two.'

They glanced at each other again. One of them had brown eyes, the other had blue. They were both shorter than Harley or the werewolf, but beyond that the masks and hoods and gloves made them all generic.

I began to try to get the ropes over my hips; once I got them that far, I could bring them over my legs, and then I could untie my legs. The chances of my loosening the ropes enough to do it at all were small, but in the few minutes I had, almost nil. Would they stop me? Would they talk to me? We had minutes of being down to just two of them, and then I figured Harley would come back. I needed options before that happened.

I wiggled toward the edge of the table. I didn't know what I planned to do, but I knew I couldn't lie there and let them bring more of my people in here to hurt.

Thing Two appeared in front of me; I knew it was him because he had blue eyes. Thing One had brown. Thing Two shook his head.

'Do you talk?' I asked.

He nodded.

'Why won't you talk to me?'

The blue eyes just stared at me.

I got my legs over the side of the table and debated what he'd do if I tried to jump off the table. Would he catch me? Would he touch me? Touching me seemed to affect all of them. It was as if the *ardeur* and my beasts had combined to be something new, different. I didn't understand all of it, but I was pretty sure that if I could have physical contact with one of them for long enough I could roll their minds like any vampire victim, or that was the plan. I'd had better plans, but we were about to run out of time, so any plan was better than none. Or that was what I told myself as I pushed off the table.

37

Thing Two caught me around the waist and arms. It put me up against him, and the moment my chest touched his, I knew it was a her. I'd known that some of them were women, but I'd expected to notice it before we were pressed breast to breast; so much for my powers of observation. My face was tucked into the bend of her neck, between the mask and the hood, but there was no skin to find. The mask was part of the hood. I was betting it was snapped in like the gloves. But I didn't need skin to smell the lion inside her. She lifted me easily and sat my ass back on the table edge.

She shook her head at me, blue eyes very serious.

'Are you forbidden to talk because you're both women?' I asked.

'They're not both women.' It was the growling voice of the werewolf, back again. 'They're a mated pair of lions, or want to be, but their vampire masters see them as theirs. They will share them with other vampires, but not allow them to be with each other.'

The female Harlequin moved in front of him, blocking his path. She shook her head.

'Their masters cut their tongues out with silver. It's something they can cut off us that won't harm our fighting skills.'

'Why?' I asked.

'The tongues will grow back, eventually, and they are supposed to learn to obey their vampire masters. The Harlequin that stayed loyal to the Mother are very old-school, Anita Blake. Animals to call, no matter how skilled, are still animals, and they treat us like animals.'

The female looked back at the male. There was another shared look.

'If the Mother of All gains her body, then all the shapeshifters will go back to being animals,' the werewolf said.

'Is the other Harlequin, the one that carried in my friend, a lion, too?'

'No, she's another leopard.'

The werewolf drew a blade and knelt by my feet. The woman touched his shoulder, but when he went to cut through the rope on my ankles, she didn't stop him. I heard chains rattle and the other lion was unlocking the cuffs on Lisandro's ankles. It was too good to be true, but for once I just let him slice through the ropes on my wrists. Too good or not, I'd take it.

He handed me my own guns. 'I didn't dare take more, and we've melted down your holy objects; they're gone.'

I checked the Browning and the Smith & Wesson automatically to make sure they were loaded. They were. I tucked the S&W down the back of my jeans. 'Don't apologize, this is great.'

He handed Lisandro his main gun, too. He checked to make sure it was loaded just like I had. 'Thank you,' Lisandro said.

'Thank me when you're safe,' he said, and started for the door.

'What's your name?' I asked.

'She thinks you gain power over people with their names; it's old magic.'

'Sorry, didn't mean to be rude,' I said.

'Thaddeus,' he said. 'My real name is Thaddeus.'

'No matter how this turns out, thank you, Thaddeus,' I said.

He nodded, and led the way to the door. The silent werelions fanned out to both sides. Lisandro touched my arm so I'd let him go ahead of me. His thigh was completely healed already; let's hear it for no silver, and let's hope that our luck stays this good. Of course, no one's luck stays this good.

38

Once we stepped out into the corridor, I had my answer on whether we were underground: yes. I'd have said it was a basement but the single hallway was all stone, as if it had been hacked from the ground, or maybe begun life as caves like the Circus of the Damned underground. This underground wasn't nearly as impressive. In fact the main hallway was narrow enough that we could only walk two abreast. There were doors on either side like the one we came out of, and a visible end to the hallway just down from our door. The other end vanished around a curve that hid anything more than twenty feet away. A dead-end corridor with a series of doors into dead-end rooms; I'd feel sooo much better when we got around that curve, and out of this nearly perfect ambush area.

'Where are our people?' I asked.

Thaddeus motioned up the hallway. 'Last door on the left has your men in it.'

He started to lead us toward that door, but I glanced at the four other closed doors. 'Are there more prisoners down here?' I asked.

'No, just our masters and their vampire henchmen.'

Lisandro and I exchanged a look. 'We need out of this hallway,' he said.

I nodded, because I totally agreed. If it had been a normal vampire hunt we could have staked the vampires, or put silver bullets into their brains and hearts, but if the vampires died, then their animals to call might die, too. It would be really ungrateful of us to kill our rescuers, so we had to leave the vampires behind us, dead to the world for now. The back of my neck prickled with the thought of them behind the doors, waiting for night, and us having only one way out. I appreciated Thaddeus and the lions helping us, but we weren't rescued yet.

Thaddeus led the way with the male lion beside him. Lisandro insisted on going next and putting me between him and the female lion. I didn't waste time arguing. We just needed to get the others and get the fuck out of Dodge.

The door we wanted was nearly at the bend of the corridor, so the lion, whom I was still calling Thing One in my head, drew a gun and glanced around that blind curve. He didn't startle or wave us off, so apparently no nasty surprises were up ahead. Good.

Thaddeus unbolted the door. It opened almost noiselessly. He said something harsh in a language I didn't speak, and in English said, 'They are not here.'

I tried to peer around the broad shoulders and cloak, but Lisandro was actually taller and looked over his head. 'Shit,' he said.

I realized I'd never asked who they had. I understood in that moment that I'd been afraid to ask, because part of me didn't want to know who they had as hostages. I was pretty sure it was Bernardo, because he'd had the coffee just like Lisandro and me, but Nicky and Olaf hadn't. I hadn't asked if they were captured, or dead. Having Olaf die in the line of duty would solve so many problems, but he was a good man in a fight and he was a fellow marshal. I couldn't wish him dead. I admitted to myself that it was Nicky that bothered me most. Bernardo was a friend, but more a work friend. I'd be sorry, but my life would go on. Nicky dead would seriously change my day-to-day life. If he'd been my lion to call his death would have hurt me, and I'd have known, but Brides of vampires are often cannon fodder, the vampires that are left behind to delay the hunters while the masters get away. If you have the vampire ability to make brides, you can always make more. Most masters knew better than to fall in love with the cannon fodder.

'Who got captured with you?' I asked Lisandro.

'I came to with just Bernardo and a guy I didn't recognize.'

'What about Nicky and Olaf?' I asked, and I forgot to use Olaf's 'marshal' name. In that moment, I didn't try to correct it. I'd learned when accidentally giving away someone's alias that just ignoring the mistake attracts less attention than repeating and correcting. Most people edit what they hear to match what they expect to hear anyway.

'I passed out when you did, Anita.'

'Shit,' I said. 'Thaddeus.'

He turned and gave me those serious green eyes in their mask. 'While I fetched weapons they moved your friends. I have failed you.'

'Who's the man that Lisandro didn't know, and what happened to the other two men with us?'

'The red tiger mongrel that you made your lover,' he said.

'Ethan?'

'I believe that is his name.'

'I've only slept with Ethan once.'

'You have a reputation for bonding very closely with your lovers after very little contact.'

'How did you get him out of the red tiger's lair?'

'Our spy knew a way to get him to come to us.'

'Good ol' George,' I said.

'That is one of his aliases.'

I wanted to argue, but wasn't sure I could, so I pushed the thought away. I'd look at it later. I didn't ask again about Nicky and Olaf either. If they were dead, there was nothing I could do, and there'd be plenty of time for mourning. Right now, I needed to get us out alive without being possessed by Marmee Noir; until those two goals were reached nothing else really mattered. I told myself that and almost believed it.

'Fine, where would they take them?' I asked.

Then a voice called from ahead, 'Anita, we have your lovers; if you do not throw down your weapons and surrender we will begin cutting pieces off them.' It was Harley; great.

I didn't answer him. I believed he'd do it, but I also believed he just wanted to hold us here in this corridor until nightfall. All he had to do was wait for darkness and the vampires would rise behind us, and Harley and the red tiger Harlequin I'd wounded – George, if that was his real name – and the female wereleopard who'd helped carry Lisandro would have more allies.

'Answer me, Anita, or do you need proof?'

'I heard you, Harley,' I yelled back.

'That is not my name.'

'Then give me a name to call you.'

'He is Marius,' Thaddeus said.

'Okay, Marius,' I yelled back, 'you want us to surrender. We want our men safe. What happens next?'

'Wolf, you have given them my name, my real name. I curse you, wolf.'

'I was cursed long ago, Marius. You are cat and that was always her favorite animal. The wolves are worse than the meanest cur to her. I will not go back to it.'

'Traitor!' A woman's voice yelled it, so she was the wereleopard that we'd met earlier.

'Yes,' Thaddeus said.

Marius gave a wordless scream, and cursed, and then there was a muffled scream from someone else. Shit. 'Marius.' I called out his name, but there was nothing I could do to undo what had caused that scream. That bit of damage was done. Fuck.

There was a small sound, and Thing One made a sign with his free hand. Thaddeus said, 'They've thrown down a finger.' He motioned and the werelions moved up and out in the large, nearly circular open area. The stairs lay on the far side of the space. The werelions moved quickly across it, guns out, alert, but there was nothing but the thing at the bottom of the stairs.

One of them covered up the stairs while the other picked it up, and then they retraced their steps, watching behind them as if they expected the others to rush them. But they didn't need to rush us, all they needed was to outwait us. They could just wait and cut pieces off . . .

The man held out his black-gloved hand and there was a pale little finger in it. It was Ethan's; Bernardo's skin tone was darker. If they hadn't used silver, Ethan would grow another finger. It meant they weren't trying to do permanent damage. That was almost interesting on its own.

'The next thing I cut off won't be from your pet tiger. The next finger will be from your human lover and it won't grow back!' Marius yelled.

I didn't try to argue that Bernardo and I had never been lovers. I had a reputation for liking men, a lot, and that meant they'd never believe that I'd passed Bernardo up. Besides, if they knew we weren't lovers, they might hurt him more and faster. There was just no way to tell. I stared at the finger in the werelion's hand. It felt like I should do something with it, but I couldn't think what.

Lisandro spoke low. 'Anita, we need a plan.'

I shook my head, staring at the still-bleeding finger.

Lisandro grabbed my arm and spun me around to look at him. 'Anita, I'm the muscle, you're the brains. Think of something!'

'I don't know,' I said.

'The vampires will rise soon, and it will all be over,' Thaddeus said.

Then I had my idea; it was a wonderful, awful idea. 'Show me Marius, George and the wereleopards' masters.'

Thaddeus didn't even argue. He just turned and started walking back the way we'd come. Marius, George, and the wereleopard had Ethan and Bernardo, but we had their vampire masters, who were still completely helpless until nightfall. They had hostages and now so did we.

39

There were two rooms full of vampires. Each held three master vampires in coffins with about a half-dozen lesser vamps curled around their coffins like sleeping puppies; okay, sleeping dead puppies, but still the visual was clear. The vampires in the coffins were important; the ones on the floor were not.

The two lions wanted to know why we didn't just kill the others' masters immediately. 'Because if all three don't die together instantaneously, the one left could kill our people before we could finish killing their master.'

So I picked three of the lesser vamps from the floor and had the three Harlequin practice simultaneous head chopping. It's harder than it sounds to decapitate a body, and trying to get three people to do it in unison sounded almost impossible, even if they were the great and fabulous Harlequin.

I let them pick the angle they wanted for the bodies, while Lisandro stayed in the hallway and tried to negotiate with Marius and the others on the stairs. I counted down for the beheadings. 'One,' and a finger out, 'two,' another finger, 'three,' and as I sliced down on three, the three Harlequin were supposed to decapitate the vampires.

They got settled over the sleeping vampires. I counted, motioned, and their swords were a shiny blur. Two heads came off and rolled away from the bodies. The third head took a second blow. I stared at Thaddeus, who had needed two blows.

'The angle wasn't perfect,' he said.

The male lion managed to express with body language alone that they had both managed to do it just fine. I said, 'I'm with him, you had all the time in the world to set up your angle. Let's pick three more and take one more practice.'

I'd half expected them to protest just slaughtering the vampires, but they didn't. Either they were used to following orders without question or they weren't particularly fond of any of the vampires here. Either way, we had three more dead-to-the-world vampires lined up pretty quickly. It was also three fewer vamps for Mommie Darkest to possess once the sun went down; it was a win-win.

Lisandro called out, 'Anita!'

I went for the door at a jog. I prayed that there wouldn't be any more body parts at the bottom of the stairs. I wasn't that close to Bernardo, but I liked him and I didn't want to think of him having to go through life missing bits because I hadn't figured this out in time. Yes, I know it wasn't my fault, but somehow it felt like it was.

Lisandro said, 'They're going to send Bernardo's hand down next if we don't give up our weapons.'

'Shit,' I said, 'we're not ready.'

'Where is Anita?' Marius asked.

I yelled, 'I'm right here, you son of a bitch.' How did I keep him from chopping things off Bernardo that wouldn't grow back? Then I had another very bad, very good idea. 'Get one of the heads we cut off and bring it back ASAP,' I said.

Lisandro didn't argue, just ran back to the room I'd just left. I tried to reason, or at least delay them hurting Bernardo. 'Why so fucking impatient, Marius? You're blocking the only exit.'

'You are human,' the woman yelled, 'you should be honored that the Mother even wants you.'

'When she can possess your body and walk around in it, we'll talk,' I said.

Lisandro was back with a head in one hand and his gun in the other; with his shoulder-length hair flying out behind him, it was very modern barbarian.

I heard sounds of struggling. Was it Bernardo? 'I have a present for you!' I yelled. To Lisandro I said, 'Do it.'

He threw the head in a graceful arc to land at the bottom of the stairs. It was perfect placement, which with a basketball wouldn't have been that impressive, but with a human head – impressive. I'd have never gotten it to land like that.

'What is that?' the woman asked.

'One of your little vampires,' I said. 'You send more body parts our way, we send you more heads.'

'We could send you a head, too,' she yelled.

'You have only two hostages; we have a dozen, and three of them are your masters, which means if they die, you die.'

'Thaddeus,' Marius yelled, 'you wouldn't dare.'

'Thaddeus isn't in charge of these negotiations; I am, and I so fucking would.'

There was silence on their end, while they conferred. If we really planned on negotiating our way out of here, we'd need to do it before the vampires rose for the night. That was going to be soon. I couldn't explain how I knew, but even underground if I concentrated I could feel the coming of dawn or dusk. We were actually planning on killing most of the vampires and then escaping over the dead bodies of our enemies, but to keep them from guessing that, we had to pretend to negotiate. You always have to lie more to cover the first lie you tell; it's a rule or something.

'What do you want?' Marius asked.

What I really wanted was for the three Harlequin to work on their timing at decapitation, but out loud I said, 'We want safe passage for all of us.'

A moment's silence and then he said, 'Of course.' He knew that as soon as night fell and the Mother entered one of her vampire children she would come after us, but he would pretend that he could let us go and we'd really be free. I could pretend that we were so stupid we'd believe the first part. We began to negotiate in earnest; we were both lying, and both delaying.

How many beheadings do you have to do to get the timing perfect between three sword blows? Nine, as it turned out. How many vampires can you behead before wereanimals fifty yards away smell the fresh blood and death? Yep, same answer. The three Harlequin sliced the necks perfectly, like some executioner choreography, and the wereanimals on the stairs yelled, 'You're killing them all!' 'Your lovers are dead!' And the three Harlequin moved to the masters' bodies laid in their neat row. Their swords were a shine of silver, gleaming and faster than my eye could really follow. In one second a sword was raised, there was a blur of movement, and heads rolled away from the bodies. The white masks made them look like doll heads, but dolls don't bleed.

There was a scream from the stairs, and a sound almost of struggle, and then nothing. The silence was so thick, I could hear the blood in my head roaring in my ears. I wanted to call out to Bernardo and Ethan, but I forced myself to keep quiet. Were they doing the same, or were they dead?

The two lions moved toward the stairs, using the curved edge of wall to hide them from the stairs until the last minute. Then one did a quick glance up the stairs, and jerked back. He was so fast at it that I thought he'd seen the bad guys still alive, but then he took a second, longer look, and then he moved into the stairwell with the other lion following at his heels.

We waited at the entrance to the hallway. I held my breath, listening, but there was nothing to hear. Then one of the lions came down the stairs and gave the all-clear signal. We started across the open space and I felt it, night was falling. I felt it click into place, and I felt something else stir.

A cold breeze eased past me, breaking my skin out in a rush of shivers and goose bumps. A voice echoed in my head: 'Necromancer.'

'Run!' I yelled it, and took my own advice. No one argued with me. We ran for the stairs.

40

The vampires came for us, and worse yet, they took back control of Thaddeus. He didn't attack us, but he stopped moving, stopped running. Thaddeus said, 'Save yourselves if you can. It is too late for me.'

I reached back for him, but Lisandro grabbed my arm and pulled me forward. He got a death grip on my arm and ran toward the stairs. I had a choice of being dragged, or running. I ran.

Bernardo and Ethan were at the mouth of the stairs with guns in their hands. They fired over our heads at the vampires, and missed. 'They're too fast!' Bernardo said.

I stumbled, fell, and Lisandro half-carried, half-dragged me. I held on to my gun, but I couldn't run like this and aim. I started to try to pull loose of Lisandro so I could turn and fight, but something hit me so hard it drove all the air from my body, and I carried Lisandro's nail marks in my arm as the vampire slammed me into the wall. It knocked all the air out of me for a moment. Just a moment, before I was able to try to bring my gun up, but a moment was all the Harlequin needed to pin my arm and gun against the wall and snarl into my face. One minute I was looking into pale brown eyes, and the next the eyes were black, like staring into the deepest, darkest night you'd ever known. The Mother of All Darkness was here. The man's voice said, 'Necromancer,' but though the voice was deeper, the intonation was still her.

I screamed, and tried to move my arm enough to use the gun that was still in my hand. She laughed at me. 'Drop your shields, necromancer, or my Harlequin will kill them one by one.'

'Don't do it!' Lisandro yelled, and then made a pain noise. Thaddeus and another Harlequin that was probably his master had him pinned to the floor. It's harder to capture than to kill someone as good as Lisandro.

Ethan and one of the werelions were circling each other. One of Ethan's arms dangled, badly broken. The werelion had a gun in each hand. The other werelion had Bernardo shoved up against the wall, one arm behind his back, the other around his throat. Bernardo's face was bloody. It looked like they'd shoved him face first into the wall to stun and disarm him.

The vampire in front of me leaned his face near mine. 'Drop your shields, necromancer.'

'Don't do it, Anita,' Bernardo said. The werelion tightened her grip on his throat and began to slowly squeeze. I watched his face darken as the werelion choked him.

'Shall we kill your human lover first, necromancer?' the vampire asked, and leaned in, the male body pinning me more solidly against the wall.

'Why won't anyone believe he's not my lover?'

'Jokes, even now, Anita,' she said in that deep voice. 'There is a difference between bravery and stupidity, necromancer.'

Bernardo went limp in the choke hold. It takes longer to choke someone to death than you think it does, but I didn't want to chance it. Shit!

'Let him go,' I said.

'But if he is not your lover, then you shouldn't care.'

'Let him go,' I said, through gritted teeth.

'Let him breathe again,' she said.

The werelion eased the hold, and Bernardo made that terrible wheezing breath like coming back from the dead. He choked, and finally whispered, 'Don't do it, Anita.'

'He is very brave, your human lover,' she said.

I didn't correct her again. 'You've gotten inside my shields before and couldn't possess me; what makes you think this time will be different?'

'I have a body to touch you with that I already possess. You should know that physical contact makes all vampire powers harder to resist.'

I stared into that stranger's face with eyes that I seemed to have known for a lifetime. 'But you're wearing gloves. None of you is touching my skin.'

I saw the frown lines through the eyes of the mask. 'Drop your shields, necromancer, and we shall see if I need to remove the gloves.'

I hesitated.

'You will do as I ask eventually, necromancer. The only question is how many of your companions will die first.'

Ethan was on the ground, and the werelion pistol-whipped him across the face. The werelion aimed one of the guns at the fallen man.

'We will kill the wererat first. He is more dangerous than the human, and I don't like rats.'

'It's because you can't control them,' I said. 'If it's not a cat you can't force it to do anything. You have to ask, just like with me.'

'Shoot him.'

'No!' I yelled.

The shot echoed through the emptiness of the space, but it was Thaddeus kneeling over Lisandro; he'd moved his body in the way of his master's shot. He half fell over Lisandro, as his master fell to his own knees wounded as he'd wounded Thaddeus. 'I can't disobey you,' Thaddeus said, 'but I can do things that you have not forbidden.' He coughed and blood sprayed down his chin. He looked across the room at me. 'Thank you, Anita Blake.'

'Thaddeus,' I said.

'I am a slave no more.' He let himself collapse over Lisandro, and then his hand was up, his gun under his own chin. He pulled the trigger before his master could tell him not to, and they both fell in a heap, their cloaks and their bodies entwined. Lisandro lay under them and I couldn't tell how badly he was hurt.

'You are forbidden to harm yourself,' she spat out, and the werelion that had Bernardo seemed to shift her weight, as if she'd been thinking about it.

The last Harlequin went toward the last werelion. 'I forbade such things centuries ago, or he would have done himself a harm long ago, wouldn't you, my pet?'

The male werelion snarled at him, but he kept the gun steady on Ethan. They might not like what they had to do, but they'd be good at it.

'Good, pet,' the vampire said, and then he stalked toward us.

The vampire pinning me to the wall said, 'Everywhere you go you disrupt my vampires. Revolution follows in your wake like a plague after a rat.'

I wanted to make a smart remark, but my last one had gotten Lisandro hurt, and maybe worse. He hadn't moved since Thaddeus and his master fell. Some ammunition went through flesh like it was butter. It could have traveled through Thaddeus and into Lisandro. He could be dead because I had to remind her that she couldn't control wererats.

'Drop your shields or the human dies next,' she said.

'You would never fuck me, don't do this for me,' Bernardo said.

Lisandro lay very still on the floor. I didn't want to see someone else die for me, and there was one more benefit to dropping my shields. Domino was one of my tigers to call; if I dropped my shields he'd be able to sense me. If I dropped them and burned bright enough, Jean-Claude and everyone I was tied to would sense me, and there were ties between us that physical distance had nothing to do with. She'd wanted me alone, but was I alone? Was I ever really alone?

My heart was trying to climb into my throat. I was so scared my mouth was dry.

Ethan called out, 'Anita!'

'Don't do it,' Bernardo said.

'If you can't possess me, I don't want you saying it's because I didn't drop my shields enough. You said it yourself: Vampire powers work better if you touch skin to skin. Take off the gloves at least, because when you aren't vampire enough to roll my ass, I don't want you bitching.'

'You are impudent, girl.'

'You've been trying to roll my mind and take my body for over a year; don't go all high and mighty about the fact that you can't do it.' My words were brave, but my mouth was still dry and I was so scared my fingertips tingled with it. One strong emotion reads like another sometimes.

'Do you want me to hurt you? Is that it? Are you trying to anger me so I kill you instead of possessing you?'

'No,' I said.

In the end, she let the other Harlequin help hold me and disarm me while she stripped off the gloves, and then she undid snaps at the neck and lifted the mask off. 'Mistress, you reveal his face.' He sounded shocked. Everything else that she'd done, and this was the thing that shocked him.

The man's face was very ordinary. It was a face that you'd pass in a crowd a dozen times and never notice. It was a real spy's face – attractive, but not too attractive, ordinary, but not too ordinary. He was neutral, from the dark brown hair cut short to the medium skin tone. James Bond is a myth; real spies don't stand out unless they wish to, and the man standing in front of me would have blended in almost anywhere, almost.

'This body is shocked to be so naked.' Her voice sounded bemused, and just that one comment let me know that the vampire whose body she was using was still in there, still feeling his own feelings. Would that be what it was like? Would I be in there, but a prisoner in my own body? Would I have to watch her do terrible things to the people I loved and be helpless to stop it? I said a silent prayer: *Please, God, don't let her take me over.*

'If you use your fighting skills to hurt this body, your friends will suffer for it. Do you understand?' she said.

'If I hit or kick you, fight you physically, you'll hurt Ethan and Bernardo.'

'Yes.'

I nodded. 'Fine.'

She put her hands on either side of my face and said, 'Let her go.'

The vampire at my back didn't argue, but simply let go of me. We stood there for a breath, and she whispered, 'Drop your shields.'

I did what she asked. I did exactly what she asked. I dropped my shields. She'd never specified which shields. I let the *ardeur* spill up and over my skin and into hers. Her night-filled eyes widened, and she drew me in against the borrowed body.

'Sex opens us all up, Anita. I have tamed many a necromancer during sex.' She leaned down and kissed me, and I dropped another shield. I dropped the one that guarded the worst power I had ever learned, the one that I had learned in New Mexico from a vampire whose eyes were the color of night and stars. She had taught me to take the life, the very essence of a person and drink it down. It wasn't that different from the *ardeur*; they both fed on energy, except with the *ardeur* there was an exchange like any act of sex in which pleasure and energy mixed and mingled, but for this feeding there was only the taking. I fed on the body, on the energy that animated it, the life of it.

She drew back from the kiss, but her hands were still on my face, and any skin would do. 'Necromancer, you surprise me,' but there was no fear in the surprise. 'I will gain so much power when we are one.' And I saw in my mind's eye a great wave of darkness, as if the deepest, darkest part of night had suddenly formed a body and reared up above me, impossibly tall, impossibly everything.

I drank down the body I was touching. I drank his very 'life' that made that sluggish blood pump, that body move. His skin began to run with fine lines as if he were drying out. I drained his energy, but he hadn't fed for the night, and there wasn't nearly the 'life' to him that there was when I'd fed on lycanthropes, but I took what was there, and the energy filled my eyes until I knew they glowed with brown light, my eyes made blind with my own vampire power.

The Darkness crashed into me, and for a moment I thought I would drown in it. I couldn't breathe, couldn't see, couldn't . . . I tasted jasmine and rain, and smelled the scent of a long-gone tropical night in a part of the world I'd never seen, in a city that no longer existed except as sand and a few wind-kissed stones.

One moment I was drowning and the next I could taste Jean-Claude's lips on mine. He whispered through my mind, '*Ma petite.*' Down those long miles that separated us, he was there, and he offered me himself, his power to help me stand and remember that I was a vampire, too. The warm scent of wolf and Richard was there over the long miles. I could smell his skin and knew he was tucked in beside a woman's body. I could feel the curve of her hip under his hand. I smelled vanilla and could feel the cloud of Nathaniel's hair across my face, and a thousand mornings of waking up beside him. Damian's green eyes above me as we made love, his hair the color of fresh blood, red hair when it hasn't seen sunlight for nearly a thousand years. Neither of them was as powerful as Jean-Claude and Richard, but they were mine, and they added to who I was, what I was. Jean-Claude whispered, 'We cannot drown if we drink the sea.'

It took me a breathless, terrifying moment to understand, and then I went back to drinking down the vampire in my arms. It didn't matter that she was putting her energy into his; I would drink it all, and everything she offered. She wanted to put her energy into me, I'd let her.

She poured the deepest darkness into me, down my throat so that I choked on the taste of jasmine and rain, but I swallowed it down. I knew if I didn't panic, if I just swallowed and breathed in between that shivering pour of energy down my throat, I could do this. She tried to drown me; I tried to drink the blackness between stars. It was like the immovable object and the unstoppable force – she wanted to pour into me, and I let the energy fill me, but I was eating her, and she wanted to eat me.

Distant as a dream I heard gunshots, but I had to trust to someone else for that. My battle was here in the dark, fighting not to drown in the jasmine sea. The world became darkness, and I was standing in an ancient night with the scent of jasmine thick on the air, and a distant smell of rain. 'You are mine, necromancer,' she breathed.

I slid to my knees and it was her body, her first body, a dark-skinned woman who held me as we knelt in the sand, on the edge of palm trees and insects I'd never heard outside her memories. 'You cannot drink the night, there is too much of it.'

And then there was a hand in the darkness, and Domino was in the vision, pressing himself against the back of my body, not trying to take me away from her, but adding his strength to mine.

She laughed, 'White tiger and black is not enough, necromancer.'

And then there was another hand in the night, another figure that wrapped around me and Domino. Ethan, with one arm still broken from the fight, was there in the dream, and that was it, that was the key. He was all the other tiger colors that Domino wasn't. I had my rainbow of tigers. What I'd never understood was why the Master of Tigers had been her nemesis, but in that moment I understood. It was the gold tigers, and all the colors were the powers of the day and the earth and all that was alive, and she was all that was dead, no matter that she'd begun life as a shapeshifting cave lion; she was cold now, dead for so long that she didn't really understand what it meant to be alive. Maybe she never had.

I touched the men, and they touched me, warm flesh to warm flesh, and just the feel of their hands on me threw me back to making love to them both. I had images of the sheets wrapped around Ethan, his face looking up at me as he licked; Domino pinning me to the bed, me looking back over my shoulder to see his body bow backward with that one last thrust. She tried to remember sex, and there were memories, but it had been too long and she didn't truly understand it. She was like a sex symbol who had been told what it is to be sexy and to have sex, but not believing in her own sex appeal, and not really liking sex; it was an empty shell, pretend. There was nothing pretend about me. It wasn't about being the prettiest, or the best, it was about enjoying it. It was about loving the men who were with you, while they were with you, and valuing every last one of them. It was, in the end, about love. The love of a lover, of friends, and of partners, of people that I never wanted to lose, and wanted to wake up beside every damn day. It was about home. Home wasn't a place, or a building, or a tropical night full of flowers and rain. Love made home not out of boards and walls and furniture, but of hands to hold, and smiles to share, and the warmth of that body cuddled around you in the dark. I swam in the darkness of the ocean on a raft of hands, and bodies, and giving a damn what happened to them all.

We let her pour her scary, lonely, insane dark into us, and we drank it down with our comforting hands, our bodies that had made us all home, and the craziness of having too many people, too much going on, but what would we give up, who would we give up, and the answer, in the end, was not a single thing. The golden tigers were the power of the sun to bring life to the earth made flesh. They'd been created to chase back the darkness and remind us all that sometimes beauty and life triumph even on the darkest night.

When she realized that she couldn't win, she tried to pull out of the vampire's body. She tried to leave him to die alone, but she couldn't back up, we wouldn't let her. She wanted to fill us up with her power, and we let her.

Her voice in my head held the first note of panic, as she said, 'If you take my power into you, you will be as I am.'

'I'm not like you,' I thought.

'You will be.'

The power felt so good, and yet I knew I was draining the life out of two people, evil vampires, but still people. I prayed, not for help to do it, but that the power wouldn't corrupt me. That drinking in her darkness wouldn't make me evil, too.

Using the most evil power I had, I prayed, and I didn't burst into flames, and no one's holy object glowed. I ate the darkness that existed before God thought light was a good idea, and he was okay with that; he created the darkness, too. He actually liked both just fine.

41

Edward and the other marshals had come to the rescue in time to free Ethan to help me and give me Domino at my back. What would have happened if they hadn't showed up in time? It doesn't matter, they were there, and it worked. Sometimes that's all you've got; enjoy the win, don't worry about what-ifs.

The Harlequin had left Olaf and Nicky for dead, but they'd heard Edward and the others coming, so they hadn't had time to make sure of the deaths. Nicky healed and is back at my side. Olaf healed, too, but he, like Karlton who helped Edward ride to our rescue, didn't pass his blood test. I wish they had killed him, because come next full moon Olaf is going to be a werelion. He vanished from the hospital. No one seems to know where he is, or what he's doing. He's too dangerous to be out there for his first full moon alone. Edward's looking for him, and so are a lot of people who have ties to certain government agencies. I think we all agree, military, government, marshal, that Olaf was dangerous enough before; he didn't need to add superhuman speed and strength and a lust for real flesh and blood to his pathology.

Olaf left a note for me again. This one was much shorter than the last one:

'Anita, I will not be your pet cat, so I will stay away from you until I find my way as a lion. I won't let you do to me what you did to Nick. I still want you, but on my terms.' He didn't sign it, but then he didn't need to.

The nurse he flirted with was in surgery when he left, but the doctor with the short brown hair, Dr Patience, who had liked him and Bernardo so much, she's gone missing. Edward and I both think that Olaf took her, but we can't prove it. He still hasn't done anything illegal in this country. Technically, he's still a marshal in good standing, and thanks to another marshal who just won a court case worth millions because he caught lycanthropy on the job and was fired because of it, well, Karlton is still a marshal, too. Micah set her up with the local werewolf pack in her home city. He's also recommended a family counselor who specializes in helping everyone related to the victim make the transition.

Ethan came home with us, one more tiger to add to the rest. I asked my other sweeties about sending Cynric home now that we had another blue tiger, but Jean-Claude doesn't understand why Cynric's age bothers me. He feels we made a commitment to him and to the vampires and white tigers of Vegas. Nathaniel thinks Cynric is tied to me too metaphysically to take the separation well. 'He's in love with you, Anita. Don't send him away.' Micah shares some of my discomfort with Cynric's age, but what if Jean-Claude and Nathaniel are right? So, for now, our teenager stays.

The Mother of All Darkness is dead, well and truly dead, and I'd never felt power like the rush of drinking her dry. The Harlequin have all either joined us, or gone back to trying to have lives of their own. We're safe. Which means that two days a week I get to stay at my house and have windows and air and light, and Micah and Nathaniel come with me, and sometimes Jason comes, and sometimes other tigers, but my vampire lovers can't risk the sunlight. But five days and nights a week I'm with Jean-Claude. We're still working out how to live together with everyone. It's better having a couple of the tigers be female and helping with the men, and some of the newest men being more heteroflexible, so that I'm not every damn person's only squeeze. I've learned you can fuck this many people, but you can't take care of this many people's emotional needs. You can fuck 'em, but you can't date 'em. Some of the men are happy with being fuck buddies, but most of them want more. People say that women are the romantic sex, but you couldn't prove it by my life. My boyfriends are all more romantic than I am, and so are my lovers.